I DO

Joan Hohl

ZEBRA BOOKS

Kensington Publishing Corp.

http://www.kensingtonbooks.com

CONTENTS

THE
TAWNY GOLD
MAN

Chapter One

"In the name of the Father, the Son, and the Holy Spirit. Amen."

The solemnly intoned benediction seemed to hang like a pall on the chill March air long seconds after the pastor closed his prayer book. A muffled sob shattered the silence, and, as if the cry had been a signal, the large crowd around the grave site began to move in a slow, unsure manner.

Some distance off to one side, in a small, sparse stand of trees, a tall man stood, unobserved by the group of mourners. Hands thrust inside the deep pockets of a hip-length sheepskin jacket, broad shoulders hunched, wide collar flipped up against the cold, damp air, all that was visible of his head and face was a shock of sun-gold hair and a pair of amber eyes, narrowed and partially concealed by long, thick, dark brown lashes. At the moment, the eyes were riveted on the flower-draped brass casket suspended over the open grave.

The figure remained still as a statue, but the eyes, cold and unemotional, shifted to the source of the low sobs. A small fair-haired woman, dressed entirely in black, stood unsteadily, supported on both sides by two tall, slender, fair-haired young men who wore the same face. The cold eyes flashed for an instant with cynicism, gone as fast as it came, then moved on to rest on the face of a younger woman, also dressed in black, standing close to one of the young men. There was an oddly protective attitude in her stance, although she was much smaller than the man. The amber eyes grew

stormy as they studied the small, pale, wistfully lovely face,
the soft, pure lines set in fierce determination. The lids
dropped, and the eyes again became clear and cold and
moved on to briefly scan the crowd before once again coming
to rest on the coffin, gleaming dully in the gray, overcast
morning light.

"I loved you, you old bastard."

The softly muttered words bounced off the warm fleece
of the collar; then the man turned sharply and strode through
the trees to the road some yards away and a sleek black
BMW parked to the side.

Anne rested her head against the plush upholstery of the
limousine, eyes closed. She was tired and the day wasn't half
over. There would be a lot of people coming back to the
house and she'd have to act as hostess, as her mother obviously wasn't up to it. The soft weeping coming from the seat
in front of her gave evidence of that. Not for the first time
Anne wished she'd known her father, for she surely must
have inherited his character. For although except for hair
color she resembled her small, fragile mother, beyond the
surface features there was very little comparison. Her mother
was gentle natured but had always been high-strung and of
delicate health, whereas Anne had enormous stamina and
strength for such a small woman. About the only thing she
and her mother shared by way of emotions was the gentle
nature. Anne was a pushover for any hard-luck or sob story
and had been taken in by and involved with so many of her
friends' problems she had finally had to harden her heart in
self-defense.

Taking advantage of the drive back to the house to relax,
Anne's mind was going over what still had to be gotten
through that day when a disturbing thought pushed its way
forward: He didn't even come to his father's funeral. Her
head moved restlessly; her soft lips tightened bitterly. For
days now, ever since her stepfather's death, she had managed
to push away all thoughts of her stepbrother, but even so she

had felt sure he would be at the funeral. Of course it had been ten years, but still, he had been notified and the least he could do . . . She felt the car turn into the driveway and, opening her eyes, sat up straight, pushing the disquieting thoughts away.

During the next two hours Anne was kept too busy to do any deep thinking, but still her eyes went to the door each time the housekeeper opened it to admit yet another friend offering condolences.

When finally the door was closed after the last well-wisher, Anne sighed deeply before squaring her shoulders and walking to the door of the library. With her hand on the knob she paused, her gaze moving slowly around the large, old-fashioned foyer. The woodwork was dark, gleaming in the light of the chandelier that hung from the middle of the ceiling. The furnishings could only be described as heavy and ornate. Anne didn't really care too much for the house, yet it had been the only home she'd ever known, as Judson Cammeron, Sr., had been the only father she'd ever known. Sighing again, she turned the knob and entered the room.

Mr. Slonne, the family attorney, sat dwarfed behind her stepfather's massive oak desk, hands folded on the blotter in front of him. He was speaking quietly to her mother, who was sitting in a chair alongside the desk. As Anne gently closed the door he glanced up and asked, "Everyone gone?"

Smiling faintly, Anne nodded and moved to the chair placed at the other side of the desk. As she sat down, her eyes scanned her mother's face.

"How are you feeling now, Mother?"

Margaret Cammeron smiled wanly at her daughter, her eyes misty. "Better, dear." Her tremulous voice had a lost, childlike note. "I don't know how I'd have managed to get through this without you and your brothers." Her breath caught and her hand reached out for, and was grasped by, that of her son who leaped from his chair and came to stand beside hers.

"Well, you don't have to get through anything without us, ever." Anne spoke bracingly, her eyes going to first one, then another, set of matching blue eyes, in the faces of her identical-twin half brothers.

Like a small mother hen, Anne was proud of her younger brothers. Usually carefree and unhampered by responsibility, due to too little discipline and too much indulgence, their conduct the last few days had been faultless. At twenty-one and in their last year of college, Troy and Todd Cammeron had never done a full day's serious work. They had inherited their mother's sweet nature and their father's quick temper, but little of his iron will and tenacity. They were good-looking and well-liked and too busy having a good time to worry about the future. Their father was rich and they had known they would go to work in his business when they left school. Meanwhile they had been busy with girls and cars and girls and fun and girls. Their father's sudden death had shocked them, as it had everyone, but they had rallied well in support of their mother. Although only four years their senior, Anne also admitted she had had as much of a hand, if not more, in their spoiling as anyone.

Mr. Slonne glanced at his watch then cleared his throat discreetly. "I think we had better begin, Mrs. Cammeron. The time stated was two o'clock and as it is now two-fifteen I—"

He stopped, startled, as the library door was thrust open and Anne felt the breath catch in her throat as her stepbrother walked briskly into the room. He paused, his eyes making a circuit of the room, then proceeding to her mother.

"Sorry I'm late, Margaret, I stopped for something to eat and the service was lousy."

Anne shivered at his tone. So unfeeling, so cold, could this hard-eyed man be her stepbrother?

Margaret raised astonished eyes to his face, murmuring jerkily, "That—that's all right, Jud. But you—you should have come home to eat."

His smile was a mere twist of the lips before his head lifted to turn from one then the other twin, standing on either side of her chair.

"Troy, Todd, still the same bookends, I see."

Their faces wore the same strained expressions, but both stretched out hands to grasp the one he had extended. He nodded to the lawyer, murmured "Mr. Slonne" then turned to Anne. She felt a small flutter in her chest as he walked to the chair next to hers.

"Anne."

His tone was low, but so coolly impersonal that Anne again felt a shiver go through her. Was it possible for a man to change so much in ten years? Apparently it was, for the proof of it was sitting next to her.

He had left home a charming, laughing, teasing young man and had walked through that door a few minutes ago with the lazy confidence of a proud, tawny lion. And tawny was the only way to describe him. The fair hair of ten years ago had darkened to a sun gold, and his skin was a burnished bronze. His features hadn't changed, of course, but had matured, sharpened. The broad forehead now held several creases as did the corners of his eyes. The long nose that had been perfectly straight now sported a bump, evidence of a break surgically corrected. The once firm jawline now looked as if it had been cut from granite. The well-shaped mouth now seemed to be permanently cast in a mocking slant. And the once laughing amber eyes arched over by sun-bleached brows now held the mysterious, wary glow of the jungle cat. Incredibly he seemed to have grown a few inches and gained about thirty pounds and he looked big and powerful and very, very dangerous.

With a feeling of real grief Anne felt a small light go out inside for the death of the laughing, teasing Jud Cammeron she'd known ten years before.

Mr. Slonne lifted the papers that had been lying on the desk and with a sharp movement Jud lifted his hand.

"If you'll be patient just a few more minutes, Mrs. Davis is bringing me something to drink." Then he turned to Margaret. "I hope you don't mind."

Her still lovely face flushed, Margaret whispered, "No—no, of course not."

At that moment the library door opened and the housekeeper, her face set in rigid lines of disapproval, entered the room carrying a tray bearing a coffeepot, cups, sugar bowl, and creamer. Mrs. Davis had been with the Cammerons only six years and she obviously looked on this new arrival as an interloper. Placing the tray, none too gently, on a small table beside Jud's chair, she turned on her heel and marched out of the room. Hearing him laugh softly, Anne thought in amazement, *He's enjoying her discomfort. No, he's enjoying the discomfort of all of us.* And for the third time she felt a shiver run through her body.

Mr. Slonne waited patiently while Jud filled his cup and added cream. Then he began reading. The atmosphere in the room grew chill then cold as he read on. Anne, her hands gripping the arms of her chair, couldn't believe her ears. Her mother's face was white with shock. The twins wore like expressions of incredulity. Jud sat calmly sipping his coffee, his eyes cold and flat as a stone and his face a mask. When the lawyer's voice finally ground to a halt, the room was in absolute silence. After a few long, nerve-racking minutes Jud's unemotional voice broke the silence.

"Well, then, it seems, in effect, he's left it all to me."

"Precisely."

Mr. Slonne's clipped corroboration brought the rest of them out of their trance.

"I—I don't understand," Margaret wailed.

Mr. Slonne hastened to reassure her. "There is no need for concern, Mrs. Cammeron, you've been well provided for. Indeed you've all been well provided for. It is just that Mr. Cammeron, young Mr. Cammeron, will have control of the purse strings, so to speak. In effect, he will be taking over where your husband left off."

"You mean I'll have to ask Jud for everything?" she cried.

Before Mr. Slonne could answer, Jud rapped, "Did you have to ask the old man for everything?"

Margaret winced at the term "old man," then answered wildly. "But you've been away for ten years. Not once have you written or called. It was as if you'd died. He never mentioned your name after you left this house. Why should he do this?"

Jud's eyes went slowly from face to face, reading the same question in all but Mr. Slonne's. Then with cool deliberation he said, "Maybe because the business that made him so wealthy was started mainly with Carmichael money. My mother's father's money. Maybe because he was afraid there was no one here who could handle it. And just maybe because he trusted me. Even after ten years."

He paused as if expecting a protest, and when there was none he continued. "Don't concern yourself, Margaret. You're to go on as you always have. I will question no expenditures except exceedingly large ones. This house is as much your home as it ever was. I have no intention of interfering with its running."

"You are going to live here?" Dismayed astonishment tinged Margaret's tone and one not-quite-white eyebrow arched sardonically.

"Of course. At least for the next few months. As you said, I've been away for a long time. I'll have to familiarize myself with the company, its management. Perhaps make a few changes."

Anne didn't like the ominous sound of his tone or the significance of his last words. Incautiously she snapped, "What changes?"

She realized her mistake as he turned slowly to face her. He didn't bother to answer her, he didn't have to. His eyebrows arched exceedingly high, the mocking slant of his hard mouth said it all loud and clear: *Who the hell are you to question me?* Anne felt her cheeks grow warm, heard him laugh softly when her eyes shied away from his intent amber stare.

"Now, then." The abrupt change in his tone startled Anne so much she actually flinched. "Mr. Slonne, thank you for your time and your assistance. You will be hearing from me soon." The lawyer was ushered politely, but firmly, out of the room. Margaret was next. In tones soothing but unyield-

ing, Jud saw her to the door with the opinion that she should
rest for at least an hour or so.

When Jud turned back to face her and her brothers, Anne
felt her palms grow moist, her heart skip a beat. In no way
did this man resemble the Jud she remembered. The Jud she
had known ten years ago had had laughing eyes and a teasing
voice. This man had neither. His eyes were alert and wary,
and his voice, so far, was abrupt and sarcastic. This man was
a stranger with a hard, dangerous look that spoke of ruth-
lessness.

"Now, you three," Jud said coolly. "I think we had better
have a small conclave, set down the ground rules as it were."

Troy was the first one to speak. "What do you mean
ground rules? And who the hell are you to lay down rules
anyway?"

"I should think the answer to that would be obvious, even
to you, Troy." Completely unruffled, Jud moved around the
desk, lazily lowering himself into his father's chair.

"Sit down," he snapped. "This may take longer than I
thought."

"I prefer to stand."

"So do I," Todd added.

The twins then began to speak almost simultaneously. Beginning to feel shaky with the premonition of what was coming, Anne was only too happy to sink into the chair she had
so recently vacated. Jud pinned her there with a cold stare.

"I'll get to you shortly."

He turned the stare to the twins and his voice took on the
bite of a January midnight. "I will tell you exactly who I
am. As our father saw fit to leave me in control, from now
on I'm the boss. And there are going to be a lot of changes
made, starting with you two earning your keep."

"What do you mean?"

"In what way?"

He silenced them with a sharp, slicing move of his hand.

"From today on every free day you have, except Sundays,
will be spent at the mill learning the textile business from
the ground up, starting with the upcoming Easter vacation."

"But we have plans made to go to Lauderdale at Easter," Troy exclaimed angrily.

"Had plans," Jud stated flatly. "There will be no romping on the sands for you two this year."

"We're over twenty-one," Todd sneered. "You can't make us do anything,"

"Can't I?"

Anne felt her mouth go dry at the silky soft tone. Her eyes shifted to the twins' faces as Jud continued.

"Perhaps not. But I can stop your allowances. I can neglect to pay your school fees for the final term. I can demand board payment for living in this house—my house."

White-faced, Troy cried, "We still have our income from the business."

"Wrong," Jud said coldly. "You heard the terms of the old man's will. Unless I choose to sign a release, every penny of that income goes into a trust fund until you are twenty-five. I'm the only one who can draw on that fund for your maintenance. Now, unless you want to be cut off without a penny for the next four years, when I say jump, the only question I want from either of you is: How high?"

Anne closed her eyes to shut out the glazed expression of shocked disbelief on her brothers' faces. With a tingling shiver she heard Jud coolly dismiss them with the advice they attend their mother, then her eyes flew open at his crisp "Now you."

"You can't frighten me, Jud. You have no control over me whatever. I have simply to pack my things and walk out of this house to be away from your—control."

Anne felt an angry flush of color flare in her face as he studied her with amused insolence, his eyes seeming to strip her of every stitch of clothing she was wearing.

"That's exactly right," he finally replied silkily. "But you won't. The old man was no fool. His plan was beautifully simple. He knew full well the sons of his second marriage were incapable of taking over, while at the same time he wanted to insure their future, so he split up forty-five percent of the company stock between them but left me in control of the actual capital. At the same time he knew I could handle the business and the twins, and that I would. But he wanted a check rein on me, too, so he only left me forty-five percent. That leaves you, right in the middle, with the other ten percent."

"To do with as I please," she inserted warningly.

"But of course," he countered smoothly. "But as I said, the old man was no fool. He was reasonably sure you would not surrender your share to me, thus giving me full control. On the other hand he could also feel reasonably sure you would not throw in with the twins, as you are as aware as he was that they would probably run the company right into the ground. Does it give you a feeling of power, Anne?"

"You can't be sure I won't sell or give my share to Troy and Todd." Very angry now, she lashed out at him blindly. Everything he'd said was true, and she hated his cool smugness.

"Right again," he mocked. "But, like the old man, I am reasonably certain, and being so, I'll call the shots. And I'll give you one warning: If you decide you can't hack it, and to hurt me you sign over to the twins, I'll ruin them—and I can, easily."

Wetting her lips she stared at him in disbelief. He meant it.

"But you'd be destroying your own interests as well."

Mocking smile deepening, he shrugged carelessly. "I'll admit that I want it, but I don't need it to survive. The twins do. And don't, for one moment, deceive yourself into thinking I won't do it. I will."

She believed him. He wasn't just bluffing or trying to scare her, though he did. He meant it. Confused, frightened for her brothers, she cried, "Why are you taking this position? Do you hate us all so much?"

"Hate? The twins?" Again the brows rose in exaggerated surprise. "You forget, the twins are my brothers too. I'll be the making of them."

The fact did not escape her that he referred to Troy and

Todd only. Shocked by a pain she had thought long dead, she argued. "You're being too hard on them."

"Hard?" He gave a short bark of laughter, shaking his head. "You call it hard to expect them to learn a business they have almost a half interest in? Good grief, they are twenty-one years old and have never done a full day's work. Do you know how old I was when I went to work for my father?"

Subdued by his sudden anger, Anne shook her head dumbly.

"I was fourteen. Fourteen." His tone hardened on the repeated word. "And how old were you? Don't answer, I know. You've had almost sole care of those two ever since you were six. You've cared for, protected, and played general guard dog to them from the time they could say your name. How old were you when you went to work in the old man's office?"

"Eighteen."

"Eighteen," he repeated softly. "No carefree college days for Anne."

"I wasn't his daughter," she protested. "I never expected—"

"No, you weren't his daughter," he interrupted. "You were, for all intents and purposes, his slave."

"He was very good to me." She almost screamed at him.

"Why the hell shouldn't he have been?" he shouted. "You never made a move he disapproved of."

Anne drew deep breaths, forcing herself to calm down. This was proving nothing. Her voice more steady, she said quietly, "I won't argue anymore about this, Jud. If there is nothing else you want to discuss I'll go up to moth—"

"There is," he cut in firmly. "If you have any papers or anything else pertaining to the office here at home, I'd like you to get them together. My secretary will be in the office tomorrow and it will be easier for her if—"

Now it was Anne's turn to interrupt. Her voice hollow with shock, she cried, "Your secretary? But that's my office."

Even though his voice was bland, it chilled her.

"I don't need you in that office, Anne; that's what I pay my secretary for. So if there's anything here, collect it before tomorrow. Now if you'll excuse me, I have some phone calls to make."

Turning quickly, Anne left the room. She heard him dialing as she closed the door. Then she stood staring at her trembling hands. That easily, that coolly, she had been dismissed, not only from the room but from the office as well. Fighting tears, she ran upstairs to her bedroom. What was she supposed to do now?

Chapter Two

Anne paced the deep rose carpet in her bedroom, Jud's words still ringing in her ears. If she wasn't going to go to the office and he didn't want her to move out of the house, what was she to do? Get another job? Work for a rival company? That didn't make much sense. Maybe he meant her to stay at home, run the house, live the kind of life her mother did. Women's clubs and bridge games and shopping week in, week out. Anne shivered. She would go out of her mind. Maybe if the twins were still small enough to keep her running, but not now. She was too used to the office. Tears trickling down her face, she riled silently. Didn't he realize she knew almost as much about the managerial end of the business as his father had? She could be of help to him while he was familiarizing himself with it. Why had he turned her out? Did he hate her that much?

In frustration she flung herself onto the bed and stared at the ceiling. He had changed so drastically. Uninvited and unwelcome, a picture of him as he was the last time she saw him formed in her mind. How young she had been then. Young and naive and so very much in love. Anne's face burned at the memory of how very gullible she had been at fifteen.

It had been Jud's twenty-fifth birthday and Anne had waited with growing impatience for him to come home to dinner. She felt her spirits drop when her stepfather came home alone and when he told her mother that Jud would not be home for dinner as he had a date, her spirits sank completely.

The hours had seemed to drag endlessly as Anne, unable to sleep, sat in her room, ears strained for the sound of his car on the driveway. On the table beside her small bedroom chair lay a tiny birthday present, its fancy bow almost twice the size of the package. At intervals Anne touched the bow gently, lovingly. She had saved so long to buy this gift, had been so eager to give it to him. Eager and also a little nervous. It was not quite a year since she had first seen the brush-finished gold cuff links and she had known at once she wanted to give them to him. At first she had thought of giving them to him at Christmas but she had not been able to save enough money. So she had taken the money she had and had talked to the store manager. He in turn had removed the links from the display window, put her name on them, and had set them aside for her. She had made the last payment on them the previous week. Now, staring at the small, wrapped box, she saw the matte surface of the gold ovals, could see the initials engraved on them. J.C.C. Judson Carmichael Cammeron. How she loved him. And how she prayed he'd like her offering.

The slam of the car door startled Anne out of a daze. The front door being closed brought her fully aware. She heard him come up the stairs, pass her door, and close his own door farther down the hall. What should she do? It was past two thirty. Would he be angry if she went to his room now? Should she wait until morning?

Anne hesitated long minutes. The she thought fiercely, *No, it won't be the same. By morning his birthday will be truly over.* Without giving herself time to change her mind, she slipped out of her room and along the thickly carpeted hall on noiseless bare feet. She tapped on his door softly then held her breath. It seemed to take a very long time for him to open the door, but when he did she knew why at once. He had obviously just come out of

the shower, as his hair was damp and he was wearing
nothing except a mid-calf-length belted terry cloth robe.
At the sight of him Anne felt her resolve weaken, but
before she could utter an apology or whisper good night,
he caught her hand and said with concern, "Anne! What
is it? Is something wrong?"

Her voice pleading for understanding, Anne shook her
head quickly and answered softly, "No, nothing. I'm—I'm
sorry to disturb you. I'm silly. I wanted to give you your
birthday present and I couldn't wait till morning."

Jud sighed, but his voice was gentle. "You're right; you
are silly." He paused, then chided, "Well, where is this present you couldn't wait to give me?"

Flushing, Anne slid her hand into the pocket of the cotton
housecoat she'd slipped the gift into before leaving her room.
As she withdrew the gift, he gave a light tug on the hand he
was still holding and murmured ruefully, "You had better
come in. We don't want to wake the household for the event
of giving and receiving one gift."

She stepped inside and he reached around her to close the
door before taking the small package from the palm of her
hand. Silently he removed the wrapping and silently he
flipped the case open and stared a very long time at the cuff
links. When he raised his eyes to hers they were serious,
questioning. Fear gripped her and she blurted breathlessly,
"Don't you like them, Jud?"

"Like them? Of course I like them, they're beautiful. But,
chicken, they must have cost a bundle. Why?"

More nervous than before, Anne plucked at the button on
her robe.

"I—I saw them in the window and—and I wanted to buy
them for you."

"When was this?" he asked softly.

"Almost—not quite a year ago."

"And you've been saving all this time?" His voice was
even softer now and Anne shivered. His tone—something—
was making her feel funny.

"Are you angry with me, Jud?"

"Angry? With you? Oh, honey, I could never be really angry at you."

"I'm glad," she whispered. "I wanted to give them to you tonight so badly. I could have cried when you didn't come home for dinner."

His beautiful amber eyes seemed to flicker, grow shadowed and he carefully laid the jeweler's box on the night table by his bed, then brought his hand to her face. Again a tiny shiver went through her as his fingers lightly touched her skin. Now his voice was barely above a murmur. "And do I get a birthday kiss too?"

"Yes." A mere whisper broke from a suddenly dry throat.

His blond head descended and then she felt his lips touch hers lightly and tenderly. The pressure on her lips increased and then he groaned softly and pulled his head away with a muttered growl. "You had better get out of here, Anne."

She felt stricken, shattered, and as he turned away she cried, without thinking, "Jud, please, I love you. What have I done wrong?"

He swung back, his eyes filled with pain.

"Wrong? Oh, chicken, you've done nothing wrong. Don't you see? Can't you tell? I want to kiss you properly and you're so young. Too young. I think you'd better get out of here before I hurt you."

His eyes burned into hers, and with a feeling of fierce elation she couldn't begin to understand running through her, she pleaded, "Oh, Jud, please don't make me go. Tell me, show me, what to do, please."

He moved closer to her, his eyes searching hers as if looking for answers. Again his hand touched her face lightly, then his forefinger brushed, almost roughly, across her lips. Her lips parted fractionally in automatic reaction and leaning closer he whispered, "Like that, honey." Again his finger brushed her mouth, this time the lower lip only, and she could hardly hear his murmured "Part your lips for me, Anne" before his lips were against hers. She obeyed him and felt a shock of mingled fear and joy rip though her as his mouth crushed hers. Never could she have imagined the riot of sensations that stormed her senses.

When his mouth left hers, she gave a low "no" in protest, and grasping her arm, he whispered, "Come."

He led her to the side of the bed, sat her down, then sat down beside her. Cupping her head in his hands he stared broodingly into her face a long time before saying quietly, "Sweetheart, if you're at all frightened, tell me now while I can still send you back to your room."

Her eyes clear, she faced him without fear. "I could never be afraid of you, Jud. How could I be? I told you. I love you."

"Yes, you told me," he groaned. Then he was on his feet, moving away from her. "But, honey, I'm not talking about brother-sister love. You know the facts of life?"

She looked up indignantly at the sharp question. "Yes, of course I do."

His tone lost none of its sharpness. "Then you know what I want?"

Unable to voice the answer, Anne lowered her eyes, nodded her head.

"Honey, look at me."

Some of the edge had left his tone and in relief Anne looked up.

"Ever since the day you first came to this house, I loved you. Like a brother with a small sister, I loved you, wanted to protect you. A little over a year ago, some months after your fourteenth birthday, I began to feel different." Anne felt a pain twist at her heart and she would have cried out but he held up his hand to explain. "Suddenly one day I realized I did not love you as a brother loves a sister. I was in love with you, the way a man loves a woman." His eyes closed but not before Anne saw the pain in them.

"Jud." She made to get up and go to him.

"No." It was an order. Anne stayed where she was. His eyes were again open. His voice wracked with torment, he went on. "I don't know how. I don't know why. But, dear God, Anne, I love you and you are too young. Get out of here, chicken. Go back to your room while I can still let you go."

"No."

"Anne."

"No, Jud," she repeated firmly then more softly, "Jud, please. I don't want to go. I want to stay with you."

In three strides he was back beside her, his hands again cradling her head. "You are a small, beautiful fool. And I will very likely burn in hell, but, honey, I need you so, want you so."

This time when his mouth touched hers she needed no prompting. Eager to experience again that wild riot of sensations, her lips parted beneath his searching, hungry mouth. His hand dropped to her shoulders then moved down and over her back, drawing her slight, soft body against his large, hard one.

Slowly, reluctantly, his lips released hers, moved over her face and she felt her breath quicken as he dropped feather-light kisses across her cheeks, on her eyelids, and along the edge of her ear. Breathing stopped completely for a moment when his teeth nipped gently on her lobe and he whispered urgently, "Anne, I want you to touch me. Put your hands on my chest, inside the robe."

Her hands had been lying tightly clasped on her lap and at his words she relaxed them, brought them slowly up. Slowly, shyly, she parted the lapels of his robe, then placed her palms against his hair-roughened skin. Enjoying the feel of him, she grew braver and slid her hands across the broad expanse of his chest. He shuddered, then moaned deep in his throat when her fingertip brushed his nipple. Made still braver by his reaction to her touch, she whispered. "Do you like that, Jud?"

"Like it?" he husked. "Lord, sweetheart, I love the feel of your hands on me. I just hope you enjoy the feel of my touch half as much." His hands moved to the buttons of her robe, unfastening them quickly. His lips close to hers, he murmured, "I don't think we need all this material between us."

He slipped the robe off then gathered her close against him, his mouth driving her to the edge of delirium as he explored the hollow at the base of her throat. Anne stiffened with a gasp when his hand moved caressingly over her breasts, his touch seeming to scorch her through the thin cotton of her short nightie, but the heady excitement his gently teasing fingers aroused soon drowned all resistance. His mouth sought hers over and over again, becoming more urgently demanding with each successive kiss and Anne felt desire leap and grow deep inside.

She felt a momentary chill when his arms, his mouth, released her and he leaned away from her. Dimly she was aware of his movement as he shrugged out of his robe and tossed it aside. The flame inside her leaped higher when he pulled he close against his nakedness. Afire with a need she didn't fully understand, inhibitions melting rapidly in that flame, she slid her hands along his body, loving the feel of his smooth warm skin. When she ran her fingers up and over his rigid, arched spine, he shivered and groaned against her mouth. "I could kiss you forever but, Anne, baby, it's no longer enough. Raise your arms."

She obeyed at once and sat meekly as he tugged her nightie up and over her head. When she was about to drop her arms, he caught her wrists in one of his hands and pulled them high over her head then forced her down against the bed. Stretched out below him, she felt her cheeks go pink as his eyes went slowly, burningly, over her body. Her color deepened when his hand followed the route his eyes had mapped out and her eyes closed with embarrassment when, without conscious thought, her body moved sensuously under his fingers.

"Open your eyes, Anne," he ordered softly, and when she did she found herself staring into warm liquid amber.

"Don't ever be embarrassed or ashamed with me. From tonight on, you are mine. You belong to me. No, we belong to each other, for I am surely yours. There's no reason for you to be shy with me. You are beautiful and I love every inch of you. Do you understand?"

Unable to speak around the emotion blocking her throat, Anne nodded. He kissed her hard then whispered, "Tell me again that you love me, Anne."

"I love you, Jud, more than anything or anyone else on this earth."

Anne heard his breath catch and then his head lowered and his mouth followed the path of his eyes and hands, branding her with his ownership. They were both breathing heavily, almost painfully, when his hard body moved over hers and between short, fierce kisses, he vowed, "I love you, Anne. I'll always love you."

Neither one of them heard the door open and they both went rigid when Jud's father said coldly, "Get away from her, Jud."

Jud hesitated a second then through clenched teeth spat out, "Get the hell out of here, Dad."

"I told you to get away from her and I mean it. Now, move."

Judson Cammeron had not raised his voice, but there was an icy, angry command in his tone. Overwhelmed with disappointment and shame, Anne moaned softly, "Jud, please."

Jud remained still, every muscle in his body tense with anger; then he moved, slowly, pulling his robe over her body as he went.

Shaking with reaction, Anne lay listening to the silence crackle angrily between father and son. Her stepfather finally broke the silence. "Haven't you had enough with all the girls you've had in the last year? Must you bring your appetite home? Use your stepsister? Good God, man, she is little more than a child."

Jud started tightly, "Dad, you—" His father cut him off. "I'm taking Anne to her room, but I'll be back." He tucked the robe around her shaking body, then lifted her in his arms. At the door he paused, his voice thick with disgust. "Get some clothes on."

He carried her to her room, laid her on the bed, then turned his back to her, saying, "Put on a nightgown and get into bed. I'll be back, I'm going to get you something to help you sleep."

Tears running down her face, she leaped off the bed the minute he closed the door. With jerky movements she pulled a clean nightie over her head, crawled back into bed, turned her face into her pillow, and sobbed brokenly.

By the time he returned she was shaking so badly he had to help her sit up and hold the glass for her while she chokingly swallowed the two pills he handed her.

"Don't cry so, Anne, you'll make yourself ill. I don't blame you in this, you're too young to understand."

"Mother?" Anne sobbed.

"She's asleep and I give you my word she, or anyone else, will not hear of this."

He left her and slowly, as the pills, whatever they were, took effect and she grew drowsy, the sobs subsided.

It had been late when Anne woke the next morning. A beautiful Saturday morning that didn't fit at all with her depressed state. Feeling hurt, uncertain, very young, Anne showered and dressed, afraid to think about Jud and what had happened. She felt ashamed that her stepfather had found them the way they were, but she felt no guilt. She loved Jud and he said he loved her and their lovemaking, aborted though it had been, was a natural outpouring of that love. Things might be uncomfortable for a while, but somehow she felt sure Jud would make it right. On that thought she had squared her shoulders and gone downstairs.

The twins were nowhere around, but her mother and stepfather were having a midmorning coffee in the living room. Anne started into the room, then stopped, a finger of fear stabbing her heart at their expressions. Her stepfather's face was set, stony. Her mother looked upset, near tears. Fearfully Anne asked, "What happened? Is something wrong?"

Judson opened his mouth, but before he could speak her mother cried, "Oh, Anne, it's Jud. Sometime during the night he packed his bags and left. He left no word of where he was going or when he'd be back, nothing."

Feeling her knees buckle, Anne dropped into a chair.

"But—"

The sight of her stepfather's eyes dried the words on her lips, for although his face was set, his eyes were filled with disappointment and despair. When he spoke, his voice was cold and flat.

"Margaret, I don't want his name mentioned in this house ever again, do you understand?"

"Judson!" her mother's voice mirrored her astonishment.

"I mean it," he went on in the same flat tone. "Talk to the twins, make them understand. Not ever again. Anne, do you understand?"

Anne had nodded her head bleakly, not understanding at all.

Anne, coming back to the present, stirred restlessly on the bed, eyes closed against the tears and pain that engulfed her. She had thought she had left the pain behind a long time ago. At first she had waited hopefully for a phone call or a letter. But as the weeks became months the hope died, only the pain went on. As one year slipped into two, then three, the pain dulled, flaring at intervals as word of him began to reach them.

He had come into a sizable inheritance from his mother's estate the same day he left and had used it well. Jud had always had a flair for the use of fabrics in clothes and he used that flair by opening an exclusive menswear shop. Somewhere he had run across two budding but avant-garde designers and he hired them. They had obviously worked well together, for by the time Anne and his father heard of it, he had expanded to four stores in key cities. The first contact between Jud and his father had been made through Jud's assistant four years before.

Anne would never forget the look on Judson Cammeron's face the day he had called her into his office and silently handed her a letter. It had been a request for an interview to discuss the possibility of the production of a particular fabric and it had been signed by a John Franks, assistant to Judson Cammeron of Cammeron Clothiers. The only word that could describe her stepfather's expression was stunned.

Maintaining a rigid control she had asked quietly, "Will you see this John Franks?"

He had hesitated, then replied heavily, "We may as well, Anne. If we don't they'll only go to the competition. Besides which, I'm curious to know what he has in mind for this fabric." He, of course, being Jud.

The meeting was held, a deal was struck, and they had been supplying Jud with special fabric off and on ever since. But never at any time had personal contact been made between father and son. And at no time did Jud's name pass his father's lips although Anne knew by his attitude that he was pleased by even this small contact.

At last report Jud's stores numbered eight and he was reputed to be becoming a very rich man. The word that had filtered down to them was that there were some very wealthy men who bought almost exclusively from Jud and that their numbers were growing by the week.

And now, Anne thought, he would have it all. The company that produced the fabric, the designers who whipped up the original clothes, and the stores where they were sold. *Not all,* Anne corrected herself, *not if I can help it.* She had no right to any part of the company, but Troy and Todd did, and somehow she had to make sure they got it.

Suddenly Anne realized that her train of thought, the last few minutes, had alleviated, to a degree, her pain and shock. The tears were gone, replaced by determination. She had taken care of the twins since they were toddlers. Her protective, mother's instinct was to the fore replacing the hurt, humiliated feeling of the long-ago fifteen-year-old girl.

Her lips set in a determined line, Anne slid off the bed and walked to the window. The light was gone from the day that had never brightened above gray. Anne's room was on the side of the house and below, some distance beyond, the bright lights above the doors of the triple garage lit the surrounding area in an artificial glare. Eyes bleak as the weather, Anne studied the dark tracery of bare, black tree limbs. The stark branches in that eerie light had the effect of many arms raised in supplication to the heavens.

Restlessly she turned from the harsh etching, her eyes moving slowly over the muted pinks of the room bathed in the soft glow of the bedside lamp. She had felt a measure of security in this room the last few years, had thought her shattered emotions healed, her heart becoming free once more. Now she felt scared, vulnerable, not unlike that tree outside with limbs lifted as if in yearning. She knew a longing deep inside that had to be quickly squashed.

Moving with purpose, she slowly undressed. She could show no sign of weakness with Jud, for if she did, she was sure he'd trample her as completely as would a wild, fear-crazed mob. She had allowed, no, invited, his trampling before. She wasn't sure she could survive it a second time.

Anne's head came up in defiance and her spine went taut with determination. She may have allowed him to hurt her, but she would not let him hurt her family. The thought that they were his family, too, was dismissed out of hand. He had disclaimed all rights to any of them ten years ago. The clock could not be turned back. All long-ago hurts—and words—were best forgotten. With a firm step she went into the bathroom.

Chapter Three

I love you, Anne, I'll always love you. Single-minded determination was hard to hang onto with those words coming back to torment her. As she showered and dressed for dinner Anne berated herself for allowing the memory to creep back. There was no comparison between the Judson Cammeron who walked into the library today and the Jud who whispered those words so fervently all those years ago.

Misty-eyed, Anne stared at her reflection in the mirror, eyeshadow applicator poised over her right lid. She had managed to erase most of the evidence of her earlier weeping, and now, with the help of carefully applied makeup, was camouflaging the last traces.

She was definitely not looking forward to dinner. Would there be a replay of that earlier unpleasantness? Anne hoped not, but she had an uneasy feeling her hopes would be in vain. Jud seemed to be on a determined course of disruption with every one of them. Although, in all truth, he had been considerate of her mother's feelings, and his plan for Todd and Troy's future could, as he had said, be the making of them. But to her, his attitude bordered on vindictive. Why? Was it possible that those words of love rankled now? That hardly seemed possible. And anyway she, if anyone, had been the injured party in that farce.

Cloudy gray eyes studied their own reflection. What exactly did he have in mind? Anne puzzled at the question as she stroked smoky taupe shadow over her eyelid. And why this insistence on his own secretary? Word of him in that department had filtered down to them too. If only half of the rumors they'd heard could be believed, Jud was a very busy boy indeed. She remembered the first time one such story had been circulated, and Jud's father's face when he'd relayed it to her. With something like pity she'd studied the warring emotions of pride and disgust he had revealed. It seemed, when it came to women, it was no-holds-barred with Jud. And, it appeared, the women were always exceptional. Beautiful, talented, rich.

Anne was an extremely fortunate young woman and she knew it. She was small and delicately formed. Her bone structure was good and covered by very soft, fine-textured skin. Her hair, a rich chocolate brown, was full and thick with a silky feel and healthy shine. Her eyes, normally a clear gray, changed color with her emotions. When she was happy or excited they grew lighter, almost silvery. But when she was angry, hurt, or felt something very deeply, they turned dark and stormy. Anne sighed as she brushed blusher onto her pale cheeks. She had been called lovely and, in all honesty, she supposed that was true, but she was not, in her own opinion, beautiful. Nor was she rich or very talented.

Her own thoughts brought her up short, and with a muttered "damn" she stood and moved away from the mirror. Why ever would she want to be any of those things? She did not have to be beautiful, rich, or talented. Just smart. Smart, and quick enough to protect her brothers' interests. She had no wish, she told herself, to attract Jud's interest, either physically or otherwise. Her Jud, the tender, loving Jud she'd secretly kept hidden inside her heart these last ten years, was just a figment of a young girl's romantic imagination. And the past was dead and buried. As dead and buried as the man who, unbeknownst to her, had saved her deep shame and humiliation when he'd walked into Jud's bedroom that night.

Squaring her shoulders resolutely, Anne left her room and walked quickly along the long hall and down the stairs. She was late. She could hear the others already in the dining room, and her mother's petulant voice ask, "Where is Anne?"

"Here." Anne spoke softly as she entered the room. "Sorry I'm late. You should have started."

The moment Anne was seated Mrs. Davis came through the door from the kitchen carrying a soup tureen and set it on the table, giving Anne a reproving look as she did so. Then, to Anne's astonishment, in a manner completely opposite of her earlier surliness, Mrs. Davis smiled ingratiatingly at Jud and murmured, "Would you like me to serve the soup now, Mr. Cammeron?"

"Yes. Thank you, Mrs. Davis." Jud's tone was quiet, pleasant, and authoritative all at the same time.

Anne felt a flash of irritation followed by a touch of fatalism. It certainly hadn't taken Mrs. Davis long to sniff out which way the wind was blowing.

During the early stage of the meal, conversation was minimal and stilted, and in the case of Troy and Todd, close to being rude. Anne herself had very little to offer and jumped with a startled "What?" when Jud rapped at her, "Who is the lucky man, and when is the big day?"

In confusion her eyes followed the direction of his and came to rest on the cluster of diamonds on her left hand. Andrew! Oh, Lord, she hadn't thought of him at all during this whole, horribly long day. Not since his call early in the morning. A deep flush mounting her cheeks, she lifted her eyes to Jud's face.

"Andrew Saunders, and we haven't set a date yet."

"Andrew Saunders." He repeated softly, then, his eyes mocking, his lower lip curled slightly. "Not the same Andy Saunders I chased home from school regularly?"

Anne felt her color deepen, but before she could form a suitably cutting retort, her mother chided, "That was a long time ago, Jud. Andrew is now a most respected, well-liked attorney. As a matter of fact he works for Mr. Slonne, and you know how particular he is."

Jud looked anything but chastised. One eyebrow rose mockingly and he turned to Anne with a bored drawl.

"And where is the most respected and well-liked Andrew now?"

Anne moistened her lips, resentment burning through her at the ease with which he could put her on the defensive. Glancing up, she felt a funny catch of pain in her throat. Jud's eyes, a strange glow in their depths, were fastened intently on her mouth. A shock of pure, blind longing hit her like a blow and to negate the feeling she rushed into speech.

"H-he had to go out of town on business two days ago." Appalled at the breathless sound of her voice, Anne forced herself to slow down before adding, "Otherwise he would be here now. He will be back late tomorrow afternoon."

"I see."

Two words. Two very small words. And yet they seemed to speak volumes. His tone, that one brow arched so mockingly, seemed to say he saw far more than the simple fact that Andrew would return the following afternoon.

He can't possible know, Anne told herself fiercely. No one can ever really know the depth of someone's feelings for another. Not really, can they? With a sigh of relief Anne heard her mother's soft voice change the conversation.

"Breakfast has always been ready at seven for your father and Anne, Jud. Will that be convenient for you also or would you prefer a different time?"

Finally Jud's disturbing gaze turned away from Anne's face to rest thoughtfully on his stepmother.

"I have already told you, Margaret, that I have no wish to disrupt the normal routine of this house," Jud answered quietly, then, on a snort from Todd, tagged on sardonically, "No more than absolutely necessary, that is."

He glanced up and smiled as Mrs. Davis entered the room to serve dessert and coffee. He waited until she was finished and was at the door to the kitchen again before he stated, "Breakfast at seven will be fine, Mrs. Davis. But don't plan on me for tomorrow morning, as I won't be here."

"Yes, sir."

The deference conveyed by Mrs. Davis's tone as she went

through the door to the kitchen set Anne's teeth on edge. Yet her eyes swung, as did her mother's and the twins', to Jud, in question. Margaret voiced the question.

"But, Jud, where will you be?"

An expression of annoyance crossed Jud's face and, though it was fleeting, it left little doubt in any of their minds about his irritation at having his movements questioned. Then, sighing softly, he answered. "I'm flying to New York in exactly"—he glanced at his watch—"two hours. There are some things I want to collect from my office and my apartment." Glinting amber eyes flashed to Anne's face as he added, "Including my secretary. I'm booked on the early flight back tomorrow morning and I'll go right to the plant."

Anne barely heard his last sentence. Her mind was hung on his "including my secretary." His phrasing had made it sound as if his secretary was at his apartment. What was his secretary like, Anne wondered. Beautiful? Talented? Rich? A feeling of intense weariness swamped her, leaving her weak, slightly sick. *It's none of my business,* she told herself, angrily forcing her attention back to the others as her mother asked, "Will you be home for dinner tomorrow night?" Margaret paused, then added nervously, "Andrew is coming to dinner and it would give you two a chance to get reacquainted."

"I wouldn't miss it for the world," Jud drawled, eyes again flashing mockingly at Anne. "Now, if you'll excuse me, I think I'd better make tracks or I'll miss my plane." He stood and strode to the door, then paused, turned back to the room, and asked, "Did you do as I asked, Anne?"

Anne felt the sense of weariness deepen, but lifting her head proudly she replied coolly, "Yes. Everything is in the briefcase on your father's desk."

His eyes grew sharp at her tone. Then, shrugging lightly, he murmured "Thank you" and left the room.

Quiet. Anne bit her lip, steeling herself for the storm that would surely follow this calm. Then it broke as the other three began speaking all at once. One hurt and two angry voices hurled questions at her. What were they going to do? What about their plans for Lauderdale? Did she think there was a chance of contesting the will? Who the hell did he think he was anyway? These questions and more along the same line, came from Todd and Troy. Wasn't it unfair to have to go to him for every penny? How could they possibly maintain a normal routine with his disruptive presence? Was there really anything any of them could do about it? Her mother had joined the questioners too.

Anne fielded the barrage as well as she could, knowing full well there was not a thing they could do. If there had been, she was sure that Mr. Slonne, being Mr. Slonne, would have indicated as much that afternoon.

Then it came. The question Anne had been dreading. What was she going to do?

"There really isn't too much I can do, is there?" Anne answered guardedly.

Three faces stared at her in astonishment long moments before Todd exclaimed, "What do you mean? Of course there is something you can do! All his big talk doesn't mean a thing if you stick with us. His hands will be tied, at least as far as the business is concerned."

"Todd is right, Anne." Her mother's voice held a mild tone of reproof. "Surely you don't intend to let him have his way?"

"I don't know exactly what I intend as yet." Anne sighed. "But I can't openly oppose him. He warned me that if I did he'd ruin the business. He assured me he could do this. I believe him; he wasn't bluffing."

"But that's stupid," Troy cried. "He'd stand to lose as much as we would. I think you're wrong. I believe he was bluffing."

Anne's head was moving from side to side in negation before Troy had finished speaking.

"Although you are right about Jud losing as much as you, you forget he has another very successful operation to fall back on. You don't. Also, have you forgotten, he has control of the capital. He could cut you all down to the bare essentials. I'm not saying he would do that, just that he could, if his hand were forced. I'll leave it up to you. Do you want to take that chance? I do not appreciate the position your father has put me in, so I'll leave it up to you. If you want to make a fight of it I'll help you all I can, but I must be honest, and, in my opinion, we can't possibly win. Jud is smart and fast and, I'm afraid, more than a little ruthless. He won't quit until he has done exactly what he said he would."

"You want us to meekly obey every one of his damned orders?" Todd's face was a study of hurt disbelief, and Anne felt a shaft of irritation at the immaturity of both the question and the expression.

"What I want doesn't mean a damn thing," she snapped in exasperation. "I have merely pointed out the options open to you. What, exactly, do you expect me to do? I hold a very small amount of stock and I remain in this house on Jud's sufferance. So, you tell me, what do I do?"

Anne's voice had risen and she was visibly trembling. Breathing deeply, she brought herself under control and was about to add that she had already been ejected from the office but bit back the words. If they decided to make a fight of it, it wouldn't matter, and if they didn't, they'd know soon enough.

Glum silence had settled on the room at Anne's outburst and the expressions on all three of the faces in front of her were the same. They were stunned, shocked, and Anne knew they had expected some sort of miracle from her. Her inability to perform this miracle was a hard fact they did not want to face. But that she was as upset, if not more than they were, was evident, and after a long pause Todd said earnestly, "I'm sorry, Anne, I didn't think." He paused, wet his lips nervously, then went on. "I guess none of us thought this through. Too much has happened too fast. First the shock of Dad's death, then the sudden appearance of Jud, followed by the will and Jud's incredible dictums. I see now we have little choice, at least for the time being, but to follow Jud's lead. At least Troy and I can escape back to school; you have to face him every day."

"I just don't understand why Judson did this," Margaret sobbed, "after forbidding us to even mention Jud's name."

Anne considered then discarded the idea of telling her mother Jud's thoughts on why his father had acted as he had. What good would it do? she asked herself tiredly. It would just agitate them more and everyone was agitated enough already.

As they left the dining room, Troy slid his arm around Anne's waist. "This is one hell of a mess Dad's left us in," he murmured. Then he repeated Jud's statement of that afternoon. "And you're right in the middle, Anne."

Excusing herself, Anne went to her room and sat there staring moodily into space. It was a hell of a mess and she didn't want to be in the middle of it, didn't want to be exposed to Jud's obvious dislike and biting sarcasm.

Was there really anything she could do for Troy and Todd? Maybe if she could have remained in the office, but here? Anne shook her head. She doubted she'd see much of Jud at home. He didn't strike her as the type to spend his evenings in quiet companionship with his family. Especially this family.

Then a new idea struck her. Maybe Andrew could advise her. True he knew little of the business, as Mr. Slonne and his partners had handled all of the company's legal work. But as a member of the firm, even a fairly junior member, he'd handled some of the minor work. And Andrew was an intelligent young man. Although reluctant to involve him in her family's infighting, Anne clutched at Andrew's name as at a lifeline. At the moment, she felt utterly helpless and Andrew was a ray of hope. It didn't occur to her that Andrew, being her fiancé, should have been the first person to turn to.

Anne had a restless night, dozing and waking repeatedly, and when she did finally fall into an exhausted sleep close to dawn, it was tormented by a nightmare.

They were swimming in a place Anne didn't recognize, and Troy and Todd were out much too far. About to call to them to come back, Anne saw them begin to flounder, then cry out for help. She struck out boldly to go to them, when she was brought up short by strong, hard fingers grasping her ankle. Two hands of steel, moving hand over hand up her leg, towed her back. "Let me go," she screamed wildly. "They'll die out there."

"You know the rules of the game." The voice was cold, menacing. Jud's voice. "It's sink or swim, live or die, winner take all."

Frantically she fought the coils of steel on her body, sputtering and choking on the churning water that splashed into her mouth. Her struggle was meaningless, for the hard hands grasped her shoulders, hauled her around to face him. In sheer terror she cried out at his look. Tall enough to stand where she could not, he seemed to tower over her, and the expression on his face was threatening, almost diabolical. Fear and panic increased her struggles and she fought desperately to free herself.

"If you insist on fighting me," he intoned icily, "there is only one thing I can do." With that he shoved her back, away from him, and, although she knew the impetus of the motion would completely submerge her, she felt a wild surge of hope as she felt his fingers loosen their painful hold. The hope was quickly dashed as she felt his arms slide around her back. He was going to follow her under—no, he was forcing her under, his large frame on top of her forcing her down, down. As the water covered her chin, she drew a great breath of air, then felt shock grip her mind, for Jud's mouth covered hers, forcing her lips apart, at the same instant the water covered her head, cutting off the life-sustaining air.

What was he doing? Was he trying to drown them both? But no, Jud was an expert swimmer; he had always amazed everyone with the length of time he could remain under water. Terror crawled through her veins like a slithering reptile. He was going to kill her! A scream grew in her chest and lodged in her throat, unable to escape, and her mind throbbed with the words "I don't want to die! I don't want to die!" Panic increased her struggles and the sinewy arms tightened, crushing her against his hard, slippery body as his legs encircled hers in a pincer embrace. Then the pressure against her mouth subtly changed, became caressing, sensuous and suddenly the fear coursing through her body changed too, became a searing tongue of desire, licking and consuming all other emotion. Their frenetic spiral under water became an erotic ballet, with his possession, and her death, the finale. And she didn't care. More, she welcomed it, somehow knowing his possession would be worth it. Roughly the panties to her bikini were torn from her, and, joy singing through her, she arched her body to his.

At that moment Anne surfaced from the nightmare, her body bathed in a cold sweat. Her hands were clutching the bedcovers and she was shaking and sobbing low in her throat. Breathing deeply, Anne finally brought her shattered emotions under control, except for the occasional shudder. The dream had been so real, was still so vivid and clear in her mind.

Afraid to go back to sleep again, she lay back against the pillow and stared at the window, watching the pale gray first light turn to shell pink day.

Anne's cheeks flushed the same shell pink as flashes of the dream skipped in and out of her mind. There were some parts of it she thought she understood. Troy and Todd's drowning, her effort to save them, Jud's keeping her from doing so. If she could find no way of helping them, Troy and Todd would go under—financially. And Jud had made it quite clear he intended to keep her from helping them.

But the rest of the dream? Anne felt a tremor slide down her spine. Did she believe, subconsciously, that Jud would go as far as physically harming her to get what he wanted? Her mind firmly skirted around the sexual connotations, putting that part down to her memories of ten years before. Nevertheless she felt a warmth invade her body, a longing ache tug at her throat. Was it possible to want someone so badly you would even welcome oblivion to taste that sweetness just once?

Anne shook her head firmly. *Nonsense, forget it, it was only a dream, all of it.* Yet, at the back of her mind she felt a small, but very real, twinge of fear.

As dawn blossomed into full morning, anxiety grew inside Anne. If she'd been able to keep to her usual routine, she assured herself, she could have controlled it, but with time on her hands, her mind ran rampant with speculation.

She was pacing her room when her mother called her to the phone. Glad for any excuse to escape her own confused thoughts, Anne raced down the steps and across the foyer to the telephone table. Breathless from her run, she almost gasped, "Hello?"

"Where the hell are you?" Jud's voice was a hard rap against her ears.

"Obviously I'm here at home," Anne snapped, all her fears of the last hours lacing her tone with ice. "What do you want?"

"What do I want?" he repeated angrily. "I want you, that's what the hell I want. You have exactly thirty minutes to get that pretty little tush of yours down here. If you're not here by then I'll come after you, so snap to it."

Chapter Four

Anne winced at the loud noise that assaulted her ear as Jud slammed down his receiver. Confusion and shock kept her immobile a few moments then the words "snap to it" echoed through her mind and, spinning on her heel, she ran up the stairs. His tone had left little doubt that he'd do exactly as he threatened.

Thirty-two minutes later she walked into the office she still thought of as hers and came face to face with a tall, willowy, gorgeous redhead.

"May I help you?"

The cool, well-modulated voice perfectly matched the appearance of the redhead and Anne felt a disquieting, sinking sensation. So this was the secretary Jud had to have in his office. She was certainly beautiful and more than likely very talented, and with the first two attributes, rich hardly seemed important.

Breathing deeply, Anne managed to answer quietly. "Yes, I'm Anne Moore. Mr. Cammeron is expec—"

At that moment one of the two doors behind the redhead opened and Jud snapped impatiently, "It's about time. Come in here, Anne." He held the door to what had been his father's office open, his amber gaze steady on her face as Anne walked past him into the large room.

It seemed like weeks rather than days since Anne had been in this office and she glanced around warily somehow expecting changes. Of course there were none, except for the fact that the top of Judson Senior's large oak desk, usually so neat and orderly, was a welter of folders and loose papers. The room was exactly the same.

Anne's eyes noted the desktop as they quickly scanned the brown and white tweed carpet, the tan burlap-weave draperies, the crammed bookshelf along one wall, and the three leather-covered chairs in front of the desk. At the same time her mind registered the warmer shading of Jud's tone as he spoke to his secretary.

"I'll be busy for the rest of the day, Lorna. I'll accept no calls except from the list of names I gave you earlier. Take your lunch at the usual time. And would you bring back a couple of sandwiches for Miss Moore and me?"

"Yes, sir."

The secretary's reply was punctuated by the soft click of the door being closed. Anne turned, a small lump catching at her throat as she viewed Jud. He leaned almost indolently against the door, his gold hair and bronze skin set off by the deep brown of his suit and the crisp white of his shirt.

"All right, Anne." His voice was soft and silky. Too silky. "What's the play?"

"I don't know what you mean." Anne had trouble covering the tremor in her voice.

His mouth took on the by now familiar sardonic twist. His eyes mocked her. "Were you going to show as much disrespect of me as possible by coming in very late or weren't you going to come in at all?"

Anne stared at him in disbelief a moment then rushed her words angrily. "You said you didn't need me in this office!"

"No, I did not," he stated flatly before jerking his thumb over his shoulder at the door. "I said I didn't need you in that office."

Since entering the room, Anne had been aware of scraping, shuffling noises from the adjoining, smaller office, the office Jud had occupied over ten years ago. His next words explained the muffled sounds.

"I'm having my old office cleaned up for you. I take it it has been used for storage for some time now?"

Anne nodded dumbly.

"Yes, well," he grimaced, "until it can be made ready for you, you'll have to work in here with me."

"Doing what exactly?"

"For heaven's sake, Anne, what do you think?" Jud sighed and pushed himself away from the door and moved across the room toward her. "I'm no more a fool than the old man was. For the next few weeks your help in here will be invaluable to me. That's why I brought Lorna back with me. To free you of the outer office work."

Her voice strained, Anne asked, "And after the next few weeks?"

Jud paused, his eyes raking her tight, closed face. "I'll probably dump even more work on you. I have two separate companies to run, Anne. And I have no intention of giving up the reins to either one of them. If the going gets tough you can cry on John Franks's shoulder. As I'm sure you already know, John is my other assistant."

His assistant! A small shiver of pleasure shot through Anne. Not only was he not banishing her from the office, he wanted her for his assistant. Anne felt tears of relief sting her eyes and blinked quickly; then her eyes flew wide as he stepped in front of her and grasped her shoulders tightly.

"I expect you to give me the same loyalty and everything else you gave the old man." His voice had taken on a thick roughness. A small shiver slid down Anne's spine. "Beginning with this." His head dipped swiftly, then his mouth was crushing hers in a brutal, painful kiss.

Anne went rigid with shock, unable, for a moment, to think or move. Then her mouth was released and he moved back, away from her.

"What do you think you're doing?" Wildly confused and angry, Anne nearly choked on the words.

"I just told you," Jud answered in a bored tone, turning his back to her as he walked around the desk. "I expect all the fringe benefits the old man had." He turned back to her sharply, his voice nasty. "Were you naive enough to think that your—how should I say it—devotion to my father had gone unnoticed? Or that the word hadn't spread?"

As his words hammered at her, Anne's mind filled with horror. What was he saying? Surely no one in their right mind would think that she and her stepfather were . . . Unable to bear the thought, Anne cried, "What do you mean? Exactly what are you accusing me of?"

"Come off it, Anne, it's been whispered about for some time now." Jud's face and voice were cold, his mouth an unremitting, hard line. "It's nothing very new or novel. An older man seeking the virility of his youth with a young woman. Or, in this case, you endeavoring to show your gratitude in whatever way he wished. Or did you convince yourself you were in love with him?"

Struck speechless, anger gripping her throat, Anne stared at him for several long minutes. Then the anger exploded from her mouth. "Are you out of your dirty little mind? He was my mother's husband."

"Are you telling me there was nothing of a personal nature between you?" Jud's tone was skeptical, his eyes sharp.

"I am telling you exactly that." Anne drew a deep breath in an effort to control the tremor of anger in her voice. "Not only do you insult me, you smear your father's memory. Have you grown so cynical, so jaded over the years that you'd believe something like that about a man like your father? I don't know what happened between you to cause the break in your relationship, and it's none of my business. But I'll tell you this. At no time was your father other than kind and considerate toward me. He treated me like a daughter, and yes, I was loyal and I was grateful. He was a good man, the closest thing to a father I ever knew. Now, if you are quite through trying to humiliate me with your filthy suggestions, I'll leave. I have a lot of packing to do."

Anne's fingers loosened from the back of the chair she was gripping and she turned and took two steps toward the door, only to stop at Jud's ordered "Stay where you are."

She was almost relieved to obey his command, for her legs were shaking so badly she wasn't sure she could take another step. Although his hands were gentle, she flinched when he touched her arms, turned her to face him.

"I'm sorry, Anne." His amber eyes were shadowed, cloudy with some emotion Anne couldn't define. His voice was soft and contrite. "I had no right to say what I did. I should have challenged the innuendo when I first heard it. I was bitter and, in that bitterness, believed it. Time and distance and circumstances can have a big effect on a man's thinking. I was out of line and I apologize. Don't leave, either this office or the house. Your mother, Troy, and Todd need you at the house. And whether you believe it or not, I need you here."

Anne lowered her eyes, fighting the tears that had been building for the last ten minutes. Her instinct for self-preservation urged her to run, but she wanted so badly to stay. Breathing slowly, she regained control and lifting her head proudly she said, "All right, Jud, I'll stay. At least temporarily. I owe that to Todd and Troy. But I warn you, if ever I hear you mention anything about your father and—"

"You won't," Jud cut in firmly. "Not from me or anyone else. You have my word on that."

The atmosphere was heavy with tension as Jud turned from her to pick up a chair and place it next to his own behind the desk. Anne stood motionless watching him until, lifting his head, one eyebrow raised, he said softly, "There really is a lot of work here, Anne. And I really could use your help."

Anne sighed as she slipped out of her coat and hung it up before moving around the desk to sit down beside him. He could still be persuasive if he wanted to, she thought ruefully, that was one area in which he hadn't changed.

"What I want to do first is go over the personnel files of everyone in any kind of a managerial position down to the last foreman and forelady and quality control person."

Pulling a folder from the pile he opened it on the desk between them and began firing questions at her.

The tension in the room soon dissipated as Anne, at times, found herself reaching for answers to Jud's sharply incisive queries. She became fully absorbed in the work and didn't notice the passage of time until a soft tap on the door and Jud's growled, "Come in" brought her head up.

"Your lunch, Mr. Cammeron."

Anne watched as Jud's secretary walked gracefully across the room. Before she was halfway to the desk, Jud was out of his chair and relieving her of the tray she was carrying.

"Thank you, Lorna. I'll settle up with you later."

"Yes, sir." The door closed quietly on the softly spoken words.

As he slid the tray onto the edge of the cluttered desk, Jud said crisply. "Come on, Anne, take a break and have something to eat."

Suddenly hungry, Anne's eyes went to the tray of food. On it were two Styrofoam cups of soup, a paper plate piled with sandwiches, a pot of coffee, a small sugar bowl and creamer, two mugs, and two paper napkins. She reached for a cup of soup at the same time Jud did, and when his fingers brushed hers she jerked her hand away as if burned.

Cold amber eyes mocking her nervousness, lips twisting in a sardonic smile, Jud picked up both cups of soup, and handing one to her, carefully drawled, "I don't bite, Anne. At least, not very often."

Pink-cheeked, Anne lowered her eyes only to lift them again as she heard him sigh in exasperation and turn away to walk to the window behind the desk. Sipping the creamed tomato soup, Anne studied him through the fringe of her lashes. The bright afternoon sunlight slanting through the window struck sparks of glinting gold off his hair, brought a glistening sheen to his bronze skin. Anne shivered as the words tawny gold crept into her mind. Even as a teenager Jud had been handsome. Now, with maturity and experience etched onto his face, he was devastating.

Wanting to look away but unable to unfasten her eyes from his broad back, a second shiver followed the first when Jud arched his spine and flexed his shoulders. During the morning, while they had been deep into the work, he had shrugged out of his jacket, loosened his tie, and opened the top button of his shirt. Now, the play of muscles under the fine material of his shirt as he stretched, one hand going to massage the back of his neck, sent a shaft of feeling through Anne so intense it robbed her of her breath.

Jerking her eyes away, she forced herself to finish her soup and reach for a piece of sandwich she didn't want.

"Why don't you get up and walk around awhile, Anne?"

Concentrating on eating the unwanted food, Anne hadn't heard Jud move away from the window and his voice, so close beside her, made her jump. Impatience laced his tone as he snapped, "For God's sake, will you relax? From the look on your face, anyone walking in right now would think I had hit you."

Anne glanced up as he moved around the desk, his face and body taut with anger. He filled the mugs with coffee, picked up the cream, and raised his brows in question, his hands pausing over the mugs. She nodded as she stood up. "I'm sorry. You startled me, I thought you were still at the window." He handed her one of the mugs without speaking, his eyes, hard and cold, searching her face. Unable to withstand his intent gaze, Anne took the mug with a murmured "thank you" and turned away to retrace his steps to the window.

Anne gulped her coffee, tears stinging her eyes when the hot liquid scorched her mouth. *What have I let myself in for?* she thought frantically. *How can I work with him if every move he makes, every word he utters unnerves me like this?*

Jud moved to stand behind her, making deliberate noises as he walked across the room. Even so, when his fingers lightly touched her arm she could not repress a small shiver. He sighed softly, then said quietly, "Anne, look at me."

Anne stiffened, then forcing her unseeing eyes from the parking lot in front of the large factory building, she turned to face him.

"We're never going to be able to work together if you tighten up like this every time I come near you, Anne." Jud's tone was still soft, but a definite firmness underlined his words. "I realize this isn't easy for you, especially after my behavior earlier. But if you intend to stick to your word and stay, you are going to have to push your dislike of me to the back of your mind at least here in the office."

"Jud—" Anne began, but he raised his hand and interrupted, all softness gone now.

"Let me finish. I'm going to be under a lot of pressure during the next few months. Besides the work here I have a number of things on the fire in connection with my clothing business. I'm probably not going to be the easiest man in the world to get along with and I can't have you around if you're going to be this uptight all the time. I've admitted I need your help here, so I'll leave it up to you. If you can't handle it, tell me. If you're going to stay, you'll have to bury your resentment." He paused, his cool eyes raking her face. Then he snapped, "What is it going to be, Anne, go or stay?"

"I told you before I'd stay, Jud. I haven't changed my mind," Anne answered steadily.

"Good." His right hand was held out as he added, "Peace?"

Anne hesitated, then placed her hand in his, felt a tiny shock run up her arm as his hard fingers clasped hers, but managed a calm, "All right, Jud, peace."

The afternoon flew by even faster than the morning had and when Jud's phone buzzed around four thirty Anne was grateful for the opportunity to stretch while Jud answered it. She heard him say, "Who is it, Lorna?" then, "Okay, put it through." Then he held the receiver out to Anne. She gave him a surprised glance, but he didn't say anything, just smiled—mockingly, she thought.

"Hello?" She spoke uncertainly.

"Anne? Is that you, darling?" Andrew's voice came warm over the wire.

"Yes, Andrew. When did you get home?" Somehow Anne infused some warmth of her own into her tone, wondering why it should be so difficult.

"Just now, who answered your phone?"

"Jud's secretary." Anne said without thinking.

"Jud?" Andrew's voice had sharpened. "Jud Cammeron? When did he get back and what's he doing in your office?"

Anne sighed. Of course Andrew wouldn't know about the will and, by the way Jud's face was tightening in anger at the interruption, she couldn't tell Andrew now. Hurriedly she said, "He's not in my office, I'm in his," and looked up to see one white brow arch arrogantly. "I can't talk now, as we're very busy. I'll explain tonight. You are coming for dinner?"

"Yes, but—" he began, but Anne cut him off. "I have to go now, Andrew, see you at the house. Goodbye." Before he could reply, she hung up, sat down at the desk, and picked up the folder she and Jud had been working on.

"So the legal eagle is back," Jud chided smoothly, the very smoothness of his tone irritating. "How nice for you. Now, do you think we could finish this folder before you have to rush home to get ready for him?"

"Jud, really—" Anne began warningly.

"Anne, really," Jud cut in sarcastically, then his tone softened. "Okay, I'm sorry for the dig. Tell you what. I promise to be on my best behavior tonight at dinner, if you will."

"What do you mean, if I will?"

"Just what I said. I'll be polite and charming to Andrew, if you'll reciprocate with Lorna."

"Lorna?" Anne repeated, stunned. "Lorna is coming to dinner tonight?"

"Yes."

"But—"

"But nothing," Jud said icily. "I called Margaret this morning and told her. She understood, even if you don't."

Oh, I understand perfectly, Anne thought scathingly, trying to ignore the sudden twist of pain that shot through her chest. What's to understand? A man brings his mistress to town, what else does he do but invite her home to dinner! *Oh, God, I feel sick.* Why? Before she had to face an answer to that why, she rushed into speech.

"Of course I'll be polite to her. Why shouldn't I be?" She hesitated, then added, "She's a very beautiful woman."

"Yes, she is." Hard finality in his tone, cold and flat as his eyes. Unable to maintain that intent stare, Anne turned back to the work on the desk, shocked at the way her fingers were trembling.

Sinking into the scented bathwater, Anne sighed wearily. She was tired. It had been a long, emotionally charged day, with Jud not letting up until almost six o'clock. Now, little less than an hour later, Anne wished for nothing more than to lie back in the tub and forget the evening ahead. She couldn't, of course. In fact, she should be downstairs at this moment as Andrew would be arriving any minute.

Sighing again, Anne finished her bath, stepped out of the tub, gave herself a quick, vigorous rub with a large bath towel, and swung around to lift her robe from the hook on the bathroom door. A flashing reflection made her pause, then stop completely to contemplate the nude young woman gazing back at her from the full-length mirror on the door.

Beginning at the top of her head, Anne's eyes critically evaluated the image before her. Her hair, dark and sleek, was cut close to her head on the top and sides, a natural wave giving it a sculptured look. The back was a little longer, turning in softly to caress her neck. The face, to Anne's eyes, though pleasing, held a sad, somewhat wistful look, too thin, too pale, and the eyes seemed enormous, with a vaguely lost expression. Her small frame was slender, too slender. Although Anne admitted it was well formed—the small breasts high and rounded, the waist tiny, the hip and legline smooth and supple.

Anne's sigh this time was deeper, almost painful. Her head and shoulders sagged and she closed her eyes to shut out the vision before her. The girl in the mirror was pleasing, yes, but hardly competition for the tall, willowy, exquisitely beautiful redhead who would be joining them for dinner.

The thought jerked her upright and eyes wide and incredulous stared back at her. Competition? Why had she thought that? She was in no way in any kind of competition with Lorna or any other woman in connection with Jud. Jud was everything she disliked in a man. Arrogant, ruthless, prob-

ably even conceited. Also, probably not above using his blatant good looks to get what he wanted.

A picture of him formed in her mind. She could see him
as he'd been at times that afternoon when her answers had
not quite satisfied him. He had pushed back his chair impatiently and prowled—prowled, exactly like the lions she had
gone to see at the zoo in Philadelphia as a little girl—back
and forth, as if trying to wear our the carpet. She had felt
breathless and strangely excited by his powerful, masculine,
overtly sexy look. Even now, hours later, the memory
brought a shallowness to her breathing, a tight ache to the
pit of her stomach.

In self-disgust Anne pulled open the bathroom door and
hurried along the hall to her bedroom. Quickly, but carefully,
she dressed and applied a light makeup, all the while telling
herself that Jud Cammeron meant nothing to her. He was a
force to be reckoned with, but that was all.

Really? chided a small, amused voice at the very edge of
her consciousness. *Then why does the mere thought of going
down those stairs and entering the living room set your heart
thumping into your throat?* Swallowing painfully, Anne hesitated, her hand pausing in the act of opening her door. *Because,* she told that tiny voice, *because I'm afraid of him.
He is a dangerous adversary who holds my brothers' futures
in the palms of his strong, capable hands. Without warning,
he could close those hands into a tight fist and crush all
their hopes and plans.*

And possibly your spirit as well? the small unrepentant
voice asked slyly.

As if fleeing a demon, Anne tore out of the room and
down the stairs, forcing herself to slow down as she reached
the entrance to the living room.

Andrew was there, and yet the first person her eyes went
to was Jud. Good Lord, he was devastating in close-fitting
brown corduroys and a tan linen shirt. The clothes, combined
with his hair and skin coloring, lent an all-over tawny appearance. *A tawny gold man,* Anne thought crazily, fighting
to control the jumbled sensations eating away at her poise.

"There you are, darling." Andrew's voice, as he came across the room to her, helped restore some of her equilibrium. "I was beginning to think you must have fallen asleep." His tone was light, teasing and as he bent to kiss her he added softly, "I've missed you. Was it very bad? And what's the story with Jud? Your mother seems almost afraid of him."

Anne managed a strained smile and whispered, "I'll explain later, when we're alone. I missed you too."

Thankful for the support of Andrew's hand at her waist, Anne moved into the room, a shaft of dismay sliding through her as her eyes encountered Jud's secretary. The red hair that had been drawn back neatly into a twist at the back of her head during the day had been set free to become a loose, glowing flame around her beautiful face. The tall, sleek body was encased in a hot-pink sheath that gave proof to all of her perfect figure.

With the urge to turn and run crawling up her spine, Anne was amazed at the cool composure of her voice as she acknowledged Jud's formal introduction.

"In my haste to get started this morning I'm afraid I forgot to introduce you two," Jud lied smoothly. Then his voice seemed, to Anne's ears, to change to a warm caress as he drew Lorna toward her. "Lorna, I'd like you to meet my"— he paused—"stepsister, Anne Moore, Anne, my secretary, Lorna Havers."

Cool fingers touched Anne's equally cool ones as Lorna murmured throatily, "I'm pleased to meet you, at last, Miss Moore."

Anne barely had time to reply, "Call me Anne, please, Lorna," when Jud informed, "I have already introduced Lorna to Andrew and your mother, Anne." His voice went hard before he added, "The twins haven't put in an appearance as yet."

He couldn't have said anything more calculated to inject steel into her spine if he had tried. Anne opened her mouth to fly to her brothers' defense, when they strolled into the room, completely unaware of the tension within. As a single unit they stopped dead in their tracks, eyes widening as they caught sight of Lorna.

A small smile of amusement tugging at her mouth, Anne turned to Andrew, and the smile and amusement vanished. Andrew's eyes reflected the admiration evident in Troy's and Todd's, and along with it was an expression Anne could only interpret as calculating speculation. Turning away quickly, Anne felt a small flicker of alarm, for Jud stood watching the tableau, a cool, mocking gleam in his amber eyes, the familiar sardonic twist on his mouth. And what caused Anne's alarm was the fact that Jud was observing Andrew closely.

With relief Anne heard Mrs. Davis announce dinner. Her relief was short-lived for after they were all seated, all the conversation except for the occasional remark tossed to her mother and herself centered on Lorna. And through it all Jud sat, the same amused expression on his face, watching—watching.

Watching for what? Anne asked herself irritably, pushing the food around on her plate. Watching for those three fools to make complete asses of themselves over his secretary-mistress? Unable to decipher the expression Jud wore, Anne had to admit she didn't know what he was watching for, and she hastened to assure herself that she didn't really care.

What an unbelievably long night, Anne thought tiredly some four hours later, as she slid between her sheets. Long and not too good for her ego. As dinner had begun, so had the evening progressed—all the men's attention on Lorna. Her mother had retreated shortly after dinner, leaving Anne to her own devices, of which she had few. And to top it off she had not had that private talk with Andrew. She had so longed for the chance to tell him all that had happened, ask his advice. Now she was almost glad the chance had not come her way. The wish to confide in him had curiously vanished.

All evening—as Jud had watched all of them—Anne had observed Andrew in growing disbelief. Quiet, calm, clear-headed Andrew was as bowled over by Lorna as the immature, lighthearted Troy and Todd. What had happened to the almost pompous seriousness of the man she was engaged to?

A few years younger than Jud, Anne had known Andrew most of her life. Their mothers had been friends for years, although he hadn't seemed aware of Anne at all until a few years ago.

Twisting Andrew's ring around her finger, Anne compared the smiling, eager, handsome man who had danced attendance on Lorna all evening with the coolly reserved, sharp-minded Andrew she had become engaged to. She had never heard him laugh so much, had never seen him so animated. Strangely the most surprising thing he'd done all evening was rake his fingers through his hair, ruffling its usual dark smoothness. Anne had never seen him with a hair out of place. Even she would not have dared to bring disorder to that neatness, and oddly, she had never had the urge to do so.

She had always felt safe and secure with Andrew. Now that security was shaken. Disturbed and confused by the events of the last few days, Anne felt alone and vulnerable, and more than a little afraid.

Chapter Five

Jud kept Anne so busy during the following weeks, she barely noticed the last dying gasp of winter or the slow, inexorable advance of spring. He set a grueling pace for himself and, in determination, she strove to keep up with him. She fell into bed exhausted every night and grew even more alive in her life. Jud seemed to charge everything and everyone around him with electricity, and his energy seemed endless. Unfortunately his temper had a much shorter span and Anne had felt or witnessed the sharp edge of his tongue too often for comfort. No one, from top management to the night watchman, escaped his notice, be it to administer a rebuke or praise. What amazed Anne was that, by April, when Todd and Troy came home for the spring break, the majority of the employees looked on Jud as a kind of god.

Anne herself had mixed feelings about him. Honesty made her admit he had a brilliant business mind. He missed nothing, however small and seemingly unimportant, and had succeeded, more than once, in making Anne feel incompetent. Grudgingly she admitted to herself he did not do it on purpose. She ached with the need to find fault with his handling of the company, and with growing frustration realized that need would not be assuaged.

She had moved into her own office at the end of the first week, then wondered why Jud had even bothered to have it made ready for her, as the connecting door between the two rooms was always left open and his barked "Anne come in here" had her running back and forth as if she were a yo-yo at the end of a string he had tied around his finger.

By the end of her second week, to her surprise, Lorna returned to his New York office, having trained a replacement in a few days' time. Jud's new secretary—a Mrs. Donna Kramer—was a highly qualified, thirty-eight-year-old widow, with three teenage sons. An attractive, friendly woman, Anne liked her at first meeting and despite their age difference a warm friendship was developing. More surprising still was the fact that Jud hardly seemed to notice Lorna's absence, even though he had been out of the office until after lunch on the day her plane left.

To Anne Jud was an enigma, never quite behaving as she would expect. She had not expected him to spend much time at home, so, of course, he was there most evenings. Even though he did close himself in the library, he was home. She had expected him to treat her mother with cool reserve, so, contrarily, he was all warm consideration toward her. The reserve he saved for Anne, who had expected mockery and sarcasm.

And as if she didn't have enough on her mind keeping up with Jud, Andrew baffled Anne. He seemed to be changing somehow, and Anne found herself wondering if she really knew him as well as she had thought she did.

On the Saturday night after Jud's return, he took her out for dinner and his choice of restaurant was in itself unusual. The inn, on the outskirts of Philadelphia, though expensive, was quiet and secluded. As a rule he chose a restaurant closer to home and always a place where he could see, and would be seen by, his friends and colleagues. From the beginning of their relationship Anne had been aware of the fact that Andrew was very ambitious. He intended to move up in the legal profession, not only in their own small community some fifteen miles outside of Philadelphia, but in Philadelphia itself. He had never confided to Anne how he planned to do this, but that his plans were rigidly laid out in his own mind had always been evident.

Anne had accepted Andrew's first invitation to go out with

him the previous spring, less than a year ago. She had accepted his proposal and ring three months ago. Yet, in all that time, he had never found it necessary to share a quiet intimate dinner with her. When he ushered her into the subdued, underplayed elegance of the old inn, the questions, and a vague uneasiness, began to stir in Anne.

Their dinner was expertly prepared and delicious and as they sipped their after-dinner coffee and liqueur, Anne studied Andrew through the shield of her lashes. His height was the only thing average about him. His smoothly brushed dark hair looked almost too perfect to be real, as did the matinee idol handsomeness of the face beneath it. His body was slender and compact, kept in peak condition by vigorous workouts at the local racquet club. His manners were impeccable and his attitude toward her had always been one of polite consideration. In essence Andrew was a cold, analytical mind in a well-dressed, attractive body.

Their relationship, so far, had been comfortable and emotionless, a fact that had gone a long way in her decision to accept his proposal. His casual lovemaking had always been just that—casual and undemanding. Anne felt safe with him because, for reasons she did not care to examine too closely, she herself shied away from any deep emotional involvement. But tonight there was a subtle difference in Andrew, a difference that made Anne uncomfortable.

"Where are you, darling?"

Andrew's quiet voice nudged Anne out of her reverie. Her eyes refocused on his somber face and she laughed shakily.

"I'm sorry, Andrew."

"What were you thinking about?" he probed. "Are you having problems in the office?"

Anne knew by the tone of his voice that he was feeling excluded. Andrew was still not fully in the picture as to her stepfather's will and its aftereffects. She had been so busy all week, thanks to Jud, not only during the day, but in the evenings as well. He had asked, no ordered, if politely, her into the library the last two nights to explain some business papers he'd found in his father's desk. Therefore the opportunity to talk to Andrew had not materialized.

Now, seeing Andrew's face grow grim and stubborn, Anne plunged into an explanation.

"You mean you are literally under his thumb?" he asked in astonishment when she'd finished.

"To a degree, yes," Anne answered softly. "Needless to say Troy and Todd resent him and his dictates like hell. But there is very little any one of us can do about it. He's a veritable slave driver in the office, and yet no one there seems to resent him too much. Possibly because he drives himself harder than anyone else."

"But this is untenable for you, Anne. You cannot possibly go on working day and night for this man simply because his father saw fit to insult you with ten percent of the stock. I find it hard to believe that he, or the twins for that matter, has not offered to buy the stock from you."

He, this man—Anne had not missed Andrew's refusal to use Jud's name. Sighing softly, she said wearily, "As a matter of fact they offered to buy the stock. All of them. I do not want to sell it."

His eyes narrowed, but before he could voice his objection, Anne held out her hand placatingly, pleading, "Andrew, let me explain, please."

He looked on the verge of refusing, then nodded angrily.

"All right, but I'm damned if I can see a reasonable explanation for you putting up with his arrogance."

"In the first place," Anne admonished, "I do not feel insulted by Judson's bequest. True, as practically everyone has been eager to point out, he virtually left me in the middle, between his sons. But equally true, as Jud was only too happy to point out, Judson was fairly certain I would not sell or give my share to any of them."

"But why, for heaven's sake?" Andrew's growing impatience was beginning to show in the tone of his voice, the brightness of his usually cool, brown eyes.

"Simply because, in all conscience, I can't. Oh, Andrew, surely you of all people understand. If I sell, or give, the stock to Troy and Todd, they'll force Jud out and in their inexperience ruin the company. And if I sell"—no hint at the word *give* here—"to Jud, he'll take over completely. At least this way he is under some control."

"Precious damn little, I'd say, with a man like him," Andrew snapped. Then his legal mind reasserted itself, and he added, "But I do see your position. Not an enviable one either. But, Anne darling, how long is this tug-of-war likely to go on?"

"I don't know," Anne answered tiredly. "Right now the twins are in silent rebellion, but I'm hoping they pull themselves together and get down to the business of learning the business. The moment I feel they can handle the company, and Jud, I'll gladly hand over the stock. I don't really want it, as I feel I have no right to it in the first place."

"What! But that's ridiculous," Andrew exclaimed. "You were like a daughter to Mr. Cammeron. I would have thought he'd leave you much more. And when the time comes there will be no talk of giving anything to anyone. You have as much right to your legacy as he has, if not more. He's the deserter, not you."

Anne glanced up sharply, the unease she'd felt earlier doubling in proportion. What had gotten into Andrew? Never before had he assumed that proprietorial attitude toward her. But even more disquieting was the nasty edge to his tone whenever he spoke of Jud. As if he actually hated while at the same time envied him. But why? Anne had no answer to that, and so felt totally lost and confused. Besides which, she was just too tired to go into it with him. Reaching across the table, she touched his hand lightly.

"Andrew, please, I'm really very tired. Could we leave this discussion for another time?"

For a moment Anne thought he would argue, but then he shrugged and murmured, "As you wish."

They left shortly after that and back in the car Anne rested her head against the seat, eyes closed. It had been a very long day. Unable to sleep past seven, Anne had finally pushed the covers back and dragged her tired body out of bed. She was not sleeping well, and when she did sleep, her rest was broken by dreams. Wild, distorted dreams that made no sense and left her shaken and frightened. Most upsetting of all was the recurrence of the drowning dream she'd had the first night Jud was home. It was always the same, never varying, and that alone shook her. She had promised herself she'd sleep late that morning and the fact that she was unable to do so sent her to the breakfast table irritable and snappy.

Jud had been sitting at the table, his breakfast finished, drinking his coffee while his eyes scanned the morning paper. His "good morning" had been coolly polite and when Anne barely mumbled a response, one bleached brow went up mockingly.

"Fall out on the wrong side of the bed this morning, Anne?" His silky tone had irritated her even more. "Or is the boss running you ragged?"

"The boss," she emphasized scathingly, "hasn't seen the day he could run me ragged. I will be fine as soon as I've had some coffee."

Brave words. Too brave in fact, for he took her up on it at once.

"In that case I'm sure you'll be happy to join me for an hour or two in the library. I have a few questions on some legal papers of the old man's that I found in the desk. Perhaps you could supply some answers."

An hour or two, a few questions, the man was an expert at the understatement. He had grilled her endlessly, chiding softly "why not?" whenever she had to tell him she had no answer. He had had Mrs. Davis bring a lunch tray in to them and had given her barely enough time to finish her salad before firing questions at her again. By three thirty Anne was on the verge of tears, inwardly appalled at how little she really knew of her stepfather's business affairs, when she'd thought she'd had a very good grasp of it all. Lord, if Jud could shatter her this soon, what in the world would he have done to the twins?

He had been studying a paper, head bent, when he calmly asked yet another question she had no answer for and in frustration she had almost screamed at him "I don't know." She'd paused, swallowing hard to force back a sob, then added chokingly, "I—I thought I had his complete confidence, but it's more than obvious I was wrong."

Jud's head had snapped up at her outburst and his eyes, those damned cat eyes, watched the play of emotions cross her face with cool intent. It was that watchfulness that drove her to turn away abruptly and head for the door. More unnerved than she'd ever been before, she'd whispered, "I—I'll understand if you want to replace me in the office, get another assistant."

She had reached the door, hand groping for the knob, when he grasped her by the shoulders, holding her still, her back to him.

"Throwing in the towel already, Anne?" he taunted softly. "I really thought you had more guts than to fall apart at the first obstacle. If you go, who is going to run interference for Todd and Troy?"

She had listened to his words in disbelief and when he'd finished, she'd gasped, "You mean you want me to stay?"

He shook her gently, then drawled, "My sweet Anne. Do you have any idea how long it would take me to train someone to replace you? I simply do not have the time. Besides which, I have known all along that you couldn't possibly know all of the old man's business. I was merely trying to ascertain exactly what facts you were cognizant of."

He'd hesitated, turned her halfway around to him, then stopped, dropped his hands, and stepped back, away from her. "You're tired," he snapped impatiently. "Take off and get some rest. You'll need it, for we still have one hell of a lot of work before us."

He'd walked away from her, the very set of his shoulders a dismissal. Anne had been only too happy to escape, for the touch of his hands on her arms had caused a feeling of extreme weakness in her legs, a tight breathlessness in her chest.

Anne moved restlessly against the plush covering of the car seat; then her eyes flew open as she felt the car slow down and then stop. Surely they couldn't be home already? They weren't. Andrew had brought the car to a stop on the side of a dark country road. He pulled the hand brake, then turned to her, an unfamiliar sheen in his dark eyes.

"Andrew, what—" that was as far as she got, for, without speaking, he pulled her into his arms and cut off her words with his lips.

At first Anne returned his kiss, but within seconds she was struggling against him, her hands pushing at his chest. This wasn't a kiss, this was an assault, and she went cold and unresponsive. Never before had Andrew kissed her in this demanding way and not questioning the feeling of revulsion that swept through her, Anne fought him frantically. Her struggles just seemed to add fuel to his fire and the pressure on her lips grew brutal, his teeth ground against her, bruising her soft mouth. She went stiff when his hand clutched painfully at her breast and in desperation she tore her mouth from his, cried out, "Andrew, have you gone mad? Let me go, please."

His breathing was ragged and uneven, his voice harsh as he released her, flung himself back behind the wheel.

"You don't give an inch, do you Anne?" His voice heavy with disgust.

Completely bewildered, Anne gasped, "I don't know what you mean."

"Don't you?" He almost snarled at her. "I'm human, Anne, a man. How long did you think I'd be satisfied with cold, chaste little kisses?"

"But—but you never said anything," Anne stammered.

"Good Lord, what do you suppose I was just trying to do? We've been engaged for three months. I need a woman and the woman who has agreed to be my wife has just turned away from me."

Overtired, overwrought, Anne stared at him, stunned. What could have caused this change in him? Not for one minute could she believe in his sudden overwhelming need of her. No, there was more to his about-face than that. But what could it be?

It wasn't until later, when she was safe in her own bed, that Anne realized Andrew had not actually said he needed her. That his exact words had been "I need a woman" not "I need you."

Even though Andrew had apologized after bringing her home, Anne begged off seeing him the following day. His attack—she could not even force herself to think of it as lovemaking—had left her feeling sick and in some way soiled, and for the life of her she could not think why. True, he had been rough, but she was a young woman and although she lacked actual experience, she was aware of the fact that there were times when men did get rough with women. She was going to be Andrew's wife, had known all along there would eventually have to be a physical side to their relationship. So why had she felt that revulsion, that near panic?

Anne spent all day Sunday unconsciously avoiding the answers to her own questions.

Her second week as Jud's assistant followed the same pattern as her first. Jud driving ahead tirelessly, Anne pushing herself to keep up with him. The only difference being that now she had an office of her own. It was there, she had seen it. She kept her handbag in one of her desk drawers but she was rarely ever in it. Also, in open defiance, she now left the building at lunchtime. If Lorna could go out for lunch, she'd asked herself angrily, why couldn't she? Her defiance was wasted on Jud, who merely glanced up when she'd informed him of her decision, smiled, and murmured, "Why not? It'll do you good to stretch your legs, clear out the morning cobwebs," and turned back to his work.

Although Anne had her doubts about the employer/employee status between Jud and Lorna, she observed no evidence to the contrary during the time Lorna was there. Their behavior was always office-procedure correct, her manner toward Anne respectful. Even so Anne breathed a silent sigh of relief when Lorna left the office early Friday afternoon, leaving Donna in possession of her desk.

Andrew called her several times during that week, but Anne put him off pleading either tiredness or work. Both of which were true, for Jud, having finished with the managerial files, had plowed into the mill employees' folders. Anne found herself enclosed in the library with Jud most evenings, folders covering the large desk until, usually around nine thirty, her mother would rescue her with a softly chided, "Jud, really, you can't expect the girl to work all day and all night. Why don't you both come into the living room, relax, and have a nightcap with me?"

Every night Jud's reaction had been the same. He had dismissed Anne at once, declined her mother's offer with a gentle, "Thank you, Margaret, but I want to give this a few more minutes. I would appreciate a drink in here, if you don't mind." He would turn back to his work, giving Anne the impression that both she and her mother were immediately forgotten.

Friday night Anne and Jud were in the middle of a heated, though impersonal, argument concerning company policy on employee vacations when Mrs. Davis knocked quietly on the door and told Anne she was wanted on the phone. As Anne left the room Jud taunted softly, "Hold that last thought, because I'm prepared to destroy it completely."

Anger burning her cheeks, Anne snatched up the receiver and snapped, "Yes, who is it?"

"Hello to you too," Andrew replied, the very coolness of his tone causing the flush to deepen in her cheeks at her bad manners.

"I'm sorry, Andrew," she apologized quickly. "Jud and I were in the middle of an argument and I'm afraid I carried my impatience to the phone."

"You're not still working?" Andrew asked in amazement. "What in the hell is the matter with that man? Is it his goal in life to see you drop in your tracks?"

"Don't be silly," Anne soothed. "I'm sure Jud hasn't the vaguest idea of the number of hours I've put in the last two weeks. As to his wanting to see me drop in my tracks, I doubt he'd notice if I did. He'd probably just step over me and calmly go about the business of finding a new assistant."

Andrew made a very impolite noise at his end, then said, "Not very complimentary to you. Try and break it up soon, will you, darling? We've been invited to a small dinner party at the home of a very important client tomorrow evening and I want you looking your best."

This sounded like the Andrew she knew and Anne wondered if he'd decided to ignore the incident of the previous Saturday.

"Anne?" Andrew's voice nudged.

"Yes, yes, of course. What time should I be ready?"

"We've been invited for pre-dinner drinks at seven thirty, so I'll come for you at seven. Will that be all right?"

"Yes, I'll be ready." Then a little devil inside made her tease. "And I promise I'll try not to disgrace you with my haggard appearance."

The teasing apparently went over his head, for he added, "I should hope not. As I said, this is a very important client."

Seconds later, as Anne cradled the receiver, she asked herself what had happened to Andrew's sense of humor, and realized, with a shock, that she'd never seen much evidence of his having one. Head bent, puzzling at her own lack of perception of the man she'd agreed to marry, Anne started back to the library. She had taken only a few steps when she was brought up short, her eyes encountering a pair of feet, one crossed negligently over the other. Slowly she lifted her head, her eyes following on an angle, long, jean-clad legs to slim hips and waist, a broad chest and shoulders, covered in a loose knit pullover and finally coming to an abrupt stop at two glittering amber eyes, the lids narrowed in amusement.

"Poor baby," Jud crooned softly. "Is the big, bad boss overworking you?"

Breathing deeply in a vain attempt to control her suddenly erratic heartbeats, Anne glared into those odd, felinelike eyes. Instilling a coolness she was far from feeling into her voice, she asked sarcastically, "Do you make a habit of eavesdropping on private conversations?"

Unabashed, unruffled, he leaned lazily against the door frame and allowed his eyes to roam slowly over her. When his eyes paused then fastened intently on her slightly parted lips, Anne had the weird sensation she could actually feel his hard, sardonic mouth touch hers.

Stifling a gasp, she stepped back, then stood still again as his soft laughter swirled around her.

"What are you afraid of, Anne?" Jud purred silkily. "You're as nervous as a prudish old maid at her first X-rated film."

Anger lent ice to her tone and covered her breathlessness.

"I am neither afraid nor nervous. I am simply too tired to play at words with you."

"Really? Then you'd better run along to bed, little girl." The purr deepened and slid along her skin like crushed velvet. "Do you want me to come along and tuck you in?"

Out of her league, and aware of it, Anne turned on her heel and started for the stairs, praying her shaky legs would carry her as far as her room. She had placed one foot on the first step when she paused again, her hand gripping the banister, caught in that soft web.

"By the way, Annie, you can rest assured that should I ever find you sprawled at my feet, the last thing I'd ever consider doing would be to step over you."

Anne ran, his soft laughter chasing her all the way to her room. Safely inside, she dropped onto her bed, fighting the sudden, hot sting in her eyes. *What is wrong with you?* she lashed at herself impatiently. *Why do you let him upset you this way? He's deliberately trying to un-*

dermine your confidence with his taunts and jibes, and you're allowing him to succeed by standing by meekly and taking it. Why? Why?

Tired of the questions that seemed to have no answers, Anne undressed and went to bed, resigned to another restless night. It seemed she'd no sooner closed her eyes than they flew open again at the racket filtering into her room from the hall. Her room was flooded with bright, spring sunlight and, glancing at her bedside clock, she was surprised to find she'd slept the clock around. She felt good and a small indulgent smile curved her soft lips as she identified the cause of the upheaval in the hall. Todd and Troy were home for spring break, bringing with them laughter and loud voices and all the attendant noises of youth.

"Cool it, you guys." The sharp command issued from down the hall came from Jud. "Your sister is still asleep and your mother doesn't want her disturbed. It's been a long two weeks."

It was wonderful to have the twins in the house again. Their constant banter, their incessant teasing, their forever dashing in and out, went a long way toward bringing a measure of calm to Anne's frayed nerves.

By Sunday night Anne faced the thought of going back to the office with much more composure than she'd left with on Friday.

She had enjoyed the dinner party she'd gone to with Andrew. And as he had seemed to have made another about-face, becoming once more the Andrew she'd always known, she found herself relaxing with him again.

That week Anne's work load in the office was somewhat lighter as Jud divided his time between the office and the mill, where he was overseeing Todd and Troy's training.

On Good Friday Anne and Jud worked alone in the office, the day being a legal holiday for employees. They worked steadily all day and by late afternoon Anne finally closed the last of the employee folders. Sighing wearily, she straightened and turned, then gave a softly gasped "Oh!" a second before Jud's mouth touched hers in a gentle kiss. It was over almost as soon as it had begun, and yet the havoc it created inside Anne was unbelievably intense.

"What was that for?" Anne whispered.

"That was a little reward for a job well done," Jud whispered back.

"Do—do you reward all your female employees that way?"

"You don't understand," Jud teased. "Your reward will be in your paycheck next week. The kiss was my reward."

Chapter Six

The weeks flew by. Busy weeks. Exciting weeks. The more Anne saw of Jud's business acumen, the more anxious she became for her brothers. She was way out of depth with Jud. Troy and Todd would have drowned in no time. Grimly she hung on, and yet she was loving every minute of it. Even the quarrels she had with him—and they were frequent—left her feeling tinglingly alive, if mentally exhausted.

By mid-April, one month after Jud took over, Anne faced the knowledge that she could not prevent him from doing what he wished with the company. His mind had absorbed all the information on the mill's management like a well-programmed computer and that, along with his keen judgment of people, seemed to keep him three steps ahead of everyone else.

Anne had hardly been aware that spring had breathed life and growth back into the land until one evening as she drove home from the office. Suddenly it was all around her, the soft green of new grass and leaves, the elusive, sweet fragrance on the mild breeze, and the more mundane fact that she was uncomfortably warm in her suede jacket.

After parking her car Anne skirted around the garage and went into the yard behind the house. Slowly she walked along the flowerbeds, drinking in the scent of hyacinths, gently touching tulip and daffodil petals. After a complete circuit of the beds she sat down on the wrought-iron bench that encircled an old, gnarled apple tree. She had almost missed it, she mused wonderingly. She loved spring and she had almost missed it.

Sighing softly, she leaned her head back. What else had she missed since engaging in this battle of wits with Jud? She could not remember a single discussion she'd had with Andrew lately, or with her mother either. Had anyone mentioned how Troy and Todd were doing in school? She didn't know, hadn't known for weeks. Ever since Jud came home.

Jud.

Without warning tears filled her eyes, overflowed, and ran down her cheeks. Defenseless and vulnerable to the gentle tug of spring, Anne closed her eyes, made no effort to wipe away the tears. In rapid succession images flashed through her mind—Jud prowling the office, the library. Jud, hands on hips, taunting her, mocking her. Jud, gold hair glinting in the sunlight, a blaze of white teeth in a bronze face. Jud, amber eyes gleaming, watching—watching, and yet unable to see.

Jud.

With a small, strangled sob Anne lifted trembling fingers to her lips. He had kissed her on impulse to tease her. That had been weeks ago and still her mouth could taste the sweetness of his, feel its tenderness.

A wave of longing and raw hunger swept through her, washing away all pretense. Her hands covering her face, she sobbed hopelessly. She was in love with him again. No, she had never stopped being in love with him. And she was afraid. Afraid that one day those watching eyes would see and know.

A shudder tore through Anne's body and she sat up straight, eyes wide. The mere idea of Jud finding out how she felt made her go hot then cold. She had been so badly hurt by him ten years ago. She had never really stopped hurting, she admitted to herself now. She could not give him the chance to inflict deeper pain. Now her recurring dream of drowning in Jud's arms made somewhat more sense, for if he got even a hint of how she felt, he'd overwhelm her as surely as the water in her dreams did.

She would have to be very careful. Step lightly and cautiously if she was not to give herself away. It would not be easy. The results of the kiss Jud had dropped playfully onto her lips warned her of that. That meaningless kiss had rocked her world, left her trembling and yes—Anne admitted it—hungry for more. She wanted him and he was not for her.

A bitter smile curved fleetingly across her lips. No, he was not for her. And now, soul bared to herself at last, she identified the disquiet she'd felt every time Jud was out of town, as he was now.

Jud had told her, two weeks ago, that as his familiarization program was over he would spend at least two days a week in his New York office. Her disquiet had begun at that moment and had ballooned in size later that same day, when she overheard his phone call to Lorna informing her of his plans. Jealousy, pure unvarnished jealousy was eating away at her insides. That was the true name of her disquiet.

And he was there now, in New York with Lorna, and the thought of them together was tearing her apart. Visions of them swirled and formed in her mind. The tall, willowy redhead enfolded in Jud's arms, their mouths clinging, bodies entwined—on a bed.

A low moan of pain escaped through her lips and she felt nausea rise in her throat. The sound of her own voice started her. *Stop it at once,* she told herself frantically. *How do you expect to get through the coming weeks if you fall apart every time you think of him with her?*

He had said, that first day, that he planned to stay a few months. One of those months was gone already, and somehow she had to make sure that when he did finally leave for good, he went away no wiser about her love for him than when he arrived.

The very thought of his eventual departure brought a flood of fresh tears to her eyes and she shook all over, as if with an illness. She jumped to her feet, and hurried toward the house. She had to get a hold on her emotions if she was not to betray herself.

Tears streaming down her face, Anne rushed through the back door, past an astonished Mrs. Davis and along the hall to the stairs. Her mother came out of the living room as Anne reached the stairs and at her ravaged face cried, "Anne, what in the world is wrong? Why are you crying?"

"Nothing, it's nothing," Anne choked. "I'm—I have a blazing migraine. I'll be all right if I can just rest for a while."

Margaret's anxious voice followed her up the stairs.

"But you've never been bothered with mi—"

Anne closed her door on her mother's words, stumbled across the room and flung herself onto her bed. Sobbing uncontrollably now, shattered, all defenses gone, she let the storm of weeping have its way.

Later, when the tempest had subsided to an occasional hiccupy sob, Anne lay staring at the ceiling, telling herself she was seven different kinds of a fool, one for each day of the week. And when her bedroom door opened, she didn't bother to turn her head, sure it was her mother.

"What caused the headache, Annie?"

Jud! It couldn't be. He wasn't due back until tomorrow. Gulping down an errant sob, Anne turned shocked eyes to stare at him. He stood by her bed, hands on his hips, every line of his body taut as if held still by a rigid control.

"Who knows what causes a migraine?" Anne hedged. Oh, Lord, just the sight of him was like a blow to her chest. Forcing a coolness she was anything but feeling into her voice, she flipped, "Don't concern yourself, these headaches usually disappear as fast as they appear."

"Can it, Anne," Jud growled. "Your mother informs me you've never had a migraine in your life. So what's caused you to fall apart like this?" His tone went low, fiercely demanding. "Has Andrew said or done anything to upset you?"

Andrew! Anne had the urge to laugh hysterically. Poor
Andrew. At no time had Andrew had the power to shatter
her in this way. Never had Andrew's nearness set off this
chain reaction of breathlessness, trembling, warm flushes,
and cold shivers.

Desperate to have him go, Anne shot back icily, "That's
a personal question, Jud, and none of your business. You're
the boss in the office, not here. Please leave my room.
And don't ever come in here again without knocking."

His body went even more taut, his face set into grim,
angry lines, and his eyes, through narrowed lids, seemed
to glow with a burning intensity. Suddenly he moved, bent
over her, and brushed a surprisingly gentle finger across
the still damp hollow under her eyes. His voice was a
frightening low snarl.

"If he's hurt you, I'll—"

Slim, cold fingers were placed over his lips, cutting off
the intended threat. For brief seconds that seemed to
stretch into eternity, cloudy gray eyes stared into angry
amber.

"Annie."

The hard male lips moved against her fingers as he
whispered her name. Tiny electrical shocks ran up her arm
and through her chest to set her heart beating in crazy,
pulsating thumps. Solid amber was melting to a soft liquid, threatening to absorb her willpower. How very easily
she could be lost in their depths. Her fingers moved across
his smooth, hard cheek, delighting in the feel of him. His
scent, a mixture of spicy aftershave and normal male
muskiness, sent her senses spinning. She knew she should
not be allowing this intimacy, she just couldn't remember
why.

"Chicken."

The whispered word sent a screaming alarm through
her mind. He had called her that ten years ago, then he
had left her without a word, alone and hurt. How dare he
accuse Andrew! She had to get him out of there before
she made a complete fool of herself a second time.

Pushing at his chest with her other hand, she rolled away and off the bed on the other side. Eyeing him warily, her breathing ragged, she watched as he straightened slowly, his eyes steady on hers. The width of the bed between them gave her the courage to order, "Go away, Jud. You have no right to be here. I'm going to marry Andrew."

"Are you, chicken?"

Something in the tone of the softly spoken question made her uneasy, as if he knew something she didn't.

"Yes, of course I am." Anne rushed into speech in an effort to negate her unease. "Being left ten percent of the company stock has not tied me to the Cammerons for life. My plans are unchanged. I am going to marry Andrew."

To her amazement Jud stepped back as if she had struck him. Fleetingly a small, bitter smile twisted his mouth, then he turned and walked to the door. As he left the room his soft words reached her ears, confusing and, strangely, frightening her.

"I don't think so, honey."

Anne didn't go downstairs for dinner and she refused the tray her mother offered to send up to her. Sitting crosslegged in the center of her bed she stared vacantly at the wall, her mind darting wildly in an effort not to think of Jud.

No luck. Amber eyes seemed to glow inside her head and his soft voice taunted silently. *I don't think so. I don't think so.* Why not? Nothing had happened to give Jud the idea the relationship between her and Andrew had changed.

But it had changed! Anne frowned as the realization hit her. The blank look left her face, replaced by one of concentration. How had it changed? Being so busy the last few weeks she had seen little of him, and when they were together, she was tired and preoccupied. And yet it was more than that. Something about Andrew was different. Thinking back, Anne tried to pinpoint exactly when Andrew had changed. Uneasily she remembered that night she'd had to fight him off in the car. But that hadn't been the start of it, she had felt uncomfortable with him all evening. She cast her mind back further, to when he had left to go out of town before Jud came home. But no, the change had not yet started. He had told her he was sorry he couldn't be with her for the funeral and had kissed her, coolly and unemotionally. No, at that time he had been the Andrew she had always known. So when had the change started?

Then it struck her. Of course! The day he returned from that business trip, the day after Jud came home. Did Jud's return have something to do with the change in him? Surely Andrew didn't feel threatened by Jud. Anne puzzled at the thought a few minutes, then a new thought jumped into her mind. Jud's wasn't the only new face at dinner that night. Lorna? A picture of the beautiful redhead formed and with it one of Andrew, a surprisingly animated and attentive Andrew.

Ridiculous, Anne chided herself. Lorna had left weeks ago to go back to the New York office, and the change in Andrew remained. But then, she mused, Andrew's been going out of town on business more than ever before the last few weeks. Could there possibly be a connection? Come to think of it, he hadn't told her where he was going, or why. Could Andrew be interested in Lorna? Was there a man who, having met her, wasn't?

Wrong thought. Anne's mind veered to Jud. Jud, who had just that day come back from the New York office, and Lorna. Were they lovers? Anne moaned softly in protest against the searing pain the thought caused. Uncrossing her legs, she curled up on the bed, head cradled on her arm. Jud and Lorna. Jud with Lorna. Jud making love to Lorna. No. No. No. The pain grew inside as once again her mind filled with pictures of the two of them together.

Dear God, what was she going to do? How was she going to get through the coming weeks working with him in the office, living in the same house? If he came near her, showed even the slightest concern, as he had earlier, she'd fall apart.

She had so desperately wanted to feel his arms around her, have his mouth touch hers. A last, tiny bit of sense had saved her this time. But could she hold off against him if he should come that close again? Did she want to?

Her thoughts revolved around and around, always coming back to the same conclusions. She loved him, she wanted him, and, should he make a determined move toward her, she did not honestly know if she'd even try to repel him.

Andrew was forgotten. Lorna was forgotten. The only thing that remained was the stark realization that should Jud want her for any reason she was his. Anne sighed in defeat, she was his if he never wanted her.

It was an alarming thought and Anne closed her eyes tightly, giving in to the truth and the torment that truth brought with it.

I love you. I'll always love you. Long-ago words, returning to add to her torment. Anne felt she'd gladly give up another ten years of her life if she could hear those words again, feel the warmth of his body close to hers. Tears of regret slid silently down her cheeks. Why did it have to be Jud? Why couldn't she love Andrew this way?

Rolling onto her back, Anne wiped the tears from her face and stared at the ceiling. She'd have to break her engagement to Andrew. She couldn't marry him now, it would be unfair to both of them. But what was she going to tell everyone? What would they think? What would Jud think? Would he think about it at all? Or care? She doubted it. Jud was interested in only one thing—the company. That's what had brought him home and that was the reason he stayed. But he had set his own time limit. A few months, he'd told Margaret. He'd been home over one month now and had completely familiarized himself with the management of the firm. A month or two at the most, Anne thought, and he'd be gone. Somehow she would have to get through those weeks with composure. She would have to play it very cool, for she was determined he'd leave as ignorant of her love for him as he'd arrived.

Anne finally slept, only to awaken several hours later shivering and scared. She had had that drowning dream again; only this time it was so clear, so real, she could still feel the coolness of the water, the heat of Jud's mouth. And, Lord forgive her, it would be worth drowning to be that close to him, if only for those few short moments.

Sanity returned with full wakefulness and Anne shuddered. *I must be cracking up,* she thought derisively. *The sooner that man goes back to his mistress the better. If he stays much longer, I'll be flinging myself into his arms and begging him to love me.*

It proved a lot easier to break her engagement to Andrew than Anne had dared hoped. That Saturday night they went to a small party at the home of one of Andrew's friends and surprisingly Anne enjoyed herself. It was the first time in weeks they'd been in the company of people their own age and as several of Anne's friends were there, there was no lack of conversation. The party was in the way of a double celebration—an engagement party and to celebrate the promotion of the newly engaged young man.

Anne observed the couple during the evening with something close to envy. They were so happy and so obviously in love. This is the way it should be, Anne thought sadly, her resolution to break her own engagement strengthening.

It was after two in the morning when they left the party and Anne, only half awake, barely heard what Andrew was saying until he said sharply, "Did you hear what I said, Anne? I'm leaving Slonne's office."

Fully alert now, Anne turned startled eyes to him.

"But why? When will you go? Do you have another position lined up?

"That's what I've been telling you for the last five minutes," he snapped exasperatedly. "I'm going into a very prestigious firm in Philadelphia. Tax work mainly."

"Philadelphia?" Anne was stunned, and it showed. "But

Andrew, surely this hasn't happened overnight. Why haven't you told me before?"

For a moment Andrew looked uncomfortable; then he shrugged. "I wanted to be certain before I said anything. I accepted this firm's offer yesterday and told Mr. Slonne this morning. I'll be leaving in two weeks."

"Andrew," Anne hesitated, then plunged, "I think you'd better take your ring with you when you go."

The car was filled with silence for some time and Anne saw his hands tighten on the wheel then relax again. Sighing softly, in what Anne thought sounded very much like relief, he flicked her an evasive glance.

"I assume there's a reason you no longer want to marry me?"

This was the Andrew she had always known—cool, almost pompous.

"I just don't think it would work," she answered softly. "I'm sorry, Andrew, but I'm afraid we're moving in different directions. Do you realize that tonight is the first time in weeks we've been with our friends? Whenever we go out it's in the company of clients or contacts. You're ambitious to the exclusion of everything else."

Andrew smiled cryptically. "Not quite everything, Anne."

Neither inclined or curious enough to question him on exactly what that meant, Anne rushed on. "I'm not saying that kind of ambition is necessarily wrong, it is just not for me." Anne paused, then honesty made her add, "Andrew, I don't love you. At least not enough to make a lifetime commitment to you."

They were almost home and Andrew was quiet as he drove up the driveway and parked in front of the large, old-fashioned house. His face somber, he turned to her, his arm resting on the steering wheel.

"You know, Anne, you've changed lately."

Anne felt a stab of pure panic. Had she given herself away? Then she sighed with relief as he added, "You always were quiet, but now, I don't know, you seem withdrawn and preoccupied. I suppose all the upheaval in the office hasn't been easy for you. You've really declared war on Jud, haven't you?"

"Andrew, it's not—"

"Never mind," he cut off. "You don't have to pretend with me. It's fairly obvious that you can't stand him. Don't misunderstand me, I don't blame you. I don't like him either, and I do understand you wanting to protect your brothers' interests until they are out of school."

He paused and Anne stared at him in wonder. Most of what he'd said after "It's fairly obvious you can't stand him," had barely registered. Fervently she hoped that everyone had the same impression of her feelings about Jud. Including Jud himself. Andrew's quiet voice intruded on her thoughts.

"As you've been honest with me, I think it only fair if I tell you I've been having doubts of my own about us."

Curious now, Anne had to ask, "Is there someone else, Andrew?"

He glanced away, then back again, a small, dry smile on his lips.

"Well, yes and no. I'm attracted to someone. I'm not sure if the attraction is mutual. I think it is, but I'm not sure. If you don't mind, that's all I have to say on it."

"No, of course I don't mind." Anne slipped his ring off her finger and handed it to him, adding, "Your private life is none of my business."

He looked rueful a moment as his fingers closed over the cluster of diamonds, then he shook his head once.

"No hard feelings, Anne?"

"No, Andrew, no hard feelings. I think we can be glad we realized our mistake now. It would have been much worse later. I will miss you though."

"I'm going to Philadelphia, Anne," he laughed softly. "Not the end of the world. If you need anything," he grinned, "like free legal advice, call me. Oh, by the way, I will still expect an invitation to Troy and Todd's graduation party."

"You'll have it." Leaning to him, she kissed him lightly on the cheek.

"Good luck, Andrew, with the new firm and—everything."

As luck would have it, Jud was the first to notice the lack of adornment on Anne's finger, and then it would have to be when they were all at the dinner table on Sunday, while Mrs. Davis was serving the soup.

"Your hand appears strangely naked, Anne," he drawled. "You haven't misplaced your engagement ring, have you?"

All eyes, including Mrs. Davis's, swung to Anne's hand. Pink-cheeked, hating him, she snapped, "No, I haven't misplaced it; I gave it back."

"Anne!"

Her mother's shocked voice had Anne wishing she hadn't avoided everyone all day on the pretext of having things to do in her room. She had known she should go to her mother with some sort of explanation, but she had shied away from it. Now she was sorry she hadn't.

Anne drew a deep calming breath before saying quietly, "It's all right, Mother. I—I—Andrew and I—well, we've decided to call it off."

"But why? Anne, I don't understand." Margaret's voice held a plaintive note. "I don't understand you anymore. You're changing. Everything's changing." She sent a bitter glance at Jud, who received it with a look of total unconcern, before she went on, her voice rising an octave. "I seldom see you anymore." She glanced from Troy to Todd. "I seldom see you two anymore. I feel like a stranger in my own home. And now this." Her voice rising even more, she turned again to Jud. "You, you said you would not disrupt this house, yet, since you came home, there's been nothing but disruption."

"Mrs. Davis, I think you'd better wait a few minutes before serving the rest of the meal. I'll call you when we're ready to resume eating." Jud's flat tone dropped into the silence that had gripped the room after Margaret's outburst.

"Yes, sir."

He waited until the door swished closed behind the housekeeper, then turned eyes as hard as flint to Margaret.

"Actually, Margaret, what I said was I had no wish to disrupt the normal routine of this house. I'm sorry if Troy and Todd's absence upsets you, but, as that is how it has to be, you may as well get used to it."

"Now look here, Jud, you—" Todd began.

"Don't interrupt," Jud snapped. "I never said there wouldn't be any changes. The old man indulged you, I won't. I haven't the time or the inclination. Margaret, you have no cause for complaint. In the last month I've paid bills for you to the tune of three thousand dollars."

Anne's eyes flew to her mother. What in the world had she bought? Her silent question was answered defensively by Margaret.

"I needed some new spring clothes, darker colors. I'm still in mourning for your father."

"I don't think the question of need applies here." Jud's tone was dry. "But that's beside the point. The point being, I have not questioned these expenditures. As stated, the bills are paid." One pale eyebrow was cocked in Troy and Todd's direction. "Yours too."

A frown creasing her smooth brow, Anne watched as a flush mounted in her brothers' faces. Good grief! Todd and Troy too?

But why? They received a more than generous allowance. This time Jud answered her silent questions.

"Don't delude yourselves into believing I don't know what the game is. The name of the game is Test Jud." Jud's eyes moved slowly around the table and the smile that twisted his lips made Anne's blood run cold. "There will be no more games, no more tests. Is that understood?"

Silence and three pairs of eyes guiltily turned to Anne with a mute appeal for help.

"Jud, really, I don't think there was any intention—"

"Shut up, Anne."

Anne gasped at the hard finality of Jud's tone. Who the hell did he think he was?

As if he could read her mind, Jud told her exactly who he was.

"I know what the intention was and I'm having no more of it. I made it perfectly clear at the beginning that I am the boss. I wasn't playing with words and I wasn't kidding. Now for the last time, is that understood?"

Anne found herself nodding her head in unison with the three he had addressed his question to. Awareness of the docile action brought a stillness to her body, a flare of anger to her eyes. Jud's sharp glance did not miss the flare and, as if in a deliberate attempt to fan it into a full flame, he prodded, "I haven't received any of your bills, Anne. Strange, but it would seem that the only one of you that does any real work is also the only one not spending like a drunken sailor."

Anne's head snapped up, eyes now blazing.

"I pay my own bills," she stated emphatically. "I always have. As for Mother, Troy, and Todd, your father set the life-style by which they live. Why should it surprise or annoy you if they expect to go on as before? They know the money is there; and the company is doing very well. Dammit, Jud, you can't expect them to adjust to all these changes overnight."

"Ah—the champion jumps in to beard the lion." Jud's soft purr scraped like a rough file against Anne's anger. "Little mother to the rescue," he taunted. "I really hate to stamp on your act," he lied, "but I hardly think five weeks can be classified as overnight. I am not my father. It was his company solely. I have no intention of working myself into the grave just so my family can live in the same life-style. Not for forty-five percent of that company, or, for that matter, anything at all. There will be changes. Get used to it."

"As easy as that?" Troy snapped his fingers, his expression full of contempt.

"No, Troy, I didn't say it would be easy." Jud's words

were slow and measured, each one underlined verbally. "But by the time you come into your own in the company, you'll know you've earned it. And believe me, that knowledge cannot be measured in time or money. Now, will it upset anyone if I suggest we finish dinner?"

Chapter Seven

As she drove to work the following morning Anne had the feeling of being reprieved, if temporarily. The topic of her broken engagement had been submerged under the barrage of angry words that had been hurled around the room and Anne had escaped to her bedroom before it could be revived. She knew she would have to give her mother a fuller explanation, but meanwhile she had the whole day in which to form the words plausibly, she thought.

When exactly was it that your brain stopped working? Anne asked herself ten minutes after she entered her office. That was right after Jud walked through the door from his office, stood, hands on his hips, in front of her desk and said bluntly, "You never did say why you and Andrew decided to call it off."

Damn the man. Anne held her breath a moment, then let it out very slowly. Why did he have to look so good? In a buff-colored suit and cream shirt he was tawny all over. Was he aware of the effect? Anne wondered. Very likely. Needing to put some distance between them, Anne pushed back her chair, stood up, and walked to the window, tossing over her shoulder, "I didn't realize I was obliged to say why."

"To me? Or anyone at all?"

Anne jerked at the sound of his voice right behind her. How in the world did the man move so silently? It was enough to give you the goose bumps.

"To anyone, really."

Her voice betrayed her shakiness and in defense she kept her head turned to the window.

"Annie, are you hurting?" he asked softly. "You sound on the verge of tears. And you were crying Friday night. Has he hurt you very badly?"

"It's nothing I won't live through," she murmured. Lord, how easy it would be, and how tempting, to let him believe it was Andrew she'd been crying over and who put the tremble in her voice now. But it wouldn't be fair to cast Andrew as the heavy. She would just have to bluff it out. Her voice stronger, she added, "I told you Friday I had a bad headache. I've had several lately. I guess I've been working too hard. As for Andrew, no, he hasn't hurt me. It was a mutual decision. We want different things from life, that's all."

"And it took you all these months to discover that?"

Jud's tone conveyed his disbelief and in desperation Anne cried, "Yes. I knew he was ambitious, but I didn't know how much so until just lately."

"There's something wrong with ambition?"

"No, no. Oh, you don't understand."

"I know," he replied quietly. "That's why I'm asking."

Exasperated, Anne spun around and went taut, her breath catching in her throat. He was so close she could see the dark brown flecks in his amber eyes, eyes that roamed slowly over her face, then settled on her mouth. Barely able to breathe, Anne choked, "He—he no longer wants to socialize with anyone but business contacts and he's leaving Mr. Slonne's office, going into a bigger firm in Philadelphia."

"So," Jud purred, "he finally landed it."

"What do you mean?" Anne whispered, eyes widening. "Did you know about this?"

"For several weeks now." Jud paused, studying her closely as if trying to decide whether to tell her more. Suddenly he shrugged in a why-the-hell-not sort of way and said, "Lorna's father is a senior partner in a very high-class law firm in New York." He smiled slightly at the surprise on her face and chided, "Yes, Annie, Lorna doesn't have to work as a secretary. Not for me or anyone else. She chooses to do so.

A smart girl is our Lorna. But that's beside the point. Anyway, not long after Lorna went back to New York, Andrew ran into her. He took her to lunch and during the course of conversation she mentioned her father. That was all your ambitious Andrew needed. Through Lorna he met some people, made some of those business contacts you just mentioned and, from what you've said, they have paid off. This move he's making is really for the best, Anne," he tacked on softly. "He would never have been content here."

Even though Anne didn't love Andrew and the engagement was irrevocably broken, she felt cheated and in some way betrayed. All this time he'd been seeing Lorna, making plans to change firms and he hadn't said a word to her. Why? Anne had no idea that her thoughts gave her face a wistful, lost look and the harsh tone of Jud's voice startled her.

"Forget him. You wouldn't have been happy with him anyway. You couldn't have given him what he needs."

"What?"

The tone and the words were like a slap in the face, an insult to her femininity and the pain they caused laced her voice.

"Exactly what I said." The tone was softer, but the words just as hard. "Andrew is a man on the make. For position, power. He needs the kind of woman who's willing to keep up with him, if not one step ahead. The kind of woman who, if she doesn't have them already, will go out and make contacts and friends, who'll help him move up. You're not that kind of woman, Anne, and you'd tear yourself apart if you tried to be."

Andrew's words "I've been having second thoughts myself" were now very clear. He had reached the conclusion that she was not the right kind of woman. What kind of woman was she? Was she any man's kind of woman? She only wanted to be one man's kind of woman and it was obvious from the way they were always arguing that she wasn't that. The thought sent a wave of defeat through her and fighting tears she closed her eyes. The next moment her shoulders were being grasped and she was pulled roughly against a hard, exciting chest.

"Don't look like that," Jud rasped. "Dammit, Anne, there are other men in the world. Men worth one hell of a lot more than he is in all the ways that count."

Oh, Jud. There is only one man in this world I'll ever be able to see. Oh, God, I love you. If you knew what sweet torture it is to be held in your arms like this. Don't ever stop holding me. Don't ever go away again. Name your price and I'll pay it, whatever it is. Just don't leave me like you did before, hurting, longing, wanting.

The very intensity of Anne's emotions frightened her, made her draw back. *I have got to stop this,* she thought wildly. If I don't clamp down on my feelings, I'll shatter like a piece of glass when he finally does go. Help me, Jud, she pleaded silently. *Insult me, fight with me. Anything, only please, please help me.*

Maybe prayers are answered, even silent ones, for at that moment Jud released her and stepped back, his fingers raking through his hair. His face seemed a little pale, his breathing not quite even as he prowled around the small room; then he strode into his own office, slamming the door behind him. A few seconds later the door was flung open again and he ordered, "Anne, come in here."

Anne smoothed clammy palms over her skirt, adjusted first her blouse, then her jacket, then, composing her face, walked as calmly as possible into his office. He was perched on the corner of his desk, the fingers of one hand drumming impatiently on the gleaming surface. A deep frown drew his eyebrows together and he had an unleashed, dangerous look.

"I know this is probably not the right time," he began quietly enough, "but I have to ask you something."

Completely mystified by his tone, she asked equally quietly, "What is it?"

He hesitated, not looking at her; then he turned the full blast of glittering amber on her.

"I want you to sell me your stock."

Stunned, Anne dropped into the chair in front on him. Was

he out of his mind? Or did he think Andrew had so wounded her she would be grateful to sell out, creep away somewhere and lick her wounds?

"Sell you my stock," she replied dully. Then anger took over. "Jud, you know very well I won't do that!"

She moved to get up and his hard hands came down onto her shoulders, holding her in her chair.

"Wait, hear me out."

It wasn't a request, it was an order. From the boss to the assistant. Anne threw him a mutinous look, but she made no further move to rise.

Jud went on the prowl, back and forth, around his desk, while Anne sat, her back straight as a yardstick, hands clasped tightly on her lap. Finally he came to a stop in front of her, fists jammed aggressively on his hips.

"I've got a deal in the works," he stated flatly. "A very large deal. It would mean a leap forward for this company. So far it's on simmer, but I know I can pull it off. It will give this company new life and we need it. But to do it I have to have control."

He stopped, waiting, his eyes hard and steady on hers, as if willing her to give him what he wanted.

Anne squirmed under that intense stare, longing to give him anything he wanted, knowing she dared not.

"What do you mean, we need it?" Anne began carefully. "We're not in trouble, our profits are good."

"We're stagnating." Jud's tone challenged her to deny his word. "With the rate of inflation our profits have remained static for the last few years. I've gone over the books, Anne. The old man was letting it drift. You can get away with that only so long. Nothing remains static, and the handwriting is on the wall for this firm. If we don't move forward, we'll slip back and once that starts, forget it."

Anne stared at him, unwilling to believe him, yet convinced he was right. If she had learned nothing else about him over the last month, she had learned one thing: In business matters Jud was thorough. But one point bothered her.

"All right, if you say we must make this deal, whatever

it is, I'll believe you. But why must you have complete control? For all intents and purposes you are the head of the company. You have run things since the first day you stepped into this office. Why must you have a majority to close this deal?"

Jud sighed, then patiently, as though he were explaining something to a slow-witted child, he proceeded to enlighten her.

"First of all let me briefly outline what this contract would entail. Expansion, new machinery, a bigger work force. With what this company wants we'd need some new, innovative designers. They know what they want. It would be our job to produce the finished product."

As Jud warmed to his subject, Anne could actually feel the excitement building in him. He had taken the bit between his teeth, now he was all set to run with it.

"We can do it, Anne," he finished forcefully. "I know we can do it." He paused then added softly, "And I want it."

"You still haven't explained why you must have my stock."

He frowned, then grimaced. "I would have thought that was self-evident. They won't go with me."

"They," Anne asked softly, "being the twins?"

"Who else?"

He turned away abruptly, his fingers raking through his gold-kissed hair. His tone, his actions, every taut line of his powerful body screamed his disgust at her.

"But why?" Anne cried, almost frightened by the restless, charged aura that surrounded him. "It would be to their advantage too, wouldn't it?"

"Hell, yes," he spun on her with very much like a growl. "But you are and have been aware of their attitude. They are in open revolt. So far in the short amount of time they have spent in the plant, they have made it their business to learn as little as possible about its actual workings. Oh," he snarled, "they have gotten to know a lot of people, have made a lot of friends. They are charming and easy to like, when they want to be. And the employees feel flattered that

Judson Cammeron's sons have gone all out to be friendly." Jud's voice grew even thicker with disgust. "But, dammit, Anne, charm and friendliness don't keep the plant running, nor does it scrape together the payroll. In short, Anne, I have talked to them. And they've given me a loud, resounding no. Or, as our so charming Troy put it, 'We're doing fine as we are. Let well enough alone.' "

She should have known without asking. She really should have known. She was, as Jud had pointed out, very well aware of her brothers' attitude toward him. She was also aware of their ignorance in business matters. She had the very uneasy feeling that simply by asking she had set a match to a very short fuse. Keeping her voice low in an effort to dampen some of the fire raging inside him, she offered, "I'll talk to them. Make them see it would be advantageous to everyone if they went along with you."

"Terrific," he snapped sarcastically. "Problems solved. Dammit, Anne, they informed me—smugly—before they left to go back to school, that they will not be home again until after graduation. What the hell do I do in the meantime?"

Anne felt her own anger stir. Who did he think he was talking to? Did he think she was that stupid?

"You negotiate, as you damn well know," she snapped back. "Graduation is only a few weeks away. I promise I'll speak to them at the first opportunity. There's more than enough time."

"And if there isn't?" Jud jibed. "What will you do then?"

He is deliberately pushing, trying to force a commitment from me, playing the odds that I don't know exactly how long a deal of this kind can take to close. Fighting down her mounting anger, Anne arched her eyebrows, widened her eyes innocently and smiled sweetly.

"Cry?"

Jud acknowledged defeat with a quick, rueful grin.

"Okay, you win. I was pretty sure you knew your job, but I had to take the chance." He shrugged, then his voice took on a no-nonsense edge. "But I'm not taking any chances with this contract, Anne. You had better be able to convince those two airheads of this, because I meant what I said last night. I'm through playing games. If they insist on fighting me I'll chew them up and spit them out."

The weeks that followed dragged interminably. Not since she'd been a little girl waiting for Christmas had Anne remembered time moving so slowly. She rehearsed and re-rehearsed what she'd say to Troy and Todd, and each new argument she came up with seemed more ineffectual than the last.

She fretted and worried and tried to hide from everyone, including herself, the deep, empty longing that enveloped her whenever Jud was away, which was most of the time. He had, he said, meetings to go to, conferences to attend, his New York office to check out and people to see. Including Lorna? Just the thought of the redhead twisted through Anne like a bent blade. Lord, she asked herself at least every other day, if she was like this now, what would she feel when he left for good? That eventuality didn't bear thinking about, so she didn't. Instead she concentrated on the twins, her work, her mother, the weather. Anything, anything but the pain in store for her.

But time did, as it always does, move forward and the day finally came for Anne and Margaret to drive upstate for Troy and Todd's graduation exercises.

Jud had been in New York for the last four days and when he sauntered into the dining room as Anne was finishing her breakfast she was so surprised she nearly choked on her toast.

"When did you get home?"

"Early this morning," he grunted.

Anne studied him from under her lashes as he walked to the swinging door to the kitchen and asked Mrs. Davis for orange juice, toast, and a pot of coffee. Then she quickly lowered her eyes to her plate when he turned back to the table. He looked tired and harassed and in a very bad humor, but even so, he was the best thing Anne had seen in close to a week and her eyes devoured him hungrily.

He was quiet until after Mrs. Davis had placed his breakfast in front of him and swung out of the room again; then he asked in the same low grunt, "What time are we leaving?"

Try as she would, Anne could not keep the astonishment out of her voice.

"You're going with us?"

As they had the day he came home, his eyes went over her with slow insolence, his expression putting her firmly in her place.

"My dear Anne," he purred silkily, "I think I had to remind you before that Troy and Todd are not your exclusive property. At the risk of repeating myself, they are my brothers, too. And, yes, whether you approve, or not, I am going with you. Or rather you are going with me, as I'm driving."

"The Beemer?"

"No, I drove the Navigator back. I thought it might come in handy if the twins want us to lug some of their junk home for them. That's why I didn't get back last night. I cancelled my plane reservation and left New York soon after midnight."

Anne wasn't sure she could believe what she'd heard. Jud explaining his actions to her? He must be even more tired than he looks, she reasoned.

"I didn't know you had a Navigator. Or isn't it yours?"

The minute the words were out Anne wished them unsaid. She had no right to pry into what was and was not his and she waited for his verbal slap down. Strangely it didn't come. Instead, Jud refilled his coffee cup, leaned back in his chair, took a sip, then, with a small smile playing at the corners of his mouth murmured, "Yes, Anne, it's mine. It's a gas guzzler of course, so I don't drive it very often. Most of the time it just takes up space in the parking garage at my apartment building. I've considered either selling it or bringing it here, but I haven't decided just what I want to do with it." He paused, then added seriously, "You wouldn't want to use it, would you? That car of yours looks like it has about had it. You're welcome to it, if it takes your fancy."

Tired! The man must be near unconsciousness. Unable to

resist taking advantage of his sudden mellowness, Anne teased, "No, thank you. But if you want to keep it here and drive it yourself, I'll gladly run the BMW for you."

"You like the Beemer?" Pale brows went up in question.

"Of course I like it," Anne laughed. "It's a super hunk of machinery, and you know it."

"All right, I'll leave the Navigator here and use it myself." He shrugged. "You can have the Beemer."

He meant it! He really meant it!

"No! Jud, really, I couldn't." Flustered, Anne's words tripped over one another. "I didn't mean—I mean I was only teasing—I couldn't take your—"

"Anne, be quiet," Jud sighed. "I know you were only teasing. But I wasn't. I don't trust that heap you drive."

Anne opened her mouth to argue, then closed it with a snap when he chided, "And don't go all moralistic on me. I'm not making you a gift of the car, simply putting it at your disposal. The car will be here, you have my permission to use it, that settles it."

"That settles what?"

Margaret followed her question into the room, her eyes studying Anne's flushed cheeks before swinging to Jud.

"I've just been telling Anne that since I brought my other vehicle back with me, she may as well make use of the BMW, retire that pile of scrap she drives."

"About time too," her mother agreed promptly. "I've been after her for over a year now to buy a new car. I don't think the one she has is entirely safe."

"Mother," Anne sighed in exasperation, "I told you I'll get another car when I can afford it. My car is not all that bad; it passed inspection, you know. Besides which, I can't use Jud's car, I'd be too afraid of something happening while I had it."

"Don't be silly, dear," Margaret brushed aside her argument. "You are an excellent driver and I really think you should accept Jud's offer."

Anne fumed and stared icicles at Jud, who sat back lazily in his chair, a look of smug complacency on his face.

"Mother," Anne breathed angrily.

"Now, Anne, please don't go on about this. As Jud said, it's settled." The subject closed as far as she was concerned, Margaret calmly poured herself coffee.

Simmering, not daring to look at Jud, afraid that if she did and he still wore that self-satisfied expression she'd throw something at him, Anne spoke through clenched teeth.

"What time would you like to leave, Mother?"

Margaret glanced casually at her wristwatch, then answered calmly, "In a half hour."

"A half hour!"

Two outbursts, one male, one female, as both Anne and Jud jumped out of their chairs. As she went out of the room, Jud at her heels, Anne heard her mother laugh softly.

"Do hurry, children. We'll have to stop for lunch on the way, and you know how I dislike rushing through a meal."

Unbelievable, Anne thought in wonder, as she rushed up the stairs. Apparently even her mother was not immune to the electricity Jud generated, or to his brand of humor either.

"Anne."

Jud's voice stopped her as she reached her door. Anne turned, impatient words hovering on her lips, but all that came out was an angry "Oh," for she saw a set of car keys dangling in front of her face, and two amber eyes glittering with steely purpose.

"Why don't you give in gracefully, Anne? Take the keys."

He is so sure of himself, Anne raged inwardly. *So damned confident he's won.*

"You know what you can do with your keys."

Spinning around, she grasped the doorknob just as his other arm shot out and his hand was placed flat, fingers spread, on the door panel.

"You're not getting in until you take the keys." His voice was a quiet taunt. "Better hurry, Annie, time's a-wastin'."

She didn't want his damned car. She didn't want anything from him, but the one thing he couldn't give her. Her anger way out of proportion to the situation, Anne turned, sputtering, "You—you have no right insisting I use your stupid car.

You have no right insisting I do anything. Take your hand away and let me . . . Oh!"

His blond head was lowered, and his lips, very close to hers, murmured, "There is only one way to calm a stormy woman."

Her protests were smothered by his mouth, in a kiss Anne felt certain he had meant to bestow lightly. But suddenly he groaned deep in his throat and his arms crushed her against the hard length of his body, his mouth fastened greedily on hers, demanding a response she had no will to refuse.

If only time could stop right here, right now, Anne mused dreamily, allowing her arms to coil up and around his neck, her fingers to slide possessively through his golden mane.

Anne could have remained locked within his arms for the rest of her life, but the old grandfather clock, which had stood in the foyer for as long as she could remember, struck the half hour and brought Anne to her senses.

Pulling away from him, she husked, "All right, I'll take your damned keys. But will you please let me go, we've only a few minutes."

His arms seemed unwilling to release her, his eyes held a strange, moody look and his face was a study in conflict.

"Anne, Annie—wait—I . . ."

Sure he was going to apologize, and not wanting to hear it, Anne pushed gently against his chest.

"Jud, please. We have got to get moving. Mother will have six fits if we are not downstairs when she's ready to leave."

Right on cue, her mother's voice floated up the stairs to them.

"Anne, Jud, why are you standing around the hall talking? Do you realize what time it is?"

With an impatient grunt, Jud dropped his arms, grimaced, then strode down the hall to his room.

Much to Anne's surprise, the drive upstate was pleasant and in the soft leather seats of the luxurious Navigator, very comfortable.

At first conversation was minimal as Anne made a pretense of admiring the scenery, Jud concentrated on his driving, and Margaret, ensconced on the back-seat, sifted through the small stack of mail she'd picked up from the hall table as they left the house.

"Oh, Jud, here's a note from Melly," Margaret murmured after some twenty-five minutes of total silence. "She says that as Franklin is doing so well now she'll be able to come up for the twins' celebration."

Melly was Melinda Cammeron Stoughten, Judson Cammeron's twin sister and Jud, Troy, and Todd's only aunt, which was one more than Anne had.

"Yes, I know," Jud answered quietly. "I spoke with her a few days ago. I was going to tell you, but it slipped my mind."

"How is Franklin, really, Jud?" Margaret asked anxiously. "It was so hard on Melly to lose her—" she faltered, then went on, "her brother, so soon after waiting through that horribly long operation on Franklin, being unsure for days if he'd live. I know that it tore at her heart not to be able to attend Judson's funeral, but it was impossible for her to leave Franklin at that crucial time."

"Yes, it was a hard time for her." Jud's voice had gentled to a loving softness. "I was with her the day before the funeral and she was in pretty bad shape. As you know, like a lot of twins, Dad and Mel were on the same wavelength."

Turning her head to stare out the window at her side, Anne fought to control her trembling lips, the tears stinging her eyes. She had become resigned to him referring to his father as the old man, even though her mother still winced when he did, but now, not only had he said Dad, he'd said it in a tone that revealed to her some of the pain losing his father had inflicted. Anne ached for him, for the right to comfort him, and she ached for herself too. His expression had been so tender, so full of loving warmth. If he could look like that for a much-loved parent and aunt, what would he be like with a woman he was in love with?

Anne blinked rapidly as an errant thought stabbed her mind. Was Lorna the recipient of his loving glances? She had seen no evidence of it while the beautiful redhead had been in the office, but that meant little. Both Lorna and Jud were too intelligent not to be circumspect in a business atmosphere.

Jealousy, pure and simple, consumed every fiber of Anne's being and along with it an emotion both alien and frightening. Hate—ugly, soul-destroying hate for Lorna—tore at her mind so viciously she had to clamp her lips together to silence a snarling moan.

This can't be happening to me, her mind screamed in protest. *I can't let this happen. I feel like I'm losing my mind and I can't bear it. What I feel for him can't be love. Love is supposed to be a tender emotion, overflowing with compassion and understanding. If I loved him, really loved him, I'd want his happiness more than anything else, even if that happiness could only be achieved with someone else. But I don't feel that way,* she cried in silent anguish, *what I feel is totally selfish. I want to be the one he reserves his most loving glances for; I want to be the one he hurries to when he leaves his office, and I want to be the only one he can't wait to have in his arms, in his bed.*

Unnerved, scared stiff by the raw intensity of her thoughts, Anne forced her attention to Jud's quiet voice. He was still discussing his aunt and uncle with her mother—could it only be a few minutes that she'd burned in the hell of her own emotions. In desperation she grasped at the threads of their conversation.

". . . that was two weeks ago," Jud said calmly. "But when I talked to her the other day she said his improvement had been so great they think they'll be able to dispense with the live-in nurse within a few weeks."

"Oh, I'm so glad, Jud." Margaret sighed softly, her gentle heart touched by her brother-in-law's suffering. "I wish she could stay longer than one day, although I can fully understand her wanting to get back as soon as possible. I truly like your Aunt Melly, Jud. I always have."

"So do I." Jud laughed softly, then added seriously, "I know you do, Margaret. And I also know the feeling is returned." Then, as if to lighten the serious mood, he added, "I also wish she could stay longer than the one day. Mel is so full of life and joy herself, she seems to infuse it into everyone she comes into contact with."

The conversation drifted easily into more general subjects and Anne, though adding little, hung on to every word as to a lifeline. The balmy weather was discussed, and the beauty of the rolling Pennsylvania countryside on which spring had once again settled itself so gracefully.

Turning her head dutifully to observe the yearly phenomenon, Anne's eyes were caught then held by two horses running across a white-fenced paddock. The stallion was large and as he pranced along he alternately tossed his beautiful, regal head and nipped playfully at the daintily dancing mare at his side. Anne heard a low chuckle beside her, then she winced as Jud murmured, "Go get her, big fellah."

Chapter Eight

Even with the graduation exercises over and the twins, with all their assorted belongings, home again, Anne could not get them together in one place long enough to have any kind of serious discussion. They were too busy with the hours they put in at the mill, settling in at home, and getting things organized for their party at the end of the week to go into a conference, they insisted.

Jud was beginning to positively scowl at her and, as if that were not enough, she was facing a problem that worried her more than a little.

The problem, in the form of John Franks, showed up the day after the twins' graduation. Why he was there was self-explanatory, for Jud was methodically feeding him information about the textile business. Why his presence at and understanding of the company was necessary at all was what worried Anne.

Questions tormented her every waking hour, the main one being, was Jud training John to replace her?

About the same age as Jud, John Franks was a good-looking, easy-going man whose demeanor belied his sharp mind. He had taken Anne to lunch a few times, on the occasions when he'd been in town negotiating for Jud with Mr. Cammeron, and Anne liked him very much. He had been amusing and entertaining and had not stepped out of line once.

On his first day at the office he had looked pointedly at

Anne's third finger and, eyebrows raised slightly, said, "The fool surely didn't let you get away?"

"No getaway necessary, John."

Anne's reply was made without strain. She had always been easy and relaxed in John's company. Then in a gently scolding tone, she added, "And Andrew is not a fool, John."

"Couldn't prove that by me," he retorted amiably, seating himself on the corner of her desk. "Personally, I thought he was not too bright in not rushing you to the altar the minute you said yes."

"Of course," Anne laughed lightly. "Words of wisdom from a man I strongly suspect is a confirmed bachelor."

"Only because, by the time I met you, you were already spoken for."

John's words were spoken in such earnest, Anne felt the laughter die in her throat. Before she could form a reply, Jud's voice drawled from the doorway.

"If you can tear yourself away from my assistant, John, I'd like to get down to work."

John's fair cheeks flushed a ruddy hue and his eyes flashed warningly as he turned to face the doorway.

Jud's stance, with his shoulder propped against the door frame, was the only indolent thing about his appearance. Pale eyebrows arched arrogantly over two glittering chips of amber stone, his face set firmly and his lips were twisted in the now familiar sardonic slant.

Obviously on the verge of an angry reply, one look at Jud seemed to change John's mind, and with a mild shrug he murmured, "You're the boss, Jud."

"I know."

Jud's silky purr had the same effect on Anne as an ice cube being drawn down her spine. Biting her lip to keep from shivering, Anne stood mutely as Jud stepped aside to allow John to walk by him into his office; then, his smile mocking, Jud pulled the door to, closing John in, shutting her out.

* * *

Saturday, the day of Troy and Todd's party, dawned bright and warm, perfect weather for a party that would, in all likelihood, spill out of doors.

Anne found herself on the move from the moment she finished her breakfast. Suddenly her mother discovered half a dozen errands for Anne to run and she was kept too busy to think, dashing around in the BMW.

Jud absented himself from this frenzy of activity until lunchtime. Anne, her mother, Troy, and Todd had started their meal, thinking Jud would not show up, when he strode into the room, a very reluctant-looking John at his heels.

Jud waved John to a chair, seated himself, and favored Margaret with a charming smile.

"As John is on his own here, I insisted he join us. Not only for lunch, but for the bash tonight as well."

Without batting an eyelash, Margaret returned his smile with one of equal charm.

"Well, of course he must stay." She then turned the smile on John.

"I'm sorry I didn't issue the invitation myself, John, but I've been so busy the last few days. I'm sure you'll understand."

John hastened to assure her he did, while Anne pondered on the changed relationship between her mother and Jud. She had no idea what she'd missed in the conversation the day they'd driven to commencement exercises, but whatever it was had caused the cessation of hostilities. The baffled expressions on the faces of her brothers told her they were even more mystified than she was.

With everyone on their best behavior in front of John, lunch was a pleasant, if brief, respite from the bustle. But from the moment they left the table Margaret began issuing orders like a field marshal and this time even Jud did not escape.

On her way from yet another trip between the kitchen and living room, Anne's arm was suddenly grasped and she was pulled unceremoniously into the library. Hearing the door close with a soft click, she turned and saw Jud leaning against it, a furtive look on his face.

Anne opened her mouth to ask what he was up to, then closed it when he placed a long forefinger to his lips and breathed a soft "Shush" as he pushed himself away from the door and came toward her. He didn't stop when he reached her, but kept on going, taking her with him with a firm hand placed in the middle of her back. When, at the far end of the room, he finally did stop, she spun on him.

"Jud, what in the devil—"

"I had forgotten what an organizer your mother is," he interrupted in a stage whisper. "Maybe I should put her to work somewhere in the company."

"Jud," Anne sighed warningly.

The teasing light left his eyes and he smiled ruefully.

"I wanted to talk to you, obviously." Jud's tone had changed from that of conspirator to one of control. "When the hell are you going to talk to Troy and Todd? I can't keep dodging around these people indefinitely, you know."

"I know, and I'm sorry." Anne raised her hands placatingly as Jud frowned. "I haven't been able to get them alone for longer than three minutes since they got home. I was hoping to corner them tomorrow sometime."

"Don't hope, do it," Jud ordered. "And I want to see you in here the minute you have." He paused, then added resignedly, "Now I suppose we had better get on with Margaret's craziness before she sets the bloodhounds on our missing trail."

By mid-afternoon all the preparations were completed to Margaret's satisfaction and Anne gratefully fled to her room to have a hasty shower and change of clothes before the guests began descending on them.

She spent more time than she really should have getting dressed, wanting, for some un-obvious reason, to look her best. Finally finished, she stepped back from the mirror and critically surveyed her reflection. She had bought the dress she was wearing on impulse, and now was somewhat amazed at the vision before her eyes. The rich apricot raw silk sheath set off her dark hair to perfection and gave a glow to her smooth pale skin. The scooped neckline revealed just a hint of a curve at her breasts, while the snug shaping outlined the enticements it covered.

Giving a nod of satisfaction to the young woman in her mirror, Anne smiled and left her room. As she hurried down the stairs, the sound of voices drifted to her from the living room; one in particular brought a glow of pleasure to her eyes.

Melly had arrived and it seemed everyone was talking at once. Hanging back, Anne watched Jud's aunt as she laughingly replied to their questions. Tall and slim, still lovely, Melly seemed to be plugged into the same high voltage circuit that Jud was, for she charged the air around her as forcefully as he did.

Within minutes of her entering the room, Anne saw Melly's and Jud's eyes meet in understanding and communication and felt a small stab of envy of the older woman.

"Anne, darling, why are you hovering there in the background?" Melly's soft, melodious voice chided. "Come here, dear, and let me look at you."

"Hello, Melly. You look wonderful, as usual."

Anne walked across the room and into the arms of the older woman, who then stepped back and let her eyes run quickly over Anne's small frame.

"Anne, I don't know how you manage it. But I swear you grow more lovely between my visits." Then Melly's eyes narrowed slightly and she sent a sharp glance at Jud. "Jud, are you working this child too hard? If she gets much thinner she'll float away on the air."

"Really, Melly—" Anne began, only to have Jud cut in.

"Anne has been working very hard the last month or so, Mel. But not to worry, I'm working on an arrangement now that will give her more free time."

Jud's tone was casually teasing, yet Anne felt suddenly chilled. What arrangement was he working on? Were her suspicions correct? Had John Franks been brought in to take over her job? Pushing the questions away, she made herself join in the conversation. This was her brothers' celebration, she would not spoil it for them by letting her worries show. All the same she decided to stay away from Jud as much as possible that evening.

The guests began arriving, and within the hour the house was filled with laughing people. While Jud, at Margaret's side, played the host, Anne circulated around the room, greeting people she knew, meeting people she didn't, making sure no one went long without a drink or something to eat.

The house became steadily more crowded and, as the one half of the large double living room had been cleared of furniture, quite a few of the young people were dancing. As Anne had suspected, the less physically inclined drifted out through the French doors onto the side patio. The evening was warm and still, the scent of first roses heady, but Anne barely noticed as she moved around—avoiding Jud—making numerous trips between the living room and the dining room to keep an eye on the food supply.

Anne was returning from one of these buffet checks when the sound of new arrivals brought her head up sharply. Stepping back into the shadow of the stairway, Anne stood perfectly still, hands clenched, observing the group of people talking in the foyer.

Although she couldn't hear his words, Andrew's cool precise voice was unmistakable, as was the throaty laugh of the woman on his arm. Lorna, here! And with Andrew! Margaret's voice was a low murmur as she greeted the couple and the twins stood, just looking at Lorna, idiotic grins on their faces. At that moment Jud strode into the foyer from the living room, hand outstretched to grasp the slim one extended to him. He said something softly that brought a dazzling smile to the redhead's face, then nodded coolly to Andrew.

Anne stayed where she was for several minutes after the group had moved into the living room, eyes closed, breathing deeply to regain her composure. Damn him! Damn him for inviting her here. Anger surged through her and she thought bitterly, *He hasn't been to New York in almost a week,*

*couldn't he bear being away from her any longer? And what
was she doing with Andrew? Had they become such close
friends she could ask him to escort her to the home of her
lover?*

Just thinking the words made Anne feel ill, and for a fleeting second she considered running to her room. Fierce pride
made her reject the idea. Squaring her shoulders, she formed
her lips into a bright smile and headed for the living room.
She hesitated a moment in the doorway, then saw two men
moving toward her from opposite directions. Jud advanced
from the left, his face set in grim determination, and from
her right John approached, a smile of warmth lighting his
face.

Not wanting to be anywhere near Jud, let alone talk to
him, Anne walked quickly to meet John, seeing Jud stop
dead out of the corner of her eye.

"Come dance with me." John smiled coaxingly. "You've
been busy long enough. Time you relaxed and enjoyed the
party."

Pliantly Anne allowed him to draw her into the cleared
area, and into his arms. The music was slow and dreamy and
as John turned her to him she caught a glimpse of Jud. He
stood taut and angry where he'd stopped, his eyes hard and
cold. Turning her head away, Anne was filled with fiery resentment. What right did he have to be angry? If she chose
to dance with John instead of greeting Jud's lady-love, why
should it bother him?

With a concentrated effort she pushed Jud from her mind
and gave full attention to the dance. She loved to dance, had
in fact, taken several classes in modern dance and she found
John a polished partner.

"Hey, you're very good!" John's surprise amused Anne.
"I should have dragged you onto the floor sooner."

"Thank you, kind sir," Anne laughed up at him as the
music ended. "You're pretty good yourself."

The young man who had taken over the stereo must have
decided it was time for a change, for the record that dropped
onto the turntable was upbeat, the tempo fast and inviting.

Anne felt the beat in every muscle and agreed eagerly when John murmured, "Are you game?"

Within seconds Anne realized that John was not only good, he was very, very good, and Anne gave herself up to the enjoyment of the intricate, somewhat sensuous movements of the dance. As John moved beside her, at times spinning her away from him, then, one arm coiling her back close to his body, she became aware that the other dancers had moved back, leaving them in sole possession of the floor.

When the music stopped there was a burst of applause and several calls of "one more time."

Shaking her head, laughing and pink with embarrassment, Anne walked off the dance area.

"That was fun." John's arm, still around her waist, tightened. "Will you dance with me again later?"

"We'll see." Anne hesitated, then added ruefully, "But definitely not as the evening's entertainment."

Glancing around, she saw Jud again moving toward her and with a hurried, "Excuse me, I must go check on the food," she slipped out of the room.

Moving quickly, Anne went through the dining room, casting a cursory glance at the buffet, and on through the kitchen and out the back door. The enclosed garden at the back of the house was quiet and very dark. Not stopping until she was at the very back of the garden, Anne stood trembling with reaction. Jud's face had been so hard, his eyes blazing with fury. The brief glance she'd had of him before she'd fled had filled her with something very much like panic.

"Who are you hiding from, Salome?"

The softly sardonic words coming out of the darkness startled Anne so badly she jumped, and with a gasp she turned on her tormentor.

"I'm not hiding from anyone, Jud. I just wanted some fresh air." Fighting to control her trembling breathlessness, she snapped, "Why did you follow me? What do you want?"

"I followed you because I'm curious." The disembodied voice blended into a blurred form as Jud stepped closer to her. "What exactly was that performance on the dance floor for? Was it simply a come-on to John? Or were you trying to get at Andrew by showing him what he'd given up?"

The suppressed rage in Jud's tone sent an arrow of fear zinging up Anne's spine and in an effort to hide it from him she laughed lightly, if a little shakily.

"Maybe a little of both." She heard his sharp intake of breath and added impishly, "Do you think it was effective?"

The next instant she was wishing she'd held her tongue, for his hands grasped her arms and pulled her hard against his chest.

"I think," he gritted through clenched teeth, "there was not a man in that room who didn't feel the effect. Myself included."

His hands loosened their painful hold on her arms, only to move up to clasp her face tightly.

"There are times, little girl, when you infuriate me." He drew her face so close to his she could feel his breath against her skin, could smell the fumes of the drink he'd had. "Then there are the other times, like now." His tone had dropped to a low rasp that sent tiny darts of excitement into her nerve ends.

"What do you mean?" she whispered.

"The answer to that is the same as the answer to what I want."

His mouth was almost touching hers and Anne felt a shock ripple through her when the tip of his tongue touched her upper lip.

"I want what was offered to me ten years ago," he murmured huskily. "I want what should have been mine before any other man's."

Anne gasped and would have denied his inference, but he wasn't finished, for he added harshly, "I want you."

His mouth crushed hers, his lips forcing hers apart, while his hands moved from her face to her back to pull her roughly to him. Struggling was futile as his arms tightened, holding her still, and as his kiss deepened she gave up the pretense. With a soft sigh she relaxed against him, savoring the possessive sweetness of his mouth. As her body softened, his seemed to grow harder, the muscles in his arms, shoulders, and thighs tautening in urgency. His mouth released hers, slid slowly across her cheek.

"Annie, chicken, come with me now," Jud urged.

"Come? Where?"

"Anywhere," he husked. "My room. Your room. The car. I don't care as long as I can have you to myself awhile."

"But, Jud, we can't. We have a house full of people. Andrew, John, Lo—"

"The hell with Andrew and John," he gritted savagely. "The hell with all of them."

His mouth caught hers again, sensuously, lingeringly, until he felt her begin to tremble. His hand moved slowly over her ribcage, then her breast. Her small gasp was smothered by a swift hard kiss.

"Annie, come with me to my room," his softly purring voice enticed. "I don't care anymore what happened before. I don't care about Andrew or any others that may have been before him."

In between the whispered words his lips had moved over her face, down the side of her neck to explore the hollows at the base of her throat, while his fingers caressed and teased the growing fullness of her breast. Almost beyond sanity, on the verge of agreeing to anything he wanted, Anne felt a chill spear through her with his last words.

"Jud, you—"

"I think you'll find," he continued as if she hadn't spoken, "I'm just as competent at pleasing you as they were. You may even find I'm better."

The chill nosedived into a frigid cold and, not unlike the first day in his office, she pushed at him, tore herself out of his arms. Hurt and angry, Anne was past caring what she said.

"You overbearing clown," she snapped furiously. "Are you trying to drive me away?"

"Anne, what the hell—"

"If you are," she interrupted, "you don't have to humiliate

and insult me to do it. Tell me you want me to go and I will. Gladly."

She moved to walk around him, but he caught her at the waist, pulled her so hard against him the breath was knocked out of her body.

"Andrew was not your lover?"

Strangely his tone was soft.

"That's none of your business," she hissed.

"Answer me, Anne."

A command, Jud was again the boss.

"No." Her voice was low, but emphatic.

"After being engaged for three months? I find that a little hard to believe."

Anger mounting, Anne struggled to free herself, but his arms tightened to make her sure he'd crack her ribs if she moved.

"I don't give one damn what you believe," she whispered harshly. "Andrew never made love to me. And there were no others."

Although his hold did not loosen, he went completely still, not even seeming to breath; then his breath relaxed in a long, slow sigh.

"It seems I owe you an apology again."

"Keep your apologies," Anne replied wearily. "They come too fast and glib after your insults."

"Annie, I said I was sorry. I mean it." The purr was back in his voice and against her will Anne felt her anger dissolving. "I wasn't trying to insult or humiliate you. Good Lord, woman, I know myself and had I been Andrew you would not have been able to answer no."

"Anne—Jud, are you out here?" Todd called from the back of the house. "Anne, Mother's looking for you, and Jud, Lorna's looking for you."

Anne stirred feebly against him.

"Jud, we must go—oh!"

His mouth touched hers, then covered it fully in a short tender kiss. As he lifted his head, he murmured, "Don't be angry with me, little girl. For if you're angry, you won't let me kiss you. And I sure as hell don't want that."

Flustered, Anne could find nothing to say and with a soft laugh he released her, all but her hand which he grasped firmly until they reached the back door.

The rest of the evening was a confused blank for Anne. Unable to erase the feel of Jud's mouth, his arms, and his perplexing words, Anne laughed and joined the conversation and could not remember afterward a single word that was said.

Anne slept late and woke to a June morning dark and overcast with storm clouds. Praying the weather was not a harbinger to what the day had in store for her, she went in search of the twins.

She found them at the breakfast table, slightly hung over, discussing the party desultorily. Receiving only nods and grunts to her bright "Good morning" Anne seated herself and picked at her breakfast in silence. When Todd and Troy left the table and headed for the stairs, she slipped out of her chair and followed them. When she reached the door to her room, they were a few steps ahead of her and she called softly, "Troy, Todd, I want to talk to you."

"Oh, Anne, must it be now?"

"Later, maybe, I have a rotten headache."

"I'm sorry, but it can't wait any longer." Turning the knob, she pushed the door open and, before they could object further, she nodded her head at the room. "Now."

They grumbled something about bossy older sisters, but they followed her, Troy dropping onto her small, padded chair, Todd flopping onto the bed.

"I think you know what this is all about," she began, then proceeded to outline what Jud had said to her, omitting that he had asked to buy her stock.

"Dammit, Anne, we told Jud weeks ago we wanted no part of this."

Troy sprang out of the chair and walked around the room

impatiently. Todd merely grunted his agreement with Troy and massaged his temples.

"But I think he's right," Anne argued. "It is time for expansion, for moving ahead. If we stand still, we'll stagnate, become second-rate."

"God, she sounds like Jud's echo," Todd told the ceiling disgustedly. Then, giving her a sharp look, rapped, "Whose side are you on, anyway?"

"Oh, Todd," Anne sighed wearily. "You sound like a little boy. I want what's best for the business, because in the long run it will be best for you two."

"Anne, listen." Sensing her growing impatience with them, Troy spoke soothingly. "We've talked to a lot of people in the mill this last week. Most of them agree with our opinion that we just can't handle a contract of this size. Regardless of what Jud thinks. The general consensus seems to be that if we take it on it will be the end of us."

"Honey," Todd began as soon as Troy had finished. "There is one thing you're forgetting. Jud is for number one, first, last, and always. I don't know what he is planning here, but you can bet he won't come out the loser. We will."

"But—"

"No buts," Troy stated firmly. "We're not going into this, Anne. That's final. And the sooner he's told the better. Maybe, if he's convinced he's not going to get his way, he'll get the hell out of here, go back to New York. He's in the library, why don't you go and brighten this dull day for him?"

His last words were delivered in a malicious way and Anne found herself asking him the same question she'd asked Jud weeks before, only in reverse.

"Do you hate Jud, Troy?"

Oddly there were only minor differences in the answer.

"Hell, no," he replied mildly. "He is my brother. If you'll remember, both Todd and I had a pretty bad case of hero-worship for him before he went away. The way he went, the fact that he never appeared again until Dad died, well, I resent it. And I just don't like him very much anymore."

"Ditto." This from Todd as he crawled off her bed.

After they left, Anne sat on the side of her bed, brow puckered in thought. Could they be right about Jud? She didn't want to believe it, but, then, what she wanted had very little to do with it. She had heard the rumors that had run like wildfire from the mill to the offices. One claimed that this other company was really planning a takeover and that all the employees would lose their seniority. Another that Jud was deliberately taking on more than they could handle in order to run the company at a loss and thereby claim a tax write-off.

As always with scuttlebutt she had shaken her head and dismissed it. Now she had doubts and she didn't like it. She had realized from the beginning that Jud was dangerous, ruthless, and bitter. But would he ruin the company his father had worked all his life to build? She couldn't believe it. She wouldn't believe it. At least not without more proof. And she wasn't going to learn anything sitting here thinking in circles. Jumping to her feet, Anne went to her dresser, brushed her hair, straightened her turtleneck shirt and ran damp palms over her jean-clad hips. Giving one last nervous glance into the mirror, Anne grimaced, turned, and left the room.

When she reached the library, Anne hesitated; then, straightening her shoulders, she knocked on the door and pushed it open. Jud was speaking on the phone but he ended his conversation as she entered.

"Good morning," he murmured, then went straight to the point. "Have you talked to Troy and Todd?"

"Yes." Anne sat down on the edge of the chair he nodded at before adding, "They were—ah—difficult."

"Tell me about it," Jud drawled.

Anne wet her lips and stared at him. It seemed he was going to be somewhat difficult himself.

"Jud, they absolutely refuse to consider it."

"You explained my reasoning?"

"Yes, of course. I—"

"Well?"

The tone of his voice warned her he was going to be very difficult.

"They've been discussing it with some of the mill employees this week and, well, it appears everyone is of the opinion that it can't be done."

Pale eyebrows shot up in a face turned cold and haughty.

"My dear Anne." The sarcastic note flicked along her nerves. "Company policy is not necessarily made on the workroom floor."

"Jud, they're afraid it's a takeover bid, or worse."

"Really?" he snapped. "And you?"

Anne was beginning to understand the feelings of a cornered animal.

"I don't know, I . . ."

She stopped and leaned back in her seat, for Jud stood up so violently she felt threatened.

"Come here."

Without taking his eyes from hers, he flipped open a folder on his desk. Before she could move, he was around the desk and in front of her, suppressed fury in his eyes.

"It's all in there," he indicated the folder. "Plans, proposed changes, approximate costs, minutes of the negotiations, everything to date."

He turned to the door as he added, "While you go over it, I'm going to hunt up some coffee. Do you want some?"

"Yes, please," she replied, then winced as the door slammed behind him.

It didn't take long. A few pages into the folder and Anne knew the twins and whomever they had talked to were wrong. She was still reading when Jud came back into the room, a mug of coffee in each hand, but she really didn't have to see any more.

Jud handed her a mug, then propped himself on the edge of the desk, his eyes glittering with anger.

"Are you satisfied?"

"Yes."

Anne bent her head to stare into the creamy brew.

"And are you going to sell me your stock?"

Her head jerked up and she had to grasp her cup to keep from spilling the hot liquid.

"Jud, I can't. You know that."

"Can't has nothing to do with it." The purr was back in his voice and Anne decided she'd rather hear the anger.

"What you mean is, you won't."

"Jud, please, try to understand my position."

"I understand it perfectly. You're afraid that if you sell to me I'll force them out. You refuse to trust me, refuse to believe I have their interests as much on my mind as you do."

He paused and Anne began to feel prickly under his brooding stare. What could she say? She wanted to trust him. But he was right, she was afraid. Even loving him as much as she did hadn't changed that.

His soft voice intruded on her thoughts. "I have an alternative, Anne."

"An alternative? What possible alternative could there be?"

Her mind darted back and forth but, for the life of her, she couldn't come up with one.

His softly purred words went through her like an electric shock.

"Marry me."

Chapter Nine

Marry me. Marry me. Marry me.

The words seemed to reverberate through her mind like the aftereffects of an explosion. Stunned, feeling as if she were caught in a vise that was slowly squeezing the air out of her body, Anne stared at him mutely, unable for several minutes to articulate even the smallest word. Had he gone mad or had she? He couldn't be serious. Or could he? The idea that he'd even consider giving up his freedom just to get control of the company was beyond her comprehension. When finally she managed to loosen her tension-taut vocal cords, her voice came in a strangled squeak.

"Marry you? How could that solve anything?"

"I would think the answer to that would be evident," he replied smoothly. "Actually the benefits would be twofold."

Her throat working spasmodically, Anne brought a measure of normalcy to her tone.

"I must be a little slow this morning, since I fail to see—"

"Anne," Jud chided gently, "get with it. If you marry me, you could support me in this, and possibly future deals, without actually giving up control of your stock. At the same time you'd still hold the check rein the old man intended. Being my wife would in no way compel you to go along with anything I wanted to do. But, at the same time, as my wife I'd know that once given, your support would not be withdrawn."

"As you suspect it would be otherwise?" Anne asked sharply.

"Might be," he corrected. "You have one very weak spot, Anne, and that's your love for Troy and Todd. There would always be the outside chance they would get to you. I don't care to take that chance."

"But, but if I agree to be—" She couldn't even think the words—be your wife—let alone say them. "To go along with your idea, Troy and Todd will think—"

"Of course," he interrupted impatiently, "for a while. Until they finally realize I'm not out to rob them of their inheritance. They are Cammerons, and I don't think it will be too long before their basic intelligence overrides their resentment."

And then what, Anne thought dismally, the dissolution of a marriage made in expediency? Before she could voice her thoughts, Jud veered from Troy and Todd.

"I said the benefits would be twofold. The first, of course, would be to me, but the second would be solely yours."

An intriguing piece of bait thrown out casually, Anne bit at once.

"In what way?"

"You could save face by beating Andrew to the altar."

Beating Andrew to the . . . Anne's eyes went wide.

"Andrew is getting married?"

"Well-ll—" Jud drew the word out thoughtfully. "I can't answer a definite yes on that. I do know he has made a proposal. I also know the lady is giving it serious consideration."

The idea of Andrew getting married didn't bother her in the least, but she was curious.

"What lady?"

The answer came fast, flat, and emotionless.

"Lorna."

Anne's eyes closed against the sudden pain in her chest. Change twofold to threefold, and number three is the real and most important one. How any woman could consider Andrew over Jud mystified Anne. But then, perhaps Jud had never made a proposal to Lorna. At least not of a legal nature. Anne didn't like the direction her thoughts were galloping in, but one in particular would not be denied. Lorna could not give Jud what he coveted the most. The control of the company he thought of as rightfully his. How much he coveted it hit Anne where she hurt the most. Not only was he willing to give up his freedom to get it. He was willing to give up the woman he loved as well.

"Well, Anne?" Jud prompted.

Anne kept her eyes tightly closed, her mind working furiously. Could she do it? Could she commit herself to a man so ruthless he'd cast aside the woman he loved to achieve his ambition? The answer came clear and simple. Yes. Only a few short weeks before she had begged him silently to name his price, had vowed she'd pay anything. Her feelings had not changed, except perhaps to grow stronger. Being his wife and not his love would not be easy to live with. But the eventuality of being separated from him completely was totally unbearable. So, right or wrong, she was still willing to pay the price.

"Anne?"

To Anne's distracted mind Jud's tone seemed to hold a note of anxious hesitation. Jud anxious? With a brief shake of her head, Anne dismissed the possibility. Lifting her lids, she looked steadily into Jud's hooded amber eyes.

"All right, Jud. I'll do whatever you say."

His breath was expelled slowly, indicating how anxious he really had been. Well, of course he was, Anne mused unhappily. He had taken a shot at his own particular star; now he could relax, his shot had hit its target.

"Anne, I—" He hesitated, as if groping for words, then, becoming brisk, all business, he stated, "I want to do it as soon as possible. These people are getting edgy and I'm not going any further on this contract until I have my ring on your finger and your word on your compliance with my wishes. We'll set the wheels in motion tomorrow morning, but meanwhile, I think we'd better make an announcement to the family at the lunch table." He eyed her warily before adding, "Does that meet with your approval?"

Anne sighed in resignation. What did it matter? It was a

business arrangement, wasn't it? To insist on the usual fuss and flutter would not only be farcical, it would be blatant hypocrisy.

"I've already said I'll do whatever you say, Jud." Anne paused, then added softly, "It really doesn't matter when or how, does it?"

In the action of leaning back to pick up the folder on his desk, Jud turned back to her sharply, his eyes glittering with an emotion totally unfathomable to Anne.

Certain she did not want to hear what he was about to say, Anne jumped to her feet and hurried to the door.

"If we have an announcement to make, I think I'd better freshen up and change."

She had just stepped into her room when he caught up with her and, giving her a gentle push, he followed her in and closed the door.

"Anne, we have got to discuss how we're going to handle this."

He strolled across the room and dropped lazily into the chair Troy had vacated such a short time before.

"If your mother and the twins get even a hint at the reason for this marriage, the silent rebellion they've been engaging in will turn into open warfare."

He ran his eyes over her speculatively, then asked dryly, "How good an actress are you?"

"Actress? I don't understand."

Raising his eyes, as if seeking assistance from above, he sighed heavily.

"Sweetheart, I think the remark you made earlier about being a little slow today was a gross understatement. I mean, darling"—the darling was heavily emphasized—"that we are going to have to play to the gallery. Convince them we have suddenly fallen deeply, urgently in love. In other words, we have got to clean up our act. If we continue taking verbal potshots at each other they'll be on to the play in no time. Now, do you understand?"

"Oh, perfectly, darling." She added even more emphasis

to the darling but some of the impact was lost as her voice wobbled. "Curtain up, let the play begin."

His soft laugh attacked her nervous system and, feeling her suddenly weak legs would no longer support her, she sank onto the bed.

"You are one fantastic little girl, you know that, chicken?"

If his laughter had undermined her poise, the silky purr he used on her now threatened to destroy her completely. In one fluid movement he was on his feet and moving across the room to her. One long finger hooked her chin, lifted her head.

"As they said in practically every cowboy movie ever made"—his voice took on the twang of a heavy Western drawl—"you'll do to ride the river with, pardner."

Dipping his head, he placed his mouth against hers and murmured, "A kiss in lieu of a contract, Anne." Then the pressure of his lips increased and his mouth, causing her heart to jump like a demented acrobat, drove out all reason and sanity.

"Yes, indeed," he whispered as he lifted his head after a few long moments. "You'll do very nicely. Now, I'll let you get changed, as Margaret and Melly are back from church and ready for lunch."

He had reached the door before Anne had gathered her wits enough to ask haltingly, "Jud, about this marriage. Will it be . . . I mean will you want—" She faltered, searching for the words.

"A normal sexual relationship?" he supplied softly.

Anne swallowed hard, then nodded. His face gave away nothing of what he felt, his eyes remained steady on hers.

"Yes."

A finally, no-questions-asked yes.

"But, I never—" Anne bit down on her lip. "I mean, I don't know if I can. I—"

"Oh, you can," he countered. "The way you respond to my kisses convinces me of that." He studied the pink stain spreading across her cheeks a moment, then added gently,

"But don't worry, honey. I'm a patient man, and I'll be very careful not to rush or frighten you."

After a quick shower Anne slipped into a light, cotton dress, applied a touch of color to lids, cheeks, and lips, and was finishing her hair when her door opened. Jud stood in the hall freshly showered and shaved, looking far too attractive in dark brown moleskin pants and a soft fawn shirt.

"Are you ready to go down?" he asked quietly. "I think it would be best to confront them together and get it over with."

Nervous, and trying hard not to show it, Anne licked her dry lips.

"Yes, I'm ready."

She left the room and walked beside him down the hall to the top of the stairs, where she paused, throwing him a quick glance.

"Do you want me to tell them or will you?"

"I think I'd better." He shot her a brief, devastating grin. "Your voice is none too steady." He started down the stairs, his hand grasping hers. "Don't give yourself away, Anne," he cautioned. "Or all hell will break loose. Just follow my lead and we'll be home free."

As they entered the dining room, Jud's hand released Anne's and slid protectively around her waist.

The action did not go unnoticed. Anne saw the surprise that filled her mother's eyes, the question that narrowed both Troy's and Todd's. Only Melly seemed unaware of the sudden tension in the room.

"About time you two showed up," Melly scolded lightly. "I'm famished. For some strange reason a long, uninspired sermon always makes me hungry. Now we can eat."

"In a moment." Jud's quiet, serious tone sent his aunt's eyebrows up. Anne felt his hand tighten at her waist, then he said calmly, "Anne and I are going to be married."

He could not have achieved a better effect if he had dropped a snake onto the table. Melly looked stunned, Todd and Troy jumped out of their chairs, and Margaret gave a small disbelieving shriek.

"You are what?"

"Getting married."

Jud's unruffled reply seemed to incite rather than calm them.

"But you can't," Margaret gasped.

"Can't?" One pale eyebrow arched arrogantly. "I assure you we can."

"But, Jud," her mother moaned. "Anne is your stepsister."

"Step being the operative word," he retorted. "It has no bearing at all."

"Now who's playing games, Jud?" Troy's voice was nasty. "And what's the name of this one? Force the twins into line?"

Todd's eyes, their cloudy color with an equal mixture of anger and hurt, fastened on Anne's.

"Or should we substitute the word blackmail for games? I might have expected something like this from him, Anne. But not you. Never you."

Anne paled. Jud's face went rigid and Margaret cried, "Todd!"

During the exchange Melly's head had swiveled from one to the other, her confusion mirrored on her face. Her glance settling on Jud, she sighed.

"I don't understand. What is the problem, Jud? Personally I'm delighted."

Jud's face softened, and he smiled gently at his aunt.

"Thank you, Mel. Don't be alarmed. There is no problem here I can't handle."

"Big man," Troy spat. "You're not forcing me into anything. You'd sell your soul to get your own way down at the mill, wouldn't you? Well, you can go to hell." His furious glance pierced Anne, and she gasped as he added, "And you can go with him."

Anne felt Jud go stiff beside her, felt the sharp pain as his fingers dug spasmodically into her waist. He frightened her. Everything about him frightened her, from his contempt-filled, cold eyes, to the still, coiled menace that emanated from every inch of him. Finally his chillingly soft purr broke the silence that had gripped the room.

"I don't have to force you into anything, Troy. You'll do as you're told." His voice went softer still, causing a shiver to tingle along Anne's arms. "And if you ever speak to your sister like that again, I will take the hide off your back. Strip by slow strip. Now make your apology."

Again the room was smothered in silence and Anne's fingers curled into her damp palms. When she felt Jud move in Troy's direction, she moaned softly.

"Troy, please."

Troy's eyes, weary and fear-filled, shifted to Anne's pale face and with a soft sigh of defeat he murmured, "I'm sorry, Anne."

"Jud?"

Although her voice was steady, Melly's eyes betrayed her unease.

"It's all right, Mel."

The change in him was almost unbelievable. Relaxed and easy, he laughed lazily, then drawled, "As a wedding gift to Anne, I'll let him live—this week."

The tension was broken. Melly's eyes laughed back at him.

"You're a devil, you know that?" she chided teasingly. "How dull my life would be without you." Her eyes lit with a mischief of their own. "Do you think you could stop playing El Macho long enough to give me some lunch?"

Jud threw back his head and laughed, the warm sound melting the ice Anne seemed to be enclosed in. Lunch was served and, although Troy and Todd remained resentfully quiet, Margaret finally gave in and joined the conversation to back up Jud's invitation to Melly to stay over for the ceremony.

"I wouldn't miss your wedding Jud—" Melly's eyes shifted to the twins "—any more than I'd miss Troy and Todd when they decide to take the plunge. Of course I'll have to call home but, as Frank's been doing so well, I'm sure it will be all right. Your Uncle Frank will be disappointed he can't be here as well."

The meal proceeded at a leisurely pace, Margaret, with Melly's prodding, getting into the swing of the sparse arrangements when she suggested, hopefully, that Anne and Jud wait, if only long enough for her to plan a proper, as she put it, wedding, but Jud shook his head uttering a decided "No."

Neck muscles tight with tension, pain beginning to throb at her temples, Anne thought the meal would never end. When finally they left the table, Anne sighed in relief and excused herself.

"I have a slight headache," she murmured when Jud asked quietly if something was wrong. "It must be the excitement."

Wanting to run, forcing herself to walk, she hurried up the stairs and into her room. She was standing at the window, staring at the black, angry-looking clouds, when the sound of her door being opened was muffled by a loud nerve-jarring crack of lightning that rent the sky directly overhead.

Anne gasped, startled by the sudden violence of nature, then gasped again when large, masculine hands came down onto her shoulders.

"Getting cold feet, Anne?"

Jud's voice was low and, coming as it did with the sudden downpour of rain, Anne could not suppress a shudder or the tight note in her voice.

"No."

"Good, because I'm not about to let you back out."

His cool breath ruffled across the top of her head, his soft tone ruffled across her heart. Drawing a deep breath, steeling herself against the craziness of her body's response to his nearness, she replied steadily.

"The thought of backing out hadn't occurred to me."

"No?"

His fingers loosened and he moved closer until, his forearms resting lightly on her shoulders, his body was only a tingling whisper away from hers.

"Then why did you come tearing up here the minute lunch was over?"

"I really do have a headache, and I was upset." She hesitated, then added sadly, "I knew Todd and Troy wouldn't like the idea of us getting married, but I didn't expect—" She broke off, a sigh replacing the rest of the words.

His arms came toward her, crossed at the base of her neck, drawing her closer still to his body. Bending his head until it was lying beside hers, he said softly. "They'll get over it, Annie. You've all spoiled them, but I don't believe they're vindictive. They'll come around."

"I hope so, Jud." A small sob caught in her throat as she added, "It will all be so pointless if they don't."

At her words he went taut, his arms tightening their hold. "Annie!"

At that moment another loud crack of lightning knifed the sky, followed by a window-rattling roll of thunder. Cringing back against him, she closed her eyes with a shudder. His teasing laughter tickled her earlobe.

"Surely you're not afraid of storms, little girl?"

"No, of course not." Her answer was quick and emphatic. "It was just so close, it startled me. And I wish you wouldn't call me little girl."

"Why not?" he murmured against her ear. "You are little and you sure as hell are a girl."

His hands moved caressingly over her shoulders, down her arms, causing a chill to feather her spine, fire to lick her blood.

"Soft too." His lips moved maddeningly down her neck, and she gasped when his tongue slid lightly along the curve of her shoulder. "Taste good, too. No doubt about it. You are definitely a girl."

The earlier unpleasantness, the tension, her headache, all combined with a sudden onslaught of desire that left her trembling and teary. Shaken by the depth of her own hunger for him, she went stiff.

"Jud, you must stop this."

"Why must I stop?"

His hand moved from her arm, fingers bringing devastation as they slid across her collarbone, down the V of her dress.

"I don't want to stop, Anne, I want you and I think you want me too."

His confidence, his obvious experience against her total inexperience, made her wary. And with her caution came the bitter thought, He's getting everything he wants so easily that now he thinks he can have me easily as well. The very idea that he could think of her as easy quenched the fire in her veins. Bringing her hands up to grasp his arms, she pulled them apart, stepped away from him.

"You're mistaken, Jud," she said flatly, then barbed coldly as he moved toward her. "You're using me to get what you want in the firm. I won't let you use me physically as well."

Incredulity, followed by blazing anger, narrowed his eyes. In an oddly strained hoarse tone, he growled, "Use you? That isn't what I would have said, but never mind."

He turned abruptly and walked to the door; then with his hand on the knob he turned back and said coldly, "Don't worry, Anne. I won't bother you with my attentions again. And I hope you freeze in your bed."

The soft click of the door closing behind him sent a shaft of pure misery through Anne. Anyone coming along the hall and hearing his last words may have looked out of the window and been puzzled, for it was June—stormy, warm, and sticky. But Anne knew what he meant and she was very much afraid that his hope would be realized.

The following week was full of uncertainty and unhappiness for Anne. At the breakfast table Monday, Jud stated calmly that Anne was not to go into the office that week. Anne and Jud were alone in the dining room, as Margaret and Melly were not yet up and Troy and Todd had already left the house, presumably choosing to go without breakfast rather than sit at the table with Jud and Anne.

"Not go in?" Anne felt the first strings of uncertainty. "But why?"

"Anne," Jud sighed patiently, "I told you I want to do this as fast as possible and one assumes that every woman has things to do the week before her wedding."

"But this isn't a normal wedding," Anne insisted rashly. "And I'm not the usual blushing bride."

Jud's eyes and tone went hard. "I know that. But no one else does, do they? You agreed yesterday to play this to the hilt. Have you changed your mind since then?"

Her uncertainty deepened at the sharp edge to his voice and with surprise she realized he was very, very angry. But why? Did his anger stem from frustration at being rejected the night before? Not wanting to even think about that, Anne answered quickly.

"No, I haven't, but I don't see what that has to do with—"

Her words faltered when he pushed his chair back angrily and stood up. Looking down at her coldly, he seemed to tower over her and unconsciously Anne shrank back against her chair. His eyes and face mirrored his scorn and he grated, "Relax, I'm not going to touch you, and I have no time to stay here arguing with you, either. I have a lot to do this week if I'm going to be out of the office next week."

"Out of the office," she repeated in astonishment. But why?"

Apparently his patience had reached the end of its tether.

"If you can refrain from interrupting," he snapped, "I will explain why."

Speechless for the moment, Anne nodded mutely.

"I would like to have the ceremony Sunday." He paused, then added sarcastically, "If that meets with your approval?"

Again the mute nod.

"Very well. I would also like to leave for New York immediately after the ceremony, as I have several appointments there next week I can't miss. Are you with mc so far?"

Uncertainty was being nudged aside by his condescending tone, and Anne hissed, "Yes."

"Good," he hissed back. "I want you to meet me for lunch at one at the Elegant Spoon. While we eat I'll outline the arrangements I've made to that point. All right?"

Anne nodded angrily.

"Okay. Now, if you'll excuse me," he jibed nastily, "I have work to do."

He strode from the room and Anne sat perfectly still for several minutes, her hands clenched into tight fists. Who in the hell did he think he was? she fumed. The memory of his cool voice taunted, *"The Boss."*

Her anger still a fierce glow inside, Anne met Jud at the restaurant. The anger was soon coupled with amazement as, forcing food down her throat, she heard him tick off the arrangements he'd made during the morning. Everything was taken care of, he told her smoothly, ignoring the warning flash in her eyes, from their stop directly after lunch at the license bureau, on through the name of the district justice who would perform the ceremony and the time of their flight to New York afterward.

Anne's mind latched onto the last of his plans.

"I'm to go with you to New York?"

Jud opened his mouth, then closed it again with a snap, glancing around the well-filled room as if suddenly aware of where he was. White lines of anger tinting his lips, he drew a long, deliberate breath through nostrils flaring in fury.

"Of course you're to go with me, you fool. By then you will be my wife."

Reaching across the table he grasped her hand painfully and, although his voice was low, none of its fierceness was lost.

"My God, woman, how would it look if I left you alone on our wedding night? Will you start thinking, please?"

His attitude toward her the rest of that afternoon was one of cool, withdrawn politeness. In growing wonder Anne observed the deference Jud was accorded wherever they went and the speed with which his smallest request was carried out. She had had no idea he had so many friends, and in such high places. It became increasingly obvious to her that as far as Jud was concerned, when he set a ball in motion, that object damned well better roll, and smoothly. For herself Anne was beginning to feel as if it were rolling over her, somewhat in the manner of an avalanche.

By the time Anne slid into bed that night, the bemusement and wonder that had kept her quiet and docile all afternoon began to burn off, leaving in its wake a residue of cold resentment.

Other than the actual day of their marriage, she had not been consulted at all about the other arrangements, she thought furiously. And if she was not to go to the office, exactly what was she to do with the rest of the week? Twiddle her thumbs like a good little girl? *Bump him,* she decided scathingly. She damned well would go to the office, and just let him try and send her home again. The decision made, Anne rolled over and went to sleep.

Her rest deep and undisturbed for once by nightmares, Anne woke refreshed and prepared to face any obstacle the day might bring, including Judson Cammeron.

In a mood of defiance she abstained from joining Jud at the breakfast table, waited at her bedroom window until she saw him back the Navigator out of the garage, then, avoiding her mother and Melly, slipped out of the house and drove to the mill—in her own car.

She had no sooner closed her bottom desk drawer when Jud's voice barked from the connecting room, "Anne, come in here."

Swallowing back the sudden brackish taste of fear that rose in her throat, Anne squared her shoulders, set her chin at an obstinate angle, and walked slowly into his office.

Leaning back lazily in his swivel chair, his hands toying with a pen, he looked deceptively relaxed and pleasant.

"I thought we'd agreed you would not come in this week." His voice matched his demeanor in deception.

"I don't remember agreeing to anything of the kind," she replied with forced mildness. "You said you have a lot to do this week; well, so have I. And it's not going to get done if I sit at home cooling my heels all week."

He moved forward with a snap and, casting aside all pretense, he let his annoyance show by flinging his pen onto the desk.

"Have you no sense of self-preservation at all? Why the

hell do you even want to be here this week? Do you have masochistic tendencies?"

Taken aback by the force and harshness of his attack, Anne stepped back in alarm.

"I—I don't understand?"

"Don't you, really?" he sneered. "Tell me you haven't heard the rumors."

Jud stared at Anne intently a few seconds; then, apparently deciding she was truly ignorant as to what he was talking about, he walked around his desk to her. His face inches from hers, he raised his brows exaggeratedly.

"Where have you been the last few weeks, permanently out to lunch? How did you manage to miss the stupid female, and male, twitters emanating from the outer offices?"

His exasperation with her was a tangibly felt presence reaching out to figuratively shake her. Feeling stifled by that presence, she snapped, "Do you think you could leave off with the insults and tell me what these rumors were?"

"Of a very basic nature," he bit back. "Having to do with the convenience of us living in the same house, if you get my drift?"

Anne's eyes flew wide with shock.

"But that's ridiculous!"

"How well I know it," he drawled sarcastically. "But not unexpected from a certain type of malicious mind."

Stunned beyond speech, Anne just stared at him biting her lip savagely. He watched her, hard-faced, for some time; then, with a sigh that sounded like one of defeat, he said softly, "Anne, you know as well as I do that our sudden decision to marry will run like wildfire through this place. And that the general consensus will be that you are pregnant. By asking you to stay away this week I was simply trying to spare you the embarrassment of listening to their stupid gossip. Now, will you go home?"

"No."

Unable to withstand the renewed flare of anger in his eyes, Anne lowered her own, studying the carpet as if it were the most fascinating thing she'd ever seen.

"Dammit, Anne, why must you be so stubborn?"

Grasping her arms, he gave her a little shake, jerking her head up in the process. Shrugging herself free of his hands, she moved away from him.

"Probably because I grew up surrounded by Cammerons."

He rewarded her with a quick grin and made bold by his softened expression, she went on, "I'm not all that fragile, Jud. If I overhear the gossip, I'll dismiss it, as I've done with all the gossip I've heard here."

With a shrug that said "Do as you please," he gave in with a brusque, "Okay, if you're determined to stay, let's get to work."

Being in the office helped her get through the week, but even so, as Sunday loomed ever closer, her stomach proceeded to tie itself into tiny little knots.

Chapter Ten

It was over. She was his wife!

The enormity of the step she'd taken didn't hit Anne until she was strapped into her seat and the plane was making its takeoff run. What in the world was she doing here? she asked herself a little wildly. Had she gone totally and completely crazy? For one very small moment panic clutched at her throat and she had to fight the urge to flip open her seat belt and run. Run where? The plane was airborne and in less than an hour they'd be landing in Newark.

Reason swiftly reasserted itself, but even so, Anne sat, body pressed against the cushioned padding, hands gripping the arms of her seat.

"Does flying frighten you?"

Caught up in her own thoughts, the sound of Jud's voice strongly tinged with concern startled Anne so much that she jumped.

"For heaven's sake, Anne, relax." Jud's hand covered hers, pried her fingers loose, and laced his long ones through hers before adding, "Flying's safer than driving."

"I know that."

Anne moistened dry lips, casting about in her mind for a plausible excuse for her tension, when she caught a flash of gold out of the corner of her eyes. Although the morning had dawned bright and sunny, by lunchtime the brightness had turned a brassy color and the air had grown oppressive; and by the time they had left for the airport black clouds were building in the west, long fingers of lightning poking through them. Anne grasped at the weather for an excuse.

"Generally I love flying," she said slowly, darting a quick glance at the small window. "But not when there's a storm brewing. I don't like taking off and landing when there's lightning about."

Jud laughed softly, a gentle, reassuring laugh that rippled along Anne's tension-tight nerve ends.

"We'll be down before you know it," he soothed; then, his fingers tightening, he leaned closer to her and murmured, "Hang on to me, honey, and everything will be all right."

In confusion Anne lowered her eyes. Had there been a double meaning to his words? That amber gaze had been so intent, as if trying to tell her something. But what? You're being fanciful, she chided herself scathingly, her eyes fastened on her small hand, held so firmly and securely in his much larger one. *He is merely trying to keep me calm,* she reasoned dismally, *insuring himself against the embarrassment of a hysterical woman.*

The plane landed smoothly and, in an amazingly short time, their bags had been collected and Anne found herself being ushered into the back of the hired limo that was waiting for them. Jud settled himself on the seat beside her, recaptured her hand, then asked softly, "Better now?"

Idly his fingers played with the thin gold band on her finger, sending tiny shivers up her arm. In an effort to cover the small sound her catching breath made, Anne laughed shakily and nodded an answer.

"Good," Jud murmured lazily, then cocked an eyebrow at her. "Would you like to stop for dinner on the way or do you want to go straight home?"

Home? The word doubled her shivers, pushed them up and over her shoulders, down into her stomach.

"I—I think we'd better go straight h—to the apartment," she finally got past the lump in her throat, "if we don't want to get caught in the deluge," she added, turning to look out the window at the steadily lowering black clouds.

"You may be right," he agreed in an unconcerned tone.

"Although, at the rate of speed this traffic's moving, we may be caught in it anyway."

They just made it. For no more than five minutes after reaching the apartment the greenish-black sky seemed to be torn apart by the fury of the storm.

Jud's apartment was in a tony neighborhood, large, and obviously expensive. Consisting of two bedrooms, one bath, a small, fully equipped kitchen, and a large living room, it had the added advantage of several large windows which afforded at least a glimpse of Central Park.

Nervous to the point of feeling sick, Anne moved silently beside Jud as he gave her the grand tour ending in the kitchen and nearly jumped when his soft voice broke the quiet.

"Are you hungry? The fridge has been stocked and I'm sure that between the two of us we could rustle up something edible."

"I—I'm not too hungry," she hedged, the very thought of food causing her stomach to jump.

He was standing indolently, one hip propped against the countertop, and the sardonic expression he wore prompted her to add quickly, "I could drink some coffee, though." Then hesitantly, "Are you hungry?"

"Actually I'm famished," he drawled. "But I can make do with a sandwich. I have before."

A small twinge of guilt put a touch of color to her pale cheeks. He was hungry and she had turned down his offer to stop. The least she could do was make him something hot to eat, she told herself contritely. Besides which, it was a way of filling in some of the hours that stretched between now and bedtime.

"A sandwich isn't enough, I'll cook something." Jud's look of mild surprise prompted her to add, "Although I'm no Cordon Bleu chef, I can get a meal together."

"I didn't suggest you couldn't," he retorted softly. His face thoughtful, he studied her a moment. "There's no hurry. I'll get some steaks out of the freezer to thaw. You look washed out. Why don't you go have a shower and rest for an hour or so?"

"Rest?" Anne was almost afraid to ask. "Where?"

His soft sigh told her of his impatience as clearly as hard words would have.

"I put your suitcase in the spare bedroom, Anne." Long fingers raked that fantastic gold hair. "Go. Get some rest. It's been a long day." His hand slid to the back of his neck, massaging slowly as he flexed suddenly bunched-up shoulder muscles. "Hell, it's been one long week. Go on," he urged. "You have a shower and a nap. I'll have a shower and a drink. On second thought, maybe I'll have several drinks."

"On an empty stomach, Jud?"

He had turned to stare out the small window above the sink, but on her hesitant question he whirled around, his face hard, his eyes mocking.

"Good God! Did I acquire a wife or a mother this afternoon?"

Stepping back at his harsh tone, Anne could actually feel her face pale. Wide eyed, hurt, she stammered, "I—I'm—sorry. I—"

"Yes, Anne," he interrupted wearily. "So am I. Don't concern yourself, I'll have some pretzels with the booze." Giving his shoulders another sharp jerk, he ordered, "Get out of here, and don't come back for at least"—he glanced at his watch—"an hour and a half."

"Jud."

"Beat it. You may have the bathroom for exactly twenty minutes. If you're not out of the shower by then I'll join you in it."

Anne spun around and fled, his derisive laughter chasing her through the living room.

Fourteen minutes later Anne stepped out of the bathroom feeling cool and refreshed, if still somewhat shaky. In the few steps required to reach her room she had neither sight nor sound of Jud. With a sigh of relief she slipped inside the room, closing the door quietly.

The room, though not as large as Jud's, was of adequate

size, furnished with an attractive pine suite. The walls were covered by a rough-textured, burlap-weave paper, the woodwork painted a satiny white. Draperies, bedspread, and carpet were all in a matching pale aqua that lent a restful color to the decor. This room, Anne decided, was at once comfortable and impersonal. A fact that suited her mood.

Dropping onto the bed, Anne turned her head to the window, studying the nubby weave of the draperies as she relived the earlier part of the day with a vague feeling of unreality.

She had wakened that morning encased in a deadly calm which, by mid-afternoon, had deepened into a cold numbness. Both her mother and Melly had flittered around the house all day, seemingly very busy. For the life of her, Anne could not imagine what kept them so occupied. Except for a few minutes at lunchtime, Anne did not see much of Jud and she didn't catch hide nor hair of the twins until they tore into the house an hour before it was time to leave.

Someone had gotten to them. Either her mother or Melly or both. Anne suspected that Troy and Todd had been subjected to lectures from both their mother and their aunt. In any case, their attitude, at least toward Anne, had softened. They accorded Jud a very thin civility, which, if his own attitude was anything to go by, did not bother him at all. Most surprising was that they had agreed to stand up as witnesses for Jud. Melly, flushed and delighted at being asked, would do the honors for Anne.

Even dressing for her own wedding had very little effect on Anne. She went through the motions slowly and carefully, standing back automatically to observe the finished product. The dress she wore, a simple summer shift in oyster white raw silk, was not new. Anne had bought the dress the previous summer, along with her shoes and bag in bronze patent leather. As she ran a practiced eye over her small form, Anne decided the overall impression was definitely blah. But then that was exactly how she felt, so, with a light shrug of her shoulders, she silently declared herself ready.

The actual ceremony could not have taken more than eight minutes but, even though she was still in a numb, unfeeling cocoon, two things filtered through and registered with Anne. First, the words of the service were the traditional ones, including love, honor, and obey. Second, the district justice, a slim attractive woman in her early forties, read them with such solemnity and force, Anne was left in little doubt as to how serious the woman considered the act of marriage.

Her calm had remained unshaken during the cheek-kissing and fervent wishes of happiness she received from her mother and Melly as they paused a few moments beside the car outside the district justice's office. Not even the last-minute surrender of Troy and Todd, given in the form of a fierce hug from each in turn and the softly muttered "I pray you'll be happy, Anne" from Troy, had really touched her. It was not until she was actually on the plane that the full realization of it all struck her like a physical blow.

Now, some three hours later, she lay in an unfamiliar bed in the guest room of Jud's apartment and the shock had worn off, leaving in its stead the sick cry—what have I done?

Exactly at the time stipulated, Anne, in brown chinos and white gauze shirt, went into the kitchen. One step inside the archway that separated the kitchen from the living room she stopped, a bubble of disbelieving laughter catching at her throat, a forlorn pain catching at her heart.

Jud stood back to her at the countertop, chopping vegetables for a salad, his just-shampooed hair glinting like a newly minted gold coin, and he was dressed, amazingly, in brown brushed denim jeans and white gauze shirt. On hearing her enter, he turned, and Anne could see a tiny piece of glittering gold chain at the unbuttoned neck of his shirt.

"The steaks have thawed enough to remove the wrapping and I've opened a bottle—" Having turned fully around, he stopped, eyes narrowing as they went slowly over her. Then, with what looked like a bitter smile tugging at the corners of his mouth and what sounded like a muttered "unreal," he turned back to his task, continuing, "I've opened a bottle of Cabernet to let it breathe awhile. Did you rest at all?"

"Yes," Anne lied calmly. "What can I do to help?"

"Put the steaks under the broiler, set the table, and start a pot of coffee, in that order," he returned with equal calm.

As she set the glass-topped, circular table, Anne felt positive she would not be able to eat. But one piece of the tender Delmonico and several sips of Cabernet seemed to revive her appetite and she not only finished all her steak and salad, she managed a small dish of fresh strawberries as well.

Conversation during the meal and the cleaning up was practically nil and Anne preceded Jud into the living room with trepidation when it was finally over.

Whatever would they talk about? Anne asked herself, warily eyeing the dark brown leather furniture. Choosing the smallest of the two single chairs in the room, she slipped off her sandals and curled herself on it, sighing in relief as Jud strolled to the entertainment unit and began looking through the CD collection.

The music Jud chose did not have the calming effect Anne had hoped for. In fact the husky quality of Garth Brooks's voice combined with lyrics that too often touched a raw nerve increased her tension.

The second hand had chased itself some ninety times around the face of the clock, and Anne was beginning to fidget, when the arm lifted off the last record on the stereo. The sudden silence in the room was short-lived, for Jud's soft but harsh voice cracked it.

"For God's sake, Anne, go to bed."

Somewhat fearfully Anne lifted surprised eyes to him. He was sitting in the exact center of the huge sofa, legs stretched out, head back, and Anne could not remember ever seeing him look quite so tired. His voice matched his expression in weariness.

"You sit there looking as if you'll jump out of your skin at the slightest move from me." He paused, his mouth twisting in mockery. "I assure you you'll be perfectly safe if you go to bed. Pouncing on unwilling women has never been my thing."

The bitterness and disgust that overlay his tone on his last words brought her to her feet in self-defense.

"Jud, I didn't mean to—"

"Get out of here, Anne," he sighed in exasperation. "Just shut up and go to bed."

He closed his eyes and Anne had the feeling that not only had he closed out the sight of her, but her entire existence as well. Cheeks pink, she retreated without another word.

A light tapping roused Anne and, coming awake quickly, she glanced around the room in confusion before realizing where she was. The last thing she remembered, after sliding under the comforter, was that she probably wouldn't sleep and now the room was bright with sunlight.

The tap sounded again; then the door was pushed open and Jud took one step into the room, looking brisk and all business in a khaki-colored summer-weight suit, crisp white shirt, and chocolate silk tie. His tone matched his appearance in briskness.

"Good morning. Sorry to wake you, but I'm ready to leave for the office and as I hate leaving notes, I thought I'd better warn you about Mrs. Doyle before she arrived and startled you. Mrs. Doyle comes in twice a week to clean the place and she's a regular whirlwind. If you don't stay out of her way she's liable to dust you along with the furniture so I'd advise you to vacate the premises. Do a little shopping. I've left you some money, it's on the kitchen count—"

"I don't need your mon—" Anne interrupted, only to be cut off herself.

"I don't have time to argue, Anne," he snapped, glancing pointedly at his watch. "I have an appointment in less than an hour. There's fresh coffee and muffins warming in the oven if you're hungry. I don't know what time I'll get home, probably not before six thirty, so don't bother about dinner. We'll go out somewhere. Take the money."

He was gone and Anne sat staring at the empty doorway, angry words of refusal dying on her lips. Gritting her teeth, she sat fuming for several minutes; then a thought struck her, propelling her out of the bed with a muttered oath. This

Mrs. Doyle would be coming to clean the rooms, including the bedrooms. Damned if she'd allow the woman to see the true status of their marriage.

Causing something of a small whirlwind of her own, Anne tidied and dusted her bedroom then moved on to Jud's performing the same tasks there, while studiously not looking too closely at his personal things. Showered and dressed to go out, Anne was sitting at the table with her first cup of coffee when Mrs. Doyle arrived.

"You must be Mrs. Cammeron," the small, round woman began in a bland manner.

"Yes, but how—" Anne started, only to be cut off with an airy wave of a small, pudgy hand.

"Mr. Cammeron called me at home. Asked me not to disturb you if you'd gone back to sleep." Then she tacked on, "Oh, yes, congratulations. I hope you'll be very happy."

"Thank you," Anne murmured, amusement tugging at her lips. "Would you like a cup of coffee?"

"No, thank you. I have two other places to get to today, so I'd better get started."

She turned to the closet for the cleaning utensils and Anne, going to the sink to rinse her cup, said quickly, "Well, I've saved you some time, I did the bedroom, so all you have are the kitchen, living room, and bath." At the look of alarm that crossed the other woman's face, she added, "There will be no difference in your salary. I—I guess I just wanted to play at housewife a little." Although Anne considered her last words an inspiration, she nonetheless had to force them through her teeth. And with the strange look Mrs. Doyle gave her, she fled with a short, "I'm going shopping. Nice meeting you."

Feeling like a complete idiot, she left the apartment almost at a run, not slowing down until she was several blocks away.

For an hour Anne strolled listlessly through the shops, barely seeing the merchandise displayed, feeling none of the enthusiasm her previous shopping trips to New York had generated. Finally giving up, she walked for some time before coming to a stop before a movie theater. On the spur of the moment Anne bought a ticket and slipped inside to lose herself for several hours in the dimmed theater and the twisting, involved plot of a foreign film.

Anne was curled into one corner of the sofa leafing through a magazine when Jud came in just before seven. He looked tired and short-tempered, his eyebrows inching up as he ran his flat amber gaze over her jeans and pullover, making her so nervous she stumbled over her explanation.

"The s-salad's tossed and—and there's a lasagna in the oven."

"That wasn't necessary, we could have eaten out."

He crossed the living room, shrugging out of his jacket as he spoke, but although his tone was indifferent, Anne had the distinct impression he was relieved at not having to go out again.

It was not until they were back in the living room, dinner finished, this time listening to the upbeat sound of Tito Puente, that Jud threw out casually, "We'll go out tomorrow night, Anne. Maybe after dinner we'll take in that Swedish film everyone's talking about. They say it's very good."

"It is."

Anne sat biting her lips as he slowly straightened, the unasked question plain on his face.

"I—I didn't feel like shopping today," Anne spoke hurriedly. "So I went to a movie. I'm sorry, Jud."

He stared at her a long time, his expression strange, almost hurt, and Anne had to force herself to sit still and not squirm. Finally, when Anne thought she'd scream if he didn't say something, he said quietly, "Doesn't matter."

They stayed in New York until Friday, and Jud did not suggest going out again, either to the theater or dinner. In fact he didn't come home for dinner, saying the same thing to her each morning before he left. "Don't wait for me for dinner. I'll grab something somewhere close to the office. I have no idea what time I'll be home. Enjoy your day."

Enjoy your day. Anne raged silently. How does one go about enjoying anything when they're torn apart with uncertainty and—yes—jealousy. Was he really working? Surely not until after ten every night. If he's not working, where is he? Elementary, dummy—Lorna's place.

In an attempt to keep these, and other even more self-defeating thoughts at bay, Anne filled the hours of the day with sight-seeing and shopping, mostly on foot. At night she roamed the apartment, tired by unable to sleep or even sit for longer than a few minutes at a time. She made several surprising discoveries, however. Apparently she and Jud shared more than their interest in his father's company. She found most of her favorite authors in his large collection of both hardcover and paperback books. She found they had like taste in popular as well as classical music as, by Thursday night, she had listened to almost every one of his CDs. And she loved the apartment. He had obviously decorated it himself, for everything about it seemed to whisper his name. Given free rein, Anne knew she'd have made very few, if any, changes. With so many things in common, why couldn't they be together for longer than thirty minutes without fighting? No answer presented itself to her silent question.

Anne boarded the plane for home Friday afternoon with mixed emotions. Relief at giving up her solitary existence in the apartment vied with unease at how Jud planned to carry off their mock marriage surrounded by family. She needn't have worried. As usual Jud had overlooked nothing.

"I've had a few changes made at the house while we've been away. I hope they meet with your approval."

Anne felt a flash of irritation at his bland, indifferent tone. As the changes were already made, did it make any difference if she didn't approve? In an effort to keep her voice calm, she pushed her question through stiff lips.

"Changes? What changes?"

He shot her a sharp glance, studying her tightly drawn features slowly before answering.

"Nothing earth-shattering, so take that trapped look off your face."

"What changes?" Anne hissed.

"I've had your things moved to the guest room on the other side of my bathroom."

Jud's room and the one her mother and his father had shared were the only bedrooms with private baths. Anne and her brothers had used the central bathroom that was entered from the hall. Unable to see the reason for the move, Anne said sharply, "Why?"

"Why do you think?" he snapped. Then he sighed and added softly, "I've also had a doorway cut into the wall between the guest room and the bathroom. Are you beginning to get the picture?"

"Perfectly. Will there be a lock on that door?"

His lips twisted scornfully. "You don't pull your punches, do you, Anne?"

For a moment his eyes glittered with anger; then with a shrug of indifference, he turned away from her, his tone bored.

"Yes, Anne, there will be a lock."

Chapter Eleven

The arrangement worked better than Anne would have suspected, even though she had bad moments, like entering the bathroom when the mirror was still cloudy from his shower steam and the air redolent with his cologne. At those times she was struck by a wave of longing so intense it took every ounce of willpower she possessed to keep from stepping through the door into his room.

Spring slipped into summer and Jud's plans for the company slipped into high gear. The much opposed contract was signed and the entire place was a beehive of activity and confusion. Jud moved through it all like the only sane man in a madhouse. He made a point of keeping Anne apprised of every move before it was made and for that she was grateful, for otherwise she'd have been as certain as practically everyone else that they would fail.

By mid-September Anne could see positive results emerging from what had looked like hopeless chaos. And as Jud's prediction that they could do it was proven correct, the attitude of the employees slowly changed from pessimistic to positive and supportive.

Anne had never worked so hard in her life. The amount of work Jud relegated to her as his assistant was enormous. No longer could she allow herself the luxury of going out for lunch, she simply could not spare the time. Instead she swallowed massive amounts of coffee and much smaller amounts of sandwiches at her desk, and not only at lunchtime but quite often at dinnertime as well.

She lost weight and, through the sunniest, hottest summer she could remember, acquired a decidedly unbecoming pallor. Her mother was vocal with concern, and when it became evident that Anne was not listening, she switched her complaints to Jud. Within days Anne's work load was cut considerably and she could feel Jud's brooding glance at regular intervals. His close observance of her had the opposite effect of what her mother had intended. Anne became even more pale and drawn and added to it was the tension that comes with being watched.

The fact that by summer's end Troy and Todd were following Jud like a pair of teenage-idol worshipers didn't do much for Anne's morale either. Convinced that the twins would have capitulated just as quickly if she hadn't married Jud, Anne felt the whole thing had been an exercise in futility. Jud had given up his freedom and Lorna, and Anne could feel herself turning into a tired, frustrated shadow. And all for what? The question tormented her incessantly.

By mid-October the major part of the upheaval was over and it was obvious that Jud had made a brilliant move for the company. The employment list was up, production was up, and most important of all, everyone's morale was up.

At the end of their first almost normal week, Jud sauntered into Anne's office, stood behind her a few nerve-wracking seconds while he ran his eyes over the order she was working on, then calmly plucked it out of her hand and dropped it onto the desk.

"John will take care of that," he said flatly. "Get your handbag and jacket, we're leaving."

"Leaving? But why? It's only three thirty and—"

"And we have a plane to catch at six forty-five," he interrupted smoothly. "So don't argue, just move."

"I'm not moving anywhere until you tell me what this is all about," Anne retorted. "A plane to where? And why?"

"We're tired, both of us." His eyes ran over her critically. "Frankly you look like hell. We're going away for a few days, soak up some sun and rest. Mel has a house on a tiny island in the Lesser Antilles and she has offered us the use of it. I graciously accepted for the both of us."

Smarting over his remark about her looks, Anne shook her head.

"I don't want to go away with you."

His eyes narrowed and his tone went low with a silky warning.

"Want to or not you're going if I have to drag you by the hair. And if you want to pack some things, you'd better snap to it. As I said, our plane leaves in a little over three hours."

Anne bristled but pulled her desk drawer open and removed her purse. She knew better than to argue with that tone of voice.

Anne woke the following morning to the soothing sound of the ocean, the scent of lush tropical growth, and the raucous noise of brightly plumaged birds she couldn't begin to name.

The trip had been accomplished smoothly and without incident but, as it was dark when they arrived, Anne had seen very little of Melly's delightful house. She couldn't wait to explore and with an eagerness she hadn't felt in months, Anne jumped out of bed. After a quick wash she donned jeans and t-shirt, then followed the mouthwatering aroma of frying bacon to the kitchen.

Whistling softly, Jud stood at the stove, alternately sipping from a cup of coffee and poking at the bacon with a long-handled fork. As she entered the room, he turned and gave her a smile that robbed her of breath.

"Good morning, wife. Your timing is perfect. If you'll set the table we can eat."

Stunned, Anne couldn't move. His easy bantering tone after weeks of strained politeness had thrown her. His taunting voice brought her to her senses.

"Wake up, lady, and get the table ready. Unless, of course, you like your bacon burned."

His tone set the mood for the day. Together, at times hand

in hand, they explored the house and grounds. Anne loved every inch of it and was only too happy to follow wherever he led her.

The house was solidly constructed to withstand the hurricanes that ripped through these islands in the fall, with a wide deck that ran completely around the single-story building. But as beautiful as the house and grounds were, the best thing about it as far as Anne was concerned was that one had only to walk down a short, gentle incline to the dazzling white sands of the beach, and thus into the unbelievably blue water.

After a very late lunch, both Anne and Jud were content to stretch out on lounge chairs on the deck and be lulled to sleep by the whisper of waves caressing the shore.

Anne woke late in the afternoon and lay quietly, allowing her eyes to roam over the sleeping form on the lounger next to hers. The last weeks had taken their toll on Jud as well as her. He looked honed down to a fine edge, not an excess ounce on his large frame, and there were new grooves cut into his face at his mouth. Fighting off the urge to reach out and smooth away those grooves, Anne slipped silently off her chair and into the house.

Fifteen minutes later, unable to resist the sun-sparkled water, Anne put on her bikini, scooped up a large bath sheet, and left the house. She dropped the huge towel on the sand and walked slowly into the water, savoring the feel as it lapped at her legs.

Some minutes later, floating on her back completely lost in her newfound, buoyant world, Anne gave a short, terrified scream when something caught and tugged at her leg. The word shark filled her mind and in blind panic she kicked her legs wildly. Her leg was released and in the next second a hard, sinewy arm slid around her waist and Jud growled in her ear.

"For God's sake, woman, relax. It's only me."

"Oh, Jud," she sputtered, "you frightened me. I thought you were a—"

The breath was knocked out of her as he pulled her against

his chest and then, with a muffled curse, his mouth covered hers savagely.

With a feeling of unreality, Anne felt herself being forced down under the water. *This can't be happening,* she thought frantically. It was her nightmare all over again only now she was awake and terrified. Struggling desperately, she tore her mouth from his, heard him whisper, "Damn you, Anne," and filled her lungs with great gulps of air. Then his mouth caught hers again and she was going under—deeper, deeper.

She felt his fingers at the clasp of her bikini top and then the wisp of material was gone, lost forever in the restless waters. His hands moved with a wet silkiness over her body, molding her against the hard length of him and with a low moan Anne stopped fighting.

As it had always done in her dreams, Jud's mouth drove out all fear, ignited a fire in her veins that spread rapidly through her entire body, filling her with a hungry need. In total surrender, she slipped her arms around his neck, arched her body to his and became flamingly aware that he had not bothered to put on swim trunks. She felt his hands tug at the material at her hips and then the brief panties were floating off to join their other half.

Mouths clinging, bodies entwined, they were caught up in a wave as it broke and were flung tumbling toward the beach. The force of the wave separated them and scrambling to her feet, gasping in the sweet taste of air, Anne ran out of the water and across the sand to drop choking and exhausted onto the towel.

Jud followed her slowly and watching him walk toward her, Anne's heart thumped wildly in her chest and throat. In the last rays of sunlight Jud's tall, lithe frame seemed to be cast in glowing bronze, the gold chain around his neck, with its oddly familiar egg-shaped medallion, glinting at her wickedly.

When he reached her, he stood unmoving and silent until she was forced to look up at him.

"Back there, in the water"—his voice was a ragged whisper—"you wanted me as badly as I want you. Don't turn away from me now, Anne. I need you now. I need you to be my wife."

Anne stared at him wordlessly for long seconds, then slowly raised her arms. With a low groan, he dropped to his knees beside her, pulled her into his arms and crushed her mouth with his. Within seconds she was back in that fiery world his lips and hands set ablaze so effortlessly.

Gently he unlocked the door that guards all maidens, and when the pain came she heard him grunt as she unknowingly sank her teeth into his shoulder. Pleasure soon consumed all memory of pain and he grunted in an altogether different tone when she full well knowingly nipped at the other shoulder.

Later, drained of everything but the wonder of being a woman, Anne lay in Jud's arms, purring for all the world like the cat that had finally caught the canary.

When he felt her shiver from the touch of the evening air, Jud rose, scooped her up in his arms and carried her to the house. Without pausing, he went into the bathroom, adjusted the shower spray with some difficulty, and stepped into the shower with her still held firmly in his arms, all the while ignoring her squeals of protest. When the last grains of sand were sluiced away he dried, first her, then himself, then carried her to his bed, where he proceeded to teach her how to pleasure, as well as be pleasured.

Anne woke in a state of euphoria, in love with life, in love with the world and more deeply in love than ever before with the man who filled her being to the exclusion of everyone and everything else. She was alone and, wanting to rectify that, she slipped on a robe and went hunting for Jud.

She heard his voice before she reached the doorway to his uncle's small study and not wanting to disturb him she paused. A moment later she was wishing fervently she hadn't. He was speaking to John Franks and his words were like a blade, plunged into her chest.

"Yes, I know it's close on the heels of the other deal, but we can handle it. What? Oh, no problem there. She's relaxed and calm." He laughed softly. "She looks like a new woman."

Anne backed away from the doorway, fighting the urge to run. *Where could she run to?* she wept silently. There was nowhere in the world far enough.

When he found her on the deck ten minutes later, she was every inch the calm, new woman he had laughingly said she was.

"Good morning, chicken," he began as he started toward her, but the words died on his lips and his eyes narrowed as he took in her withdrawn expression.

"What's the matter, Anne?" His tone was now low, urgent. "Is it about last night? I'm sorry if I was rough at first, but—"

"There is nothing to be sorry for, Jud," she answered coldly. "I've put it from my mind, as if it never happened."

"Never happened?" he repeated in a hushed tone, then at a near shout, "Never happened? What the hell do you mean?"

"Just that, Jud." Suddenly afraid of the fury in his eyes, she turned away from him, walked several feet along the deck before turning back to him, indicating the surroundings with a wave of her hand. "I'm as human as the next, Jud. This near perfect setting," she shrugged, "I gave in to an urge." Her voice chilled scathingly. "The urge of nature. Man, woman. Male, female. Animals. Mating."

He went white and stepped back as if she'd struck him.

"Animals?" It was a hoarse groan through pale, stiff lips.

For an instant he seemed to sag with defeat, then he straightened and his eyes glittered dangerously. The old, hatefully sardonic smile twisted his mouth and he said smoothly, "Can I take it from that you are ready to go home?"

"Yes, if you don't mind."

His shrug was elegantly careless, as was his tone.

"Whatever."

They returned home that night, both of them locked inside their own frozen world. The weeks that followed were the worst Anne had ever lived through. The pain and heartbreak Anne had felt when Jud went away all those years ago were nothing compared with the anguish she lived with now. And added to that anguish was a growing confusion and uncertainty, for the deal she had overheard Jud discussing with John Franks that fateful morning had not materialized.

Jud was unfailingly polite in an icy, contemptuous way and he was watching her again. She could feel his eyes on her at odd hours of the day and night, sending cold shivers down her back, raising goose bumps on her flesh. Anne wondered desperately how long she'd be able to withstand his silent assault on her nervous system.

A week after their return he strolled diffidently into her office and tossed a square white envelope onto her desk. Anne eyed it warily, saw it was addressed to Mr. And Mrs. Judson Cammeron and that it had not been opened. She didn't touch it and after a long silence he drawled sarcastically, "Your legal eagle is getting married. He requests the honor of our presence at the ceremony."

Who cares? a voice cried inside Anne, but aloud she could barely murmur, "I don't want to go."

"Too bad, because you're going to go." His eyes raked her ruthlessly. "I have already told Lorna we'd be there."

"Jud, I will not be—"

Anne sighed; she may as well have saved her breath. Jud had turned and walked back into his own office, closing the door with a final-sounding snap.

As the weeks before Andrew's late November wedding date shortened, Jud spent longer and longer periods of each week in his New York office. Anne swung widely between being sure he was being unfaithful and equally sure he was not.

Ten days before the wedding an employee problem cropped up while Jud was in New York. As the employee involved was one of executive staff and the problem was of a delicate nature, Anne, in her present mental state, felt she could not cope with it. At the dinner table that evening, Anne outlined the situation for Troy and Todd and asked them if they'd take care of it for her. Before she'd even finished speaking, they were shaking their heads emphatically.

"I wouldn't touch it with a dirty stick," Troy snorted.

"Ditto." From Todd.

With a sigh of resignation Anne left the table and went into the library. There was nothing else for her to do; she would have to telephone Jud. On the third ring the call was answered by Lorna's husky voice.

"Hello."

Anne's eyes closed slowly. Oh, God, no, she prayed. Please let there be a mistake. There was no mistake, for clear and unmistakable, as if she stood in the same room, Lorna's voice asked, "Hello? Who is this?"

Slowly Anne lowered her arm, gently cradled the receiver. Moving like a sleepwalker, she made two more brief calls, walked out of the library, and up the stairs to her room. Twenty minutes later, suitcase in hand, she came back down the stairs and left the house.

Melly welcomed her with open arms that closed warmly and protectively around Anne's small, too slim body.

"Anne, honey, with your mother away, I'm so glad you came to me."

Margaret had left the previous week to spend a month in Florida with some friends, but even had she been home, Anne would have gone to Melly, feeling she had to get out of Jud's house.

After showing Anne to the guest room, Melly settled herself on the small, padded rocker in the room, and said bluntly, exactly as her nephew might have, "All right, let's have it. What's the problem?"

"I—I can't handle it any longer, Melly," Anne whispered. "I've made an appointment with my lawyer for next Thursday. I told him I wanted to dissolve my marriage."

Melly leaped out of her chair with the agility of a teenager, her face stark with shock.

"You are going to divorce Jud?"

"Yes." Anne's voice cracked, then grew stronger as she went on. "And I don't want to talk about it."

Melly opened her mouth to protest but closed it again when Anne raised her hand and said flatly, "I mean it, Mel. Unless you want me to leave right now, please don't question me."

"At least answer one question," Mel coaxed. "Does Jud know where you are? What you're planning to do?"

"No." Anne answered in the same flat tone. "And that's two questions."

"Just one more," Mel rushed on. "Do you think you're being entirely fair?"

"Fair?" Anne had to force back the hysterical laughter that rose in her throat. "Jud doesn't know the meaning of the word fair."

"Anne!"

"I'm sorry, Melly," Anne cried. "I know how much you love him and I'm truly sorry. But I won't discuss it. I can't. I'm so tired. All I want to do is rest awhile." Turning away she sobbed. "Maybe I shouldn't have come here."

"Nonsense." Melly turned her around and gave her a quick hug. "Of course you should have, and I promise you I'll ask no more questions. Now, I think you should hop into bed, start getting some of that rest you obviously do need."

In the days Anne stayed with Melly she did rest, and although she refused to talk about the action she was about to take, she did tell Melly the name of the motel she had booked a room at, when she went back.

She was packing to leave when Mel called her to the phone. Passing Mel in the hall on her way to the phone, Anne cast her a reproachful look. Shrugging fatalistically, Mel murmured.

"I only promised not to ask questions."

Lifting the phone with shaking fingers, Anne breathed, "Yes?"

"What time does your plane get in? I'll meet you."

No hello. No how are you. Just a cold, flat request for information.

"No, Jud." Anne's tone was equally cold and flat.

"Anne, we have to talk this out sometime," he argued patiently. "It may as well be tonight."

"I don't want to talk to you, Jud. My lawyer will talk for me."

"Dammit, Anne," he snapped, all pretense at patience gone. "Do you have any idea of the upheaval you've caused here? Todd and Troy have been ready to climb the walls. I was practically sitting on them to keep them from calling and upsetting your mother, when Mel called. Now stop behaving like a spoiled little girl and tell me what time your plane gets in."

She gave in and told him, thinking wearily, what difference did it make? He was right, they would have to talk sooner or later, might as well get it over with.

He was waiting at the airport, hard-faced and cold-eyed and, without a word, he retrieved her suitcase, grasped her elbow, and led her to the car.

After they were out of the worst of the traffic, Anne told him the name of the motel she wanted to go to only to have him growl.

"We're going home."

"But I don't want to go home."

"To tell you the truth, Anne," he returned tiredly, "right now I don't give one damn what you want. We can talk there without being disturbed. I shipped Troy and Todd to New York for a couple of days to work with John. We'll have the barn to ourselves." He grinned ruefully. "You can even scream at me if you want to."

Not bothering to answer him, Anne withdrew into a cold, unresponsive silence. When they reached the house, Anne flung her coat at a chair in the foyer and headed purposefully toward the living room. Jud's hand grasped her arm, pulled her around, and ignoring her struggles and protests pushed her up the stairs in front of him. When they reached her room he shoved the door open, nudged Anne inside, tossed her suitcase into a corner, kicked the door shut, then stood, balled fists on his hips, and demanded, "Okay, what's the story?"

The white, bulky-knit pullover he wore made his shoulders look even broader than usual and his stance, the way his eyes gleamed, frightened her. Stepping back, she moistened her dry lips.

"I'm going to divorce you, Jud. I have an appointment with my lawyer tomorrow morning."

"Why did you go away like that without a word to anyone? Why didn't you at least let me know where you were?"

His harsh voice flung the questions at her like stones and in a tone of equal harshness she flung the answer back.

"Because I didn't want you to know where I was. I didn't want to see you or talk to you."

Turning around, she walked to the window, stared at her own reflection.

"I still don't."

"Are you trying to kill me by inches?"

Barely breathing, Anne stood perfectly still. His voice had dropped to a ragged whisper and his words threw her off balance. Beginning to tremble, she turned to look at him.

"What are you talking about?"

"You, and the hell you've put me through," he lashed out at her. "I was damn near out of my mind when Mel called me."

"But why?" she cried out in bewilderment. "Jud, I don't understand you."

"Don't you?" he rasped. "Well, then, maybe it's time you did."

Had he gone mad? Eyes widening, Anne watched as his hands yanked the sweater, tugged it up his body and over his head. With a violent motion he threw it down, then lifted his head to stare at her.

"Come here, Anne."

Half afraid to move, more afraid not to, she walked unsteadily across the room, coming to a stop in front of him.

"The medal I wear on the chain. Does it look familiar, Anne?"

Anne's eyes dropped to the oddly shaped medal; then, a look of disbelief on her face, they flew back to his.

"Take it in your hand. Examine it closely."

Her eyes went back to the medal as hesitantly. Fingers shaking, she touched it, lifted it from his chest. The oval was warm from the touch of his skin, its matte finish glittering dully in the artificial light, and etched onto its surface were the initials J. C. C. Turning it over, she saw the back was exactly the same, etched with the same initials.

She had no need to speak, her eyes asked the question.

"I never wore them as links," he said quietly.

Her finger moved over the surface.

"But how? Why?"

"How? Very simple." His hands came up to cover hers, closing it around the disc. "Not long after I left, I took it to a jeweler, he removed the posts, fused the two together and attached the loop. I've worn it ever since. It's been my talisman, my good luck charm, my curse. Except when I went into surgery when my nose was broken, I've never had it off. Why? Because it was all I had of you."

The pain in his voice tore at Anne's heart. What was he trying to do to her? Jerking her hand from his, she stepped back.

"But you went away," she sobbed. "You went away."

"You drove me away."

Shocked by his suddenly renewed anger, she stood dumbly, shaking her head.

"Why did you come to my room that night, Anne? Were you experimenting? Were you curious?" His harsh voice hammered at her. Giving her no time to deny his words, he went on. "Do you have any idea what it does to a twenty-five-year-old man to face the fact that he's in love with a fifteen-year-old girl? Or what it's like to watch that girl grow into a lovely young woman? Wanting her? Needing her?"

"But there were other women, Jud," Anne cried hopelessly. "I know there were."

"Hell, yes," he shot back. "There were a lot of women before that night. And a lot more since. And for the same reason. Always the same reason. To exorcise you."

Reaching out his arm, he caught hers, drew her close to him.

"And you know what?" His voice was a tormented groan. "It didn't work. I said I'll always love you and I always have. Even while I was hating you I loved you, so no matter what you do, I guess I always will. I don't want to, Anne, but I do. And I'm not going to let you divorce me."

Anne closed her eyes, afraid to breathe, afraid to move, afraid that if she did she'd hear him laugh and say he was lying and she knew she could not bear that.

"Anne?"

The note of hesitant fear that laced Jud's tone set off a million tiny lights inside Anne, and not pausing to think she whispered, "Oh, Jud. I love you so much I can't stand it."

For one terrifying second he didn't move, and then she was hauled roughly against him and held there tightly in hard, possessive arms. Murmuring her name, he bent his head but she lifted her hand to put her fingers over his lips. She knew the mindless state his kiss could induce. She had to have some answers first.

"Jud, no."

He stiffened then leaned back, his arms loosening.

"No? Anne, what are you trying to do to me?"

"Jud, I'm sorry, but I must know. How did I drive you away? Was I too young? Too inexperienced?"

His hand came up to cradle her face, hold it still. Bending his head, he dropped a light, tantalizing kiss on her mouth and murmured, "Of course you were too young. But I was past worrying about age at that point and, if you hadn't told him you never wanted to see me again, nothing would have kept me away from you."

"Your father?" Anne's eyes flew wide.

"Yes," he sighed. "My father. We had one hell of a fight. Even after he told me how you begged him to send you away so you wouldn't have to see me again, I insisted on seeing you. He was determined I wouldn't. I came pretty close to hitting him that night, Anne. I loved him. Hell, I damned near idolized him, but I came very, very close. We were shouting at each other. I had never seen him so mad."

Dropping his hands, he moved away from her. She saw a shudder ripple across his naked shoulders and when he turned to face her again, his eyes were bleak, his face pale, ravaged with memories.

He went on the prowl, moving restlessly around the room, fingers raking through his hair.

"He called me all kinds of names, none of them pretty. He accused me of trying to rape you. Told me that I had probably scarred you for life. By then I must have seemed like someone demented. I told him I had to see you, tell you." He stopped pacing, shot her a hard look. "He kept repeating how you'd begged him to keep me away from you. Said that if I had an ounce of decency I'd get out and stay out. By the time I left, he had me feeling like I should crawl instead of walk."

Tears running down her face, Anne sobbed. "I didn't say anything. He gave me some pills, I fell asleep. The next morning—when I woke up—I—I kept thinking, everything will be all right, Jud will make it all right. And then, when I found out you were gone—Oh, Jud, I was so sure you'd come for me. I waited and waited."

Jud went absolutely still at her words, the raw pain in her voice. Growing pale under the burnished tan, his face revealed the conflict of emotions he was feeling. Lids that had gone wide now narrowed over eyes that combed her face, searched for truth. He found it in the eyes that pleaded to be believed, the anguish in the one word she whispered.

"Jud."

His face twisted with inner torment and his eyes closed completely as he expelled a long, ragged sigh. In three strides he was across the room. Pulling her into his arms he pressed her face against his rough chest.

"Damn him," he snarled. "Damn him to the same hell he put me through."

"Jud! You mustn't say that," she cried wildly. "He probably thought he was protecting me."

"He damned near protected you into marriage with Andrew." A shudder rippled through his body and his arms tightened possessively. "I came so close to losing you," his voice dropped to a hoarse growl. "Damn him."

"Jud, don't," Anne sobbed. "He's gone. Please, please don't hate anymore."

"Okay, okay," he murmured. "I'm sorry. Calm down."

His hand at the back of her head lifted her face to meet his searching mouth and in between short, hungry kisses he murmured, "Don't cry, chicken. I promise you, we'll make up for all those years."

"What about Lorna?"

"Lorna?" An expression of total blankness crossed his face. "What about her? She's marrying Andrew tomorrow."

"I—I thought you were in love with her. That you'd given her up and married me, to get control of the firm."

"Good God!" His arms tightened, his lips teased hers. "I married you to get control of you. Say the word and I'll go to the phone, transfer my shares to Troy and Todd, if you'll call and cancel your appointment with your lawyer."

"You know I'm going to cancel that appointment," she admitted, "as well as you know I'd never ask you to give up your shares."

His soft laughter did strange things to Anne's spine. It was a lighthearted, teasing sound. A sound she had not heard in over ten years.

"I know," he grinned, then he sobered again. "But I would do it, honey. I'd do just about anything to keep you with me."

While his one hand caressed the back of her head, the other moved sensuously over her back, drawing her closer, closer to his body.

"Oh, Anne," he groaned, "even when I hated you the most, I wanted you. There were times when I thought I'd go crazy with wanting you. When I first heard that rumor about you and the old man—" He closed his eyes a moment and when he opened them again they were blazing with remembered fury. "I wanted to kill you—both of you. I spent the last few years before I came home hating you. Or believing I did. When I stood in that cemetery and stared at his coffin, I knew I had been lying to myself. I loved him."

"You were at the cemetery?"

"Yes, I was at the cemetery." He cocked a pale brow at her in self-mockery. "And when I walked into the library afterward, I knew nothing had changed for me. I still loved you, I still wanted you, and I still thought of you as mine. As for Lorna, she is a good secretary and a good friend and nothing more."

"Then why did she answer the phone in your apartment the day I called?" The strident note of jealousy in her own voice startled Anne and she caught her lip between her teeth.

"What day?" The sharpness of his tone conflicted with the genuine bafflement in his eyes.

"The day I left to go to Melly's," Anne whispered, suddenly not sure she wanted to hear the reason Lorna was there. "I called the apartment because of a problem at the mill I didn't know how to handle," she explained hurriedly. "When Lorna answered, I hung up."

"Having jumped to the obvious, but incorrect, conclusion." Jud's arms tightened around her as he lowered his head, rubbed his cheek against her hair. "If you hadn't hung up, you'd have learned there were several people with me that night, including Lorna's father. We were having an informal, if serious, business meeting over dinner. Lorna was there as my secretary, nothing more." He sighed, drew his head back to look at her, a teasing light entering his eyes. "Although I must admit that a few times I deliberately used Lorna's name in the hope of getting a reaction from you." His arms tightened even more, almost painfully. "I was so damned jealous of Andrew and I wanted you to feel something, if only a tiny measure, of the pain I was in."

"But there was no reason to be jealous of Andrew," Anne exclaimed. "Not ever."

"Now she tells me," Jud murmured ruefully.

By now his hand was on her hip, pressing her tightly against him. His blatant need ignited an answering one in her. Lightheaded with happiness, starving for his love, she ran her hands up and over his chest, fingers sliding through the dark-gold hair.

"My legs are getting very tired standing here, Jud," she whispered. "Couldn't we find a more comfortable place to talk?"

His soft laughter rippled over her again and he gave her a swift, hard kiss before swinging her off her feet into his arms. "Yes, but not here." Carrying her effortlessly he went through the connecting bathroom into his bedroom. Standing her on her feet beside his bed, he stared into her eyes a long moment, the amber of his eyes seeming to glow like hot, melted honey. Then, his hands gentle, trembling slightly, he sensuously undressed her. Still moving slowly, as if savoring every minute, he eased her back onto the bed, caught her wrists in one hand and pulled her arms taut over her head.

"I had to see you like this. I had to." Jud's voice was raw with hunger, his eyes molten as they burned over her. "For almost eleven years my mind carried a picture of you stretched out across my bed. At times that picture damned near drove me mad."

"Oh, Jud." The two whispered words were all Anne could force out of her emotion-clogged throat. Desire, hot and fierce, clamored through her body and she thought that if he didn't kiss her soon, touch her, she'd go out of her mind.

"The reality puts the picture to shame." His soft, hoarse voice was a seduction in itself and Anne's body moved with the tremor that rippled through her. She heard his sharply indrawn breath before he lowered his head, brought his mouth close to hers, whispered, "Part your lips for me, Anne."

The gentle touch of his mouth on hers was a covenant, a seal, a blessing that quickly changed to an urgent, fiery demand. He did not make love to her. He had made love to her while they had been on the island. Now, he worshipped her. With his hands, his mouth, his entire body, he worshipped her.

His mouth left a trail of fire from her throbbing lips to

her aching breasts, wrenched a gasp of pleasure from her with his teasing, tormenting tongue. His stroking hands sent shivers chasing each other in a tingling cascade to the base of her spine, drew a longing moan from deep in her throat when they caressingly feathered the inside of her thighs. His hard, muscular body, tawny hide warm under her fingers, moved against her with maddening slowness until, her hands gripping his hips, she drew him to her with a sobbing outcry.

"Jud, please, please love me."

He did. Long into the night, stripping away all inhibitions, all shyness, he brought her to full womanhood, fulfilled and fulfilling.

When Anne opened her eyes, the room was bright with sunshine from outside and Jud's eyes, lazily studying her face, were bright with a light from within.

"I love you." No frills, no curlicues, his voice held a steady, truthful ring.

"I don't love you." Anne turned her head, pressed her lips to his throat.

"No?" Jud drawled indulgently.

"No. I adore you, I worship you, I—"

"Enough," he laughed softly, lowering his head to brush his lips across her temple. "I'll settle for that."

His arms drew her close, tightening in a fierce bear hug, before he released her completely and sprang out of bed. Throwing his head back, he lifted his arms high over his head to stretch luxuriously like a large contented cat.

Her eyes moving slowly over his beautiful body, Anne was surprised, after the loving night she'd been through, at the growing ache deep in her body, the tingling arousal of her nipples.

"God, I feel good," he joyfully told the ceiling, then his head swung down and around, eyes fastening on her bemused, smiling face. "Rustle that enticing tush, woman," he ordered. "We have places to go. Things to do."

"Where do we have to go?" Startled out of her erotic musings, Anne flushed pink. "What do we have to do?"

Moving around the room restlessly, totally unconcerned with his nakedness, Jud said, "First we are going to call your mother, Troy, and Todd, tell them to stay away at least two more weeks." White teeth flashed in a quick grin. "I may even set their minds at rest by assuring them that I really do love you. After that I'm going to take you for something to eat before we go shopping for a wedding gift. We were invited to a wedding today, you know."

"You really want to go to that wedding?" Anne asked in astonishment.

"I'm afraid we slept through the wedding, honey." Happy laughter rippled from his throat. "But, yet, I want to go to the reception. After we've chosen a suitable gift I'm going to shop for you, buy you the most fantastic dress we can find." His eyes lit with deviltry. "Then I'm going to escort you to that damned reception and watch every man there eat his heart out, because you belong to me."

"Jud, you're crazy," Anne laughed. "Now tell me the real reason you want to go."

"Because I want to celebrate," he grinned. "And Andrew and Lorna's party is as good a place as any. Besides, all our friends have been concerned about you. It will please them to see the completely satisfied look you're wearing."

"Completely satisfied?"

Letting the sheet slip from her, Anne sat up slowly. Doing her own impression of a stretching feline, she felt her breasts rise tautly, hardened tips point at him. Through her lashes she watched his eyes narrow, the instant response of his body.

"The hell with it," Jud purred, moving toward the bed. "We'll mail the gift."

With a delighted squeal Anne moved to get up. Jud's diving body pinned her to the bed. His lips moved against hers. "We can call the family later. Much later."

POWER
AND
SEDUCTION

Chapter One

Her long, elegant legs carrying her slender body swiftly along the sidewalk, Tina Holden Merritt was oblivious to the appreciative male glances she received as she strode by. Come to that, Tina was entirely oblivious to her surroundings, the cold bite of the late November air, and even the lowering gray clouds that threatened rain, sleet, snow . . . or possibly all three.

Though her classically structured, beautiful face appeared serenely composed, Tina's mind seethed with a hot fury that was becoming as familiar to her as her own body.

Damn him!

Her long, beautifully cut camel coat swirling around the tops of her brown suede knee-high boots, Tina swung through the entrance doors to her apartment building. Smiling vaguely at the security guard, she crossed the plushly carpeted lobby to stand before the elevator, impatiently tapping one narrow foot as she waited for the doors to open. In an effort to calm herself, Tina forced slow, deep breaths through her slightly parted, perfectly shaped lips.

Damn him to hell!

Fully aware that the breathing exercise wasn't working, she stepped into the elevator when the doors swished open and stabbed agitatedly at the floor button marked six. As the car ascended, Tina closed her anger-brightened brown eyes and deliberately conjured an image of the object of her fury as she'd last seen him.

Even viewed through anger-clouded eyes, there was no denying that Dirk Tanger was one attractive specimen of masculine virility. Tina didn't even attempt to deny it; she simply hated the man too much to be affected by it.

Who cared that he'd attained a height of at least six foot, three inches of near physical perfection? Or that every one of those inches was covered by taut, healthy-looking skin the exact shade of a gleaming bronze coin? Or, for that matter, that his tan face contrasted so gorgeously with his straight white teeth and complemented his burnished gold hair and beautiful, sapphire blue eyes?

Very likely hordes of misguided, not too awfully bright females cared, Tina though nastily, grimacing as she strode out of the elevator and along the carpeted hall to her apartment door.

But then, the poor dears didn't know Dirk as she did. Tina forgave the unknown females pityingly. Tossing her supple leather handbag onto the nearest chair, she withdrew a crumpled paper from a deep pocket in her coat before flinging the garment after the bag. Smoothing the wrinkled paper out, she read the politely worded message for perhaps the fifteenth time, teeth grinding as her eyes scanned the neatly printed lines.

At that particular moment, Tina was positive she could easily strangle one overbearing, arrogant Dirk Tanger . . . even if she had to stand on a ladder to reach his throat. Which was a bit of an exaggeration as she was only about seven inches shorter than he.

How dare that man refuse her access to her own money . . . again! Tina raged inwardly. And it wasn't as if Dirk could possibly have misunderstood the situation, either. The letter she had written to him had been clear and distinct, informing him of the fact that if he did not advance her the sum of money she requested she would very likely lose everything; the emphasis being on the word "everything."

And as if his refusal hadn't been hard enough to swallow, the bastard had had his secretary send out a damned form letter!

Crumpling the letter—again—Tina tossed it onto her desk, then stormed to the wide window that framed the tall spires of Manhattan. Staring sightlessly through the pane, Tina curled long, slender fingers into her palm; oval nails digging into her flesh, she bit down hard on her lower lip. None of her ploys to stem the flow of stinging tears worked. Overspilling her lids, the tears trickled then ran down her artfully made-up face, leaving black trails of watered mascara all the way to her usually determinedly set chin.

She had to get away before she started screaming, she realized. Drawing a ragged breath, Tina wiped at her wet face. She'd begun snapping at everybody in the shop after reading the letter this morning, and had actually come to within a hair's breadth of firing Paul Rambeau, her most talented stylist. If she kept on like this there would be nobody left to keep the shop running—not that it mattered much, since she was probably going to lose it anyway if she couldn't come up with some fast cash.

But where could she get the money? Resting her flushed face against the cold pane, Tina closed her eyes. She had borrowed to the hilt from the banks, and she'd be darned if she'd go to any of her friends for a loan; her friends weren't aware she was having money problems. Tina would just as soon keep them in the dark. So, that left one source: Dirk Tanger, Tina's financial guardian.

Raising her head, Tina looked down at her trembling hands. A bitter smile twisting her lips, she decided she could not—*would* not—go begging to Dirk looking like a washed-out, worn-out nervous wreck.

Walking slowly into her bedroom, Tina stood frowning at the pale reflection of her own image in the mirror above her dresser. The smudged mascara gave her the appearance of a woebegone raccoon, but even after she cleaned her face, Tina knew that she would still look pale and drawn, with dark circles under her eyes.

That couldn't possibly be from sleeping a mere two to two and a half hours at any given stretch, now, could it?

she silently asked the pathetic woman in the mirror. Lifting her hand, she raked her fingers through the wind-tossed mane of dark red hair that waved gently to her shoulders.

You need a rest, my girl, Tina advised her reflection wryly. A long rest in a quiet place; a place without pressures or hassles or bills marked overdue. But where . . . other than an institution? The vacation house in the mountains had been a victim of the divorce she'd been a party to nine months before, so scratch the eagerly purchased, painfully given-up hideaway in the hills.

Stepping out of her boots, then her beige wool skirt, Tina mulled escape locations while preparing for a warm shower. The figure-hugging nubby-knit sweater was pulled off, then the lacy sage green bra sailed through the air in the general direction of the clothes hamper. Slipping off sheer panty hose and lacy matching bikini briefs, Tina left them where they lay and walked into the bathroom adjoining her bedroom.

Tina loved the black-and-white tiled bathroom. In fact, Tina loved the entire apartment. Glancing around as she briskly applied a toothbrush to her even white teeth, she sighed regretfully. The apartment would have to go; she simply couldn't afford the rent on the place much longer. Blinking against a fresh onslaught of tears, she stepped under the shower, head bent to allow the warm spray to beat against the tense muscles in her neck.

First her car, she thought dejectedly, and soon her apartment. And if she didn't come up with some money—a lot of money—she was going to lose the whole ball of wax, Tina raged silently.

And all because *that* man liked playing God with *her* inheritance. Actually gnashing her teeth, Tina turned the water off and grabbed a fluffy white bath sheet, drying herself carefully before stepping onto the deep-pile bath mat that covered a portion of the black-and-white marbleized tiles.

"I could just murder that man!"

Saying the words aloud eased the tightness in Tina's chest

somewhat and, strolling into the bedroom, she smiled as various methods of bringing about Dirk Tanger's demise rose to tantalize her imagination. Contemplating the gorier of those methods, Tina absently tidied the room, a grim smile playing on her lips.

The room once again cleared of discarded clothing, she shimmied into a pale rose silk robe and drifted, shoulders drooping wearily, from the bedroom to the large bright kitchen.

Where could she go to get some rest while strengthening herself to clash with the ogre in charge of her funds?

Thinking of, then discarding, several sites, Tina prepared a cold tuna salad supper . . . knowing full well she would probably not eat it. Tina had eaten less and less each day as the financial bonds had slowly tightened around her. At five feet eight, she had sported a svelte figure mere weeks ago. Now she was beginning to look hollow and fragile, and she knew it.

Where can I go? she wondered distractedly, dipping an herbal tea bag up and down in a cup of hot water.

Go home.

Hand paused in midair above the steaming cup, Tina frowned at the answer her subconscious had provided.

Home?

Not even tasting the forkful of salad she'd put into her mouth, Tina chewed methodically as she rolled the word around in her mind.

Home.

Of course! Raising the cup to lips smiling with natural ease for the first time in months, Tina nodded her head briefly, decisively. What more perfect place to crawl into a hole to lick raw emotional wounds than a small seaside town in November?

None whatever, Tina told herself firmly, spirits rising. Polishing off the salad with renewed appetite, she sat back in the cane chair and sipped meditatively at her tea, a faraway expression in her eyes as she mused on the perfection of her hometown as a retreat.

Tina had been born in Cape May, New Jersey, and had always been proud of the fact that it was the nation's oldest seashore resort town and a historic national landmark. Smiling reminiscently, she remembered singing her hometown's praises while away at school, informing anyone and everyone of its famed Victorian architecture and its legendary visitors, from six presidents to John Philip Sousa and even Ford and Chevrolet, who, it was claimed, raced on the beaches.

Sighing with sudden, unaccountable homesickness, Tina jumped up and located the cordless phone. Without hesitation she punched out the home number of Paul Rambeau, her second-in-command at the shop she'd worked so hard to establish.

Paul answered on the third ring, his naturally deep voice pitched even lower than during working hours.

"It's only me, Paul," Tina said in a voice laced with amusement. "No need to strain your vocal cords." Grinning at his inelegant snort of disappointment, she purred, "Which one of your latest conquests were you expecting to call this evening?" Paul always kept at least three eager women on his emotional string, each woman fully aware of the other two. In that way Paul adroitly avoided any deep involvement with any one female.

"Serena," Paul replied in a tone of utter boredom that Tina knew was a part of his who-the-hell-cares act. "What's on your mind, boss lady? Or did you just this minute think of something you forgot to chew me out about this afternoon?" Paul drawled wryly. But then, of course, Paul could afford to sound unconcerned. To Tina's knowledge there were at least four of her competitors dangling lucrative bait under his nose in a bid to steal the very talented stylist away from her.

Tina winced. Had she behaved like a raving ogress that day? No, she asserted in answer to her own question, she behaved like a raving ogress *every* day! In all honesty, she couldn't blame Paul if he bit the proffered bait and left her salon.

"I'm sorry about this afternoon, Paul." Tina gave a poor excuse for a laugh. "I'm sorry about every afternoon," she said expanding her apology.

"No sweat, Tina." As usual, in private, Paul dropped the phony French accent he affected so well and slipped into the vernacular. "I know the heat's been on you lately to come up with a lot of bucks. Don't sweat it. Something'll turn up."

Tina was at once torn between laughter and tears. The idea of the ridiculously handsome, aristocratically austere-looking Paul Rambeau spouting slang brought a bubbling giggle to her throat; her comprehension of the support within that slang brought moisture to her eyes.

"Paul, I . . . I have to get away for a while," Tina said, swallowing the lump that had risen at his understanding.

"Tell me about it," Paul murmured in an exaggerated drawl.

"Can I dump the whole shooting match into your lap for a few weeks?" she asked, already sure of his answer.

"Can birds fly?" Paul queried dryly. "Is the Pope—"

Tina groaned theatrically. "Is that a yes?" she prodded.

"That is most definitely a yes," Paul assured with genuine seriousness. "Get the hell out of town for a few weeks, or even a few months, and figuratively at any rate, tell your creditors to back it up for a while." Paul chuckled softly. "I'll keep the clientele happy . . . one way or another."

Tina was still shaking her head in amusement as she hung up a few minutes later. As the majority of the shop's clientele were female, Paul had not had to draw Tina a verbal diagram of exactly how he'd go about keeping them happy if all professional services failed.

Tina's final request of Paul had been for the loan of his car, a sporty little Dodge he valued more than any woman he'd yet found. Paul's unhesitatingly swift granting of the favor said reams about the trust and friendship that had grown between them over the three years he'd worked for her. Interwoven with the friendship they shared was a deep mutual respect. Proof of this was in the fact that not at any time had Paul exerted his undeniably sexy charm on Tina.

With a lighter spring to her step, Tina swept back to her bedroom. As the arrangements were for Paul to drop his car off at her apartment in the morning before he went to open the shop, Tina decided to pack and make it an early night. Who knows, she thought wryly, dragging her suitcase from the closet, I might even sleep the night through for once!

The speedometer reading a steady sixty, Tina held the steering wheel loosely as she cruised along the Garden State Parkway. A smile softened the somber slant of her lipline as she passed the exit sign for Ocean City's business district.

And none too soon, she mused, surprised at the hunger pangs grumbling in her stomach. In less than an hour she should not only be at home but out again, shopping for food to stock the fridge. Excitement reinforced the hunger pains building inside Tina. By the time she finally drove the little car down the quiet tree-lined street, she felt half sick with anticipation.

Slowing to make the turn onto the curved street, Tina crept along, her misty gaze caressing the familiarity of it all. And there, near the very end of the street, stood her home, smaller, not as impressive as some of the other, more famous Victorian homes in the quaint community, but home just the same.

Parking along the curb, Tina sat still a moment, staring at the house she hadn't seen in over five years. Would it seem considerably smaller to her now? she wondered. Then, more practically: Would it be in terrible disrepair? Only one way to find out, she chided herself, go have a look!

Set into action by her own advice, Tina slid out of the car, strode across the pavement and up the front steps to the veranda—and stopped dead in her tracks, blinking at what had to be a hallucination. She *had* to be seeing things, Tina as-

sured herself, for that could not have been a face peering out
the narrow living room window at her!

When Tina opened her eyes, the face was gone, the lace
curtain in place again. Laughing shakily to herself, Tina
delved into the capacious handbag slung over her shoulder,
finally extracting a large, old-fashioned door key. You need
a rest even more than you thought, she chided herself, stepping to the door. Before the key touched the lock, the door
swung open.

"Oh!" Tina gasped, staring in disbelief at the face she'd
seen peering out the window. The face was part of a neatly
shaped gray-haired head that rested on a thin neck connected
to a tiny, trim body.

"May I help you?" the small woman asked pleasantly, a
smile of welcome on her plain face.

"Yes . . . ah, that is, I—"

"You're looking for a room to rent?" the woman cut in.

Room to rent? Tina frowned. In my own house? Tina
opened her mouth to speak; then not knowing exactly
what to say, closed it again. What was going on here?
Deciding to try to find the answer, Tina returned the
woman's smile.

"Do you have a room for rent?" she inquired curiously.

"In November?" The woman's laugh was every bit as
pleasant as her smile. "I have a house full of empty
rooms." Stepping back, the woman motioned Tina inside.
"And I'm aching for some company," she continued as a
dazed Tina entered the beautifully preserved foyer. "The
place is a little dull right now, but it will liven up closer
to the holidays when the tourists arrive for the Christmas
festivities."

"Ah, yes, I suppose so," Tina murmured vaguely, all too
aware of the seasonal attractions the town had to offer at
Christmastime. But for now Tina was too distracted with
glancing around, noting the changes, to dwell on the holiday
that was still over six weeks away. Suddenly realizing she'd
been staring much too long, she returned her attention to the
woman.

"Have you been here long?" Tina asked carefully.

"Going on five years now," the woman replied, waving Tina into the living room. "I'm Elizabeth Harkness, but every one calls me Beth." She smiled, then went on, nudgingly, "And what's your name?"

"Oh, ah, Tina . . . Tina Merritt."

Beth extended one tiny hand. "What a pretty name. How do you do? It'll be a joy to have you in the house." Beth made a face. "It does tend to get a little lonely here along about the middle of November. How long were you planning to stay?" Lively dark eyes studied Tina hopefully.

Captivated by the small, friendly woman, Tina laughed. "I have no definite date in mind, as a matter of fact. A few weeks or so I guess." She shrugged at her own ambiguity.

The woman's dark eyes glowed. "That's wonderful! Have a seat, dear. No! Don't!" Beth smiled at her own change of instructions. "Let's get you settled first." Whipping around, she headed for the front door. Tina had little choice but to follow in Beth's wake. "Do you have much luggage?" Beth asked as she opened the door.

"No." Tina was beside the smaller woman with a few long strides. "Just a suitcase and a carryall."

Trailing Beth across the veranda and down the steps to the pavement, Tina glanced up and down the nearly deserted street. "I suppose the car will be all right here," she mused, thinking she'd be in big trouble if anything happened to Paul's car.

"It'll be fine, dear," Beth assured her dryly. "As you can see, there's not an awful lot of traffic!"

Laughing together, they carried the cases into the house, Tina following Beth up the curved staircase that joined the building's three floors. The bedroom that Beth ushered Tina into was different, yet familiar. Tina had spent her childhood in that very room, as it had been her own bedroom from the day her mother had decided Tina was ready to graduate from the small nursery next to the master bedroom.

"It's . . . it's lovely." Swallowing against the thickness clogging her throat, and widening her eyes to contain the sudden welling up of tears, Tina strolled to the room's one narrow window which overlooked the back garden, now lonely-looking in its bare starkness. "Yes," she murmured. "Quite lovely."

"Well, then," Beth said briskly. "I'll leave you to get settled." Her hand on the doorknob, Beth paused. "Did you stop for lunch along the way?"

"No." Shaking her head absently, Tina turned to smile at Beth. "I was hoping to find some place to have lunch after I'd arrived."

"Well, you have." Beth smiled. "Lunch will be ready in fifteen minutes." She started out the door, then paused again, as if in afterthought. "Will that give you enough time?"

"Plenty." Tina nodded in agreement. "I just want to freshen up a little. I can unpack later."

"Oh, that reminds me!" Beth's eyebrows flew into an arch. "There are no private bathrooms. There's a central bath on each floor. The one on this floor is two doors down the hall." Again, Beth moved to go out, and again she paused, a chuckle running through her voice. "Of course, you'll have the bath all to yourself—at least for a week or so." This time she did leave, closing the door quietly behind her.

Standing at the window, Tina glanced slowly around the room, the thickness in her throat expanding as the tears escaped her lids to trace rivulets down her face. When she had occupied the room before, the walls had been painted a bright sunshine-yellow and the furniture had been white French provincial.

Now it was completely changed. The walls were covered with paper patterned with tiny blue periwinkle flowers, and the furniture was oak and wicker. Potted and hanging plants added a dash of freshness to the charming decor.

Closing her gritty eyes, Tina had the feeling that if she listened hard enough she'd hear her mother or father calling her for lunch or dinner. Shaking her head, Tina brushed at her wet face and walked out of the room and along the hall to the bathroom, noting the changes there as well.

No, she told herself sadly, her parents would never call to her again.

By the time Tina had splashed cool water on her face and washed her hands, she had her emotions firmly under control, and was determined to find out how her house had become a bed-and-breakfast. With a grace that was natural to her, she ran down the curved staircase and moved unerringly toward the kitchen . . . which, like the entire house, was changed but still familiar.

"Something smells delicious!" Tina exclaimed as she entered the big, old-fashioned kitchen in which the most modern of conveniences were cleverly camouflaged to appear turn-of-the-century.

"Clam chowder." Beth smiled. "Manhattan style. And spinach salad"—her smile grew into a grin—"my style. Have a seat." Beth waved at the sturdy oak table. "Would you like a cup of coffee? It's fresh."

"I'd love some, thank you." Tina slid a ladder-back chair from under the table and sat down. "I drove straight through from New York and I'm beginning to feel parched." She didn't add that her tears had left her throat feeling raw and dry as well. "Is there anything I can help you with?" The question came as naturally as breathing; Tina had always helped her mother in the kitchen.

"Not a thing, dear." Beth shook her head as she set a steaming cup of coffee in front of Tina. "You're the paying guest, just sit and enjoy."

Bending over the cup, Tina inhaled the aromatic steam. Sipping the best coffee she'd tasted in years, Tina studied Beth as she bustled about getting lunch. A very nice person, Tina decided, but how did she get here? In my house? Tina determined once again to get some answers.

After three spoonfuls of the rich, savory soup, Tina changed her opinion of Beth; Beth was not just a nice person, she was an absolute treasure!

Never reticent in lavishing praise where she thought it was due, Tina complimented Beth on both the soup and the salad—a dream with chunks of tomato, bits of crisp, real bacon, croutons, and English walnuts tossed among the dark green spinach leaves and ranch-style dressing.

Tina held her counsel until after the meal was finished when she and Beth were sipping from fresh cups of coffee; then she began probing gently.

"Does running a bed-and-breakfast rooming house pay when there are obviously off periods, like now?" Tina asked with what she thought was commendable casualness.

"It does for me." Beth laughed. "I receive my salary every week whether the house is full or empty."

"Oh, I see," Tina murmured, positive now that she really did. "You run the place for an absentee owner?" Even though she'd posed it as a question, there was no longer one in Tina's mind. And her mind was beginning to churn with the anger that had been banked by the novelty of meeting Beth Harkness.

Beth nodded. "I receive a check in the mail every week to cover my salary and whatever expenses I may have incurred—you know, for repairs and such." She smiled softly. "Dirk never questions the amount."

Tina swallowed the groan that rose to her throat. Keeping her tone coolly modulated, she repeated quietly, "Dirk?"

"Yes." Beth's smile was positively motherly. "Dirk Tanger. A wonderful man."

Tina gagged on the mouthful of coffee she'd unfortunately sipped while Beth was speaking. *Wonderful!* Sure . . . old Dirk could afford to be wonderful—and generous: the rat was spending *her* money. With the thought came the realization that she would be expected to pay for her room—*her* room!

Controlling her temper was not the easiest thing Tina had ever done but, by gritting her teeth, she accomplished it.

"How much do I owe you for one week's rent?" she asked, in a muffled tone owing to the fact that she was speaking through gritted teeth.

Smiling benignly, Beth quoted a sum that was in truth very reasonable, Tina knew—unless one was up against a financial wall, which Tina was. Doing a swift mental computation of rent, gas for the car, and the possibility of meals taken outside the rooming house, Tina figured she could stay at the house until the first or second week of January. Sighing ruefully to herself, Tina withdrew her wallet from her purse.

Beth wrote a receipt for the money Tina handed to her, then said, "The price includes all meals whenever you're here." The smile that spread over her face was pure imp. "Usually only breakfast is included, but"—Beth shrugged— "I'm so delighted to have the company, I'm throwing lunch and dinner in as a bonus."

Tina helped Beth tidy the kitchen, then she went to her room to unpack. The anger she'd felt the day before was on her again, riding her mind unmercifully. Carefully *not* slamming drawers, muttering imprecations against arrogant jerks who played lord of the manor with other people's money, Tina stashed her foldables into dresser drawers and hung the few dresses and skirts she'd packed into the one shallow closet the room contained.

When Tina was finished unpacking, she slid the suitcase and carryall under the bed, then stood, uncertain, in the center of the room. Now what? she wondered, rubbing her palms down over the expensive denim sheathing her hips. You came to rest, didn't you? Tina mutely replied to her own query: So, rest.

Shoulders drooping, she walked to the window. Dully examining the changes time and a different point of view had wrought, she let her gaze rest on a delicate-looking white-painted iron bench placed under the wide, bare branches of a tree Tina knew was over one hundred years old.

Near the bench was a brick path that ran the length of the back garden. The path had been there for as long as Tina could remember; only the placing of the dormant rosebushes and rows of hedge were changed.

The same, yet not the same. Like me, Tina thought moodily, swinging away from the window. I'm the same Tina who slept in this room and the same Tina who dreamed away rainy days sitting by that window. And yet I'm a different Tina, grown up, mature, the galling fact of a divorce in my past.

The last consideration sent Tina striding across the room. Scooping her suede jacket from the foot of the bed, she left the room and ran down the stairs. She paused only long enough to give a sweeping glance to the living room; not spotting Beth, she walked out of the house, hoping a vigorous walk would burn off some of her renewed anger.

Moving with quick, rhythmic precision, Tina's legs made short work of the streets as she roamed around, reacquainting herself with the town. Her boots kicking leaves as dry and dusty as her memories, Tina presented a calm exterior to the occasional person she passed. Inside, she was boiling again.

It was all Dirk's fault. Everything that had happened to her since her father died was Dirk's fault, she fumed, jamming her chilled hands into her pockets. At least, Tina qualified, everything *bad* that had happened to her. Even the failure of her marriage could be placed at Dirk's door!

Entering the quaint bygone-era ambiance of the Washington Street Mall, Tina slowed her breakneck pace. Breathing heavily, she strolled through the mall, glancing into shop windows, seeing nothing. She passed a coffee shop, then turned back and went inside.

Over a cup of coffee she didn't really want, Tina was immune to the charm of Victorian decor as she railed against the one man on the earth who held her entire future in his hands. Thoughtfully sipping the dark brew, Tina set her mind to work on various ways of getting what was rightfully hers from Dirk Tanger—her own money and her own life.

Rejecting each and every idea that swam into her tired mind, Tina paid for her coffee and left the shop. The sun was beginning to throw long shadows along the ground, but there was one more place she wanted to go before returning to the house.

Walking slowly now, Tina covered the short distance from the mall to the beach. Standing on the sand, she gazed out over the constantly moving ocean, her mind swept clear by the stiff wind whipping off the water.

"Makes you feel insignificant, doesn't it . . . the sea?"

At the sound of that voice, still too familiar, Tina whirled around, her breath catching in her chest.

Dirk Tanger was leaning against the beach front promenade, his burnished hair ruffled by the wind, his blue eyes intent and alive with amusement, his lips curved into a wry smile. He looked arousingly attractive, muscularly fit, and more than ready for anything.

"Hello, big-city girl," Dirk said softly. "Slumming?"

Chapter Two

Surprised, shocked, mentally rattled by the sight Dirk made as he leaned indolently against the rocky base of the promenade, Tina stared at him in disbelief. Where the devil had he sprung from . . . hell?

"Not at all." When Tina finally responded to Dirk's taunt she was rather proud of the casual note she'd managed to inject into her voice—in actual fact, she was trembling like a leaf inside. "I might ask what you're doing here."

"You might at that." Smiling lazily, Dirk pushed his deceptively slim body away from the large rock. Hands coming to rest lightly on his hips, he arched a brow that was more brown than gold. "I might even tell you." His white teeth flashed against his tanned face as his smile widened. "Over a beer," he added challengingly.

About to fling a frosty no at him, Tina caught herself just in time. In a bid to gain time to consider her options, she tilted her head, her expression blatantly bored as she slowly made a visual inventory of him. And Dirk inventoried to a staggering amount of pluses!

Even attired casually in stone corduroys, a fisherman's knit pullover in a shade that reflected the sapphire blue of his eyes, a wide-wale corduroy jacket in an espresso color, and dark desert boots, Dirk Tanger contrived to appear elegant . . . damn him.

For some inexplicable reason the tremor inside Tina deepened. I'm not ready to deal with him yet! she cried in silent protest. And yet, what better way to form a battle plan than to get behind the enemy's lines? Undecided, Tina stared down at the suede boot toe she was ruining, grinding it into the moist sand.

"Hello?" Dirk's bored tone snagged at her attention. "Is anyone home?"

Head snapping up, Tina glared at him, her eyes shooting sparks of annoyance. "You always were dreadfully amusing," she drawled with deliberate nastiness.

"I'm glad you remember," Dirk taunted softly.

"Or were you merely dreadful?" she continued sweetly, a thrill of an emotion quite like fear curling in her midriff as Dirk's eyes narrowed with anger.

"I was never dreadful to you," he retorted sharply, as if deeply stung by the barb.

"Oh, really?" Tina was suddenly consumed by the rage of memory, rage that inundated the fear. "Would you like me to quote you chapter and verse?" she asked, gaining strength from the flush of red that crept up his throat.

"Dammit, Tina," Dirk exclaimed harshly. Then as if catching himself, he lowered his voice. "Are you going to have a beer with me or not?" he asked with a sigh.

"Why not?" Tina lifted her shoulders in a careless shrug. "If . . ." Her voice trailed off. There were many if's Tina could have demanded of Dirk, if's like: If you guarantee we'll have the drink in a public place; if you promise not to badger me; or, most important of all, if you give me your word you'll keep your hands to yourself.

"If?" Dirk prompted warily.

Deciding to be prudent, Tina shrugged again. "If you'll allow me wine instead of beer," she lied with forced unconcern.

The blue gaze that raked over her was dark with inner speculation. Dirk didn't believe for one second that she'd hedged over his choice of a drink, and Tina knew it. The sardonic smile that curved his lips promised trouble ahead for her, and Tina knew that too.

"My dear Tina," Dirk said smoothly, "you can have champagne if you like." There was a brief, telling pause, then he let fly a barb of his own. "Since I'll be paying the check with your money anyway."

Tina choked off the gasp that sprang from her throat, and swallowed the bitter taste of gall. You arrogant bastard! she seethed. You overbearing son of a—

"I did mean today." Fortunately, Dirk's prodding drawl interrupted Tina's less than ladylike mental ravings. Extending one large hand, he cupped her elbow. "Shall we?" His hand dropped as Tina jerked her arm away.

"I can manage very well by myself, thank you," she said coldly, moving around him toward the street.

Tina was striding haughtily when Dirk drew alongside her, matching his gait to hers. Rigidly facing forward, Tina gave him a sidelong glance, a rush of satisfaction washing through her at the sight of his taut features.

"You really are mad because of that letter I sent you," Dirk said. "Aren't you?"

"Not at all," Tina corrected coldly. "I'm mad because of *every* letter you've *ever* sent me!"

They were approaching a restaurant-lounge that fronted on Washington Mall and, as Tina would have walked by, Dirk caught her upper arm, turning her in her tracks.

"We can have our drinks in here," he instructed tersely, when she threw him an angry look. Swinging the side entrance door open, he motioned her in.

Even now, nearing dinner time, in the off-season the back dining room contained few patrons, and those few had clustered together in one corner. Choosing a table at the other end of the room, Dirk slid a chair out for Tina. When she was seated, he circled around to sit facing her. A waiter appeared at their table as they were still adjusting their chairs.

"Maybe every letter I've ever sent you made you angry because I simply refused to let you squander all your money," Dirk suggested dryly, after the waiter had taken their order and departed.

"Squander?" Tina stared at him incredulously, "You—

you—" Sputtering, and fully aware that she was, Tina paused to draw a deep breath and lower her voice. "Damn you, Dirk! You have no right to say that. I do not squander money," she insisted with soft force. Tina's quietly outraged tone gained her an arched expression of mockery from Dirk.

"Well, at least not as often as you'd like to," he sparred verbally. "But that's only because I won't let you."

Tina opened her mouth to dispute his claim, then immediately closed it again when the waiter delivered the drinks to their table. She played with her cocktail napkin until he'd retreated to the bar again, then she launched into an attack.

"I am on the verge of losing every damn thing I own," Tina spat at him. "All because *you* refuse to advance me some of *my* money!"

"Not so." Shaking his head in denial, Dirk leaned back comfortably and drank deeply from his frosted mug of beer. "If you're about to lose *any* damn thing you own, it's because you lavished what you did have on that slime you married." Dirk's smooth tone was contradicted by the fierce light in his eyes. "And I made up my mind the day you married him that *he* wasn't getting any of *your* money." A derisive smile twisted his lips. "Not until you were twenty-five, at any rate." Dirk's smile turned downright nasty. "And he didn't, did he?"

Tina glared across the table at him. Twenty-five was the magic number for her, because when she turned twenty-five she took control of her inheritance. Of course, her marriage hadn't endured that long. Right or wrong, Tina held Dirk responsible for the failure of her marriage. Now, staring not daggers but swords at him, she let her hate show.

"No, Chuck didn't last." Tina emphasized her former husband's name deliberately. "But I blame you for the breakup of my marriage." If she had hoped to shame him by her charge—and she most definitely had—Tina was rudely shaken by his response.

"Good." Smiling serenely over her gasp, Dirk swallowed the last of his beer. Catching the waiter's attention, he indicated his desire for a refill, then lifted his brow at Tina's barely touched wine. "Not thirsty?" Dirk's gaze mocked her rising flush of anger.

Ignoring his question, Tina narrowed her eyes and glared at him. "What do you mean, good?"

Dirk laughed. "I mean . . . good." Exchanging the empty mug for the full one the waiter brought to the table, Dirk silently toasted her. "If my tight hold on the purse strings had anything whatever to do with the demise of your misalliance, well, then . . . good. I'm glad. Couldn't be happier." He smiled companionably. "Have I defined my expression fully now?"

"You really are a bastard!" Tina snarled in a whisper.

"I do try." Dirk's shrug spoke volumes about his indifference.

Frustrated by her failure to get at him, Tina raised her glass and gulped some wine, barely noticing the crisp taste of the drink Dirk had ordered for her.

Dirk observed her quietly, his eyes dancing with amusement, until she placed the glass carefully on the tiny napkin.

"Would you like another?"

Inside he was laughing at her, and Tina knew it. The knowledge infuriated her all the more. "Since I'm paying for it, why not?" Tina let all the bitterness and anger she was feeling show in her rough-edged tone.

Dirk was unimpressed, as he proved by grinning at her wickedly. "Would you like something to eat with it? Since it is dinner time . . . and you *are* paying for it?"

Dinner time. Beth Harkness. *Her* house. The thoughts tumbled into Tina's mind, reminding her of another very sore spot. Accepting a fresh drink from the waiter, she sipped daintily.

"Dinner." Tina's rough-edged tone had smoothed to a purr, somewhat like the noise one hears from a wildcat an instant before it springs. "That reminds me. Do you know, I'm paying rent to sleep in my own house?" She raised one brow delicately. "Isn't that amusing?"

Anyone who really knew Tina would have been justified in becoming uncomfortable at her soft, chiding tone. Dirk was not merely anyone, nor was he in the least uncomfortable—if his lounging form and smiling face could be believed.

"A regular riot," he concurred teasingly.

"Of course, Beth is throwing meals in with the rent." Tina's voice grew even more pleasant, and even more dangerous.

"Kind of her," Dirk observed agreeably. "But then, Beth's one of a kind."

Tina's fingers tightened their grip on the fragile stem of the glass.

"If you throw that wine at me," Dirk warned softly, "I'll shampoo your hair with this beer."

Stalemate. Tina gritted her teeth and hated him with her eyes. Dirk smiled benignly into her hate. The tension humming between them was a palpable thing, tightening Tina's already taut nerves, exciting her senses, and interfering with her breathing.

"I want to kiss you so badly I can taste you on my mouth."

Tina stopped breathing entirely. Shivering inside the warmth of the jacket she had not bothered to remove, she stared at him in mute shock. Dirk was no longer laughing, or lounging. Sitting erectly, his gaze intent, he was watching closely for her reaction.

"That—that's not funny." Tina deplored the weakness of her tone, but the strength she strove for just wasn't there.

"No, it isn't." Dirk's low tone certainly didn't lack strength. "As a matter of fact, it aches like hell."

Tina recoiled against her chair as though he'd struck her. It was so unfair of him! The memory was there; had been there from the moment she'd spun around on the beach to face him. But it simply was not fair of him to bring it into the open. Protesting inwardly, Tina stared at him in anguish.

Why, she wondered in sudden weariness, had she ever expected Dirk to be fair?

"You ache too, don't you?" Leaning across the table, Dirk grasped her hands with his. "Don't try to deny it, Tina. Your eyes betray you."

Oh, damn . . . what Dirk said was true, though she'd endure mental and physical torture before she'd ever admit it, especially to him. Merely feeling his heated gaze roam over her body set her on fire.

"You really are a son of a—"

"Oh, honey, you don't know the half of it." Dirk's soft laughter sliced across her hoarse voice. "I can be real mean when I'm hungry," he whispered, the caressing movement of his fingers on her at variance with his threat. "And I'm getting hungrier by the minute." Surprisingly, confusingly, he released her hands and sat back. "So, shall we order dinner?"

If Dirk had hoped to throw her completely off balance he'd succeeded admirably, Tina conceded wryly, clamping her teeth together to keep them from rattling. Her breath coming in shallow little gasps, she raked her mind for a suitably scathing put-down and came up blank.

"I'm going home now." Pushing her chair back, Tina moved to stand up.

"Sit down, Tina." There was no menace at all in Dirk's tone; no warning, no threat. Still, there was something, an elusive something that touched her deep inside. Tina sat down.

"Do you have any idea how much I despise you?" Tina made herself meet his stare directly.

"Yes." Dirk's brilliant eyes clouded for an instant, as if with deep pain, then they cleared, glittering with a sexuality that was as terrifying as it was exciting. "And while you're away from me, you can hate me with the fervor of a purist." His lips curved in a knowing smile. "Isn't it a bitch that when we're near each other, the hate gets muddled by physical attraction?"

Tina wanted to scream a denial to his face. She wanted

to but could not, simply because she knew he'd know she was lying. In an effort to combat the strange sensation that she was crumbling inside, Tina raised her glass and drank thirstily.

"My room is directly across the hall from yours."

Tina choked on her wine. Coughing, she gaped at him helplessly.

"Oh, Tina." Shaking his head, Dirk got to his feet to walk to the bar area. When he returned he was carrying a glass of water and two menus.

"Here, drink this and calm down," he advised almost tenderly. "I have no intention of kicking your door down in the middle of the night to have my evil way with you." One eyebrow arched in devilment. "Even though the idea is rather intriguing." Dirk watched in amusement as she sipped gratefully at the cool water. When the choking spell was drowned, he returned to his chair.

"No, Tina. You'll never find yourself in the position of having literally to fight your way out of my arms." Dirk's eyes caressed every feature of her face, setting off a tingling shiver she was beyond masking. The evidence of her response to his visual lovemaking lit a flame in the depths of his eyes and curved his lips in a smile.

"Ah, no, Tina." Dirk's tone of rough velvet ignited a blaze in her body. "You won't have to fight me."

Dirk had no need to elaborate and he knew it. Tina was well aware the battle was with her own unbridled response to him. Dirk was as aware of the fact as she.

Biting her lip, Tina drank more carefully, riling at the fate that had sent him to Cape May at this particular time. If she'd had more time to pull herself together, to rest and get a grip on the despair and anger driving her to near exhaustion, she felt sure she could have controlled this physical thing between them. Sighing, she watched him warily, knowing that if he touched her she'd go up in flames, and then she'd hate herself as well as him.

"Settle down and choose your dinner." Dirk handed her

a menu. "You didn't think I was considering a wrestling match here, did you?"

"You're disgusting!" Snatching up the menu, Tina hid her face behind it, hating him even more because she knew that, were he to attempt seduction in a very public dining room, he'd very likely succeed!

"We could begin with oysters." Dirk's dry tone drew her suspicious glance. "Never know when you'll need fortification."

"I'll start with onion soup." Tina smiled sweetly.

Dirk's laughter, when natural and free, was a sound of beauty. "Thanks, honey. I haven't laughed that easily in a very long time."

His eyes were so honest, so open, Tina hated having to sink a needle, but she couldn't pass up the opportunity.

"Trouble with the little woman, Dirk"—she hesitated briefly—"honey?"

Dirk's reaction was immediate, and chilling. A coldness settled over his face that froze his features and hardened his eyes. And he used those hard-looking eyes to advantage, slicing through to Tina's core.

"Not anymore." His tone was as hard as his eyes. "And I'm not planning to have any with you, either."

"No?" Tina dared to smile. "Then I'd advise you to re-think your plans . . . *honey*. I'm going to give you more trouble than your wife ever dreamed of." Leaning an elbow on the table, Tina propped her chin on her hand and smiled beguilingly. "I think I'll have grilled ham"—she fluttered her lashes flirtatiously—"as my main course."

From behind her teasing pose, Tina watched as the tension eased out of Dirk's strong body, her chest heaving along with his in a long sigh of release.

"Excellent choice." He applauded her tactics. "Oddly, I'd forgotten how much fun it is to fight with you."

Pretending interest in the patrons on the other side of the room, Tina glanced away from him. "I can assure you, this time the fight will not be fun," she said tightly, damning him once more for raking up the past.

"Maybe not for you," he observed blandly. "But that's understandable, you're going to lose."

Turning her head very slowly, Tina stared into his incredibly blue eyes. "Rather than divorce you," she said scathingly, "I'm amazed your wife didn't kill you."

"She didn't divorce me." Dirk's lips curved with scorn . . . for his wife or her? Tina wondered. He cleared the issue bluntly and succinctly. "I divorced her."

Tina had never met his wife, had never wanted to meet her, yet at that moment she felt compassion for the woman who'd made the mistake of loving such a ruthless man. Glancing down at the menu still clutched in her hands, she sighed and closed it.

"Suddenly not hungry?" Dirk taunted.

Tina shook her head briefly. "I just remembered that Beth will be expecting me for dinner," she lied, longing for nothing more than to get away from him.

The movement of Dirk's head reflected hers. "No, she won't. I told her we'd be having dinner out."

"You told her?" Tina blinked. "When? I only left the house a few hours ago!"

"And I arrived less than fifteen minutes after you left." Dirk blinked back at her mockingly.

Again cursing providence for sending him here at this time, Tina deplored the necessity but asked the obvious. "But how did you know I was staying there? Did Beth tell you?"

"Of course." His gaze roamed her face, lighting with amusement at the evidence of anger tingeing her cheeks. "But I already knew. Where else would you have gone?"

Adding one and one, Tina came up with the obvious: Dirk had known she was coming home. And there was only one person who could have provided him with the information. Gritting her teeth, Tina promised herself she'd fire Paul Rambeau the moment she returned to New York.

"I asked Paul not to tell anyone where I would be." Tina sighed. "How did you get the information out of him?"

"Is that his name? The one with the bogus French accent?" Tina nodded curtly.

Dirk's eyes glittered with some emotion Tina couldn't quite identify. "Your new boyfriend?" His tone was as smooth as glass—or ice. Refusing to give him the benefit of any reaction at all, she simply stared at him. "What does he do?" Dirk's brow arched. "At the shop, I mean?"

"He's my top stylist." Tina replied grudgingly, fully aware of what his reaction would be. Dirk's bark of laughter proved her correct.

"A stylist!" Dirk's condescending tone grated on Tina's nerves. Still, she maintained a stoic silence. "How sweet." His laughter subsiding to a deep chuckle, Dirk raised his glass in a mock salute. "Here's to Paul . . . just one of the girls."

"You fatuous jerk!" Bristling, Tina jumped to Paul's defense, conveniently forgetting her vow to fire him moments ago. "Paul is not only one of the most sought-after hairstylists in New York, he's one of the most sought after bachelors! He has more women than a rich Arab sheikh!" Her lip curled jeeringly. "Save your ridicule—or apply it to yourself."

Dirk's eyes glittered warningly. "Are you one of those women?" he asked very softly.

Her expression haughty, Tina mirrored his action by raising her glass mockingly in a salute to him. "Mind your own business," she said pleasantly.

With a deceptively frightening calm, Dirk placed his glass on the table, then leaned forward in his chair. Only the flash in his sapphire eyes revealed the fury raging inside him. Lifting his hand, he grasped her chin with his thumb and forefinger, drawing her face close to his.

"Are you sleeping with him?"

Incensed, Tina glared into the shocking blue depths of Dirk's eyes, hating him—and suddenly wanting him more than she wanted air to breathe. Determined not to humiliate herself by struggling against his hold, she sat perfectly still, refusing to answer, defying him with her eyes.

"Answer me, damn you!" Dirk's voice had gone very low and scratchy. "Are you sleeping with him?" His grasp tightening, he shook her head slightly.

"No!" Tina spat the word through gritted teeth. "Paul's an employee and a friend, nothing more. Now take your hand off me."

Though Dirk obeyed her command, he did so with a lingering caress, trailing his fingertips over the satiny texture of her cheek. The shivering response Tina could not hide brought a satisfied smile to his lips. The tips of his fingers still burning her skin, he leaned closer to her.

"Come, Tina," he whispered coaxingly. "Come one inch nearer and kiss me."

God, she was tempted! Her senses exploding from the musky, arousing male scent of him, her lips tingling with the need to taste his, Tina stared at him, inwardly fighting the urge to lose herself inside the blue depths of his eyes. She was losing the battle when Dirk inadvertently turned the tide.

"Come, my love, let me have your mouth."

A spasm of agony slashed through Tina at his hoarsely voiced endearment. The sudden urge she had to fight was violent. Dirk had called her "my love" that afternoon five years ago. Like the young fool she'd been, Tina had taken the endearment at face value, living to regret it with every fiber of her being. The impulse to strike out at him searing through her body, Tina drew a deep breath and slowly sat back, putting a measure of distance between them.

"Go to hell." A confusing mixture of pleasure and pain washed over Tina at the way Dirk's head jerked back, as if she'd struck him a physical rather than a verbal blow.

"I've been there." Dirk's smile held bitter humor. "I prefer taking you to heaven." Tina's involuntary gasp made his smile real and breathtaking. "I distinctly remember being there with you." His gaze caressed her paling face. "Have you been there since, Tina?"

The implication contained in Dirk's question was unnerving and insulting at the same time: unnerving for Tina and insulting to her former husband. Recoiling, yet determined not to reveal how deeply his shot had penetrated, Tina forced herself to be still.

"You really are a conceited beast," she grated coldly.

"Very likely," Dirk surprisingly agreed. "But along with my enormous conceit, I am also very honest." He smiled with wry self-derision. "And in that honesty I must confess that my king-sized marriage bed never afforded me the exquisite pleasure I found in your narrow, virginal twin-sized one."

Abruptly Tina was on her feet and moving to the door. She had to get away from him or face the consequences he'd most assuredly mete out when she hit him . . . which she was sorely tempted to do!

Tina was halfway down the next block before Dirk caught up to her. Grasping her upper arm, he brought her to a jarring halt.

"You're always running," he said in an exasperated tone. "Haven't you learned yet that you can't run away from the truth?"

"Truth?" Amazing herself, Tina dragged a ripple of laughter from the depths of her churning emotions. "One man's truth is another woman's fiction." Feeling the encroachment of hysteria, she jerked her arm sharply in a bid for freedom; Dirk's hold remained firm. "Damn you, let me go!"

"No." Dirk's tone was adamant. "Not now. Not ever again."

Before Tina could find the breath to question his rather ominous statement, he began walking, forcing her into motion beside him. "You didn't have your dinner." Glancing at her, he added, "And I think you're beginning to get a little light-headed." Without pausing, he started back to the restaurant.

"Dirk! Stop this!" Tina's voice held an edge of shrillness that carried clearly on the cold night air. Digging her heels in, she attempted to slow his determined stride. "I want to go home. I'll get something to eat there."

Surprisingly, Dirk stopped. Turning to face her, he caught her other arm and held her still. "Okay, Tina, we'll go home." His tone went low with emphasis. *"We'll* go home." Ignoring her gasp of outrage, he released her arms only to capture her hand inside his own. Striding along once again, this time toward home, he pulled her along with him.

Even with the long stride Tina possessed, there was no way she could match Dirk's loping gait. Impelled into a trot to keep up with him, she was robbed of the breath necessary to vent her anger and frustration at him. By the time they had traversed the few blocks to her house, Tina was panting from exertion and seething with fury. Presenting a composed exterior to Beth Harkness was one of the most difficult things Tina had ever done in her life.

"You two back already?" Beth smiled in surprise when Tina was practically flung into the living room by a less than gentle shove at the back of her waist.

"We decided to come home for dinner," Dirk informed the older woman tersely.

Beth's smile vanished. "Oh, dear! I've already cleared everything away—not that there was all that much to clear away." Her shoulders moved in a helpless shrug. "I wasn't very hungry." Laying aside the large lap rug she was knitting, Beth moved to get to her feet.

"Don't get up." Dirk's gently voiced order arrested Beth's movement. "We can help ourselves. Can't we, Ms. Merritt?" He slanted a warning glance at Tina.

"Yes, of course," Tina responded, somehow managing a smile for the other woman. "Is there any of that soup left from lunch?"

"Yes, it's in the plastic container on the top shelf of the fridge." Beth frowned. "Oh, Miss Merritt," she murmured reproachfully, "why didn't you tell me who you were?" Before Tina could reply, she moaned, "And I charged you rent!"

Tina shot a glance of sheer rage at Dirk before crossing the room to Beth. "I guess I was too surprised," she admitted candidly. "I expected to find the house empty." As Beth continued to frown, Tina added softly, "I might add that receiving such a warm welcome was a very pleasant surprise . . . and I'm still Tina," she chided gently.

"Of course she's still Tina," Dirk drawled from right behind her, his nearness causing a tremor along her spine. "And now Tina and I are going to raid the fridge." Curling his arm around her waist, he drew her close to his hard, warm length. "Come on, kid, let's dump some food into you." Tina smothered a gasp as he slid his hand over her hip. "We've got to fatten this gal up, Beth," he tossed over his shoulder as he led Tina toward the kitchen. "She feels like a bag of Tinkertoys."

"We'll do our best, Dirk." Beth's delighted laughter followed them out of the room.

Tina wasn't laughing; she was hanging on to her temper by sheer willpower. The instant they were out of Beth's sight and hearing, Tina pulled away from Dirk's encircling hold.

"Tinkertoys?" Tina hissed, swinging away. "You—"

"Can it, honey." Dirk cut her off with a chuckle. "You're skinny, kid. It's as simple as that."

On the point of opening the refrigerator door, Tina spun to glare at him. "I am not skinny," she snapped, planting her hands on her hips aggressively. "I'm svelte."

Dirk's chuckle grew into full-throated laughter. "Call it what you will." Walking to her, he brushed her hands from her hips and grasped them with his own. "You still feel skinny to me." Although Tina stiffened with resistance, he drew her rigid body into contact with the angular contours of his. "Very exciting," he whispered, his smile fading. "I actually like the sensation of being prodded by your pelvic bones."

Against her will, against her simmering anger, against all common sense, Tina's heartbeat kicked into high gear. Her sense of self-preservation urged her to protest this intimacy, to step away from him and ridicule the fire of passion flaring in his eyes. Staring into the heat of that passion, Tina's breathing became shallow as she slipped beyond protest. Feeling her skin grow warm from the blaze in his eyes, she watched, mesmerized, as Dirk lowered his head to hers.

Chapter Three

Dirk's kiss was everything Tina remembered—and much, much more.

Drowning in the sweetness of his persuasive mouth, Tina sighed and parted her lips to the searing probe of his tongue. As she softened against him, Dirk slid his hands from her hips to imprison her within the tight circle of his arms, crushing her to his chest with a growl in his throat.

"Tina."

Tina felt more than heard the aching sound of her name groaned into her mouth and, at the same time, felt a liquid flame race wildly through her veins. Oh, Lord, she wanted him. And the wanting was as much of heaven as she ever hoped to know, and more of hell than she ever wished to experience.

Tina knew, somewhere deep inside, that she had to stop him, and she would, soon . . . but first, she had to taste him, just this once.

Curling her arms around Dirk's strong neck, she drank as greedily from his mouth as he did from hers, thrilling to the shudder of responsive need that shook his long body. Clinging to him a moment longer, Tina parried the urgent thrust of his tongue, then dipped daintily with her own. When the restless movement of his hands brushed the outer curve of her breasts, Tina broke free of his arms and ran for the safety of the stairs and her room.

Locking the door behind her, Tina slumped back against it, dragging deep, sobbing breaths into her chest. Slowly, testingly, she glided the tip of her tongue over her kiss-bruised lips, yearning for more of him.

"Tina." Dirk's soft call from the other side of the door sent a chill to mingle with the heat in her veins. "Open the door, love. We've got to talk."

No. No. Moving her head back and forth on the solid barrier between them, Tina closed her eyes and mind to the entreaty in his voice. Dirk's use of that particular endearment again quenched the blaze his kiss had ignited.

"Tina!" Though still soft, Dirk's tone had taken on the edge of impatience. "Open this door."

"No." This time Tina said the word aloud, if in a strained whisper.

Even so, Dirk heard her. Cursing softly, he rattled the doorknob. "Honey, come on! You haven't eaten. Come have supper with me."

Supper? Sure. He wanted *her* for supper! Biting her lip, Tina shook her head more fiercely. "I'm not hungry," she declared truthfully. "Go away, Dirk. I'm not going to unlock the door." Pushing herself away from the door, she straightened her shoulders. "I'll talk to you tomorrow . . . maybe."

"What do you mean, maybe?" Dirk snapped angrily. "You can't hide in your room forever, Tina." There was a pause. Then, his voice menacing, he warned, "And don't even think of running back to New York during the night, because this time I'll come after you." He paused again. "I mean it, Tina. If you run I'll find you, wherever you go to hide. You're not a kid anymore." Dirk lowered his voice, pitching it so she could hear him while Beth, downstairs, could not. "I want you, and I'm going to have you. Even if it means following you straight to hell."

Beginning to shiver, Tina clasped her upper arms, hugging herself as she stared at the door. After a moment, cursing again, Dirk strode purposefully down the hall.

This time I'll come after you. Hearing his promise reverberate inside her head, Tina walked to the window and sank onto the brightly patterned cushion on the white wicker chair placed to one side of it.

You're not a kid anymore. A kid. Tina swallowed in an attempt to dislodge the lump of emotion in her throat. It seemed like forever since she'd been a kid. Closing her eyes, she conjured a picture of the kid she'd been—the kid Dirk had indulged more than he ever had his own younger sister.

Tina could hardly remember a time when Dirk had not been around. Yet she knew that he'd first come onto her scene the summer she was five years old and he was fourteen. Tina had fallen into a very bad case of hero worship that summer. Her hero had been Dirk. She had never really fallen out of it.

Smiling sadly, Tina sent her mind skipping down memory lane in much the same manner she had skipped along that summer she was five. In point of fact, she'd been skipping around the kitchen table as her mother prepared lunch when her father entered the room, a tall, gangly, towheaded boy trailing at his heels.

"Here's Dirk . . . finally, Pam." George Holden drew the youth forward to meet his wife.

Eyes wide with awe, Tina stared up at the young man who, at least to her eyes, looked like the Prince Charming in her picture book.

"How do you do, Mrs. Holden?" Dirk said very formally, sticking out a bony right hand to grasp hers.

A gentle smile played on Pam's lips. "I'm very well, thank you," she replied softly. "And delighted to, as George correctly put it, finally meet you." Her smile grew wide. "I've heard many good things about you, Dirk."

"And you're as beautiful as Mr. Holden claimed!" Dirk blurted, a red stain flushing his cheeks. "Ah, I mean . . ."

"Don't be embarrassed." Pam laughed softly. "It's very nice to hear that George still thinks I'm attractive after all these years."

"I think you'll always be beautiful," Dirk responded with quiet dignity.

"Didn't I tell you this boy was something else?" George laughed heartily. "And this little imp here"—he reached out to draw Tina to his side—"is our Tina." Parental pride was evident in his tone.

"Hello, Tina," Dirk said soberly, shaking her little hand as formally as he had Pam's.

It was at that moment that Tina had fallen in love.

Dirk was invited to lunch and accepted readily. Pulling out the chair next to Tina's, he kidded, "I'll sit beside scrawny here."

At Tina's stricken face, Pam consoled, "Don't fret love, you're merely growing faster than your weight can keep up with. I'm sure Dirk was only teasing." Lifting her hand, Pam smoothed her palm over Tina's one long braid. "You're going to be a real beauty someday."

"And then I'll marry you." Grinning boyishly, Dirk yanked on her braid.

The terribly heartbreaking thing was, Tina had believed him.

From that day on Dirk seemed to become a permanent fixture around Tina's home, at least during the summer months. From the Saturday before Memorial Day until the day after Labor Day, he spent more time at the Holden house than he did at his own parents' summer home a block and a half away. For Tina, Dirk became friend, brother, protector, and knight in shining armor all wrapped up in one tall, lanky frame.

That first summer, his already broad hand holding the padded seat securely, Dirk taught Tina how to balance and ride a two wheeler without training wheels. Subsequent summers brought lessons in swimming, body-surfing, sailing, kite-flying, and fishing from a pier and from a deep-sea boat.

The rest of the year, except for Christmas, which always arrived with a gift under the tree for her from him, Tina heard nothing from Dirk—not a card, not a note, not a telephone call. When, during the course of that first winter, Tina became moody because of Dirk's lack of communication, her father had drawn her onto his lap, stroking her hair as he explained the circumstances of Dirk's life.

"You probably won't understand all this," George began, correctly. "You see, honey, Dirk's winter months are very busy and full, much more so than the average boy of his age."

Being a normal five and a half, Tina had gazed up at him owlishly. "Why?" she demanded sulkily.

"Well, for one, he attends a private school instead of a public school like most of the children you know." George tickled her under her chin in an attempt to tease her out of the blue devils. "He is very bright, you know."

Well, of course, Tina had known that. Her hero was the smartest person in her world . . . at least *she* thought he was. Tina nodded solemnly.

"His daddy owns a bank in Wilmington and, even at the age of fourteen, Dirk is being trained to take over for his father someday." At that point George smiled in a way that meant nothing to Tina, but would have conveyed empathy to a more mature person. "Summertime is the only time Dirk has to be young," he continued with a sigh. "And I know he wanted very badly to play football," he'd gone on softly, before smiling down at her. "Oh, well, I'm sure Dirk's father knows what he's doing."

"Indeed!"

It was the unusual acerbic note in Pam's tone that drew Tina's glance to her mother, not the meaning behind the single word she'd spoken. There would be many years after that January evening before Tina would come to understand the brief conversation that had followed between her parents.

"Now, Pam," George cautioned mildly. "Howard Tanger is a fine man, and he's been a very good friend to me, as you well know." His smile was tender, as it always was for Pam. "Where do you think I'd be today if it hadn't been for Howard?"

"Really, George," Pam scolded gently, "I know and understand the esteem you have for Howard. And your loyalty is commendable, but—"

"But—without Howard, I'd still be working for someone else," George interrupted gently.

Pam sighed. "All right, yes, the man was the only banker with enough faith in your idea to approve a loan for you to start your own business, but I will not accept the premise that you would be a failure today if it weren't for him!" She

held up a dainty hand when he would have interrupted again.
"No, dear, let me finish. It might have taken you longer
without Howard, but you would eventually have found a way
to start the business. As to Dirk"—Pam sighed more
deeply—"he's everything you wanted in a son." Her voice
trailed to a faint whisper. "The son I couldn't give you."

"Darling, don't." George would have jumped to his feet
to go to her had he not been holding Tina. "You know I
wouldn't have traded you for half a dozen sons."

"Yes, I do know." Pam smiled brightly. "And now you
have Dirk, at least from June until the beginning of September. It simply saddens me that the boy has only three short
months every year to *be* a boy. Childhood is such a short
period of time as it is, and he's missing it!"

As nothing her parents were talking about made any sense
at all to Tina, she had chosen that moment to fall asleep on
her father's lap, still missing her new friend Dirk.

Winter wore on, but as summer always does, it came again
to the seaside town, and with it came Dirk, a little taller but
as gangly as before. And so the years of their childhood spun
out, more quickly for Dirk than for Tina. And with each
successive summer, the changes were noted as to wintertime-
acquired height and filling out, again more quickly for Dirk
than Tina.

For Tina, the memories of summer were precious gems to
be hoarded more greedily than any miser ever hoarded his
gold—for Tina the memories *were* pure gold.

Gold! The noise Tina made deep in her throat was part
sob, part derisive snort. On closer inspection, the gold proved
to be cheap spray paint that had chipped away badly over
the last four years, Tina thought tiredly.

Shivering with a chill that had more to do with her mental
sojourn than the wind rising outside the window, Tina stood
up stiffly, then froze. The footsteps coming along the polished hardwood hallway were not really heavy, yet not light
enough to be those of Beth Harkness. In the seconds the
steps paused outside her door, Tina ceased to breathe. The
ragged breath that eased past her lips when the steps resumed

again hurt her chest, and her heart. At the soft click of a door closing across the hall, Tina sighed and switched on her bedside lamp. It was safe for her to get ready for bed now: Dirk had retired for the night. Scooping her nightgown from the foot of the bed and her robe from the narrow closet, she inched open her door, then crept along the hall to the bathroom. Five minutes later she scurried back into her room, locked the door, and dove under the covers, switching the light off even as she burrowed into the warmth of the down-filled comforter that covered the bed.

By the time Tina finally fell into a fitful slumber hours later, the comforter was a tangled mass around her slender body, and her eyelashes fanned over smudges of exhaustion under her eyes.

Sometime during the morning a ringing phone drew Tina partially from the depths of the deep sleep she'd drifted into after bouts of lighter, dream-disturbed rest. For some time after the ringing stopped, she hovered in that dark tunnel between wakefulness and sleep. She was sinking into the arms of peace again when she dreamed she felt gentle fingers smoothing errant strands of tousled hair from her temple and brow and heard a soft, familiar voice close to her ear.

"Don't run away. Please, wait for me, love," the dream voice pleaded. "This time, wait for me."

When Tina woke fully, it was on the heavy side of mid-morning. Her eyes still closed sleepily, she frowned. There was a strangeness here, but what was it? The muted, mournful cry of a sea gull turned the frown to a wistful smile; she was home, not in the apartment above the crowded streets of New York City.

Dirk.

The smile faded and Tina closed her eyes again. She would have to leave, go back to the city and the shop; she simply could not deal with Dirk in the state she was in.

But would Dirk let her go? The question nagged at the edge of Tina's mind as she pushed herself from the tangled comforter and made her way to the bathroom.

As she bathed, Tina recalled Dirk's warning the night before. A prickling sensation ran down her spine as her mind replayed the low, intense sound of his voice.

I want you, and I'm going to have you. Even if it means following you straight to hell.

Dirk had meant what he'd said, and Tina knew he'd meant it. She also knew precisely what he'd meant by it.

Beginning to shiver, she stepped out of the old-fashioned tub, firmly assuring herself the tremor coursing through her was caused by revulsion and *not* anticipation.

Catching sight of her reflection in the medicine-cabinet mirror, Tina frowned at the shimmer of excitement flaring in her sherry-brown eyes.

"Grow up, you fool!"

The reflection blinked at the scathing sound of the advice she muttered aloud.

"If you want to commit emotional suicide, there has got to be a better way to do it than through Dirk Tanger!"

Tearing her gaze from the mirror, Tina quickly dried herself, shrugged into her robe, and after carefully scanning the hallway, dashed back to the relative safety of her room.

Tina was midway to the bed where she'd laid out her clothes when she stopped short, a puzzled expression stealing over her face. The day had progressed to within striking distance of noon . . . why was the house so very quiet? Was she alone in the house?

Her curiosity aroused, Tina dressed in lacy underwear, a deep pink, cowl-necked sweater that should have clashed with her dark red hair but didn't, and jeans. After putting on her boots, she punished her unruly mane with a brush; then, her face free of makeup, she descended the curving staircase slowly, warily searching for Dirk.

At the bottom of the stairs she glanced around; the house did indeed appear deserted. The aroma of freshly brewed coffee told her it wasn't.

Feeling ridiculously like a child again, Tina tiptoed through the dining room to the kitchen, steeling herself for the sight of her nemesis.

"Whatever are you doing?" Standing at the refrigerator,

Beth tilted her head and leveled a quizzical look at Tina. "Why are you pussyfooting through the house? You don't need to worry about waking anyone. You're the last one up."

Her cheeks growing pink with embarrassment, Tina sighed with relief at finding Beth alone in the room. "I. . . ah . . . didn't know," she said lamely. "It was so quiet, I thought perhaps Dirk was still asleep."

Beth chuckled. "Heavens, Tina, he's been gone for hours."

Tina sauntered into the room with her more usual loose stride. "Gone?" she repeated, almost afraid to hope. "Gone where?"

"Back to Wilmington." Taking a carton of orange juice from the fridge, Beth closed the door, then glanced at Tina, shaking her head. "Poor dear, and he only arrived late yesterday. I don't believe that man has had a vacation in three years."

"Really?" Trying to sound and look casually interested, Tina dropped into a chair. The odd sinking inside couldn't be caused by disappointment . . . could it? Lifting a slender hand, Tina flipped her hair back over her shoulder in a defiant gesture; of course she wasn't disappointed. Dismissing the strange hollow feeling, she forced her concentration on what Beth was saying.

". . . And he works so hard too." Beth was now at the slate-topped counter next to the sink, pouring orange juice into a delicate-looking stemmed glass. "Did you hear the phone ringing this morning?" Her eyebrows arched as she set the glass in front of Tina.

"Umm." Tina sipped at the juice before murmuring, "Vaguely."

Beth smiled understandingly. "Sleep is rarely restful the first night away from home." Moving with what Tina was beginning to recognize as her normal briskness, she crossed to the stove. "Now, what would you like for breakfast?"

Information. Tina bit back the response. If she was patient, maybe, just maybe, Beth would get around to telling her why Dirk had left so precipitously.

"I'm not really much of a breakfast person." Tilting the

glass, she finished the juice. "Toast will be fine." Rising with a fluid grace that was both unconscious and natural, she carried the glass to the sink.

Beth ran an assessing glance over Tina's too slender form. "It seems to me you're not much of an *any* meal person," she chided gently. "Tina, I really think you should eat something substantial. You have an absolutely fragile look." Beth smiled coaxingly. "I have waffle batter all ready to pour into the iron and, if I do say so myself, I make heavenly waffles." Her eyes twinkled. "There's blueberry sauce to top it off with."

"Hot blueberry sauce?" Tina's mouth actually watered; she hadn't had waffles with hot blueberry sauce in ages.

"Hot blueberry sauce," Beth concurred with a grin, sensing a victory.

"Sold." Tina grinned back.

Awash in a pool of buttery-colored sunlight, Tina savored every bite of the berry-drenched light-as-all-made-from-scratch waffles. Her fork spearing through the last small piece, she mopped up the remaining sauce before popping it into her mouth.

"Oh, Lord," she moaned, sipping at the coffee Beth had set in front of her. "That was so good." Gazing at Beth, Tina smiled. "I don't suppose you'd consider coming back to New York with me, would you?" she asked hopefully.

Although she shook her head, Beth flushed with pleasure. "I couldn't do that. Dirk would have a fit!" Refilling Tina's cup, she chided, "Especially after he practically ordered me to find a way to get some food into you."

Tina's pulses leaped. With anger, she assured herself, staring at Beth with eyes widened with incredulity.

"Dirk did . . . what?"

"Asked me to at least try to get you to eat," Beth replied complacently.

Tina shook her head in confusion. "When?"

"This morning, before he left." Beth flashed a smile as she poured a cup of coffee for herself. "While *he* was mopping up the sauce with his last piece of waffle."

Ridiculous as she knew it was, Tina felt a glow of pleasure

at the idea that she and Dirk had enjoyed the same breakfasts. The glow was short-lived as she ruthlessly asked herself, So what? Curiosity finally getting the better of her, Tina asked, too offhandedly, "Why did Dirk have to cut short his first vacation in years?" Try as she might, she didn't succeed in keeping her tone free of sarcasm. Beth's startled expression caused a twinge of remorse in Tina's conscience. Watch your mouth, her better self warned. It's not Beth's fault you detest the man; *she* obviously adores the beast.

"That phone call this morning was from his secretary," Beth explained in a tone that conveyed consternation. "It seems that some sort of a deal that was simmering on a back burner came to a boil sooner than expected." Her shoulders lifted in a helpless shrug. "He had to go back, since he's the president of the bank, you know."

Oh, yes, Tina grimaced inwardly. *She* knew better than most. President and controlling stockholder. Tina swallowed an unladylike, disdainful snort.

"Yes, I know," she managed to reply with commendable calm. "Too bad his deal cooked over at the start of his vacation." How very like Beth to equate business with what she knew best, Tina thought with amusement.

"Yes, well." Beth sighed. "That's the way it goes. Dirk did say he'd be back, though."

As Beth had offered that tidbit while she was rising from the table, she missed the spasm of shock that shuddered through Tina's slight frame. Her haunted gaze following the older woman's progress to the sink, she moistened her suddenly dry lips.

"He did?" she asked carefully.

"Mm, hmm." Beth turned to smile at her. "Left a message for you too."

"What . . . sort of message?" No amount of applied willpower could keep the wary note from Tina's voice.

"Dirk said you were to rest and eat to build up your strength for when he returns." The smile Beth gave Tina was beautiful, and innocent. "He must be planning something exciting for the two of you."

Exciting? Oh, God! Tina shivered in the warmth of the fall sunshine. Dirk's message was equivalent to a declaration of war.

Run!

The command screamed through Tina's mind as she stared at Beth with deceptive composure. Where could she run to that Dirk would not eventually find her? Not for an instant did Tina even try to convince herself that Dirk's warning of the night before had been issued capriciously; he had been serious. Whatever his reason, Dirk was determined on a course of action. And *she* was the target at the end of that course.

Suddenly feeling crowded and stifled in the large room, Tina jumped to her feet. "I think I'll take a walk," she said with forced brightness. Starting for the door, she paused as her glance skimmed the dishes in the sink. "Oh, would you like help with the dishes?" she asked contritely.

"Tina!" Beth laughed. "Let's not get things confused here. I work for you, remember? I get paid for doing the dishes." She made a small, shooing motion with her hand. "Go drink in some fresh sea air, it just might give you an appetite for dinner." She favored Tina with her pixieish grin. "I'm preparing chicken and dumplings. That should put a little meat on your bones."

Hands jammed into her jacket pockets, Tina strolled the quiet streets of her childhood, the familiarity of it all tugging on her memory and emotions.

Much like any tourist in a city, but without the usual guidebook in hand, she wandered about, up one street then down another, falling in love with her hometown all over again.

Standing across the street from the stately Chalfonte Hotel, Tina chuckled aloud as whispers from the past tickled her memory. The chuckle faded to a loving smile as her gaze caressed the ornate Italian style of the town's oldest hotel, which had always made Tina think of New Orleans for some reason.

Steeped deeply in the past, her own and the town's, Tina continued her stroll through memory's byways.

There was the Queen Victoria, as regal-looking as ever. And over there The Mainstay Inn, Cape May's Victorian mansion. Oh, how she loved each and every one of the town's beautifully restored homes in the historic district. But as deeply as the old structures touched her, there was an even older love that lured Tina. Having paid due homage to the town, she turned her steps to the sea.

For some time Tina ambled along the long promenade, filling her lungs with the tangy sea air, and her senses with the lost and lonely cry of the gulls. At that moment Tina felt in complete empathy with the swooping sea birds. Only civilization's veneer kept her from issuing a lost and lonely cry of her own.

Turning her back on the imposing old hotels and newer motels that were strung out like jewels along Beach Avenue, Tina loped down the steps to the beach and the swishy siren call of the ocean.

The tide was out, revealing a width of sand that Tina quickly crossed. Walking along the edge of the foaming surf, she tried to visualize the bygone activities that had taken place on the broad strand. How often, she mused, had she heard the tale of how Henry Ford and Louis Chevrolet, among many others, had raced their cars on the then-wide beaches? Or of the sailing sloops and later the steamers that had journeyed from Philadelphia, New York, Baltimore, and Washington full of summer visitors? On reflection, Tina humorously wished she had a dollar for every time she'd heard those and a host of other turn-of-the-century stories.

And all the stories, all the sights and sounds, and the ever-restless, ever-mesmerizing sea added up to one irrefutable fact: Tina was home.

And home, to Tina, meant Dirk. A less palatable, but irrefutable, fact.

A bittersweet smile played along Tina's suddenly vulnerable-looking lips. Feeling her lower lip beginning to tremble, she caught it between her teeth.

If nothing else, Dirk had been correct about one thing, Tina thought tiredly. She most assuredly did need to rest, and very likely needed several good solid meals to fortify her. In truth, she couldn't remember ever feeling quite so tired before.

But were a few days of rest and food enough fortification for the clash of wills she knew was coming? Somehow Tina doubted it.

The chill that permeated Tina's entire body had little to do with the November air or the cold ocean spray that set her dark red hair shimmering with tiny beads of moisture. Even so, Tina chose to believe it did. Walking at an angle, she scuffed through the sand toward the promenade, but instead of remounting the steps, she leaned against a huge supporting boulder in much the same way Dirk had the previous afternoon.

Had coming back here been a mistake? Sighing, Tina raised her face to the westering sun. This place, and its special ambiance, held far too many memories for her, both good and bad.

Yes, perhaps coming home had been a mistake. What she needed was time to regroup her strengths, shore up her weaknesses, and gird herself for the battle that was approaching as surely as sunset.

Here, in this town where she had laughed and cried and come early to the emotion of innocent adoration, Tina felt her chances of winning were cut by half. And the biggest undermining factor was the object of that youthful adoration, Dirk himself.

Her own inner speculation startled Tina into awareness. What in the world was she thinking of? she berated herself. The time of naive hero worship was long since past. The braided Tina was no longer alive. She had emerged from the chrysalis a sleek, independent businesswoman. Yesterday could not hurt her, it was tomorrow that held danger.

Pushing her lethargic body erect, Tina walked up the steps to the promenade, then down the ramp to the street. As the road was practically devoid of traffic, she crossed against the light, grinning at a patrolman who called to her to be careful.

Run. The earlier panic came back to tease her mind. Lifting her head, Tina thrust out her delicately formed chin. Run? Ha! No way! She had a business to save from financial ruin. And what promised to be a battle royal with the only man who could help her save that business was yet to be faced.

Tina unconsciously straightened her spine as she walked. She had worked damned hard for her shop. And nothing, nobody, was going to take it from her—not even the overbearing, arrogant Dirk Tanger.

As she turned the corner onto her street, Tina decided that whatever she had to do, she'd do, but save the shop she would.

Chapter Four

In a conference room rich with the gleaming patina of dark wood and expensive plush carpeting, Dirk sat unmoving in a leather curved-arm chair.

His hands resting lightly on the smooth table, his features set into austere lines, Dirk's sapphire-bright gaze was fixed on the middle-aged businessman who was presenting his request for a large loan to save his company from a takeover.

To the rest of the men at the long conference table, Dirk's concentration appeared as usual: unnervingly direct. The rest of the gentlemen at the table would have been shocked out of their staid minds if they knew Dirk's thoughts.

She's going to run. In fact, she's probably on her way to New York right now—if she hasn't arrived there already. Dammit! Why did this takeover panic have to come to a head today?

Revealing nothing of his inner turmoil, Dirk tuned the older man's voice out, fully aware that he was going to grant the loan. His eyes as clear as a bottomless blue pool, Dirk stared at the man sightlessly.

So, the very elegant, very independent Ms. Tina Holden Merritt needed money, did she? Blasting angry and ready for war, is she? Absolutely detests Dirk Tanger, does she? How very interesting.

Catching a smile of satisfaction before it reached his uncompromisingly straight lips, Dirk savored the warmth of the smile as it curled and wended its way through his taut body.

He would go after her, of course. Hadn't he warned her that he would? The thought of the chase turned the curl of satisfaction to a wave of heat. For a moment, Dirk found it difficult to remain motionless in his chair.

This time, you fool, don't let her get away from you! Dirk chastised himself mercilessly. If you had kept your head together five years ago, she never would have rushed into the avaricious arms of that—that *user*. She was yours, and you let her slip away. Don't make the same mistake again.

His gaze riveted to the man speaking across the table from him, Dirk made himself a solemn promise. If he had to follow Tina halfway around the world, if he had to force her to do things his way, he would do it. Nothing was going to stand in his way this time. Not his conscience. Not her antipathy for him. Nothing.

Groaning with repletion, Tina sat back in the kitchen chair and lifted her coffee cup in a salute to Beth.

"Oh, Beth, that meal was fabulous! I believe you whipped those dumplings out of clouds and air." Relaxed, Tina sipped her coffee. "And that sour-cream salad dressing is delicious. I feel as if I've gained five pounds!"

"I seriously doubt it." Beth's sparkling eyes belied her dry tone. "But I'm glad you enjoyed it. Cooking for one gets pretty boring." Beth beamed at Tina. "Now, how about dessert?"

"Dessert!" Tina exclaimed, shaking her head. "I'd absolutely explode!" Her voice softened, coaxingly. "Are you sure you wouldn't like to come back to New York with me?"

"Yes, Tina, I'm sure." Beth chuckled, and pinked like a young girl. "But thank you anyway. It's always nice to hear compliments."

The two women were quiet for several minutes, savoring the rich-bodied flavor of the coffee. As she refilled their cups, Beth gave Tina a quizzical look. "What do you do in New York, Tina?" Before Tina could reply, she added, "If you're not, you should be a model."

Tina's soft laughter danced around the quiet room. "I'm not a model, Beth. I own and operate a salon."

"A beauty salon?"

"Well, sort of," Tina explained, "but not exactly. It's more like a spa, but not exactly that, either."

Beth's expression drew laughter from Tina. "Well goodness! What exactly is it then?"

"I suppose you could call it a combination of the two," Tina replied with a slight shrug. "We offer all the services of both, from a simple haircut to a personal detailed fitness program. The name of the shop is The Total Person, and that's what we cater to—for women, men, and children." Tina smiled. "We even have individual sessions on fashion."

"Very expensive?" Beth teased.

Again Tina's laugh lit up the room. "Of course! I employ some of the best in all the various fields: cosmetology, physical fitness, and fashion." Her laughter faded to a soft smile. "I have one stylist who can do the most fantastic things with the most problematic head of hair." Tina's voice was tinged with awe. "I swear, Paul is a stylistic genius!"

"A man?" Beth looked skeptical.

"Oh, yes." Tina chuckled. "Very definitely a man."

"How intriguing," Beth said interestedly. "In fact, I find the whole idea of your salon intriguing. Tell me more."

Beth's request was like dangling a carrot in front of a race horse. Tina happily lunged at the bait. All through the kitchen clean-up routine, Tina expounded on the whys and wherefores of how she'd conceived and then executed her idea for the salon. The only thing Tina didn't tell Beth was that, unless she could pry her money out of Dirk, the reality was doomed to fade into never-never land.

Tina and Beth spent the remainder of the evening quietly in the comfortable Victorian-decorated living room. While Beth's knitting needles clicked away at an amazing rate of speed, Tina sat engrossed in a recently published book on nutrition.

Having slept restlessly the night before, Tina was smothering yawns midway through the eleven o'clock news on the

small television set that was neatly concealed inside a delicate cabinet with beveled-glass doors when not in use.

"I'm for bed," Tina declared, giving up the effort of keeping her eyes open.

"You'll miss the weather forecast," Beth observed teasingly.

"Hmm." Getting to her feet, Tina stretched her long, lim-
ber body. "I'll stick my head out the window tomorrow
morning." She yawned again. "That method is more accurate
anyway."

Beth's commiserating laugh followed Tina as she slowly
mounted the curved staircase, her hand trailing loosely along
the polished wood banister. Within minutes of entering her
room, she was crawling under the cocooning comforter, no
longer making even a token attempt to cover her yawn. Settling onto the welcoming mattress, Tina closed her eyes
wearily . . . and suddenly found herself wide awake.

After shifting restlessly for a few minutes, she threw the
covers back and slid out of bed, deciding the room was air-
less and stuffy. Crossing to the window, she ran the shade
up, flipped back the latch, and opened the window a few
inches, drawing deep gulps of sea air into her chest.

The room quickly lost its stuffiness; Tina quickly lost her
desire to sleep altogether. Sighing, she drifted back to the
bed, burrowing her cold feet under the covers.

Now what?

Lacing her hands behind her head, Tina stared at the ceiling. She was tired, extremely tired, yet her mind raced at a
speed that obstructed sleep. Her problem was that she didn't
want to examine the subject her mind raced with. Frowning
into the darkness, Tina tested the name of her nemesis on
her tongue. "Dirk."

What did he want with her? Tina's lips twisted wryly. Well,
of course she knew *what* he wanted! The question was, Why?
And why now? For, other than two abrasive meetings, she'd
had no contact with him for five long years. They had both
married during that time. The twist to her lips grew bitter.

She had no idea what had gone wrong with Dirk's married life, but she knew what had interfered with hers.

The grating noise of Tina's teeth grinding together sounded loud in the quiet bedroom. If it hadn't been for Dirk's obstinacy, she would still be married to Chuck.

Indeed? Tina winced at the nagging, ridiculing nudge from her conscience. Well, she temporized, perhaps the failure of her marriage wasn't *all* Dirk's fault. But his firm refusals to release her funds had certainly contributed greatly to it.

And Chuck's other women? her conscience persisted. Tina's soft sigh betrayed a sense of an inadequacy she would never reveal to anyone else. Squirming in discomfort caused more by her thoughts than the awkward position she was lying in, Tina clamped her lips against a cry of despair. Why? Why? What had she lacked, how had she failed Chuck so very badly that he sought comfort with other women?

Was she too strong? Too weak? Too outgoing? Too retiring? Had she laughed too often? Too little? Had she disappointed him both emotionally and physically? Had she failed to fill his needs?

But what about her needs?

Tina closed her lids over the hot moisture welling in her eyes. Didn't her needs count? If Chuck had felt unfulfilled he had certainly not been alone!

While Tina had looked forward to recreating the same type of homey atmosphere she had grown up in, Chuck had insisted on an exorbitantly priced showplace, a frame for his spectacular good looks. While she had hoped for intimate evenings at home, with quiet dinners and communicative conversation, he had demanded bright lights and hordes of flashy people. But in the final analysis, Tina's biggest shock came when she finally pinned Chuck down to a discussion about children. She admitted to longing for at least two, ideally a boy and a girl. Chuck laughed in her face. Tina was sure she'd remember his taunt for the rest of her life.

"Children! Are you serious?" Chuck had actually sneered. "Procreation is for the middle-class mentality. The last thing I want is even one of the little brats cluttering up my life."

What an absolute fool she'd been to allow Chuck to sweep her off her feet and into a whirlwind marriage. As is usually the case when one acts on impulse, Tina found the product fell far short of its gorgeous outer wrapping. Besides which, Chuck had been an unimaginative if not downright lousy lover.

Of course, Tina had had only one previous encounter on which to base a comparison. Dirk.

Tina's head moved reflexively in denial of the memory that rose to torment her. No, she would not think of it! She could not bear to think of it. She was simply too vulnerable now, too tired, too burnt out. Curling into a ball of misery, Tina erected a mental roadblock against the memory of Dirk and that beautiful afternoon they had shared.

Love's young dream! An impressionable teenager's romanticizing of a very basic physical act, Tina chastised herself ruthlessly.

Bitter laughter shattered the midnight peace of the bedroom. Rejection at any age is emotionally demeaning; at nineteen it had been traumatic. In sheer self-defense, Tina had pushed the incident out of her conscious mind for a long time.

Now here it was, back to torment her, undermine her anger and hatred, and make her burn for him all over again.

Unaware of the tears that ran down her flushed cheeks, Tina clenched her hands, viciously digging her nails into her palms in an attempt to neutralize one pain by the infliction of another.

"Oh, damn you, Dirk Tanger." The muffled cry sliced through the night and Tina's heart. For, damn him as she often had—and would again—the truth was as undeniable as the pulse that beat through her bloodstream: she loved him.

"I won't love him!" Angrily.

"I don't want to love him!" Rebelliously.

"He doesn't love me." Despairingly.

Exposed, the wound throbbed and bled in the form of hot tears. Her face turned to the pillow, she sobbed herself to sleep like an abandoned child.

Tina woke to the pervading chill of an early morning mist

creeping on gray padded feet through the open window, and the ever-present soulful calls of the gulls. Her own emotions echoing the cries, she dragged her tired body from the bed, moaning a protest as she caught her reflection in the cheval mirror that stood near the wall opposite the bed.

Walking slowly to the glass, she peered at her reflection, frowning at the telltale signs of too many restless nights.

"Exercise, and plenty of it," she murmured to the pale face staring back at her. "That's what you need, my friend."

Still clad in the short pullover nightie, Tina moved fluidly into her warm-up routine, stretching and bending to wake up her muscles. After half an hour of the workout, she dressed in jogging pants and jacket, socks and running shoes, and put a terry sweatband around her forehead. After leaving her room, she made a quick stop in the bathroom to scrub her teeth and splash cold water on her face. Then, draping a towel around her neck, she ran lightly down the stairs and out the front door, heading for the beach with the determination of a lemming.

Arms loose at her sides, elbows bent, Tina shook her hands lightly as she jogged at an easy pace to the promenade. Standing on the walkway, she drew deep drafts of the misty air into her lungs before skipping down onto the beach.

Once again Tina went through a warm-up of stretching and bending. Once the nighttime kinks loosened, she took off on the packed yet resilient sand near the water.

There were a few hardy souls like herself on the beach, jogging at various speeds from a fast walk to a flat-out dash. Tina, in for the long haul, maintained a steady, rhythmic pace.

She really didn't like to jog; in fact, she loathed it. It hurt. And the longer she ran, the more it hurt. Working like a bellows, her lungs burned and screamed for air, her heart pounded until she thought it would burst from her chest, and she became light-headed. No, Tina did not enjoy running; Tina enjoyed feeling fit. Tina ran, each and every day—as a rule—to stay in shape.

This morning, Tina was paying dearly for laying off the previous two days. What she really wanted was a steaming cup of Beth's coffee. What she was getting was the result of two days laxity. Still, the soles of her shoes beat a regulated slap on the sand. When her mind whispered that with just a tiny bit more effort on her part she could very likely fly, Tina packed it in and went home.

"That you, Tina?" Beth called from the kitchen at the sound of the front door closing.

"Yes," Tina called back from the foot of the stairs.

"Are you ready for breakfast?" Beth came to stand in the doorway to the dining room. At the sight of Tina her eyebrows arched. "Oh. Have you been jogging?"

"I'll say!" Tina rolled her eyes. "Give me ten minutes to shower and dress and I'll be ready to consume anything you put in front of me. I'm starving!"

"Take your time." Beth laughed. "I'm not going anywhere."

Neither am I. The realization flashed into Tina's mind as she dashed up the stairs. She had been working, sometimes nonstop, for so very long, the idea of not having *anything* to do was unsettling.

How in the world was she going to fill up all the hours in the day? Tina wondered, turning her face into the shower spray. Perhaps she could help Beth with some of the housework. In actuality, the responsibility for the property *was* hers. After all, she owned the place.

On reflection, a warm glow of ownership seeped into Tina. Too bad the house was so far away from New York. If it were just a little closer, she could live here and commute. Then it wouldn't matter so very much that she had to give up her apartment.

At the consideration, Tina went still, oblivious to the water cooling as it cascaded over her body. What was she thinking of? she chided herself harshly. She loved her apartment. Hadn't she come here with the firm intention to rest and gear herself for a showdown over money with Dirk? Had she lost sight of her goal after only two days?

Twisting the water faucet off, Tina shook her head sharply. Get your act together, she advised herself grimly, stepping onto the bath mat. Hold fast to your original plan to have the final round with Dirk.

And it's not merely a question of the apartment, remember, Tina continued her silent lecture as she patted her glistening limbs dry. It's your business, the car you loved that you had to give up, all the years of begging for what is yours, and all the years that arrogant man laughed in your face as he turned you down!

Turned you down. The phrase resolved in Tina's mind as she dressed in soft wool slacks and a long-sleeved tailored shirt.

Damn him! Tina stamped her narrow foot into a supple leather boot.

Double damn him! Tina repeated the process with the other foot.

How dare he turn her down? Although Tina refused to examine the exact cause of the fury searing her mind, the issue had grown cloudy. Five years. Five long years, and still it hurt so very badly that Tina masked the pain with fury. But deep inside, where she absolutely would not look, a tiny voice wept with anguish.

Why did he reject me?

If I were a man, I'd beat him up! Uncaring of the childishness of the thought, Tina savored the idea of it as she dried her hair, then brushed it out. Fiery strands crackled with electricity as she stroked the bristles through the shoulder-length mass. Tossing the brush onto the dresser, she met her own stormy eyes in the mirror. The very idea of her administering a thrashing to Dirk brought a rueful smile to Tina's soft, delicate lips, and her sherry eyes lighted with grudging humor.

Okay, scratch the much-needed thrashing, but she'd find a way to make him pay for all the indignities he'd heaped on her over the past five years. Her mouth set in a grim smile, Tina made a silent vow. She'd get Dirk . . . somehow. He'd been leading her on a merry dance long enough. The time had come to pay the fiddler. And in this instance, Tina

Holden Merritt *was* the fiddler . . . and it was her time to call the tune.

Feeling extraordinarily light, as though a weight had lifted from her shoulders, Tina began humming softly to herself as she went down the stairs. She was still humming as she time-stepped into the kitchen.

"Well, how do you do?" Beth smiled. "If jogging has that kind of effect on everyone, maybe I'll take it up myself."

The laughter that rippled from Tina's smooth throat widened the smile on Beth's lips. "Actually, I'm feeling great!" she admitted, the delightful sound of her laughter ringing out again. "Ready to face just about anything . . . or anybody!"

"I'm so pleased." Beth's chest heaved with a sigh of relief. "To tell you the truth, Tina, you looked just about beat to your knees when you arrived here two days ago." Tilting her head, she scrutinized Tina's glowing face. "I know Dirk will be pleased when he gets back. He was very concerned about you, my dear."

Talk about crash landings. Tina came down to earth with a decided bang. Dirk, Dirk, Dirk. All things considered, she was thoroughly sick of hearing his name. With a dismissive shrug, she plopped onto a kitchen chair.

"Dirk is not my keeper, Beth." Though mild, Tina's tone had an edge of impatience to it. "I can't say I care whether or not Dirk is pleased."

In the process of pouring grapefruit juice into a glass, Beth's hand paused in midair as she glanced down at Tina in shock. "But . . . Tina, Dirk is obviously very worried about you," she exclaimed. "And isn't he your guardian or something?"

"No!" Immediately contrite for the sharpness of her tone, Tina bit her lip in vexation. "Beth, I'm sorry." Tina sighed, thinking, good-bye good humor. "Dirk has control of my inheritance until I'm twenty-five, but that's all he has control of."

"But he's so fond of you," Beth protested, chidingly.

"Why, anyone could see that! It's as plain as the nose on your face."

"My nose is plain?" Tina made a weak attempt at changing the topic of conversation. "And here I always thought it was rather patrician."

"Your nose is elegant . . . as are all your features, and you know it." Beth frowned fiercely at Tina. "And don't try getting away from the subject, either. Dirk Tanger is a very nice man." A grin flirted with her thin lips. "Not bad to look at, either."

Wrong. The last thing Dirk is, is not bad to look at, Tina thought exasperatedly. Dirk Tanger is downright devastating. Damn his hide!

Against her will, a picture of her tormentor rose in Tina's mind, burnished-gold hair glinting in the sunlight, sapphire-blue eyes laughing at her, white teeth flashing in a teasing grin. The vivid image sent a sensuous chill tiptoeing the length of her spine.

"Be that as it may," Tina said repressively, whether to herself or Beth was beside the point, "Dirk's attractiveness has nothing to do with it. And I'm not convinced about his concern for me. Dirk looks out for number one—always."

The carton of juice landed on the table with force. "Tina, really! I think you are being terribly unfair. Why, I've known Dirk for over four years now, and he's never been less than a gentleman."

Yes, but then you have no money under his control. Prudently, Tina kept the indictment to herself. Mentally shrugging, she decided to leave the bubble-bursting to Dirk; raining on parades was simply not Tina's style. Holding up her hands in a gesture of surrender, she smile conciliatorily at Beth.

"If I agree that Dirk is definitely a gentleman," she teased, "may I then have some breakfast?"

"Oh, good grief!" Beth went into her bustling routine. "I am sorry. What would you like? Eggs? Pancakes? Swiss breakfast?"

The last suggestion stopped Tina. "Swiss breakfast?" she repeated blankly. "What in the world is that?"

"I can see you've never had breakfast in Atlantic City," Beth retorted.

"I haven't been in Atlantic City since I was twelve," Tina admitted somewhat ruefully. "First because I was too busy getting an education, then starting my business, and later, because I simply couldn't afford taking a chance of gambling away my money." Tina frowned. "But what has that got to do with this Swiss breakfast?"

"I first ate it there," Beth replied. "And I've since concocted my own version." Lifting the carton, she filled the glass in front of Tina. "What I make is pretty close to the original, if I do say so myself."

"I believe you." Tina hid a smile. "But what is it?"

"Oh." Beth grinned sheepishly. "Cold oatmeal."

"Cold oatmeal?" Tina shuddered delicately. "I think I'll pass."

Beth's smile turned smug. "Would you trust me enough to take one taste?" Without waiting for Tina to reply, Beth went to the refrigerator and removed a small dish. On the way back to the table, she scooped a spoon from the cutlery drawer. Dipping the spoon into the cereal, she passed it to Tina, who sampled it very cautiously.

Prepared to hate the stuff, Tina chewed slowly, then an expression of amazement spread over her face. "This is delicious!" she exclaimed in astonishment. "What the devil have you got in there?" Accepting the bowl from Beth, Tina dug in hungrily.

"All good things." Beth smiled serenely. "Bits of pear, peaches, apricots, raisins, and pecans, all mixed together with cream."

"Hmmm," Tina murmured. "Heavenly."

"I thought you'd like it." Beth poured cups of coffee for Tina and herself. "It's one of Dirk's favorites."

Dirk—again! Fortunately, Tina was sliding the last spoonful into her mouth; her appetite went flat. "Then it's too bad he isn't here to enjoy it," she observed diplomatically.

"Yes." Beth sighed. "I was hoping he could return today."

Tina wasn't, but refrained from offering her opinion.

"The man works too hard." Beth's tone held conviction. "Has ever since I've known him."

That did it. Rising, Tina went to the counter where the coffeepot was placed and refilled her cup. The absolute last thing she wanted was a running account of Dirk's virtues. As far as she could ascertain, Dirk had none. Suddenly deciding she needed to talk to her shop manager, she headed for the doorway.

"If you'll excuse me, Beth"—Tina flashed her a smile— "I have to check in with the shop. I'll clear out of your road." Her glance rested on the old-fashioned-style wall phone. "If there's another phone?"

"Oh, yes, of course." Beth waved her hand to indicate the second floor. "There's a mobile phone in Dirk's room, across the hall from you." Just as Tina was gritting her molars, Beth continued, "You can take it into your own room, of course."

Though Tina dreaded having to enter Dirk's bedroom, she did so boldly; after all, it was her house, she assured herself bracingly. The pep talk was not necessary, however, as the room held not a trace of his person or things.

Paul Rambeau answered the phone in the shop on the third ring, which immediately set Tina to wondering where their receptionist was.

"The great Rambeau answering the phone?" Tina asked. "What will people say?"

"People better keep their sayings to themselves," Paul retorted. "Except you, of course. But then, you're not people, you be the boss."

"And I think you be a trifle strange." Tina laughed.

"I can't call to mind a single living soul who'd refute that statement." Paul joined in on Tina's laughter. "What can I do for you, Ms. Employer?"

"Keep your mouth shut for starters." Though mild, Tina's voice conveyed her displeasure.

"Hit me with that again, my pet, you missed the bull's-eye

entirely." Paul's bafflement was genuine. "What am I supposed to have done wrong?"

"I distinctly remember asking you not to tell anyone—like in not a soul—where I was going," Tina said carefully.

There was a pause, then, "And I distinctly remember following your instructions to the letter," Paul shot back. "Which, come to think of it, hasn't been extremely difficult, as there's only been one call to that effect."

"So, how did he know where to find me?"

"The banker? How the hell should I know?" Paul's tone drew a clear picture of his frown for Tina. "Are you telling me he did find you?"

Tina relaxed at the note of sincerity in his voice; she'd hated the idea of Paul's betraying her. "He arrived here mere hours after I did."

"No sh—kidding!" Paul laughed. "That son of a—gun!"

Her sentiments exactly. Tina smiled wryly. Aloud, she probed, "You didn't give him a hint?"

"Honey, I wouldn't give him the time of day," Paul scolded. "You know that."

"I'm sorry, Paul," Tina apologized contritely. "Knowing him, I thought he'd strong-armed you into confessing."

"Over the phone?" Paul laughed. "I'd pay hard-earned money to see that trick!"

Don't be so glib, Tina advised silently, Dirk could probably do it. "Everything going all right there?" She changed the subject. "No problems or anything? Like Janise quitting, maybe?"

"I chased Janise out for a latte for me." Paul smacked his lips loudly. "I'm a sucker for that stuff. And yes, everything's perking along as usual here." His voice lowered with concern. "Will you loosen up, beautiful? You needed this break. Enjoy it. I'll hold down the fort."

For several moments after she'd ended the conversation, Tina sat staring at the phone. How would she have ever gotten through the last year without Paul's concern and affection? she wondered, rising slowly. Come to that, she thought,

Paul had been the only undemanding constant in her life ever since she'd hired him.

Paul deserves a raise, Tina decided, leaving the room. And I'm going to give him one—five minutes after I shake Dirk's dust from my boots!

Tina filled the hours of the day by running errands for Beth, a pleasant chore, since she did the running seated inside Paul's car. After consuming another of Beth's delicious dinners, she and Beth retired to the living room.

"I wonder what happened to my collection of books?" Tina mused aloud, frowning as she glanced around the room.

"Everything of yours is here, dear." Beth looked up from her knitting. "Stored up on the third floor."

Tina snapped at the idea of something to do. "I think I'll go investigate," she said, uncurling her legs and rising.

"You'll need the key, the storeroom is always kept locked." Beth smiled at her. "Dirk's orders. The key's in the cellar way, hanging on a nail."

After retrieving the key, Tina ran up the stairs to the third floor, which consisted of one large room. Unlocking the door, she pushed it open, then groped for the wall switch. The room sprang to life and a soft, shocked "Oh" whispered through Tina's lips.

Beth had not been exaggerating. Everything of Tina's was in the room, not boxed and shoved out of the way, but neatly arranged, exactly as it all had been in her room on the floor below when she'd left the house for the last time.

Transfixed, Tina's startled gaze roamed over the room as she blinked furiously against a rush of tears. All her furniture was there, placed as closely as possible to the way it had always been, as were her books and the little china pieces she'd collected as a teenager.

But the object that riveted Tina's attention was the single-sized canopy bed, looking exactly as it had years ago, the ruffled canopy crisply laundered, the matching spread smoothed over the mattress.

Biting her lip, Tina stared at the bed, unable to move as memory washed over her, flooding her senses. Five years ago, she had lost—no given—her virginity on that very bed. The recipient of her gift had used it and then thrown it back at her, tarnished forever. The recipient of her gift had been her hero from the first time she had seen him at age five. The recipient of her gift had been Dirk.

Spinning on her heel, Tina rushed down the stairs as though the room were possessed by demons, when, in truth, it was her own mind that was possessed. Crying freely, she entered her room and threw herself into the wicker chair by the window, her brain whirling with images she could no longer keep at bay.

Chapter Five

Tina had been curled up in a chair that afternoon five years before too. She had also been crying. The tears were of loss for her only remaining parent, her father. Although Tina had known that her father had never recovered from the death of his wife two years before, she hadn't dreamed that he'd simply work himself to death in his grief. Yet that was precisely what George Holden had done. At the age of nineteen, Tina had buried her father.

Friends had been kind, and Tina truly appreciated their kindness, but there was an emptiness, an ache deep inside, that seemed to be tearing her apart. And Dirk, her champion, her dearest friend, her secret love, was thousands of miles away in Germany. Dirk had teasingly kissed her good-bye less than a month earlier when she'd returned to the college she was attending in North Jersey; Tina's childhood love knew nothing of the secret she held close to her heart.

The late September afternoon back then was dark with angry storm clouds. The window was awash with the heavy flow of rain, as if the pane of glass were weeping with the pale face in its reflection. So deep into her misery was Tina that she didn't even hear the first light tap at her door. The only reason she noticed the second tap was that it was accompanied by the sound of a voice—the most beloved voice in the world to Tina now that both her parents were gone. Afraid to believe her sense of hearing, her head spun toward the door even as it opened.

"Tina."

Sounding as though the one word hurt him inside, Dirk closed the door quietly and strode across the room to lift her gently out of the chair and into his arms.

After being strong for three days, Tina fell apart at Dirk's touch.

"Dirk." She sobbed against his chest. "He's dead. Daddy's dead. And I wasn't even here. He wouldn't let them send for me until it was too late. Oh, Dirk. Daddy's dead!"

"I know, honey, I know." Dirk's voice had an unfamiliar gravelly sound. "I came as soon as I heard." For a moment, his body tensed. "Dammit, they should have notified me. I should have been here with you!"

Dirk's concern, his gentle embrace, set the tears flowing again, and Tina cried like a lost child, her arms clasped around his waist, her tears wetting his shirt.

Turning carefully, Dirk sank into the chair, drawing Tina onto his lap. "Cry, honey," he murmured into her hair as his hands stroked her arms and back. "Cry it all out. I'll cry with you." And he did. Tina knew because she could feel the warm tears as they dropped off his face onto her cheek.

The afternoon waned as Dirk sat holding Tina securely against his strength, stroking her, rocking her, murmuring to her. Even after Tina had stopped crying, and then sniffing, he held her, brushing his lips over her temple, crooning a wordless song of sympathy. The change came to both of them at the same time, innocently, naturally.

Seeking more of Dirk's warmth and strength, Tina curled into him, raising her face as he lowered his to murmur his empathy. Their lips brushed, parted, brushed again . . . then clung.

"No." The whispered protest came from deep inside Dirk's throat, a protest against himself, not Tina. Slowly, reluctantly, he drew his mouth from hers. "Tina . . . honey, I—"

Her lips burning with a strange but pleasant sting, Tina silenced Dirk's plea for reason with her mouth, her soft gasp of delight mingling with his sigh.

Reacting instinctively, Tina parted her lips, thrilling to the new and wonderful sensations radiating through her body from the sudden hard pressure of Dirk's mouth. A soft, melting moan slipped from her at the first, tentative touch of the tip of his tongue as it slid along her lower lip, igniting an overwhelming need deep within her body.

Her hands groping unsurely, Tina found the strong, taut column of his neck, and then her fingers speared into his burnished hair, the tips kneading his scalp, urging him closer still.

"Honey, I shouldn't," Dirk groaned, sliding his mouth from hers. "You're so very young, so very . . . oh, God, I want you so!" This last as Tina sent her tongue gliding along his lip in an action reflecting his.

Their mouths touched again, then fused, short circuiting the wires connecting mind to reason. In an instant the kiss went from sweet to wild. Set free of restraint, Dirk's tongue scoured the honey-coated recesses of Tina's mouth, his teeth nipped hungrily at her lips, and his hands moved with restless abandon over her shoulders and down her back.

Within seconds the storm raging inside Tina was far more spectacular than the one flinging rain against the window. Consumed by a molten heat unlike anything she'd ever experienced before, her hands moved frantically over Dirk's chest and arms, propelled by a driving need to explore him everywhere.

His mouth locked to the sweetness of hers, Dirk deepened the kiss, teaching her the sensuously erotic love play of dueling tongues. Stroking, thrusting, his tongue ripped the fabric of Tina's senses as devastatingly as the lightning outside rent the black clouds.

"Tina!" Dirk's voice was thick, a strangled cry of pain. "Sweet, love, help me. Stop me—I can't stop myself!" Even as he pleaded for her intervention, his mouth took hers again, and one strong, gentle hand curved over her breast, cupping it possessively.

The effect of Dirk's stroking fingers on her breast was like a torch to tinder, setting off a blaze that ran like wildfire throughout Tina's entire body. Reality drowned in the rising tide of first passion, and Tina blindly followed the lead of emotions out of control.

Her fingers trembling with the need to touch him, Tina fumbled at the buttons on his white shirt until, with a sigh of pleasure, she found the warm skin beneath the silky material. The touch of Tina's fingers to his bared chest shattered the last of Dirk's reserve.

A growl-like sound grating in his throat, Dirk gathered Tina into his arms and stood up to carry her to the narrow canopy bed. Beside the bed he let her go, to slide down the length of his taut, aroused body as if in warning.

"You can still stop me, love, if you want to." His warm breath feathered her ear, sending a shiver creeping enticingly down her spine. Feeling her response, Dirk groaned in defeat. "I'll try not to hurt you, love. I'd rather be tortured than hurt you."

Gently, tenderly, exquisitely, Dirk removed the barrier of clothing that separated their yearning bodies. When, at last, they stood before each other, naked, Dirk's adoring gaze worshipped the budding perfection of Tina's body.

"You're so very beautiful," he breathed raggedly. "As beautiful as I always knew you would be." Not making the slightest move toward her, he held out his arms. "Come to me, love . . . if you still want to."

Tina didn't hesitate. Her sherry eyes soft and glowing with love, she stepped into his arms, wrapping her arms around his slim waist possessively, sensuously gliding her body against his until her curves fitted perfectly his angular shape.

The move from standing beside the bed to lying on the bed was made smoothly, effortlessly, and for Tina, excitingly. The feel of Dirk's warm, naked skin sliding along hers set off tiny explosions at her nerve endings, demolishing the last of her inhibitions.

Whimpering a siren song that needed no lyrics, Tina flowed like satin under the tightened muscles of Dirk's body, her senses absorbing, flaring to the hoarse, gritty sound of his voice.

"Slowly, love, slowly." His lips roamed over her face to

her neck, then down, down. His tongue bathed the wildly fluttering pulse in her throat before leaving a moist trail to the tip of her breast. When his lips closed over that quivering tip, Tina cried out in delight at her first encounter with the promise of ecstasy.

"You're so satiny soft here"—his finger stroked the curve of her breast—"and so excitingly hard here." His teeth raked the tight nipple with gentle savagery. "I want to kiss you, and bite you, and slide my tongue over every inch of you." And as he whispered his desire, he carried out his designs, tantalizing her, driving her deeper into love madness with the biting kisses and teasing tongue he sent on a languid exploration from her breasts to the soles of her feet.

And all the while Dirk paid homage to the perfection of Tina's long, satiny body with his hands and mouth, he adored her verbally in a voice that spoke of a desire long repressed.

"I've dreamed—been afraid to dream—of doing this since the summer you were sixteen." The ragged sound of his voice fanned the flames roaring through Tina. "When I went home the fall before, you were still a twittering, gawky girl. Then when I came back the next year, I found an emerging young woman."

"Oh, Dirk. Yes!" Tina's gasped response was not in answer to his huskily murmured statement, but to the melting sensation of his teeth sinking gently into the soft inner flesh of her thigh. Writhing beneath his love bites, she was beyond coherent articulation.

"How many nights!" Dirk's groan misted her fine skin with his sweet breath. "God, love, the nights were hell since that summer . . . every night since then!"

Completely lost to reason's cautioning call, Tina filled her hands with the silky strands of his hair, shivering to the feel of it sliding along the sensitized skin between her fingers.

"I love you. I have always loved you. I will always love you." The voice was feminine, and young . . . but certain.

"I know, love." Dirk's restless hands molded her hips. "I've been your brother, protector, best friend." Tina could feel the motion of his chest against her legs as he drew a calming breath deep into his lungs. When he spoke again it was as if the words were torn from his throat. "Now I must be your lover."

"Yes." Tina's response drew a shudder from Dirk. "Oh, yes, please!"

The entreaty in Tina's voice drew his long, sinewy body up the length of hers. Finding her mouth, he drank deeply of her passion, drawing it into himself with the searing brand of his hardened, hungry tongue.

"Now I know why your hair is such a deep red," he murmured into her mouth. "You're a living flame, my Tina." Taking infinite care, Dirk joined their bodies, absorbing her moment of discomfort with his own strength, soothing her with stroking hands and beguiling whispers.

"There will be no more pain now, love." His body moved against hers gently. "Trust me, my Tina."

Tina's fingers flexed, nails biting into the smooth, vibrant skin of his shoulders. Her action was all the reply Dirk required. The motion of his body increasing, he lowered his face to hers.

"Burn for me, my flame." The lure of his enticing whisper drew Tina into harmony with his rhythm.

Her eyes closed to savor the rush of torturous pleasure sweeping through her in ever-powerful waves, Tina heard and responded to the urgency in Dirk's voice.

"Yes. Yes, love. Beautiful. Perfect. Now!"

"Now!" The five-year-old echo of Dirk's strained cry reverberated inside Tina's mind, causing quakes throughout her body. Caught up in the memory of that long-ago afternoon, she was beyond awareness of the here and now. Her body trembling with the need for one man's touch, she covered her face with her shaking hands and sobbed her despair into the silence of the room.

"I love you. I have always loved you. I will always love you." The sound of her own voice, like the scream of an animal in agonizing pain, brought reality into sharp focus. Exhausted, yet shimmering with the first real flow of life she'd felt in five years, Tina bared her soul . . . to herself.

"I will always love him."

The insistent trill of a ringing telephone later drew Tina from a shallow slumber. Prying her swollen eyes open, she frowned with the effort of remembering exactly when and how she'd gotten into bed. She lay frowning long after the phone stopped ringing.

A deep crease connecting his eyebrows over the bridge of his nose, Dirk listened impatiently to his caller for several minutes before rudely interrupting.

"Dammit, Derek! I told you to reschedule that appointment! Now do it!" Not bothering to wait for another protest from his usually dependable assistant, Dirk went on ruthlessly. "I'm leaving. Not for the rest of the day. Not for the rest of the week. But until I feel like returning. Do you read me?"

"But, Dirk! What can I possibly tell—" That was all the time Dirk allotted Derek Saunders, his very ambitious, very competent second-in-command.

One pithy expletive said it all before Dirk slammed the receiver onto its cradle.

Leaning back into the soft leather of his desk chair, Dirk smiled slowly as his thoughts replayed the phone conversation he'd had with Beth Harkness less than an hour ago.

"Well, of course she's still here," Beth exclaimed. "Where else would Tina be, for heaven's sake?"

"I'd thought, perhaps, that she'd returned to the city," Dirk dissembled, a grin of sheer relief softening the forbidding line of his lips. "To take care of business or something."

"No." Beth paused, then went on. "She did confiscate the cordless phone from your room yesterday to call the shop, but she said nothing about the need to go back. Apparently that manager, or stylist, or whatever he is, is handling everything at the shop for her." Again she paused before offering, "Would you like me to call her to the phone?" Before Dirk could reply, she added, "I'm really surprised that she's not up and out by now. She was back from her jog by this time yesterday."

Dirk was intrigued. "Tina jogs?"

"Yes." Beth chuckled. "Like a fanatic! She was sweating like a workhorse when she came in yesterday morning . . . ate like one too."

A vision of Tina, her long, elegant limbs gleaming with exertion-drawn moisture, sent a zinging shaft of fire to Dirk's loins. Gripping the plastic receiver with suddenly slippery palms, he drew a silent breath into his aching chest.

God, he wanted her. At that moment, all the longing that he'd endured for the past five years culminated into one throbbing ache that spread to every cell in his body.

"Dirk?" Beth's confused tone cooled the rush of Dirk's hot blood. "Are you still there?"

Hanging on by my teeth, Beth. Dirk smiled derisively at the explanation he silently gave the innocent woman. Aloud, he gave her reassurance. "Yes, of course. I was . . . ah . . . thinking." The grin doubled in size, lending his austere face the glow of recaptured youth. "You said Tina talked to Rambeau?"

"Yes. For quite a while, at that."

Dirk's smiling lips flattened with displeasure. If that bogus excuse for a Frenchman has had her, I'll break his fingers! Dirk promised himself grimly. *Then* we'll see how great he is as a mincing stylist!

"I see." Dirk's smooth tone betrayed none of the emotions churning in his guts.

He was about to go on when Beth exclaimed, laughingly, "I hear her moving around now. Do you want to hold on until she comes down?"

"No!" Then, more calmly, "No. It won't be necessary. I'll see you both soon."

Now, anticipation growing in his mind and body, Dirk sighed with the realization that he would be seeing Tina within hours. Breathing steadily in a bid to slow the racing beat of his heart, Dirk mentally set a seal on Tina's future. She was his first. She'd be his again. There wasn't a power on earth strong enough to take her away from him this time. Tina could run her little mercenary heart out, but she couldn't run fast enough or far enough to outdistance him. She had played at life and love long enough. It was time to face the real world . . . and him.

As Dirk's thoughts coalesced into concrete determination, the breath that had seemed to be permanently constricted inside his chest eased out through nostrils flaring with passion.

Revitalized, Dirk shot to his feet. He was through screwing around! Enough is damned well too much, he decided harshly, silently issuing the order that set him into dynamic motion.

Go get her. No matter what it takes, make her yours.

Tina's running shoes slapped rhythmically on the wet sand. Her breathing ragged, she mentally dodged the ramifications of her enlightenment of the night before. This morning, Tina was dodging ineptly.

She would not, could not, love him. She had hated Dirk Tanger for years . . . nothing had changed the situation between them. She was still financially dependent upon his less than benign guardianship. He was still a ruthless bastard.

Status quo. Everything the same. Nothing changes, especially not Dirk.

Tina should have listened to her own thoughts.

On reaching the end of the beach, where tall sea grass swayed to the eerie tune of a fresh rising breeze, Tina flung her depleted body onto the sand. Drawing her legs up, she encircled them with her arms, rested her chin on her knees, and tried to sort out her tumultuous thoughts by staring at the undulating sea.

More tired from the racing of her thoughts than the punishment she'd meted out to her body, Tina was simply not up to keeping memory barred from her conscious mind. Taking control as completely as the encroaching waves took over the beach at high tide, remembrance swept her emotions, drowning her resistance in their swirling eddies.

Dirk had loved Tina through what was left of that long-ago

afternoon and into the blackness of midnight. Seemingly insatiable in his hunger for her, he'd brought her to ultimate pleasure time and time again.

Perhaps the very fact that Dirk had given the appearance of never wanting to let her go made his abrupt rejection of her the devastating blow that it was.

"I can't go back to school now," Tina had cried, reeling from the adamant tone in his voice.

"You can, and you will." Dirk's bright sapphire eyes were shuttered, concealing whatever feelings—if any—he had. "And I have to go back to Germany," he continued flatly.

"Back to Germany?" Tina closed her eyes in fear of revealing the anguish he was causing her. "Dirk, please." She choked. "Please take me with you."

"I can't do that, and you know it." Unmoving and immovable, Dirk stood before her, coolly beating her girlish dreams of a forever-love to death with his hard tone. "You have to finish college. I have conferences to attend."

His gaze swept her stricken face and for a moment his tone softened. "Last night was a mistake, Tina. A mistake that, at my age, I should have avoided. I came to you to offer comfort." For an instant his tone faltered. "And stayed to steal the most precious gift you had to give to a man of your choice."

Very slowly, Dirk drew in his breath, as if girding himself for the hardest blow he'd ever have to bear. "I made you a woman." His lips twisted—with what? Tina had always wondered. Disgust with her or self-reproach? "Whether you were ready to become one or not. The damage can't be undone." Dirk's voice roughened. "But I can make damn sure it doesn't happen again before your maturity catches up with your body!"

Dirk stared at her through eyes gone dead, all expression drained from his features, leaving a stranger to observe her reactions. "Go back to school, Tina. Go do whatever it is young girls do at your age. I'll take care of all the school costs and send you an allowance."

"Dirk! No!" That was all the time he allowed her to protest.

"What happened last night was an accident," he went on, as if she hadn't breathed a word. "An unfortunate but understandable accident. Tina, we're both grieving and needed to share that grief. Now it's time to go on with our lives as planned."

Dirk's final words slashed into Tina's heart like a rapier: "I won't be returning to Cape May next spring."

At that moment, had Tina not blinked repeatedly against a rush of tears, she'd have seen the lines of intense pain etching Dirk's face. But Tina had blinked, fighting to restore at least a part of her pride by refusing to weep or beg him to change his mind.

By the time Tina returned to college, she had her tattered pride repaired and firmly in place. But gone was the laughing, outgoing teenager who had attended the school mere weeks before. In that young girl's stead was a woman with coolly assessing, sherry-brown eyes who had learned how to make exquisite love and how to hate with a vengeance.

During the two years that followed what Tina would secretly think of as her mental breakdown, she absolutely refused to respond in any way to overtures, written or phoned, from Dirk. She spent the money he sent her freely, carelessly, and made frequent, imperious demands for more. Dirk supplied the additional funds, and then one day she stood before him during his one and only visit to her at school; she coldly stared through him, blatantly refusing his attempt to reach her.

"Tina, please try to understand." Dirk had finally shaken her to center her attention. "I did what I had to do. You weren't ready for me two years ago. Hell! You weren't ready for a boy, let alone a full-grown man with an overactive libido!"

Dirk had not been attempting humor . . . which was just as well, for Tina wasn't amused. Narrowing her eyes, she allowed him a glimpse of the glittering hatred she held for him. The glittering hatred of a mature woman.

Stepping back, Tina shrugged out of his grasp. "You will never touch me again. Is that understood?" Her voice was as brittle as tiny shards of glass. "You rejected me once.

Rejected the friendship of our past, and the might-have-beens of our future. You will never get the opportunity to do that again, either. Is *that* understood?"

"Oh, Tina." Dirk sighed deeply, smiling with infinite sadness; Tina refused to hear or see. "I did not reject you, our past, or our future. I *had* to let you go, give you time to grow to the point of making an *adult* decision, not an emotional one." There was a long pause, then he sighed again. "You're not listening to a word I'm saying, are you?"

Lifting her head regally, Tina smiled at him as if he were a stranger . . . as indeed she thought him.

"Go to hell, Tanger." Turning gracefully, Tina walked away from him, not to see or hear from him again until that first time she was forced to go to him to appeal for money. By the time that meeting materialized, Dirk no longer heard or saw *her.*

Adrift in the ebb and flow of memory, Tina was unaware of the changing tide until the first wave lapped at her running shoes. Startled out of introspection, she jumped to her feet with a muttered "Damn fool!"

Unwilling to decide whether her foolishness was connected with her reminiscence or with her nocturnal acceptance of her love for Dirk, Tina pivoted and ran back to the safety of the house and Beth. The scene that greeted her as she rushed into the kitchen was decidedly not one of safety for her.

Dirk was sprawled on a kitchen chair, a steaming cup of coffee clasped in his hand, a relaxed smile curving his lips into lines of shattering attractiveness. Tina felt every muscle in her body tense at the heart-wrenching sight of the only man she had ever really loved. Felt it and denied it at the same time.

"Well," she drawled with what she considered commendable sarcasm, "home is the hunter, home from the hills . . . and the banker back from the . . . whatever," she paraphrased dryly.

Sapphire-blue eyes pinned Tina where she leaned with deceptive ease against the frame of the doorway. Crossing one ankle over the other, she angled her chin at him defiantly while cautiously swallowing the wad of dust that appeared to have lodged in her throat.

"Feisty this morning, aren't we?" Dirk's glance slowly raked her indolent form, then came back to drill directly into her eyes. "What have you been feeding this hellcat, Beth? Rusty nails and pieces of wrecked boats?"

"Now, Dirk, don't tease," Beth scolded laughingly. "Tina is probably starving." Beaming at Tina, Beth invited, "Come have some coffee before you go up to shower, dear. You must be exhausted. How in the world anybody can run for two hours is a mystery to me."

"Yes, Tina, come tell us all about the benefits of running one's, ah, tushy off." Dirk's tone was heavy with mockery.

"I think I'll pass." Smiling sweetly through gritted teeth, Tina strolled out of the room, calling over her shoulder, "Give me ten minutes, Beth."

The minutes required for Tina to both bathe and prepare herself for whatever Dirk had in store for her—and she didn't deceive herself for an instant that his reason for being there was strictly relaxation—tallied up to thirty-five. And during the entire time, she taxed herself to near distraction over what he was up to.

Dirk had sought her out, coolly and deliberately. That fact was obvious. But why? And why now? Those were the considerations that had Tina gnawing on her lower lip. Fortunately, for that lip and her peace of mind, she finally forced herself to return to the kitchen, minus answers, but with a myriad of related questions. It was enough to stir an urge to walk sideways and bury herself in the sand exactly like a crab did when frightened.

The urge intensified as Tina reentered the kitchen to discover Beth missing and Dirk at the stove.

Actually sidling into the room, Tina eyed Dirk warily. "Has Beth gone somewhere?" A silent groan rang in her head at the edgy sound of her voice.

"It's Thursday." Dirk made the pronouncement without turning away from the stove.

"Thank you, Mr. Answer Man," Tina snapped, beginning to feel surrounded even with six feet of tile flooring separating them. *"Has* Beth gone somewhere?" she repeated.

"Beth quilts with a group of friends every Thursday." Turning slowly, Dirk pierced her with a mocking glance. "I assured her I would be more than happy to prepare your meal."

"What are you cooking?" Tina mocked back. "Toadstools and holly berries?"

The smile that curved Dirk's lips sent a panicky shiver skittering down Tina's spine.

"Don't need 'em," he murmured. "Before too many days have passed, Tina, I just might decide to love you to death."

Chapter Six

"Close your mouth and sit down, love. You're in no immediate danger."

Tina's jaws came together with a snap that shattered the bemused trance Dirk's earlier taunt had locked her into. The jolt also brought awareness of her surroundings with it, the pale sunlight slanting through the window over the sink; the wind-tossed dance of barren branches on the trees beyond the glittering glass; the sizzle and spit of bacon frying in the black pan on the stove; the happy gurgle of coffee perking; the soft thunder of her own life-force rushing wildly along her veins. And centered in that awareness, the instigator of her chaotic condition, his burnished hair reflecting sparks of sunlight, his tall body seeming to quiver with anticipation, his jewellike eyes riveted to her arrested, incredulous face.

"Lord!" Dirk's mocking drawl shuddered through Tina's bones all the way to her toes. "I'm glad no part of my hide was under those snapping teeth!"

Poised for flight, tension shimmering the length of her nervous system, Tina delved desperately into her reserves for composure. Surprisingly, she found some.

"You have a rather bizarre sense of humor, Dirk." Raising one delicately arched eyebrow, Tina slid into the chair she had been hanging on to for dear life. "Bizarre, and a trifle dark in color."

His bleached brows arching every bit as elegantly as Tina's, Dirk gave her a crooked grin before turning back to the stove. "An integral part of frustration," he rejoined, only half jokingly.

Tina frowned at his broad, neatly tapered back. He was a fine one to talk about frustration, she sneered inwardly. *She* could easily write a thousand-page tome on the subject— with Dirk Tanger as the main cause!

"In the mood for an omelet?"

Tina blinked her eyes to refocus her attention, sheer amazement flooding her face and mind. Was Dirk serious about cooking for her? Obviously, he was, for he was already beating eggs in a spotted blue-and-white mixing bowl.

"Ah . . . an omelet will be fine, thank you." Tina's reserves of composure went on strike. "But it really isn't necessary for you to make it." Pushing the chair back, she scrambled to her suddenly less-than-graceful feet. "I'll do it!"

His back to her, Dirk slowly poured the egg-and-milk mixture into an omelet pan. "Sit down, Tina"—he didn't even bother to turn his head—"before you trip over your own feet and break one of those gorgeous dancer's legs of yours."

Ridiculously flustered by his left-handed compliment, Tina subsided into the chair, watching his competent movements as he sprinkled chunks of onion, green pepper, ham, and mushroom into the pan as he slid it rhythmically over the gas jet.

"You really do know what you're doing there," Tina murmured, a hint of respect in her voice, "don't you?"

As her question had been uttered rhetorically, Tina was not expecting an answer, and certainly not the one Dirk sardonically tossed over his shoulder.

"A man foolish enough to marry a butterfly has absolutely no reason to be surprised if she refuses to risk singeing her wings by fluttering too close to the stove."

"Is that your abstract way of telling me your wife couldn't cook?"

"Not at all." Finally, he turned to her; his contemptuous expression made Tina wish he hadn't. "It is my direct way of telling you my wife adamantly refused to cook." A derisive smile slashed his face. "She did give me a choice, though," Dirk went on dryly. "She said I could either hire a professional cook or learn to cook for myself."

Before Tina's amazed eyes, Dirk folded the mixture over, held the pan motionless an instant, then gently slid the golden brown omelet onto a plate. A satisfied smile softening his harshly drawn lips, he placed the perfect omelet in front of her.

"That's beautiful," Tina smiled, genuinely impressed.

"It's an egg." Turning from the table, Dirk walked to the counter to fill two heavy mugs with coffee. "Surely even you can cook an egg?" he taunted.

Tina sampled her first bite of the fluffy mixture chewing appreciatively. "Hmm." She nodded, swallowing. "Delicious!" she pronounced before answering him directly. "Actually, I'm a very good cook. I took a course on gourmet cooking as an elective in my junior year of college."

"Your junior year." Dirk regarded her from darkened eyes. "The year I made my one and only visit to your school."

Tina wet her lips nervously. She could see Dirk's expression settling rigidly with the memory of that bitter visit, could feel the anger tensing his body. She watched warily, all the nerves in her body knotted, as Dirk placed the mugs on the table, then dropped onto the chair beside her.

"If I recall correctly," he drawled in a quiet, dangerous tone, "you told me to go to hell that day."

I was young. I was upset. I was hurt. All these and more excuses flashed through Tina's mind; she discarded every one of them. Lifting her chin defiantly, she met his glinting blue eyes steadily.

"That's right."

A flicker of admiration feathered Dirk's eyes, then he veiled them again in frost. "I should have pulled you out of that damned school then and there." Dirk raked her body with a searing glance. "You really never used the degree you went for anyway."

"Never used it!" Tina exclaimed sharply. "Of course I used it . . . I'm still using it!"

"You need a certificate in physical education to curl some

bimbo's hair?" Dirk sneered. "You need that certificate to employ some limp-wristed—"

"Dirk!" Tina's sharp tone sliced across his jeering words. "Paul Rambeau is not some limp-wristed *anything!* Paul is a very talented hairstylist." Pausing to control her rising voice, Tina literally threw her fork onto the tabletop. "And I do not cater to bimbos!"

Dirk snorted.

Tina saw red. Incensed, she leaned close to him, spitting her words into his face.

"I use my certificate every day, in a hell of a lot more ways than I would have done by becoming a high school physical education teacher. And I make a hell of a lot more money at it too."

"Indeed?"

Had Tina not been so consumed with outrage, she would have recognized the trap Dirk had set for her. But as she was outraged, thoroughly outraged, she walked right into it.

"Yes," she enunciated clearly. "Indeed."

"Then, perhaps you'll explain to me just why you're always in such dire financial straits."

Tina could have screamed with frustration. Instead, she sputtered with indignation. "I—well, I need the money for—"

"All your creditors?" Dirk interrupted. "And to meet all the forever expenses like heat, electricity, water, and the phone bills?" He shook his head wonderingly. "Then., of course, let us not forget the exorbitant rent on your apartment, your penchant for rather expensive but terribly darling little sports cars, and the absolute necessity of being seen in the very latest designer fashions." Dirk smiled sarcastically. "Is that what you were going to say, love?"

It was not until later that Tina realized how very close she came to retaliating with a physical blow. It was also not until later that Tina realized how very fortunate it was for her that she only retaliated verbally; as it was, Dirk reacted in a way that stunned her.

"You really are a cynical bastard, aren't you?" Tina flung the accusation at him hotly.

Dirk pushed his chair back forcefully. "I've had enough of your curses, Tina." Grasping her roughly by the shoulders, he jerked her to her feet, knocking the air from her chest as he pulled her against him. "You've been cursing me in one way or another for five long years—and I'm sick of it."

"Tough!" Sheer bravado prompted Tina's sharp reply. Her bravado earned her a punishing kiss.

Muttering a rather colorful expletive, Dirk crushed her lips under his own, forcing them apart ruthlessly. When Tina began to struggle to free herself, he anchored her head by running his fingers into her hair. Still, Tina attempted to free herself by squirming frantically. Dirk merely tightened his hold and ground his mouth into hers.

Then, slowly, subtly the kiss changed, becoming coaxing, beguiling. With a groaning murmur, Dirk played at the corners of her mouth with his tongue, teasing a response from her lips that Tina was suddenly powerless to control.

Sweeping his hand down her spine, he spread his fingers at the base and drew her body up and in to meet the urgent thrust of his hips. Binding her to him with one hand entangled in her hair and the other caressing the small of her back, Dirk evoked near delirium in Tina by stroking his tongue over hers.

All the fight went out of her on a softly expelled sigh. Raising her hands to clasp his head, she let her body glide sinuously against his hard angles, shivering with the hungry groan her action elicited from deep in his throat.

By the time Dirk slid his lips from hers to trail moist kisses down the arching curve of her throat, Tina was making incoherent, urgent sounds of enticement.

"Oh, Tina." The words were torn from Dirk's soul. "Oh, God, Tina! Do you feel it? Do you feel what you do to me? Never, not with any other woman, is my response so immediate or so very painful." Running into the barrier of her shirt collar, Dirk released his grip on her hair to slip the buttons from their holes with trembling fingers.

Tina knew she ought to stop him, knew that if she didn't she would soon not be able to. The brush of his fingertips over her already heated skin decided the emotional issue. She arched back in silent invitation and cried out with remembered pleasure when his lips tasted her quivering flesh at the edge of her bra.

She had to touch him, she *had* to. The demand, more impulse than formed thought, impelled her fingers to the gathered hem of the sweater Dirk was wearing. Sliding her fingers beneath the fine knit, Tina sighed with the sensation of warm skin on skin. Slowly, deliciously, she stroked her hands upward, delighting at the moan of pleasure that rumbled from Dirk's throat as he arched his spine against her caressing palms.

It felt so right, all of it so very right. The heat of his mouth on her breast, the warmth of his body under her hands, the lassitude as her senses swam with the clean, tangy male scent of him. It all felt so perfectly right that being swept from her feet into Dirk's arms, the journey up the curving staircase, was all part of an exciting flight to paradise. Even the jarring crash of the door Dirk closed by a backward kick of his booted foot failed to alarm Tina.

Drowning in the widening pool of need expanding at her core, Tina reveled in the urgency of his arching body, the restlessness of his searching hands, the hot moisture bathing her skin, his hungrily seeking mouth.

Moving, moving, Dirk's lips blazed a trail of stinging fire from her breasts to her neck, then to her face.

"I want to take hours and hours to love you," he murmured against her ear, his tongue darting in and out evocatively. "But I can't. I can't. I've dreamed about this so long . . . so very long." His parted lips slid over her cheek to the edge of her mouth, setting a flame dancing along her nerve endings. "I need to take you now, Tina. I must have you now."

Yes. Yes. The sound of surrender was a silent moan that quivered through Tina's soul. It's been so long, so long, and I've waited, wanted . . . always, just you . . . only you . . . ever you. Even with Chuck it was always . . .

The hazy thoughts fragmented, dropping like weights into Tina's consciousness, rippling outward, gaining strength until she had to face the stark reality of their content: even with Chuck it was always Dirk she had wanted.

Oh, God.

Awareness brought a shudder of self-revulsion, and then an icy withdrawal. Feeling her stillness, Dirk lifted his head to gaze down at her, his eyes cloudy with passion and a building confusion.

"Tina?"

Opening the eyes she'd closed in pain, Tina stared into his blue depths, and down through the years to the afternoon he'd made her a woman . . . and his own.

All the dodging and twisting she'd indulged in, all the furious physical activity she'd applied herself to, all the mental gyrations she'd performed had been to one end: the desire not to face the demeaning truth.

But now the truth was staring at her out of eyes that were midnight-blue with passion.

"Tina?" A thread of concern laced Dirk's voice. "What is it?"

You. Me. Mostly me. The thoughts tumbled around Tina's brain, bringing not more confusion but clarity. Me, and what a fraud I really am. You're disgusting! Tina flung the accusation at herself silently before it erupted clearly and concisely in a whisper of self-condemnation. "You're disgusting."

His hands caressing her shoulders flexed, fingers digging into her flesh spasmodically. "What the hell are you trying to do?" Dirk stared at her as if she'd sprouted horns.

Twisting out of his grasp, Tina fumbled at the buttons on her shirt. "I—I'm sorry. I can't. I'm not—"

"What do you mean you can't?" A dangerous combination of sexual frustration and flaring rage chilled Dirk's tone. "A few moments ago you wanted me as much as I wanted you!" His body taut with suppressed anger, Dirk stepped toward her. When Tina backed nervously away, he lashed out bitterly. "What the hell kind of tease are you? Do you get your kicks by turning men on only to watch them suffer? Is that why

your husband was trying to set the record on the number of
women he could lay?"

Tina recoiled as if Dirk had struck her. Her eyes horrified, she shook her head, unmindful of the mass of hair
that veiled her vision; vision that might have noted the
lines of self-reproach scoring Dirk's strained features. But
Tina probably wouldn't have noticed anyway; she was no
longer looking out, she was looking in, and she hated the
woman she was looking at.

The buttons on her shirt fastened, if unevenly, Tina jerked
away, running for the bedroom door. Scooping her bag and
jacket from the straight-backed chair just inside the door,
she made her escape while Dirk stood, momentarily too
stunned to move. Tina was clattering down the stairs when
she heard Dirk's voice from the doorway.

"Dammit, Tina! Where do you think you're going?"

Where was she going? Biting her lip in an attempt to stem
the gathering pool of tears blurring her vision, Tina shook
her head. Where could she go to hide from the truth, when
the truth was inside herself? She had been cheating for the
last five years, cheating everyone . . . but mostly herself.

Shrugging into her jacket as she dashed down the veranda
steps, Tina glanced at the elegant silver Jaguar parked behind
Paul's Dodge. The car made a bold statement for the rewards
of wealth. Tina knew without doubt that the car belonged to
Dirk.

Digging into her bag for her door opener, Tina heard the
door of the house open, and an instant later the grating sound
of Dirk's voice. "For God's sake, Tina! Will you wait?"

Sliding behind the wheel of the little car, Tina jabbed the
key into the ignition. A moment later the car jerked into
motion and roared down the quiet street with a grinding of
gears.

Will you wait? Will you wait? Dirk's cry echoed inside
Tina's head as she made the turn onto West Perry and drove
toward the Point. A sad smile curved her trembling lips as
she realized her destination. From the time she'd learned to

drive at sixteen, Tina had escaped to Cape May Point whenever she wanted to work out a problem or cry out a hurt.

Her eyes dry but gritty, Tina ran a swift glance over the lighthouse to her left as she sped by, wincing at the memory of the first time Dirk had taken her there, giving her an outing while at the same time a history lesson on the importance of the light to seafarers.

Her direction now focused, Tina drove too fast as she made for Sunset Beach. She was out of the car and walking before the vehicle had ceased shuddering from the sudden stop. Head bent, she continued toward the water, her only reaction a mild shiver when she heard the screech of tires braking to an abrupt halt next to the Dodge.

Deserted of the summertime tourists happily examining stones in hopes of discovering one of pure quartz known as a Cape May diamond, the pebbly beach offered solitude and peace.

Tina felt that peace seep into her soul as she stared sightlessly out over the water to the *Atlantus,* the old ship lying half-sunken within a stone's throw of where she stood.

"I'd like you to tell me what happened back home."

Tina's lashes fluttered as they swept down to momentarily shadow her cheeks. Home. Dirk's use of the word, his achingly familiar, quiet tone, brought home very close.

But not the home of the bed-and-breakfast establishment that Tina had just fled. The home settling softly on her mind now was the home of her childhood, years of happiness and laughter with her parents, years of safety and security, years of hero worship and romanticism.

Years of Dirk.

"Has it sunk any deeper, do you think?" Tina's gaze rested on the hull of the old ship.

"Not noticeably." Dirk's response held the exact note of consideration Tina's query had. And in the same way it had a lifetime ago, his arm came to rest lightly across her shoulders.

Home.

Tina smiled around the thickness in her throat. She was

so very tired of fighting and felt so very vulnerable. Gone was the ruthless Dirk who would see her lose everything she'd worked so hard for. Gone was the aggressive business-woman guarding her bruised emotions behind a façade of fierce independence.

On Sunset Beach, staring out at the ship, were Dirk of the teasing eyes and protective arms and Tina of the gentle glances and grateful acceptance of any spare moments he had to offer her.

"I'm sorry for that crack about your husband." Even Dirk's voice had a different ring, echoing the tenor of the younger man.

"It was true," Tina said softly. "Even if I was, classically, the last one to know."

"I'm not apologizing for what he did," Dirk corrected her gently. "I'm apologizing for using my knowledge of it to beat you with."

Tina's lips quirked with genuine amusement. Her old Dirk had returned indeed, scolding gently when she displayed ob-tuseness. As always when Dirk chastised her, Tina moved closer to his protective warmth. And, as always, she told him the scrupulous truth.

"I failed him."

"How so?" There was no hint of condemnation in the question, merely a request for clarification.

"I accepted his marriage proposal."

The soft swish of the lapping waves grew loud in the si-lence that fell between them. After Tina's stark statement, there was really nothing else to say—at least on that particu-lar subject. Dirk introduced a new-old topic.

"How many times have we watched the sun set from this exact spot?" he asked, a thread of laughter weaving through his tone as he spoke of remember-whens.

"Four thousand, two hundred and seventy-seven."

"Are you sure?"

"Positive."

The hand grasping her shoulder tightened. "I could have sworn it was only seventy-six." After the near violence of their earlier exchange in Tina's bedroom, the relief in Dirk's voice was obvious.

Tina's tone mirrored his. "No," she said earnestly. "I always kept a running count. It's definitely seventy-seven."

"Hmm." Tilting his head, Dirk playfully frowned at her. "Is that including or excluding today?"

Tina frowned back. "Since we haven't seen the sun set today, it must be excluding."

"Good point."

Once again silence reigned, a relaxing, tension-dissolving silence. When it was next broken, Tina was indulging in remember when.

"How many times were you forced to tell me the stones I found weren't diamonds?"

"At least a million." This time the glance Dirk slanted at her was openly affectionate. "Poor mite, you never did find one, did you?"

"No." Tina shook her head. "But that didn't matter. The fun was in the search."

"Like the mystery hunts you and your giggly friends were always trying to involve me in?" Dirk chuckled. "You girls certainly did come up with some winners."

"You mean like the time we buried the 'treasure' of old costume jewelry our mothers had given us and told you we'd found a genuine treasure map?"

Dirk laughed outright, the sound shimmering on the air around them, tugging the deepest part of Tina's heart.

"What a bunch of fluff tops you all were." His eyes danced. "There wasn't an ounce of seriousness to the pound in any of you."

Their voices blending, sometimes overlapping, they recounted memories as the sun trekked toward the horizon and descended spectacularly beyond the sea. Their voices faded, then stilled as the sun, reflecting an illusion of a pedestal, seemed to rest on it a moment before surrendering its glory to the encroaching dusk. Awed by the panoramic beauty, Tina shivered. Dirk was immediately solicitous.

"Come on, kid. Time to go home."

His arm still clasping her shoulder, Dirk turned them both in the direction of the two cars.

"Drive back at, or under, the limit." A chiding grin tugged at his lips as he handed her into the car. "If you wrap this pile of metal around a pole, they'll have to pry you out of the debris with a can opener."

"Charming thought." Tina wrinkled her nose.

"No, it isn't." Her gaze flew to his face at his rough tone. "It's a sickening thought. So drive carefully." Turning abruptly, Dirk moved to the Jaguar, leaving a bemused Tina staring after his rigidly straight back.

The warm bemusement lasted throughout the drive home. Tina, sedately following the taillights of Dirk's car, smiled dreamily at the visions their ruminating created inside her mind.

Drenched in the past, their past, she parked the car and hurried to join him where he waited for her on the sidewalk, slipping under his extended arm as though there had never been a harsh word uttered between them.

Oh, it felt so good being close to him again. How had they lost that precious camaraderie they had shared from the first day her father had brought him home?

Tina's thoughts muddied the calm waters of her contentment. She knew exactly how they had lost their empathy for each other. Dirk had ruthlessly taken all the love she'd had to offer, then discarded it and her.

Carefully disentangling herself from Dirk's encircling arm, Tina hid her renewed bitterness by fussily hanging their jackets inside the small foyer closet before turning abruptly to the stairs.

"Hey, kid!" Dirk exclaimed, startled. "Where are you going? I was about to offer to make a cup of tea for you."

And sympathy? Tina paused on the third step, glancing at him over her shoulder.

"I'll be down in a minute. I want to wash up." As hard as she tried to hide it, her tone reflected the chill permeating her thoughts.

"Tina?" Dirk's sharp gaze saw more than she wanted to show. "What is it? What's wrong?"

"Nothing!" There was an edge of panic there, an edge Tina knew she must control. "Nothing, really. I simply want to freshen up. You . . . you go put the kettle on. I'll be down in a moment." Tina was moving with her last word, taking the stairs two at a time.

Inside the comparative safety of her room she stood, shoulders slumped in dejection, wondering where she'd find the courage to go back downstairs again. Dirk was up to something, she knew, but what? Shaking her head, Tina walked to the dresser. Pulling a brush through her wind ruffled hair, she stared deeply into her reflected eyes.

Dirk is completely in control, and he knows it. After years of cold withdrawal, why was he suddenly donning the cloak of friendship again? The solemn brown eyes in the mirror held no answers, only worried confusion.

Dirk wants something from me. The realization turned Tina cold to the marrow. When had it happened? she protested mutely. When had she relinquished the reins into his hands? *She* had come home to rest and devise a plan by which she could wrangle something from *him*. At what point had she lost the impetus?

The tremulous mouth in the mirror smiled knowingly. Observing the movement of her own lips, Tina winced. She knew darned well exactly when she'd started to fall apart. Her eyes shifted slightly to the spot in the room where Dirk had so recently held her to the burning hardness of his body. The sight disappeared as Tina slowly closed her eyes.

All this time, she moaned inwardly, all the years I've hated him and kept myself motivated by hating him, I have really been hating myself. And with good reason.

Tina's conscience squirmed. At twenty-four, a finally *honest* twenty-four, Tina could appreciate Dirk's actions of five years ago. She had been so terribly young, so terribly green, so terribly naïve. Her lips twisted wryly. Was it any wonder he'd run from her as though from the plague? Today, nine years difference in their ages was of no account. Five years ago it was a chasm. And because he had not fettered himself with that green girl, Tina had spent every one of those years punishing every person who dared come too close, especially her husband.

Suddenly feeling too weary to stand, Tina sank onto the edge of the bed. What an absolute waste, she thought sadly. A waste of time, and effort, and, yes, money . . . her money.

Had she married Chuck with cool, if unconscious, deliberation?

A shudder tore through Tina's slender frame at the thought. While it was true that Chuck was unfaithful as well as unprincipled, it was also true that Tina had never been stupid. Hadn't she known, from the very beginning, exactly what she was letting herself in for with Chuck? The probing thought straightened Tina's spine.

Then another, more disturbing conjecture chilled Tina's stiffened back. How had Dirk said it? *I'm apologizing for using my knowledge to beat you with.* The phrase revolved in Tina's mind.

In effect, hadn't she used Chuck to beat Dirk? Hadn't she known, while refusing to know, that Chuck would make demands for money from her? Money that she would have no choice but to ask Dirk for? Hadn't she also known that, by giving passive rather than active participation in her marriage bed, Chuck would seek satisfaction elsewhere, thereby saving her the shame of facing the unpalatable fact that while the man in her bed was her husband, the man in her heart and mind was Dirk?

"Rustle it, Tina!" Dirk shouted from the foyer. "Your tea is getting cold."

The tea wasn't the only thing. Tina shivered.

"Coming." Tina's response was threaded with anxiety and defeat. How could she face him? Not only face him but beg him to save her from the results of her own vindictive actions? But, Tina thought frantically, she had to get him to release her money. She couldn't lose the shop now, it was all she had left.

Reluctance making her movements stiff, Tina rose and

walked slowly to the door. She hadn't washed her hands, she thought with bitter whimsy, but she'd done a fairly good job of scrubbing her grimy conscience.

"Tina!" Dirk's impatient call came from the kitchen as she reached the foot of the stairs. Not bothering to answer, she continued her slow pace to the doorway of the room.

"Where the . . ." Dirk's words trailed away at the sight of her strained features. His body tensed as if preparing for a blow. "I don't know, honey," he murmured, shaking his head as he examined her face closely. "But for some reason, I have this nasty suspicion you're withdrawing from me again." Dirk's head lowered with resignation. "Okay, let's have it. What have you decided I'm guilty of now?"

Chapter Seven

Tina smiled . . . at least made the attempt to smile. "Same old story, I'm afraid." She shrugged. "I need money. You refuse to release it to me. Instant antagonism."

Standing on the other side of the table from her, Dirk ran an assessing gaze from her gleaming red hair to the tips of her dusty boots.

Watching him scrutinize her, Tina felt a frisson of unease move through her at the contemplative spark that flared in his eyes before he concealed his thoughts by narrowing his lids. That brief flare convinced Tina that, whatever his thoughts, they meant trouble for her.

"There *is* one way," he began, then frowned when the phone rang shrilly. "Damn!" With a murderous scowl, he crossed to the phone and jerked the receiver from the hook. "Hello?" he barked into the mouthpiece. Turning his head sharply, Dirk pinned Tina with a blazing stare. "Yes, she's here." Even as he spoke, his jaw grew rigid with anger. "If you must," he finally snarled, holding the receiver out to Tina.

"Do I recognize the pleasant tone of your benign banker?" Paul drawled the moment she responded.

"Yes."

"How lucky can one woman get?" he wondered in an awed voice. "First the man with the iron tongue, and now me, bearing tidings of financial woe."

"I'm almost afraid to ask." Tina sighed tiredly.

"Have you somehow overlooked the paltry sum of seven

thousand dollars still owed on Chuck's car?" Paul asked brightly.

Tina had. Groaning softly, she rested her head against the cool wall. How could she have forgotten her agreement to pay for Chuck's import when she'd made the agreement in a last-ditch effort to get her divorce? It had been blatant blackmail on Chuck's part, of course. But at the time, Tina was so desperate, she was willing to do almost anything.

"Tina?" Though soft, Paul's voice was sharp with concern.

"I'm here."

"Look, beautiful, don't go into a tailspin. I paid it for you. You can pay me back when you get it." Paul spoke quickly in an obvious bid to relieve the tension he could feel humming through the wires.

"Oh, Paul!" Close to tears, Tina bit her lip. "I . . . I don't know what to say."

"Say good-bye."

The order came from behind Tina, not through the receiver. And it was decidedly an order, one Dirk fully expected her to obey. Paul had heard the command as well.

"Is that guy for real?" The steel-like quality of Paul's tone was new and surprising to Tina; Paul *never* became perturbed. "And is he looking for a rap in the teeth?" he demanded, convincing Tina he did, at times, become perturbed.

"It's all right, Paul, I—" Tina cried out as the receiver was wrenched from her hand, then slammed onto the hook. "How dare you?" she shouted. "You have no right to inter—"

"I'll tell you how I dare!" Grasping her by the upper arms, Dirk dragged Tina close to him. "I dare, love," he sneered, "because *I* hold the purse strings. Remember?"

"Have you ever once let me forget?" Tina sneered back.

"No." Dirk shook her in an oddly gentle way. "And I'm not about to start now." Then, quietly, too quietly, "What did Rambeau want?"

"Money, what else?" Tina laughed shrilly, then wished she hadn't when his hands tightened painfully.

"You pay him?"

All the fight drained out of Tina, leaving her limp in his grasp. "Of course I pay him. He works for me."

"That isn't what I meant," Dirk said insinuatingly. "And you know it. Do you pay him in the same way you paid your husband, for services rendered?"

"No." Tina closed her eyes against the sickness welling in her throat. She heard his muttered curse an instant before he gathered her into his arms.

"Tina, don't. Oh, honey, don't look that way." Dirk crooned into her ear as he bent over her. "I'm sorry. Baby, please, stop trembling." Tina both felt and heard the deep breath he dragged into his lungs. "Why must we always claw at each other?" Lifting his head, he gazed at her tenderly. "We didn't always blindly strike first and ask questions later. Did we?"

"No." Tina sniffed. "Not before I grew up."

Raising his hands, Dirk cradled her face and tilted her head up. "Is that what happened?" Dirk's smile brought tears to Tina's eyes. "You grew out of your braids and into your bra." The spasm that moved over his face spoke of pain. "And shot a hole in my ego by discovering boys your own age."

Appalled by the very idea that she might have hurt him, no matter how innocently, Tina rushed to explain. "I never meant to hurt you, Dirk. You were always my knight in shining armor."

"Yeah, but when your father died, I rusted it."

And there it was, out in the open at last after festering in silence for five long years. As scalding moisture slipped over the edge of her eyelids, Tina closed them and lowered her head.

"Oh, Tina." Dirk's groan held the weight of every one of those years. "The worse part is that I can't make myself feel sorry it happened. I've never been touched so deeply as I was that afternoon, or felt so completely satisfied afterward." His hands less gentle, Dirk lifted her face again. "I wanted you very badly then." Slowly, irrevocably, he lowered his mouth to hers. "I want you even more now."

"Dirk, please, no—" The protest was lost inside the moist

heat of his mouth, as Tina was lost inside the need that had been a constant companion for five years.

Time, place, self, spun away and drew Tina along in the whirlwind. There was nothing but a void beyond the safe haven of the only arms she ever wanted to surround her. Greedily drinking from his parted lips, Tina surrendered her soul into Dirk's keeping. She was his now, as she'd ever been his . . . whether he knew, or cared, or wanted her or not.

Dirk's actions made it clear that he definitely wanted her—at least the physical her. Murmuring of a need too long denied, he unfastened the buttons on Tina's shirt for the second time that day. When the material was at last brushed aside and the front clasp on her bra disengaged, Dirk burned her skin with his passion-fired gaze. Then, with excruciating slowness, he lowered his mouth to her breasts.

Her throat arching as her head fell back, Tina whimpered a sensual "Yes" as she speared her fingers through the silky strands of his hair and drew his lips to one aching nipple.

The raspy grate of Dirk's tongue on her sensitized skin sent shards of desire into the lower part of Tina's body. The gentle but urgent draw of his suckling lips wrenched a cry of sheer ecstasy from her throat. The sudden, jarring ring of the phone elicited a groan of protest from both of them.

"If that's Rambeau again, I will personally travel to New York and strangle him!" Dirk snarled savagely, drawing Tina with him as he stepped to the phone. Before attempting to answer, he breathed in deeply several times.

"Hello?" Even with the calming breaths, his voice betrayed impatience. Clasped to his side, Tina felt the tension seep out of him before he spoke again more evenly. "No, Beth, I'm sorry. I, ah, was occupied." As Dirk listened to Beth his glance covered Tina's face, then went caressingly to her still-heaving breasts. "No, of course not. Go, enjoy yourself." A sensuous smile curved the corner of his lips. "Tina and I will find *something* to eat."

When Dirk hung up he allowed his smile to grow enticingly. "Beth is going out to dinner with the girls and she was concerned about us." His glance danced over Tina's body, and along her nerves. "We could always devour each other," he suggested hopefully.

With that outrageous suggestion he was back, the Dirk Tina had adored forever, the Dirk of the laughing eyes and teasing quip. Her sense of humor struck, Tina skipped out of his loose embrace, drawing her shirt closed as she went. Tossing her now wildly disarrayed hair back, she smiled beguilingly.

"I'd rather have lobster." Tina fluttered her eyelashes exaggeratedly. "And a mound of French fries. And a Greek salad with feta cheese. And hot crusty rolls. And—"

"Hey, kid!" Dirk contrived to look stern. "You eat much more than all that and you'll be sick."

Tina threw him a prim look. "I was going to say: and a tall glass of gin and tonic—heavy on the tonic."

Dirk was suddenly serious. "The mood's gone . . . isn't it?"

"Yes." Tina smiled tremulously. "The mood—or madness—is gone." Almost fearfully, she watched to see if the ruthless Dirk would return. Tentatively, she held her hand out to him. "Still friends?" she asked, unaware of her pleading tone.

Taking the two steps necessary to reach her, Dirk curled his fingers around hers. "Yes, love, still friends." His eyes clear, he stared down at her. "We're going to have a long talk, if not over dinner, then after it. Our differences have to be resolved, Tina."

Tina wet her suddenly parched lips, tingling all over when his gaze avidly watched the tip of her tongue. "I"—she cleared her throat—"I know. But let's not think about it now." Sliding her hand from under his, she took off at a run. "I'll bet I can be showered and dressed before you," she challenged in the same impudent manner she had as a girl.

"You're on." Dirk accepted, close at her heels. "Name the stakes."

Tina hesitated at her bedroom door. "The loser buys dinner?"

"Done." Dirk was disappearing into his room as he spoke.

Surprisingly, Tina won the bet, if only by some thirty seconds. Dirk was still grumbling about the possibility of her having cheated by not showering as they left the house.

"Do I look like the type of woman who would splash on half a bottle of perfume and call myself bathed?" Tina laughed, walking to the side of the car.

"No," Dirk admitted sourly. "But how the hell *did* you get ready so fast? If I remember correctly—and I do—it always took you forever to get ready for anything." A grin denied his earlier sourness. "Even to go to the beach, where you *knew* you would immediately become messy with suntan oil and sand."

"Owning and running a business keeps me clicking along," Tina admitted seriously. "I have my grooming time almost down to a science. Now it's habit. It never takes me very long to get my act together, regardless of where I'm going or who I'm going there with."

Dirk's appreciative gaze roamed slowly from her shining hair to the three-inch heels on her Italian sling-back pumps. "And you get your act together very well," he murmured, smiling at the flush of pink that tinged her cheeks. "I like the dress." Dirk indicated the soft rose-tinted wool sheath that caressed her body, his smile growing in time with the color highlighting her skin. "Will you be warm enough with that?" Lifting his hand, he tested the material of the cashmere jacket Tina had thrown around her shoulders.

"Yes." Possibly too warm, Tina added silently, breath quickening from the heat suffusing her body. Deciding two could play at this game, she examined his attire, fighting to hold an air of detachment.

Her examination only increased the flow of heat coursing through her veins. In truth, Dirk always looked good to her. Dressed to go out, he looked magnificent. His newly shampooed hair gleamed with burnished-gold streaks; his freshly shaven cheeks displayed the sheen of a year-round suntan. His pristine white shirt contrasted beautifully with the Harris tweed jacket that enhanced the breadth of his shoulders; the diagonally striped tie expertly knotted at his collar added a dash of color and panache. Even the wide-wale chocolate-brown corduroys that encased his long, muscular legs were an enticement . . . to what, Tina shakily refused to acknowledge, but her detachment slipped alarmingly. Swallowing in an effort to moisten her suddenly dry throat, she moved jerkily toward the car.

"Okay," Dirk drawled with amusement. "How would you rate me? On a scale of one to ten?"

Fifty-two. Tina could not deny the smile that curved her lips at the number that sprang to her mind. She had no way of knowing her smile hinted at her thoughts.

"That good, huh?" Opening the car door, Dirk leaned over quickly and brushed his lips over her cheek. "For that unspoken compliment, I'll happily pay for dinner." His eyes sparkling with laughter, he boldly assessed her exposed thighs as Tina slid onto the car seat. "And for that glimpse of the cradle of heaven," he whispered, "I'll even dance with you after we've eaten."

The car door closed with a solid thunk, effectively covering the gasp that escaped Tina's parted lips. The cradle of heaven? Tina smoothed the skirt of her dress down over her thighs with nervous fingers. The cradle of heaven. Was that what Dirk had found with her? A heaven of physical completion? The thought was both upsetting and exciting.

Tina's pulse hammered erratically. Was she supposed to respond to that blatantly sexual overture? A delicious tension holding her still, she slanted a guarded glance at Dirk as he slid behind the wheel.

The look Dirk returned was loaded, as was his observation. "There's no need for you to look so uneasy, love. You know I'm a smooth . . . ah . . . *gentle* dancer."

Tina stopped breathing altogether at his thinly veiled innuendo. Liquid fire suddenly racing out of control through her veins set a spark to her imagination and memory. For one brief, glorious instant she could actually feel the ecstasy she'd experienced while "dancing" with him on that long ago afternoon.

"You've always loved me."

Snapped into the present by Dirk's softly voiced but adamant statement, Tina stared at him out of anguished eyes.

"Yes." Feeling oddly defeated and triumphant at the same time, Tina straightened her spine and met his assessing regard fearlessly. "Yes," she repeated clearly. "I've always loved you."

"As a brother?" Dirk arched one golden-brown brow.

"Yes."

"As a lover?" His voice lowered seductively.

"Yes."

"As a man?" Tension filled his tone.

"Yes."

Inside the island of the plush Jaguar, Tina held her breath as Dirk's sapphire eyes scrutinized her features one by one. When those jewellike eyes captured hers, she released the breath in a sigh of surrender. She was his. She had always been his and, deep down, had always known it. Now he knew it too.

"I told you earlier that there was a way . . ." Dirk's voice trailed away, leaving tracks of question.

Bemused as she was, Tina knew what he was referring to at once. Dirk had said the words to her that afternoon just as the phone rang with the call from Paul. His response had been to her plea for money. Now, searching his face for a clue and finding none, Tina nodded her head in understanding.

"And that way is?" she asked softly, expecting, from his preceding hints, to be propositioned.

"Marry me."

Tina stared at Dirk in astonishment, but his austere expression left no doubt whatever about his seriousness. Why had she never considered the possibility? she wondered blankly. A tiny smile of bitterness tugged at her lips but was quickly gone. Why should a man buy something he can get for nothing? The old admonition silently mocked her. The light in her eyes diminished as Tina gazed at Dirk knowingly. Had he reached the conclusion that she would refuse to dance until he paid the band?

"Well, Tina?" An edge now serrated Dirk's tone.

"Is your need that great?" Tina blurted.

"Yes." The edge bit her savagely. "Is yours?"

Tina closed her eyes. It was obvious that Dirk believed he was referring to two entirely different types of need: in his own case physical, in hers financial. Lifting her shoulders in a tired shrug, Tina opened her eyes to stare into the blue depths of his. What did it matter? she asked herself, the pain she felt cutting into her heart. If she was his, she was his—whether she was with him or not. Now, given the choice, Tina knew she'd rather be with him than anywhere else on earth. What difference did it make as to why he wanted to be with her?

"Yes." Tina's softly uttered agreement was affirmation to both his questions; yes, her need was great, and yes, she would marry him to alleviate that need.

"When?" Dirk's gaze bored into her.

Attempting insouciance she was light years from feeling, Tina flicked her hair off her shoulders with a toss of her head.

"Whenever," she responded flippantly.

Dirk's eyes narrowed over a revealing leap of flaring anger. "All right." His too-even tone sent a chill that feathered Tina's nape. "Next Thursday," he decided with a grim smile. "It will give us an added something to be thankful for on Thanksgiving."

Tina had completely forgotten that the holiday was only one week away. Gazing into his flinty eyes, she lowered her head in acquiescence. "Whatever you say."

"Look at me, Tina."

At the almost coaxing sound of his voice, Tina raised surprised eyes.

"We've both tried to make it with others and failed." Lifting his hand, Dirk drew an uneven line over her cheek. "I don't know." He shrugged. "Maybe our lives are too entwined." The soft laughter that broke from his lips held scant humor. "My wanting you feels almost incestuous. You were always like a sister to me, much more of a sister than my own ever was."

"Dirk." Tina's protest went unheard and unheeded.

"But I do want you." Dirk's tone hardened. "Thoughts,

dreams, and the longing for you have tormented me long enough. The torment will end one week from today."

Or will it really just be beginning? The consideration dropped into Tina's consciousness like a stone into water, sinking into the very depths of her being. Suddenly cold, she drew her jacket around her to contain the shiver that rippled the length of her spine. Dirk felt the shiver in the tips of his fingers.

"Dinner," he decided firmly, removing his hand and turning in his seat. "You're chilled from sitting here too long and you're probably half starved." His features relaxing, he sliced a teasing glance at her. "My care of you thus far hardly recommends me as husband material . . . does it?"

"You always took very special care of me," Tina reminded him quietly.

"Because you were always special to me," Dirk responded immediately, flicking the key in the ignition with a twist of his long, capable-looking fingers.

And Dirk's fingers were capable, Tina knew. In fact Dirk had proved capable at everything he'd ever attempted, from sailing a boat to reeling in the fish he'd caught over the side. He could ride a horse with the best, ride a wave when it was up, ride a hunch that made an enormous profit for him. Bring a woman straight to heaven.

A sensuous thrill ricocheted along Tina's spine. Yes, she had glimpsed that heaven Dirk could offer a woman. And she had craved more of it every day for the last five years.

Into her own thoughts, Tina was only superficially aware of the motion of the car until it came to a stop mere minutes after they'd pulled away from the house. Drawn out of her reverie, Tina glanced around in confusion. The car was parked in the lot of the imposing Marquis de Lafayette Inn. Frowning, she turned to Dirk, who was watching her, an amused smile curving his lips.

"We're having dinner here?" Tina's brows arched.

"Obviously." Dirk's brows mirrored hers. "Would you prefer to go somewhere else?"

"No." Tina shook her head vigorously. "This is fine. I was just wondering why we bothered with the car."

"Because it will probably turn cold before we're ready to leave." Dirk ran a meaningful glance over her attire. "And I doubt you'll be warm enough in that." Not waiting for a response, he opened his door and stepped out. Tina was standing on the macadam before he'd circled the car.

"Liberated, are you?" he drawled, sliding an arm around her waist.

"Of course." Tilting her head to glance up at him, Tina wound her arms around him and gave him a quick hug, laughing softly at his contemplative look.

"Brazen too," Dirk decided dryly, setting her into motion by striding briskly. "I hope you don't make a habit of draping yourself around me in parking lots . . . or anywhere else, for that matter."

"Only the ones I've known for almost twenty years," Tina quipped, yelping when he retaliated by suddenly tightening his hold on her waist.

Laughing easily together, they entered the Inn and went directly to the Top of the Marq restaurant on the sixth floor. It was over five years since Tina had stepped foot into the restaurant, yet they were greeted with the warmth and friendliness accorded regular customers.

When Tina saw the table they were being ushered to, a small pang twisted her chest. She could vividly remember seeing Dirk at that same table on the July evening her father had brought her to the restaurant for dinner. The spear of pain stabbing Tina was two-pronged. The memory was both bitter and sweet.

Preoccupied, Tina was blind to the searing scrutiny of shrewd blue eyes.

Innocently unaware of the fact that it would be the last time she'd dine out with her already ailing father, Tina had looked forward with glowing excitement to their dinner at the Marq. Within minutes of being seated at a window table that afforded a panoramic view of the ocean, however, all the excitement faded from the evening, and all the expectation Tina had secretly harboured concerning Dirk died an agonizing death.

Dirk had not occupied the table across the room from Tina and her father in lonely isolation. The woman sitting very close to him was unfamiliar to Tina. The woman was a stunner: blond, suntanned, beautiful, and obviously enthralled with her escort.

To the silent death knell of all her girlish dreams of a happy-ever-after with Dirk, Tina had observed the couple from her window table. Intent on the menu, her father never noticed Dirk and his lovely companion. Intent on his companion, Dirk never noticed Tina and her father. Sadly, to this day, Tina could not remember what she and her father had talked about that evening, or what she'd ordered and subsequently eaten. Of course, the identity of the meal was unimportant; the conversation had been the last of any length she'd had with her father.

"Tina, where are you?"

Startled out of the past, Tina gazed solemnly at the Dirk of the present. How incredibly naïve she'd been, she thought. So naïve she hadn't even considered the idea that Dirk would enjoy, let alone need, female companionship. Seeing him with a woman hanging on his every word had shattered Tina's fantasy bubble. A tiny bittersweet smile shadowed her lips.

"Tina?" Though Dirk kept his voice pitched low, the edge of concern reached her. "I asked where you'd gone off to?"

"To an evening five years ago," Tina told him. "The night Dad brought me here for dinner." She sighed. "It was the last time he took me out. And the first time I ever saw you with a date."

"A date?" Dirk gazed at her in confusion. "Who was she?"

Tina shrugged. "I haven't the foggiest. I'd never seen her before." Since it was obvious Dirk didn't remember the woman, Tina smiled. "But she was a knockout; blond, tan, and gorgeous."

"Blond, tan, and gorgeous." Frowning in concentration, Dirk repeated the description. "Hmm, I wonder . . ." He smiled reminiscently as his voice trailed away. "Ah, the disco queen!" he exclaimed, laughing softly.

"Disco queen?" Intrigued, Tina raised a questioning eyebrow.

Dirk shook his head. "All that chick wanted to do was dance," he explained. Then, his laughter taking on a hint of sensuality that annoyed Tina, he qualified. "Well, that isn't quite *all* she wanted to do."

"She liked to swim?" Tina inquired sweetly around a patently false smile.

"Only if it was on top of a water bed," Dirk retorted dryly. "I swear, that woman was—"

"I don't want to hear it," Tina cut him off sharply, feeling her cheeks grow warm when he roared with laughter. "And I don't see anything funny, either!"

"Oh, Tina." Dirk sighed. "You haven't changed at all. You're still a very prim and proper young lady."

"And you have changed completely," Tina shot back. "You never were an arrogant bas . . ."

"I warned you about the name-calling once, Tina." Dirk's quiet tone was coated with ice. "I have no intention of spending my married life being cursed."

"Are you threatening me?" Tina asked in amazement, beginning to feel all the old anger churn in her stomach.

"Merely warning you, love," Dirk corrected gently. "I'm usually a patient man, but my patience doesn't extend to listening to my wife swear at me."

"You haven't got a wife yet." Tina glared at him. "And at this rate, you just may not get one—at least not this one." She stabbed one long-nailed finger against her chest.

"Really?" Dirk was obviously unimpressed by her tirade. A sardonic smile curving his lips, he leaned back lazily in his chair. "Then," he actually purred "whatever will you do to get the money you need to bail yourself out of debt?"

Square one. Tina could really have sworn at him then. Fortunately, the waiter chose that moment to bring the drinks she'd never even heard Dirk order. Reflecting his careless attitude with forced composure, she watched him warily while sipping the cool white wine.

"No quick comeback?" Dirk drawled with chiding humor. "No protestations of numerous financial sourccs? No assurances to the effect that you don't need me—for anything?" The sensuous curve played over his lips again.

He knows full well how very much I need him. The realization of her own vulnerability drained all the fighting starch from Tina's stiffened spine. How she longed to put Dirk down with a verbal slap. But some inner knowledge warned her that, should she attack, Dirk would retaliate harder, and she was simply too tired to deflect his verbal blows.

A self-effacing smile on her lips, Tina raised her glass in salute. "To the victor . . . and all the rest of it," she toasted him bitterly. "We spoils will endeavor to control our tongue."

The sensuous curve to his lips grew a wicked twist. "Not in *every* situation, I hope. There are times when the application of one's tongue can be quite exciting."

"You are absolutely unbelievable!" Tina exclaimed softly.

"Horny too," Dirk admitted blandly. "But then, I think I demonstrated that quite effectively on two separate occasions today, didn't I?" Not bothering to wait for a response from her, he raised his glass in a return toast. "To the blessed end of five long years of horniness."

Humiliation, shame, and pure rage combined momentarily to choke Tina. She loved him to the point of adoration, and he only wanted the use of her body. Collecting her outraged sensibilities, Tina retaliated in the only way that presented itself at that moment. "On our wedding night," she added to his toast, experiencing a small sense of revenge at the spasm of shock that flashed across his face before he could impose control.

"You're really going to make me wait?" he asked, almost teasingly.

"I'm really going to make you wait," Tina repeated.

"I might be agreeable to releasing your money sooner," Dirk suggested. "Or have you forgotten your creditors?"

"I'm really going to make my creditors wait as well." Tina

emptied her glass with a few deep swallows. "Look at it this way," she advised mockingly. "next Thursday, you and my creditors will have something to be thankful for."

Expecting a range of reactions from rage to sarcasm, Tina was amazed when Dirk laughed. She was just beginning to wonder if she should feel insulted when he quashed that idea as it formed.

"Okay, Tina, let's drink to Thanksgiving Day." Once again he raised his glass. "The feast will be all the more enjoyable for the anticipation of it."

Unable to join him in the drink, Tina merely touched her empty glass to his, thinking drolly, *And in this case, I'm the turkey.*

Chapter Eight

Methodically chewing a piece of his rare prime rib, Dirk contemplated the infuriating, tantalizing woman seated across the table from him.

Doing justice to a rather large lobster tail, Tina appeared sublimely unaffected by either his perusal or his presence.

Swallowing a curse along with the mangled piece of beef, Dirk stabbed his fork into the steaming baked potato on his plate. The very idea of blackmailing any woman into marriage was galling. The fact that he was applying force against this particular woman was actually creating a growing sickness inside.

All these years, all these years. The refrain revolved continuously in Dirk's mind. Years of caring, and protecting, and loving Tina. Tina, his sister, his friend, his confidant.

But Dirk no longer regarded Tina as his little sister, and therein lay the root of the conflict that ate at his conscience, setting him against himself.

Dirk loved Tina; there was no question about that. The question tormenting him was, In what way did Dirk love Tina?

Ostensibly viewing the unique mural of "Old Cape May" the Inn was proud to display, while actually observing Tina closely, Dirk consumed his dinner without tasting it, and his wine without feeling its effects.

Smiling inwardly, he watched as Tina daintily devoured her meal, a tremor quaking through him as the tip of her tongue flicked at a glistening drop of melted butter on her lip.

Damn. There certainly was no question of how he wanted to love Tina. Dirk had long ago admitted to himself that he wanted to feast on her like a starving man at a banquet table.

Though Dirk had mentally dodged the knowledge for months, he had finally faced the truth the winter between her sixteenth and seventeenth birthdays. And that truth was that he, Dirk Tanger, the pride of his parents and the private school he'd attended, the shrewd live wire, up-and-coming banker, the no-nonsense businessman, lusted after Tina Holden, the teenaged daughter of the man who'd been more of a real father to him than his own.

Suddenly dry, Dirk drained the full-bodied red wine from his glass. How many women had he used in a vain attempt to quench his thirst for Tina that winter? More than a few, he acknowledged ruefully. And not only that winter, either.

Lord! Dirk now thought in amazement. From the summer Tina was sixteen until that September afternoon when she was nineteen, he'd spent almost as much time hopping in and out of bed as he had amassing the fortune he now possessed. But where the business deals had been satisfying, the sexual indulgences had not. He realized now he had been trying to escape the hold Tina had on him; there was no escape.

Ignoring the remains of his dinner, Dirk refilled his glass, then bleakly watched Tina over the rim, sipping slowly as she finished her lobster.

God, she is so beautiful! So elegant in appearance. So gut-wrenchingly desirable. If anything, Dirk wanted Tina more now than he had before he had experienced the total fulfillment she could give him. And the bottom line of truth was, he'd used his wife as ruthlessly as every other woman in his determination to avoid facing his own reality.

Of course, as his wife had also been using him, Dirk forgave himself that transgression. What he couldn't forgive was his own weakness, which drove him not only to possess Tina physically but to own her soul. And that was exactly what he intended . . . he would own her, completely.

"Is there something wrong with your dinner?"

Dirk's gaze rested on Tina's lips as she posed the question. "No." Raising his glance to hers, he narrowed his eyelids to conceal the flow of desire reflected there. "I guess I'm not as hungry as I thought I was." At least not for beef and potatoes, he amended silently.

"You look . . ." Tina shrugged lightly. "Pensive. Are you feeling a little down?"

Quite the contrary, Dirk thought wryly. "I'm fine, Tina," Dirk assured her. "I'm just not very hungry. "A teasing smile charmed his lips. "But you obviously were." A nod of his head indicated her plate.

"I love lobster tail." Tina smiled. "You, of all people, should know that."

"Yes, I know that, darling." Dirk returned her smile. "I introduced you to it when you were six, remember?"

"Yes."

Tina's whispered response and the dreamy expression on her lovely face combined to send a shaft of pain through Dirk's heart.

Whenever Tina thought of the past, their past, her features softened into that dreamy expression, and she became once again his own beautiful little sister. But there were other times, times like the day he'd confronted her on the beach, when her eyes glittered with the hate she bore him in the present.

Dirk was nothing if not honest with himself about this. He knew that their former relationship bound them together in an intensely emotional way. He also knew that by stepping over the line from brother to lover, he had irreparably damaged that precious relationship. And yet the emotional ties endured, twining around them both, the loose ends of love and hate binding them securely one to the other.

With new insight, Dirk followed the trend of his thoughts. He was not alone in the hell of inner conflict; Tina also suffered the effects of emotions straining in opposite directions.

He loved her, needed her . . . and hated her for having created, however innocently, the insatiable hunger he had for her.

Tina had admitted to loving him, needing him . . . and hating him, not only for shattering her young dreams, but for the subsequent control he'd held over her through her inheritance.

He thought her a grasping mercenary, prepared to use any means or any man in her determination to succeed as a businesswoman.

She thought him a coldhearted ruthless womanizing bastard.

And so they hated each other.

And so they loved each other.

Dirk's thoughts settled fatalistically. Marriage to each other would very likely be both heaven and hell. But it was the only arrangement he'd accept, because he knew from experience that living without her was just pure hell.

He'd live with it, Dirk decided. They would both have to learn to live with it . . . and each other. Raising his glass, he tilted it in a silent salute to his bride to be. It was better that they destroy each other than still more innocent bystanders along their way.

"What are you drinking to?" Though Tina's voice was light, her eyes betrayed wary confusion.

"Us." Though Dirk's tone was smooth, his painful thoughts were centered on the real reason for his toast. To the revenge we'll wreak upon each other, love, he mused darkly. Revenge achieved by legally binding our futures. And if the pill we mutually swallow is bitter, we'll have the bleak consolation of knowing that the coating is very sweet.

"Dirk." Tina's concerned voice drew Dirk from the depths of black despair. "What is it? You look so . . . so pained!"

Sighing deeply, Dirk shook off the residue of bitter speculation. "It's nothing, honey." He grinned to back up his denial. "For a moment there, a spectre was dancing on my future grave."

Future grave? Tina shuddered. What an odd thing for Dirk to say. Sitting forward, she examined his eyes and skin color for signs of a brewing cold or flu. Dirk's color was not only good, it advertised glowing health, and his eyes were blue and clear. Still . . .

"Why are you peering at me like that?"

"I'm not peering." Sitting back, Tina frowned. "I was trying to determine if you were coming down with some sort of illness," she explained worriedly.

Dirk laughed reassuringly. "I'm perfectly all right." Then, knocking back the last of his wine, he set the glass on the table and rose to his feet. "And to prove it," he continued teasingly. "I'll chase you around the floor." Extending his hand, he smiled. "Come on, honey, Come dance with me."

Stepping into Dirk's arms was like stepping into yesterday. Sighing contentedly, Tina obligingly moved closer to Dirk's strength when his arms tightened about her waist. Her senses drowning in the intoxicating masculine scent of him, she allowed her suddenly heavy eyelids to flutter down. Immediately Tina was transported back in time to the only other occasion when Dirk had held her while dancing.

It was late spring, the evening of Tina's senior prom. Excited, she'd finished dressing long before her date, the good-looking boy who sat behind her in English, was due to arrive. Too keyed up to remain in her room, and eager to see her father's reaction to her appearance, Tina had swept down the curving staircase with all the elegance of an antebellum debutante, her wide, belled skirt swishing against the spokes in the stair railing.

Weeks before, to George Holden's mock pleas for mercy, Tina had scoured one shop after another for the perfect gown. The dazed expression on her father's face as she waltzed into the living room made the exhausting search worthwhile. But in truth it was the unexpected blazing gaze of sapphire blue that put the final stamp of approval on the billowing yards of virginal white tulle.

Off the shoulder and with a snug bodice, the dress drew the eye to the budding maturity of Tina's breasts and her tiny waist. The snowy white against her skin enhanced the creamy glow of her neck, shoulders, and arms.

Poised in the doorway to the living room, Tina held her

breath while waiting for the two most important men in her life to offer an opinion. She hadn't had to wait very long.

"Is this beautiful creature my skinny Tina?" George asked in an awed tone.

From where he'd been sitting by the narrow window, Dirk walked to her slowly. "You look like every man's fantasy come to life." His oddly hoarse tone drew her startled eyes to his face.

For one brief moment, Tina thought she saw a flash of intense pain flicker in Dirk's eyes. Then it was gone, banished by a smile that warmed her all the way to her toes.

"Since your date hasn't arrived yet," Dirk murmured, opening his arms wide in invitation, "I'm claiming the first dance."

The music wafting around the room from the stereo was slow and romantic, perfect for that moment. Dirk held her lightly and maintained several inches of space between them during the brief ballad. Yet at that distance and in those fleeting moments, Tina realized two very important things. One was that she followed Dirk's lead as easily and naturally as if they'd danced together hundreds of times. The second was that, even with the distance separating them, she would rather dance with Dirk than any other man on earth.

The appearance of Tina's date was the anticlimax to her evening. Tina had gone on to the prom, her corsage of white and pale green orchids gracing her slender wrist, and she had thoroughly enjoyed her evening. Still, while she laughed and conversed with friends and danced with different partners, she carried an inner vision of being twirled around the small confines of her living room within the thrilling embrace of her one and only hero.

"At least this time there's not a mile of material between us." Dirk's murmured observation sent a tingle feathering Tina's spine. The brushing sensation of his lips moving over her temple drew goose bumps of excitement to the surface of her shoulders and arms. "This time I can feel your body moving with mine." His breath whispered into her ear, cutting hers off entirely.

Attuned in memory and motion, oblivious to the other couples on the dance floor, they swayed to a more evocative, more basic rhythm.

Flushed, her blood rushing through her veins in time to the music, Tina placed her slightly parted lips against the curve of Dirk's neck and caressed him gently with the tip of her tongue when he drew in a quick, sharp breath.

"Are you trying to get tumbled on the dance floor, woman?" Dirk's whispered growl was nearly Tina's undoing. "Maybe it's time to get out of here before we scandalize the decent folk of this fair city." His tone was laced with amusement and a broad vein of sensuality.

Responding to his mood, Tina glanced up at him through her partially lowered lashes. "Did you have a destination in mind?" she asked guilelessly, teasing him by combing her fingers through the fine hairs at his nape.

A visible shiver ran the length of Dirk's spine and his arms flexed in reaction. "We could continue the dance at home," he suggested softly. "In my bedroom . . ." A sexy smile curled the corners of his lips at the gasp that escaped Tina's guard. "I can guarantee you'll love the beat of the music."

For a moment Tina forgot to breathe. Her insides and her resolve melting, she closed her eyes in defense against the luring gleam in his. The temptation to fling caution to the winds was great, but not quite great enough. Piercing the web of sensuality Dirk was weaving around her, a smidgeon of common sense urged Tina to think.

She loved him, and although she would trust him with her life in a threatening situation, she could not trust him with her future. Dirk wanted her now, wanted her enough to make her his wife, and by doing so make not only her inheritance but his own fortune available to her. But if she were to allow him the physical satisfaction he craved before they were legally bound, what assurance did she have that he'd carry through with his promise?

Absolutely none. The answer came from deep within Tina's consciousness. The temptation to end her five-year hunger for him was great . . . but not quite great enough.

Shaking her head, Tina swirled out of Dirk's embrace. "I think we'll take a moonlight stroll on the promenade instead." She laughed, eyes bright with mockery. "Something tells me you could do with some cooling off before crawling into your bed . . . alone." Slanting a come-hither look at him over hers shoulder, Tina made for their table, her body swaying invitingly.

A bemused smile softening his lips, Dirk trailed in Tina's scented wake. After paying the check, he escorted her from the Inn, draping her jacket securely around her shoulders as they crossed Beach Drive to the deserted promenade.

The night air was cold and heavy with salty moisture that tantalized the nostrils and clung to the eyelashes. Drawing the distinctive odor of the seashore deep into her body, Tina was again transported back in time.

How many times had she walked this path with Dirk by her side? she wondered dreamily. The soft murmur of the curling waves seemed to whisper an answer more times than can be counted.

The feel of Dirk's arm circling her waist, drawing her close to the warmth of his body, was a familiar sensation. Tina settled naturally into his easy, loping stride, more at home within the curve of his arm than in the house she'd grown up in.

"Shall we take a stroll along the silvery moonlight path?" Dirk's teasing question was as familiar as his protective embrace. Tina's gaze sought the undulating strip of silver on the inky darkness of the sea. With very little imagination, one could believe it possible to follow that path to the horizon.

"Where will the path lead us?" Tina responded as she always had, bringing her moonlight-brightened gaze back to his face.

Dirk's eyes were dark with the memory of how very often he'd answered Tina's question. "A carefree place, filled with light, laughter, and love." He repeated the words he'd first spoken to Tina the summer her father had drawn him into the circle of love surrounding the Holden family. "A place glowing with all the colors of the rainbow."

Tina blinked against the rush of hot moisture that filled

her eyes, pitying the five-year-old dreamer who had believed that such a place could exist. Smiling sadly, she shifted her gaze back to the lure of the restless sea.

"Growing up is a bitch, isn't it?"

Tina came to an abrupt stop at the harsh bitterness in Dirk's tone. What did *he* know of bitterness? The thought incurred renewed anger. Denying the need to burrow closer to his strength, she slipped out of his encircling arm, spinning away from him.

"Tina!"

Ignoring the entreaty in Dirk's commanding tone, Tina ran down the steps to the beach, unmindful of the abrasive grains of sand that insinuated themselves under the narrow straps of her sandals. She hadn't a hope of outrunning Dirk and she knew it, yet Tina fled on wobbly high heels, heading for the shoreline. Her breath a raspy sound in her ears, Tina didn't hear Dirk as he gained on her. His grasp of her shoulder came as a shock, though it shouldn't have.

Wildly angry, and not even sure why, Tina tried to shake off Dirk's detaining hand. His hold tightened, his arm jerked, and then she was falling, pitching to the ground, pulling him down with the impetus of her body. He landed with a thud beside her.

"What the hell is the matter with you?" Dirk's ragged voice growled into her ear.

"Nothing! Everything! I don't know!" Tina deplored the uncertainty threading her own gasping voice. Her arms flailing, she attempted, unsuccessfully, to scramble to her feet. Utterly spent, she lay still, staring up at the star-tossed sky. "Why did you ask me to marry you, Dirk?" she whispered.

"I think you know the answer to that." Dirk's emotionless tone was chilling.

"Yes." Closing her eyes against the brilliance overhead, Tina shuddered at the memory of his hot mouth searing her skin. "We'll destroy each other, Dirk." Her toneless statement still managed to convey despair.

He was lying so close, Tina felt the sigh he expelled. "Very likely." Dirk was quiet a moment, then he pushed the upper part of his body up to stare directly into her eyes. "But there's no turning back, no getting out of it." His trembling fingers contradicting the fierce determination blazing out of his eyes, he tenderly brushed the hair back at her temples. "Like it or not, Tina, there is a bond between us. An emotional and physical bond. I've never believed in predestination, but . . ." His voice trailed away, and shrugged. The smile that played with Dirk's mouth had the power to wound. "Who knows"— he shrugged again—"maybe we're both working off our individual karma on each other."

Predestination? Karma? Tina shuddered. Inching away from him, she struggled to her feet. Closing her mind to the possibility of what he'd sardonically suggested, she brushed vigorously at the sand clinging to her dress.

"That's ridiculous." Tina wished her voice held more assurance. "We control our own destiny, and you know it."

"Do we?" Chuckling softly, Dirk sprang to his feet before her startled eyes. "Then how do you explain the lure that keeps drawing us back together?"

"Sexual attraction." Speaking each word distinctly, Tina lifter her head proudly. "A violent reaction of our respective body chemicals."

Dirk's soft chuckle expanded into a full-throated laugh. "I'll say!" he exclaimed, choking back a fresh burst of laughter. "And if you think I'm going to deny all those chemicals going berserk inside my body, you're crazy." Grinning wickedly, he slid his hand around her neck and tugged her rigid body into contact with his own. "Sexual attraction, chemistry, or whatever, you are going to marry me." His lips teased the corner of her mouth. "Aren't you?"

Tina felt the tingle begin at the inside of her mouth, then slowly radiate throughout her body. Sighing softly in defeat, she moved her head the fraction of an inch necessary to fuse her lips with his. Disappointment racked her nerve endings when Dirk lifted his head slightly, refusing to kiss her.

"Aren't you?" he insisted, tormenting her by flicking the tip of his tongue over her lips.

"Dirk." Tina's cry was part protest, part plea.

"Aren't you?" His tongue slid fleetingly into her mouth.

"Yes." Clasping his head with her hands, Tina drew his mouth to hers. "Yes," she moaned, parting her lips for the invasion of his. Melting into him, she gave herself to the thrill of his thrusting tongue. "Yes." Her whisper was lost inside Dirk's mouth.

To what conclusion the embrace might have led, Tina had no idea—nor did she care. Swept into abandonment by the fiery onslaught of Dirk's mouth, she was soon past the point of rational thought or even instinctive self-preservation.

Not merely pliant but eager, she threw all her longing and frustration into the kiss, as if trying to absorb the essence of him into her entire being. It was Dirk, an obviously shaken Dirk, who saved Tina from herself.

Tearing his mouth from hers, he held her away from him, his breathing rough and uneven as he stared down into her passion-glazed eyes.

"Good Lord, Tina!" Dirk's whispered exclamation held a note of pain. "Now dare to tell me the only thing between us is *physical* attraction!"

Tina felt the intensity in Dirk through the tremor of the fingers gripping her upper arms. Her breath coming in shallow gasps, she closed her eyes. "Dirk . . . won't . . ." That was as far as she got, fortunately, for she hadn't thought of one word with which to plead her case.

"You will." Dirk enforced his words with a light shake of her shoulders. "You will admit it because, like me, you have no choice."

"You're wrong!" Tina's eyes flew wide in reaction to his statement. Staring up at him, she longed to lower her lashes again, to shut out the heart-wrenching image of him with moonlight striking burnished glints of his hair and sparks of blue fire from his piercing eyes. The glinting streaks in his hair rippled as he shook his head.

"No, Tina, I'm not wrong. I could control simple physical attraction, and I'm sure you could as well. But what we're dealing with here is much stronger, much more involved, and you know it." The smile that feathered his lips sent an ache radiating through Tina's chest. "No, darling, what we're dealing with here has the scent of obsession."

"Dirk!" Tina's cry of protest rang on the cold night air.

"Hush, love." Drawing her to him, Dirk cradled Tina's trembling body close to his hard strength. "Accept it. We've tasted of the forbidden fruit. The obsession is to devour the entire apple."

Obsession.

The one word stood between Tina and sleep. Alternately hot then cold as she lay on her bed, she restlessly drew the covers up to her chin only to throw them off again moments later.

Was she obsessed with the need to possess and be possessed by her friend, her hero, her one-time lover? Flopping onto her side, Tina raised her hand to wipe impatiently at the tears gathering in her eyes. Now was not the time for tears; now was the time for some heavy thinking.

When had her mental waters become so muddy? Sighing tiredly, Tina rolled to her other side. On leaving New York, her goal had been clear-cut, her thinking decisive. Confident in her determination, she'd never really doubted her ability to get what she needed.

Of course, with perfect hindsight, Tina now saw the two glaring errors in her calculations. In the first place, she had conveniently forgotten how adamant and stubborn Dirk could be. And then, compounding her foolishness, she had actually convinced herself that the emotion that ran rampant inside whenever she thought of him was hate.

Grimacing with astonishment at her own self-delusion, Tina slowly shook her head. If she lived for a thousand years, she could not hate Dirk. She could resent him, and she did, sometimes violently. But hate?

A sound, half sob, half laugh, shattered the early-morning stillness of the room. Surely even a moderately intelligent person could define the difference between resentment and hate. Unless, of course, Tina admitted with ruthless honesty, that person wanted to avoid the unvarnished truth that lay beneath the resentment.

And yes, that truth was a love so enduring that even Dirk's coldness failed to freeze it. Did that make what she felt obsessive?

Yes.

Scrambling off the bed, Tina prowled around the dark room like a caged animal; the bars caging her were all mental.

A perfectly normal urge to run gripping her, Tina dropped to her knees beside the bed, groping for the suitcase she'd stowed there on her arrival. Had it really only been a few days? she marveled, sweeping her arm along the carpet. Lord, it seemed like weeks since she'd left her apartment.

Common sense gained control as Tina's fingers brushed the supple leather case. What would running accomplish? Her turmoil was inside, it was emotional, and there was no way to run from it. No, she decided, shaking her head as she got to her feet; running was out. In a sense, hadn't she been running for the last five years? Could she face the idea of running in place for the rest of her life?

No! The cry came from deep within. She knew she had to stay and follow the path connecting her life to Dirk's to its natural conclusion.

Sliding onto the bed, Tina steeled her resolve. With luck, and a lot of hard work, maybe, just maybe, she and Dirk could make a life together . . . *if* they could reconcile their past with the present.

Tina hugged that vaguely hopeful thought to her heart as she drifted into an uneasy sleep.

Behind another closed door across the hall, Dirk lay awake and thoughtful. Had he convinced her? he wondered. Had he managed to convince himself?

Giving up on the hope of sleep, Dirk rose, raking a hand through his hair as he walked to the window to gaze sightlessly at the deserted street below.

Damn, he groaned silently. How had something that had begun so simply become so complicated?

Looking back with his mind's eye, Dirk could see himself, young, lonely, eagerly following George Holden into the house to meet his family for the first time.

Smiling softly into the night, Dirk relived the welcoming warmth Tina's mother had given him, and the glow of love that had appeared to surround the three members of the Holden family. Unstintingly, they had drawn the impressionable youth he had been into that circle of love. And he, as a man, had betrayed George Holden's trust.

Dirk's smile gave way to the bitterness that twisted his lips. And now, with cool deliberation, he was about to betray his friend a second time.

His movement violent, Dirk spun around to stalk the length of his room.

George, forgive me, Dirk pleaded mutely, but I must take your most precious possession and make her mine.

Dirk was still pacing his room, still waging war with himself, when the first streaks of dawn lit the horizon. Stepping out of his boxers, he shrugged into a terry robe and strode to the bathroom. His course was set and there was no going back: Tina would be his.

The plan sprang into Dirk's mind, full blown, as he stood under the stingingly cold shower spray. A satisfied smile tugged at his lips as he mulled the idea over while drying his body with a large white towel.

Tina was vacillating, and Dirk knew it. His own mind set on the necessity of a legal union between them, he'd worried over the possibility of Tina's balking, perhaps even running before he could marry her.

Now Dirk's smile expanded into a confident grin. He knew exactly how to proceed with her. And the answer was so damn simple too.

Pulling on his robe, Dirk left the bathroom, whistling softly as he strolled to his bedroom. Inside his mind a vision lingered, a vision of Tina, her features softened by memories, her eyes faraway and dreamy.

His voice low, Dirk sang the words to the ballad he'd been whistling. As he dressed in chinos and a finely knit sweater, the song's lyrics gave way to a rumbling chuckle.

Pulling on his scuffed desert boots, Dirk swung out of his room and ran lightly down the stairs. His battle tactics clear in his mind, he took the final two steps as one and pivoted toward the back of the house. All that is now required, he thought smugly, is to put the plan into action.

Dirk was again whistling as he sauntered into the bright kitchen. The sight that met his eyes stole the whistle from his lips and the smugness from his mind.

In much the same manner as Mrs. Holden had so many years before, Beth was standing at the stove, preparing a meal. But the figure that arrested Dirk's glance and attention was tall and slim, all graceful motion as she bustled around the table with dishes and flatware, one fiery braid bouncing merrily on her back.

The breath catching painfully in his throat, Dirk experienced an eerie sensation of déjà vu.

Completely unaware that his eyes had clouded with memory and were caressing the slender woman poised expectantly by the table, Dirk moved like a sleepwalker into the room. Having planned to steep Tina in memories throughout the week to keep her amenable to his wishes, Dirk now found himself caught in the very same web.

"Good morning, scrawny." The husky murmur was all Dirk could get past the tightness in his throat.

Chapter Nine

At her first glimpse of Dirk as he paused in the kitchen doorway, Tina felt a rush of warmth tingle through her body. At his murmured greeting, all her bones seemed to melt. Ensnared by the smoky blue of his eyes, she clutched the edge of the table to keep from sliding into a heap on the tile floor.

Within the instant required for him to cross the room to where she stood, Tina was held breathless in a time warp. She was five years old again, quivering with the expectancy of hearing her father's robust voice introduce the golden-haired young man to her smiling mother.

"Breakfast is almost ready." Beth's amused voice broke through Tina's memory warp. "And if you could coax her to eat more, Tina wouldn't be so scrawny."

Simultaneously, Tina and Dirk blinked themselves back to the present, then exchanged smiles of secret communication. Once again attuned to each other's thoughts, they moved in unison to finish setting the table, their gazes tangling when their hands, briefly touching, set off sparks of awareness between them.

"Did you sleep well?" Dirk's low tone flowed over Tina like a healing balm.

"No," Tina admitted frankly, with a rueful smile. "Did you?"

"No." A self-derisive smile shadowed Dirk's lips. "Not at all, actually." A frown drew a line across the bridge of his nose. "Did you run this morning?" Scraping a chair back from the table, he seated her before moving to the stove to help Beth.

"Yes, for a little while." Tina smiled into the arched glance Dirk threw at her over his shoulder. "I wasn't up to the long haul."

"Considering the meager amount of fuel you put into your body, I'm surprised you can run at all!" Beth exclaimed scoldingly, carrying a plate of crisp bacon to the table.

Trailing in Beth's wake with an oval serving dish heaped high with fluffy scrambled eggs in one hand and a plate of stacked toast in the other, Dirk grinned at Tina wickedly.

"Shall we confine her to her room unless she cleans her plate?" he asked Beth dryly.

"It's an idea, but it probably wouldn't work," Beth responded in kind. "What Tina needs is someone to take care of her, twenty-four hours a day!"

"A keeper?" Tina exclaimed, laughing.

"Or a husband," Dirk inserted smoothly.

Beth's shrewd glance shifted from Dirk to Tina. "Is there a husband in the offing?" she asked bluntly.

Tina felt the heat of a flush in her cheeks, but before she could reply, Dirk stole the initiative from her.

"Yes." Dirk equalled Beth's bluntness. "Me."

For long moments the room seemed to hum with tension, then Beth beamed her approval, lighting her face and lightening the atmosphere. "That's wonderful!" she cried, reaching out to grasp their hands. "When was all this decided? And when will the wedding take place?"

"It was all decided yesterday." Dirk supplied the answer, again beating Tina into speech. "And the ceremony will take place next Thursday, Thanksgiving Day." His tone was as dry as Tina's throat.

"Thanksgiving," Beth exclaimed, "how absolutely perfect!" In that moment, Tina was positive she could see Beth mentally shift gears. She was proved correct when Beth added enthusiastically, "We can have a small reception right here!"

Stunned, Tina and Dirk stared as Beth jumped out of her chair and bustled to a drawer in the cabinet next to the sink.

Exchanging confused glances, they tried to make sense of the housekeeper's excited chatter.

"A reception?" Tina whispered, appalled. "Must we have a reception?"

Dirk was already shaking his head, frowning as he glanced back at Beth. "We didn't want any fuss, Beth," he said carefully, not wanting to hurt the older woman's feelings. "I thought the three of us could have a meal out, after the ceremony."

Tina felt her body relax with relief, only to tense again at the shocked expression on Beth's face when she returned to the table, a pencil and pad in her hand.

"Eat out?" Beth's lips pursed sourly. "The three of us?" she repeated in an outraged tone. "Dirk Tanger, you have some very good friends in this town!" The look she leveled at Dirk reminded Tina of a stern teacher . . . her sixth-grade teacher, in fact. Hiding a smile brought on entirely by nervousness, Tina forced her attention back to the chastising Beth. "Not to mention your family and friends in Wilmington."

Displaying patience Tina didn't know he was capable of, Dirk smiled at Beth. "But you see, Beth, Tina and I prefer—" he began gently, only to be interrupted by a now incensed Beth.

"And you, Tina. What about your friends? Don't you think they'd feel slighted if you just sneak off and get married?"

"Sneak off?" Tina and Dirk responded in unison, their voices loud in the quiet kitchen. With a brief nod of his head, Dirk allotted the floor to Tina.

"Beth, we are *not* planning to sneak off anywhere," Tina explained as calmly as she could. "But we both prefer a quiet, simple ceremony. I mean, really," she went on, contriving a laugh she was a long way from feeling, "neither one of us is exactly dewy-eyed. We've both been married before."

"So what!" Beth snorted. "Is it chiseled on stone somewhere that a second marriage can't be celebrated?" As the query was obviously rhetorical, Beth didn't wait for a response. "Good grief!" she scolded. "Every living soul is entitled to one mistake, and most have countless numbers, come to that! You're getting married, for heaven's sake! I'd think you'd want to share your happiness with all your relatives and friends."

"Oh, Beth, you don't understand," Tina protested weakly, turning to Dirk for support. At the contemplative expression on his face, she felt a knot grow in her stomach. The knot expanded with the glittering light that flared in his eyes.

"You know, love, I'm beginning to think Beth's right."

Astounded, Tina just stared at him. Surely he couldn't be serious, she thought wildly. After a brief hesitation, Dirk set her straight on that score. Oozing charm, he leaned toward the now smiling housekeeper.

"What did you have in mind, Beth?"

Beth took off like a Chinese rocket. "Well, I thought I'd prepare a buffet. You know, all the traditional Thanksgiving foods, but with slight variations because it's also a wedding. Using the dining room as well as the living room, I'd estimate we can squeeze about forty or so people into the house."

"Forty?" Tina's squawk went unnoticed as Beth continued talking to a very interested Dirk.

"Of course, there'll be no time to send out formal invitations, but I'm sure your secretary can do the inviting by phone." She raised a narrow eyebrow at Dirk. "Can't she?"

"Certainly," Dirk drawled, obviously amused by Beth's ardor.

"Dirk!" Tina might as well have saved her breath for all the notice her companions paid her.

"I'll need a list of names from the two of you," Beth murmured, scribbling what appeared to be a grocery list on the pad of paper she'd brought to the table. "And I'll need it today." She glanced up to frown at first Dirk, then Tina. "And you also have arrangements to make, don't you? I mean, marriage license, and so forth?"

"Right." Getting swiftly to his feet, Dirk walked around Tina's chair, giving a gentle tug on her braid. "You heard the lady. Let's get crackin', kid."

Feeling slightly punchy, Tina rose and followed him out

of the room. Partial rationality returned as she stood meekly in the front hall, watching Dirk remove their jackets from the closet.

"Where are we going?" she asked, shaking her head as if to clear it of cobwebs.

"Beth was right, Tina, we do have things to do." Stepping behind her, he held the garment as she docilely slid her arms into the sleeves. "We have to apply for the license. There's a three-day waiting period. Remember?"

"Yes, but . . ." Tina came to life as he moved around her to zip up the jacket. "Hey, wait a minute!" she objected. "I have no makeup on, and I should brush out my hair."

Already at the door and holding it open, Dirk ran an encompassing glance the length of her body, from the shiny red braid to her scrubbed face, over the sweater that outlined her breasts and down to the jeans that encased her hips and legs. When he brought his gaze back to hers, Tina imagined she could feel the heat blazing out of his eyes.

"Tina." Dirk's low tone was husky with sensuality. "If we don't leave this house right now, I'm going to pick you up and carry you to my bedroom." Arching one brow, he taunted, "I'd as soon stay here. The choice is yours."

A soundless moan shivered in Tina's throat. Suddenly feeling vulnerable and very tempted, she stared at him wistfully, her eyes drinking in the sheer masculine appeal of him as he leaned lazily against the door.

A quick awareness of his sharpened gaze alerted Tina to what he was about to say.

"Honey, you better make your choice," he warned softly, "while the choice is still yours to make."

Coming to her senses, Tina dashed past him and through the open door, tingling to the rumble of the laughter that followed her. As he joined her on the porch, Dirk's laughter subsided to a teasing grin.

"Coward," he murmured into her ear as he slid his arm around her waist.

Sniffing disdainfully, Tina walked sedately down the

steps, automatically heading for the little Dodge. Long fingers flexing into her flesh brought her to an abrupt halt.

"I think we'll take my car." The gritty edge on his voice caused an altogether different kind of tingle along Tina's spine. "At least I know mine is paid for."

"So is this one." Tina indicated the sports car with a wave of her hand. "And it's not mine anyway."

Dirk's entire body went still; Tina's heart began to race erratically.

"Not yours?" A deceptive silkiness increased the thumping in her chest. "May I inquire to whom it belongs?" he asked with frightening formality.

For a moment Tina could barely articulate past the thickness in her throat. Then a rush of impatient anger swept by the obstruction. Who does he think he is? she fumed, glaring at him.

"It's Paul's," she said tightly. *"My* car was repossessed weeks ago . . . thanks to you!"

"Thanks to me?" Dirk's jaw tensed, lending an arrogance to his features that chilled Tina. "In what way, precisely?" he demanded.

Shrugging out of his grip, Tina hastened to the side of the gleaming Jaguar. "You knew perfectly well in what way," she snapped, mourning the loss of their shared camaraderie.

"Tina, stop this!" Walking to her, Dirk grasped her by her upper arms and shook her lightly. "You know why I've guarded your money so carefully."

"Oh, sure." Incensed now, Tina struggled to free herself; Dirk merely tightened his hold on her. "You were determined to keep Chuck from squandering it. Well, I've got a news flash for you, Mr. Banker. I'm this"—she held her thumb and forefinger apart a quarter of an inch—"far from losing everything I've worked so very hard for!"

"Poor management," Dirk pronounced pedantically, sending Tina's temper soaring.

"It was not poor management!" Tina had to pause to keep herself from screaming at him. "I could have handled it, if—" Realizing what she was about to admit, Tina caught herself up short.

"If Chuck hadn't demanded more and more money from you." Dirk finished for her. "Is that what you were about to say?"

All the fight suddenly drained out of Tina, leaving her feeling excessively tired. How many times had they had this same argument? she wondered bleakly. How many more times would they plow over the same barren ground?

Deflated, she watched as he unlocked the door on the passenger side of the car, and obediently she slid onto the seat at his impatient gesture. Sighing softly, Tina caressed his lithe form with dulled eyes as he circled the hood of the car to the driver's side, sadly aware that he possessed the power to arouse her even when she was furious at him. Futility left a bitter taste in her mouth and she grimaced as he slid behind the steering wheel.

"It's over, Tina." Though quiet, Dirk's tone was hard with finality. "One week from today you can write any number of checks to pay off your debts." His chest heaved with a roughly expelled breath. "And for any other whim that might take your fancy." Reaching out, he caught her chin with his fingers, lifting her head to stare into her eyes. "But the first one had damned well better be a car of your own." His fingers tightening spasmodically, Dirk bent to brush her lips with his own, muttering fiercely, "I want that vehicle returned to Rambeau as soon as possible."

Running the tip of her tongue over her lips to savor the elusive taste of him, Tina fought back a growing excitement. Was that the ring of jealousy she heard in his commanding tone? she asked herself in amazement. Her ebullience went flat with the verbal pin Dirk stuck into her ballooning hopes.

"You belong to me now, Tina. Exclusively." Eyes narrowing dangerously, Dirk visually pinned her to the plush seat. "I don't share my private property with other men. Do I make myself clear?"

Warring emotions of frustration, anger, and crushing disappointment kept Tina silent. She could feel Dirk's mounting anger in the fingers now bruising her tender flesh.

"Do you understand?" he grated in a terrifyingly soft tone. "As long as you wear my ring, there will be no other men in your life."

Sheer rage provided the strength that enabled Tina to jerk her chin out of his grasp. Dirk's insinuation concerning her lack of morals ran through her system like poison. Her chest tight with pain, her breathing shallow, she lashed out at him in a choking snarl. "You pompous bastard, I will be no man's private property!" Twisting around, she groped for the door release. "Do you understand *me?*" she flung over her shoulder.

Dirk stopped her flight by the simple method of catching hold of the braid that seemed to fly right into his hand with her swift movement. Tugging it sharply, he drew a cry of pain from her compressed lips. "Be still and you won't be hurt," he advised remotely. "I did warn you about cursing me. Didn't I?"

"Let me go, Dirk." Tina kept her face averted to conceal the tears blurring her vision. "I've changed my mind. I won't marry you." Being deliberately cruel she added scathingly, "I'll find another man to tide me over until my birthday."

"Stop it!" Dirk's voice rang with the same authoritative tone he'd always used when she'd had temper tantrums as a girl. Responding to that tone, Tina quieted and closed her eyes as his hand released her braid and curled around her neck. Sighing, she allowed him to draw her back against him.

"You know you're going to marry me—so spare me the histrionics, please." Tilting her head up to meet his descending mouth, he added, softly, "Be a good girl, darling, and part your lips for me."

"Dirk . . ." Tina's attempt at protest was swallowed by Dirk's mouth.

The very gentleness of his kiss disarmed her. Carefully, tentatively, his lips explored hers until, feeling the resistance ease out of her rigid body, his lips hardened possessively while he staked his claim with his raking tongue.

When Dirk raised his head to gaze down at her, all the anger was gone from his eyes and expression. "We're already bound to each other, Tina." His fingers trailed lightly over the satiny skin on her arched throat, leaving a path of fire in their wake that evoked a tremor Tina was beyond concealing. "The legalities are just a formality," he murmured, stroking the fluttering pulse in her throat with his thumb. "And you know it."

"Yes."

Hours later, the legalities Dirk spoke of set in motion, Tina sat at the kitchen table mulling over their hectic morning while she played with her lunch, Dirk and Beth's conversation swirling unheard around her.

"Well, I think that if you're going to do it at all, you may as well do it right. What do you say, Tina?"

"What?" Glancing up, Tina blinked. "I'm sorry, I was thinking about something."

Beth frowned. "I asked if you wouldn't rather be married by a minister than a judge?"

"Oh." Tina's frown mirrored the older woman's. "I . . . I don't see that it makes any difference. As Dirk pointed out earlier, this isn't the first time for either of us."

Now Dirk frowned, making the expression around the table unanimous. "But it will be the last," he said flatly. "So perhaps you're right, Beth." He smiled at the older woman. "Okay, you win. Call your pastor and ask him if he'll officiate."

Rising with deceptive laziness, he arched a brow at Tina. "Does that meet with your approval, darling?" he asked smoothly.

Tina shrugged her shoulders; what difference did it make who actually said the words over them? "Yes, of course," she murmured, then she qualified, "but I really don't want a lot of bother." Sliding her gaze to Beth, she cautioned, "Tell your pastor we'd prefer to be married in his study—or for that matter, right here in the house."

"Why, Tina," Beth cried, "that's a wonderful idea!" Jumping up, she whipped around the table to bestow a fierce hug on Tina. "And since the lists you two gave me are so skimpy, we can invite everyone to the wedding as well as the reception!"

At the mention of the lists, Dirk smiled dryly at Tina. Beth had scolded both of them about the meager number of people they wanted present. Nevertheless, they had remained adamant and the guest list Dirk had relayed to his secretary by phone had numbered less than twenty.

"Okay, is that it for today?" Dirk fixed a look at Beth that said it had better be.

"Yes, I think so. Why?"

"Because Tina and I are going to take a brisk stroll on a long boardwalk, that's why." Dirk's tone brooked no arguments. "Let's go, kid," he ordered a blank-faced, open-mouthed Tina.

"But . . . but . . ." Tina stuttered as Dirk grasped her arm to pull her from the chair. "Dirk!" Digging her heels in, she planted her hands on her hips diffidently. "What are you talking about?" she demanded, thoroughly exasperated. It *had* been a strange morning. "What boardwalk?"

"Atlantic City. I'm taking you to dinner and then a show." Dirk grinned. "And if you're good, I might even give you a little money to play with."

"Atlantic City?" Tina's voice betrayed the excitement beginning to curl inside; she'd been longing to see the hotel casinos for ages. "Really?"

"Yes, really," Dirk drawled. "So suppose we adjourn this conclave and get ourselves ready."

"Now?" Tina frowned. "It's only one-thirty. I thought you said we were going for dinner?"

"We are, my sweet." With a strong hand at the back of her waist, Dirk steered Tina out of the kitchen, Beth's chuckle trailing them. "But I also said we were going to stroll the boardwalk." Reaching the stairs, he urged her up the curving treads. "A good brisk walk will whet our appetites."

* * *

The trip to Atlantic City was a huge success and the start of the most enjoyable five days Tina had ever lived through. Leaving all the wedding arrangements in Beth's capable hands, Dirk and Tina drifted through the days in a world all their own, most times steeped in memories of the past they'd shared.

On one exceptionally mild day they went sailing, Dirk laughing as Tina scrambled around relearning skills she'd nearly forgotten.

And on one blustery afternoon they wandered around the ruins of the old lighthouse and gun battery, Dirk indulging Tina by playing hide-and-seek with her as he'd done when she was ten.

They walked the beach and the promenade day and night, in all kinds of weather, holding hands and reminiscing about family and friends and other such walks, countless in number.

In the mornings, Dirk ran beside Tina on the damp sand, his teeth flashing in the bright fall sunlight in an endearingly familiar grin.

Ensnared by silken threads of memory, Tina was happier than she'd been in years. Not at any time did she notice the occasional glance of assessment Dirk slid over her or the shadowy smile of satisfaction that fleetingly touched his lips.

By the time Thanksgiving—and her wedding day— dawned, bright with holiday sunshine, Tina was not only amenable to any and all suggestions Dirk made, she was anxiously looking forward to becoming his wife.

The morning was spent in a happy if hectic continuation of the communion she and Dirk had shared throughout the previous five days. Smiling secretly at each other, they performed the last-minute tasks Beth assigned them without demur, slipping out of the housekeeper's sight at regular intervals to touch with their eyes or hands or lips.

Late in the afternoon, as Tina dressed in a winter-white soft wool suit and a lacy blouse that matched the sherry color of her eyes, she tilted her head whimsically, examining the dreamy-eyed young woman reflected in the mirror, vaguely surprised at the change five short days had wrought in her appearance.

The woman staring back from the looking glass had no need of the artifice of cosmetics Tina had used mere weeks ago to conceal the taut lines of strain around her eyes and mouth. Her skin glowed with the dewy freshness of a late-blooming rose; her soft lips smiled easily with the relief from tightening stress; her eyes sparkled with anticipation.

Turning from the mirror, Tina's gaze slid over the narrow bed, then returned, a delicious tingle igniting her nerves and senses. No longer would she lie alone and lonely on that single bed, she mused, her smile growing sensuous.

Glancing at the watch that encircled her delicate wrist, Tina's lips trembled. Within a few hours she would be climbing the curved staircase again, only this time to share the wide bed of her friend, hero, lover, husband.

Even as Tina stared at the face on her watch, the hands moved and it was time for her to leave the room of her childhood, close the door firmly behind her, and go to meet her future.

Though short, the wedding was beautiful. Tina knew simply because everyone told her it was. For herself, she was too distracted by her groom to take more than surface notice of the solemnly intoned service. She repeated her vows sincerely, if automatically, only coming fully aware as Dirk bestowed the traditional sealing kiss.

Tina had invited only Paul and two of her other employees from the shop as guests. Besides his parents and sister and brother-in-law, Dirk's list had consisted of his personal assistant, who acted as best man, and two married couples from Cape May, all of whom Tina knew casually from her younger days. Beth proudly stood beside Tina as matron of honor.

After congratulations, the shaking of hands, and the kissing of the bride, the guests eagerly attacked the sumptuous array of foods Beth had so lovingly prepared, washing it all down with the champagne Dirk had supplied by the case.

Except for a hurried, serious conversation she had with Paul in the relative privacy of the kitchen, Tina hadn't the vaguest idea of what she talked and laughed about with her guests during the three-hour reception. All she remembered was wishing it would all be over, and that everyone would simply go home.

Tina's new in-laws were the last to leave. When, finally, after pitching in to help clear away the party debris and bestowing still more kisses and well-wishes, they did depart, they took a tired but happy Beth with them to drop her off three blocks away at the home of her best friend.

After waving them on their way, Tina stepped back into the hall, smiling a trifle shyly at her new husband as he closed the door with telling firmness. Her smile faltered as Dirk turned to her, his eyes colder than the night air outside.

"What was that little tête-a-tête between you and Paul in the kitchen all about?" he demanded tersely.

Dirk's tone dispelled most of the euphoric haze that had clouded Tina's thinking throughout the previous days. A frown marring her smooth brow, she shook her head as if to clear it.

"There was no tête-a-tête, Dirk." Lifting her chin, Tina faced him confidently. "For some reason, Paul thought I was considering selling my business. He made me an offer for it."

"For some reason?" A sardonic smile curled Dirk's lip as he softly repeated the words. "How naive of him," he muttered.

"What?" Tina's frown deepened.

Dirk shrugged as he moved into the living room. "Never mind. Did you accept his offer?" Turning slowly, he pierced her with eyes now glittering with blue fire; Tina was too surprised to notice.

"Of course not," she exclaimed. "Why would I even consider it?"

"Why indeed?" Dirk's expression settled into sharp lines of austerity. "Unless, of course," he went on chillingly, "you thought to consider the fact that the business is in New York, while our *home* will be in Wilmington."

Oh, Lord! Tina's teeth caught at her lower lip. Not once had she given even the tiniest thought to where they'd live.

And in all fairness, she could not possibly expect Dirk to make his home in New York while conducting his banking business in Delaware. But give up her business? Everything inside Tina rebelled at the idea.

Distractedly raking her fingers through the mass of red waves, Tina stared at Dirk, mutely beseeching him to solve the problem.

"Well?" Dirk merely stared back stonily.

"I . . . I don't know." Tina shrugged her shoulders helplessly. "I suppose we'll have to work out some sort of arrangement." It was hardly a satisfactory solution, and Tina knew it.

"I see." His sardonic smile was back, causing a twisting pain in Tina's chest.

"Dirk . . ." she began, not even sure of what she was going to say. Her voice faded as he turned abruptly, heading for the dining room.

"I'm going to lock up," he said, not bothering to look at her. "You go up, I'll be there in a few minutes."

Feeling dismissed, and angry for it, Tina hesitated briefly, then ran up the curving stairs, unconsciously dashing into her own bedroom.

Dirk was angry with her, very obviously angry, and he had every right to be. Where *had* her mind wandered off to this last week? Tina berated herself, absently beginning to undress as she paced the floor.

Images of the laughing, companionable days she and Dirk had spent together flitted in and out of her mind. Instead of playing, she sighed, they should have discussed their future—all aspects of their future. And because they hadn't as much as mentioned the future, they were facing their very first crisis on their wedding night.

Her eyes bright with threatening tears, Tina was hanging her suit in the closet when the door to her room was flung open forcefully.

"What the hell are you doing in"—the sharp edge of Dirk's voice softened as he caught sight of Tina—"here?" he finished hoarsely, his eyes devouring the look of her body, clad skimpily in a white-satin teddy, sheer hose, and sling-back high heels.

"Oh, God, Tina, you're so beautiful!" A blue flame leaping in his eyes, Dirk slowly crossed the room to her. Raising his hand, he slid his fingers into the thick waves that tumbled to her shoulders, lifting one tendril to his lips as he bent his head. "And now you're mine!" Brushing her hair back, he sought the curve of her neck with his mouth.

Tina knew she should stop him; they had to talk, come to some kind of understanding. She knew it and yet, at the touch of his moist lips against her skin, she chose to forget what she knew. Closing her eyes, she let her head drop back, giving him access, and invitation.

"My Tina." Dirk's warm breath sensitized the nerves close to the surface of her skin. "Finally," he muttered, sweeping her into his arms and carrying her to his room across the hall.

There was no hesitation, no awkwardness, no fumbling. Within moments Dirk had removed Tina's scanty clothing and his own, tossing everything carelessly to the floor. Then, his eyes worshiping her flawless form, he lowered her gently to the bed.

Covering her quivering body with his own, Dirk proceeded to drive Tina wild with his lips, his hands, and the exciting murmurs he growled deep in his throat.

"I've waited so long, so very long." Tina shuddered as Dirk's tongue tasted every inch of her. "Oh, love, the nights I lay awake, aching for your softness, for the way you fill my senses, for the sweet taste of your mouth."

Time and time again he brought her to the very edge of ecstasy, only to soothe her, calm her before arousing her unbearably once again, whispering raggedly, "I want to make it last for ever; I want it perfect for both of us."

Gasping, her mind lost to reason, needing his possession more than she would have believed it possible to need anyone or anything, Tina clung to Dirk, returning his caresses.

And when finally Dirk's hair-roughened thighs eased between the silkiness of hers, Tina cried out with joy.

Becoming one, their loving was hot, and sweet, and at times savage, so very starved were they for each other. And then, their oneness complete, they slept in each other's arms.

Chapter Ten

"Are you on the pill?"

Still lying curled against his warm strength, barely awake, Tina blinked as she gazed up into her husband's calm face.

"What?" she asked softly, shaking her head to dispel the lingering wisps of sleep.

"I asked if you've been taking a birth control pill." Dirk's voice was as calm as his composed features.

"No." Tina frowned; what was he getting at? "Why?"

Dirk's chest heaved in a deep sigh. "Well, it's too late to do anything about last night," he said wearily. "But from now on, until you can see a doctor to get a prescription, I'll see to it."

Thoroughly confused, and oddly fearful, Tina gazed at him in amazement. "Dirk, I don't understand. What difference—"

"I worried myself sick that other time, after your father died," he interrupted in a faraway tone. "I called myself all kinds of a fool for being so careless."

As Tina listened to him, her eyes widened in stupefaction. How strange, she mused; usually it was the female who worried herself sick. At the time, crushed by his rejection and consumed with resentment, Tina hadn't even thought about the possibility of becoming pregnant.

"But, Dirk," she chided gently, "that was a long time ago. Why would we need to be careful now?"

"I could say it's because I want you all to myself," he said, expelling his breath on a very weary sigh. "And although that would be the truth, it would not be the complete truth."

Disentangling his legs and arms from hers with obvious reluctance, Dirk slid off the bed.

Her still slumberous eyes cloudy with confusion, Tina stared up at him blankly. "Dirk, I . . . I don't understand."

"I think it would be better for all concerned if we agreed not to bring children into this marriage," he explained in an oddly thick voice.

"No children?" Tina repeated dully, then shocked: "No children! But why?" This time Tina's blink was against the hot sting of tears. Through the blur, she missed the spasm of pain that flickered over Dirk's face.

"Tina . . ." Dirk raked his fingers through his hair agitatedly. "Honey, you must admit that you're not the same type of woman your mother was," he said distractedly.

"My mother?" Tina echoed flatly. "Dirk, what does . . ." Her voice trailed away as he turned away from the bed.

"I know what it's like to grow up in a house where the mother is so terribly busy with her own pursuits, remember?" Sublimely unconcerned with his nakedness, Dirk strode restlessly around the room. "For all the delight and enthusiasm my parents displayed last night, you know as well as I do that they could never really be bothered with the day-to-day problems of raising children."

Spinning to face her, Dirk smiled humorlessly. "Oh, I will grant that they love me in their own fashion, but in any competition with *his* work and *her* civic duties, both my sister and I ran a poor second. The closest thing to a real home I ever knew was in *this* house."

Every bitterly anguished word Dirk spoke was true, and Tina knew it. Hadn't she heard her father voice the same opinion to her mother numerous times while she was growing up? But still, what did that have to do with *their* marriage? Tina felt even more confused than before. She would have expected Dirk to be almost fanatic in his determination to be a good father—but not to want children at all? That didn't make any sense. And what had he meant about her mother?

"Dirk?" Her eyes wide, Tina sat up as he rummaged in a drawer for underwear, a pair of jeans, and a shirt. When he paused to glance over his shoulder, she blurted, "Where are you going?"

"For a shower," he muttered. "Then for some coffee." Turning away, he reached for the doorknob.

"Wait!" Now Tina was on her knees in the center of the bed, disregarding her own nudity. Though he paused again, Dirk held firm to the doorknob.

"Well?" he asked with tired patience.

Hurting for him, and herself as well, Tina drew a steadying breath. She had to have an answer. "I'd like to know what you meant by saying I'm not the type of woman my mother was."

"Oh, Tina." The eyes that met hers were bleak. "I would think, after last night, the answer would be obvious. You hadn't even given any thought to where we'll live." His eyes closed briefly. When he opened them again, they were remote. "Or for that matter, if we'll even live together."

"But—" Tina began, flushing.

"I know," he interrupted. "Your career and business mean everything." He smiled sadly. "And that was what I meant by the comparison with your mother. The only thing your mother ever asked for from this life was this house—with her husband and daughter safely inside it. She was the homemaker-mother type." His smile vanished, leaving his mouth unrelentingly tight. "On the other hand, you need the challenge of a career—at whatever cost." Shrugging, he twisted the knob and swung the door open, unaware or unheeding of Tina's low gasp of pain.

"Dirk!" Once again her cry halted him. "I've—I've worked so very hard for it!"

"I know. I've accepted it. I won't ask you to give it up. Not the challenge or the excitement or any of it." His chest heaved with the depth of his sigh. "You're not the homemaker-mother type, Tina. I prefer not to bring a child into the unstable marriage situation we've bound ourselves to." Stepping into the hall, Dirk shut the door quietly behind him.

Tina stared at the door until the flow of tears obliterated the carved wood panels. What had they done? What had *she* done? Distractedly, she combed her fingers through the long mane Dirk had tangled during his impassioned lovemaking. More to the point: What were they going to do now? Everything Dirk had said was true—as far as it went. She did love her career, and the challenge, and the excitement. But she loved him too. She *wanted* to bear his children. Didn't Dirk realize that?

How could he? She silently answered her own question. Did they really know each other anymore? Tina sighed; how could they have gotten to know each other again? All they'd done was spar and jab at each other.

What was she going to do? she wondered, gazing around the room where she'd discovered the meaning of the word *bliss*.

They had to talk, she decided, slipping off the bed and drawing a robe over her chilled body. She should have insisted they talk things out *before* she so mindlessly agreed to marry him.

Wiping ineffectually at the tears still running freely down her cheeks, Tina sank onto the edge of the bed. Why hadn't they discussed the everyday details of marriage? Frowning, she carefully retraced every minute she and Dirk had spent together since he'd first mentioned the word marriage.

Tina's tears lessened, then stopped completely as enlightenment slowly dawned. Incredible, unbelievable as it was to accept, the realization hit her that Dirk had seduced her a second time . . . only this time he'd seduced her with memories. And she, fool that she was, had succumbed every bit as easily the second time as she had at the untried age of nineteen.

Her lovely features settling into rigid lines of anger and self-disgust, Tina shook her head slowly. Denying the pain that seemed determined to tear her apart inside, she faced the truth squarely. Not only had Dirk seduced her twice, he'd rejected her twice, the first time when he'd sent her back to school after making her a woman, and just a few moments ago, by rejecting her worthiness in mothering his children.

What kind of life could they possibly have together, Tina wondered dully. Unable to bear thinking about the barren emptiness of that life, she scrambled to her feet and fled to the now vacant bathroom.

Some thirty minutes later, carefully attired in her finest wool pants and a complementing sweater, with her hair brushed into obedience and her tear-ravaged face camouflaged with expertly applied makeup, Tina strolled into the sunny kitchen determined to appear her best before her husband.

Dirk was sitting at the table, his hair gleaming almost copper in the ray of sunlight streaming in through the window, his hands curled around a steaming mug of coffee.

As she entered the room, he glanced up and Tina felt her breath catch painfully in her throat at the weariness on his beloved face.

And it always had been, and always would be beloved to her, Tina acknowledged sadly as she crossed the room to pour herself a cup of coffee. Whatever her future, Dirk would have to be part of it. Tina had tried denying that truth once, she simply wasn't up to the subterfuge any longer.

Carrying the cup to the table, Tina sat down opposite Dirk, who had watched her every move through shuttered eyes.

"What are we going to do?" she asked with what she considered commendable calm.

"Do?" Dirk raised one burnished brow. "Why, we're going to enjoy our honeymoon." He shrugged. "At least for the next ten days" he qualified dryly. "I have to be back in Wilmington a week from Monday." Then, the sardonic smile Tina was quickly growing to hate curving his lips, he said, overpolitely, "And don't you have some financial matters to see to?"

"Yes," Tina admitted tiredly. "That is, if you release my money."

"I have." The coldness edging his tone chilled Tina to the marrow. "Any other questions . . . my love?" Dirk drawled with quiet insolence.

Refusing him the pleasure of seeing her flinch, Tina employed every ounce of willpower she possessed to retain her composure. "Just one," she responded steadily. "Are we going to see each other at all? I mean, after we leave here next Monday?"

"Of course," Dirk replied unhesitatingly, if dryly. "I suggest we meet here on Christmas Eve and stay through the first week of the new year." Again one brow arched quizzically. "Isn't that what you had in mind as a 'sort of arrangement'?"

Tina opened her mouth to protest, then closed it again. She *had* made the suggestion, and even if she hadn't meant it the way Dirk had interpreted it, what difference did it make? For even though Dirk had said *their* home would be in Wilmington, Tina now realized he couldn't care less whether they shared a home permanently or a bed every few weeks or so.

"Does that *arrangement* meet with your approval, Tina?" Dirk insisted grittily.

As she raised her cup to her lips, Tina lowered her lashes to conceal the shimmer of tears blurring her vision.

"Yes," she whispered, gulping the hot brew in a vain hope that it would warm her frozen insides.

Tina held little expectation for the remainder of their time together. Confounding her yet again, Dirk proved her assumption incorrect as soon as they left the breakfast table.

For the rest of that day and the nine days that followed, Dirk wrapped Tina in a glorious mantle of happiness. And if at times his laughter seemed a trifle strained and his lovemaking a bit desperate, Tina was far too bemused to notice.

By the time she found herself behind the wheel of the Dodge, approaching New York City, it was much too late to ask questions. Dirk had left the house in Cape May hours before she'd awakened that morning.

Her hands gripping the wheel as she had a near miss with a cab, Tina felt her cheeks glow with the memory of the reason she'd overslept.

They'd returned to the house very late after a last fling in Atlantic City, and Tina had literally danced into Dirk's arms with buoyancy, flushed with the thrill of winning fifty-five dollars at roulette. Laughing with her, Dirk had swept her into his arms and up the curving steps. But the laughter subsided, replaced by the repeated murmur of her name as he slid into the big double bed beside her.

Throughout what was left of the night and into the pearly gray dawn, Dirk was a flame in her arms, a flame burning out of control, igniting an answering blaze deep inside Tina.

Now as Tina made her way back to her empty apartment, and her emptier life, she sighed for what might have been for her and Dirk—if the love she knew he carried for her only outweighed the bitterness she also knew he harbored.

Away from Dirk, time dragged endlessly for Tina. But the slowly moving hours produced one positive resolution in her mind. Tina wasn't even sure exactly when that resolution occurred, but midway through the three long weeks of separation following their honeymoon, she realized she had lost her resentment for Dirk. Now she merely loved him.

When she'd awakened that last morning of their honeymoon, alone and already lonely, Tina had bridled at the terse note Dirk had left on his pillow. The note had consisted of four demanding words. In a slashing scrawl, Dirk had ordered: *Christmas Eve. Be here.*

Disappointed, disheartened, Tina crumbled the note up angrily, only to smooth it out again after she was packed and ready to leave. It wasn't much, just a small scrap of paper, but he'd scribbled his name across the bottom, and it was all she had of him to take with her. Folding the wrinkled note carefully, Tina slid it into a zippered compartment of her handbag; she'd carried it with her everywhere since then.

As the tension and anticipation of the approaching holiday accelerated, Tina's spirits swung from low to rock bottom. The glittering decorations, the joyous music, and the trills of excited laughter all combined to instill depression and longing in her.

Telling herself she absolutely would not do it, Tina nonetheless found herself pushing her credit card across a counter for a beautiful handmade cableknit sweater for Dirk for Christmas. As she had already written out Christmas bonus checks for her employees, her only other purchase was a lacy shawl imported from Spain for Beth.

Sleeping little and eating less, Tina was beginning to re-semble the Ghost of Christmas Yet to Come as Christmas Eve drew closer. As the holiday business was always frantic, Tina was working herself to a frazzle when, surprisingly, Paul Rambeau decided he'd had enough of it. Lingering in the shop after one particularly frantic day, he peremptorily closed the account printout Tina was laboring over.

"I want you to get out of here," he said quietly when Tina shot him an angry look.

"What?" Tina muttered, shocked by his action and his advice.

"And I mean all the way out," Paul went on assertively. "Look at yourself, Tina!" Frowning, he ran an encompassing glance over her drawn features and thin frame. "For God's sake, you're so fragile—physically *and* emotionally—you look like you'd shatter at the lightest touch."

"I'm all tight," Tina insisted.

"No, honey." Paul shook his head pityingly. "You are defi-nitely not all right. You're on the verge of crumbling, and I don't want to witness it. I think it's time to go home."

"To an empty apartment?" Tina choked through her tear-clogged throat.

Paul smiled tenderly. "No, Tina. To your banker."

"Paul, you don't understand."

"That's right, I don't. But I understand this: If you don't do something about the problem between you two, you're going to wind up in a hospital." Paul bent over to grasp her chin and raise her face to his. "There are only two days left before the holiday. I can handle everything here. Go home, Tina. Home to Cape May. Make peace with your husband . . . and yourself."

Peace. Yes, Tina decided sometime around three A.M. that night, perhaps it was time to make some sort of peace with Dirk. She had endured five years of undeclared war, both hot and cold, and she was simply too weary to maintain the battle. Paul was right; it was time she went home.

The next morning, tired, nervous, filled with trepidation,

Tina called the shop and asked to speak to Paul. The moment he came on the line, she blurted her question.

"Do you still want to buy the shop?"

"Yes," Paul responded promptly, reassuringly. "Are you ready to sell?"

Tina's response was equally prompt. "Yes."

Paul's long sigh of relief sang along the wire to Tina. "I'm positive you're doing the right thing, honey. Every man likes to believe he comes first with his woman." He laughed softly. "And as tough as Dirk obviously is, I doubt he's any different from the rest of us closet chauvinists. And I know he loves you."

"Can I come cry on your shoulder if he proves you wrong?" Tina asked tremulously.

"I'll go you one better," Paul said quite seriously. "If you like, I'll come there and flatten him for you."

Paul's promise was the one bright ray in an otherwise gloomy and overcast day. With the lowering clouds threatening snow, Tina loaded her suitcases and the two exquisitely wrapped presents into the unsporty compact she'd bought the week before and, without a backward glance, drove out of the city.

A fine, light snow began falling as Tina left the Garden State Parkway and turned onto Lafayette. The pavements wore a dusting of white when she parked the car in front of her house.

"You're early!" Beth exclaimed happily, hugging Tina as she urged her into the warmth of the house. "Dirk told me to expect you both on the twenty-fourth."

"I needed a holiday," Tina explained, laughing to keep from crying.

Stepping back, Beth ran an assessing gaze over Tina's slim body. "I'd say you needed one very badly," she murmured despairingly. "Tina, are you ill?"

"No! Of course not." Shrugging out of her coat, Tina walked to the fireplace to warm her hands near the crackling fire. "I'm just tired. I've been busy at the shop the last few weeks. All I need is some rest." And to be close to Dirk, she added silently.

"The house looks beautiful, so Christmasy," she complimented Beth, gazing around at the natural decorations of pine boughs, fruit and nut arrangements, and flickering candles. "And the tree is magnificent!" she exclaimed, staring at the shimmering six-foot blue spruce. "And"—Tina drew a deep breath—"I'd hazard a guess that you've been baking up a storm!"

"Only the usual." Beth dismissed her efforts, while still beaming with pleasure. "Cookies, mincemeat pie, and fruit cake."

"It smells like home." Impulsively hugging the older woman, Tina sniffed. "It feels like home too."

Much too close to tears, Tina hurriedly collected her things and headed for the stairs, positive that unless she moved away from Beth at once, she'd be sobbing out her unhappiness on the older woman's shoulder.

By the time Tina finished unpacking in the room she and Dirk had so passionately shared for ten days, she was wound as tight as a spring. Pulling on her jogging outfit, she determined to run off her tension. As she left the house, Tina assured Beth she'd be back shortly.

The beach was deserted. Tina's sole company was the muted roar of the waves and the occasional caw of a gull. Tina was never certain, afterwards, when she lost sight of her intention to run for only a half hour or so. Depressed, fearful of yet another rejection from Dirk, her mind revolving with images and impressions of all the times, happy and bitter, they had shared, she began running, and forgot to stop.

Her feet rhythmically slapping the wet sand, Tina ran on and on, past pain and into near euphoria. On and on, unaware that she was practically staggering, she was unsure if the call came from within or without the first time she heard her name, sounding like a cry of pain swirling in the wind-tossed snow.

"Tina."

Frowning with the effort to concentrate, she kept on, unable now to stop, unaware and uncaring.

"Tina!"

Dirk. Oh, Dirk. Sobbing, yet no longer knowing why, Tina stumbled to her knees. Her tortured breaths a sound of agony, she closed her eyes as her head dropped to the sand.

"Oh, my God. Tina!"

She vaguely heard the beloved, familiar voice as she slid into the comforting arms of oblivion.

When Tina opened her eyes she was in the big double bed and the room was flooded with morning sunshine. The details of how she'd gotten back to the house, let alone into the bed, were a mystery to her fuzzy brain. One thing was certain; it was morning. The morning of Christmas Eve? Tina asked herself.

Christmas Eve. Dirk was coming today!

Flinging back the covers, Tina sat up, groaning at the stiffness in her muscles. Then, her mental fuzziness dissipating, she remembered bits and pieces of the day before; her foolish overexertion on the beach, the sound of someone calling to her, her collapse on the sand. Had it really been Dirk calling to her?

Ignoring the aches in her body, Tina rose, scooping up her robe and sliding her arms into the sleeves as she hurried from the room.

She found Dirk in the kitchen, sitting at the table, a cup cradled in his hands, in much the same manner as the day after their wedding. However there was one glaring difference in his appearance. This morning Dirk looked overdrawn and exhausted, his face pale, his eyes shadowed, and perhaps the most startling thing of all to Tina, his clothes rumpled as if he'd slept in them.

As she entered the room, Dirk glanced up quickly and Tina's breath caught in her throat at the haggard, harried look of his face. The eyes that observed her passage into the room were dark and rimmed with red. Had he been crying? she wondered.

Shaken, yet unable to accept the idea of Dirk crying for any reason, Tina continued in a straight line to the coffeepot.

"How are you feeling?"

The hoarse, hesitant note in Dirk's voice arrested Tina's hands midway to the coffeepot. Was he coming down with a cold? she speculated, completing the action of pouring the dark brew into a cup. A cold would explain the rough edge to his voice and the redness in his eyes. Staring out the window above the sink, Tina answered without looking at him.

"I feel stiff and achey, and more than a little foolish." Turning slowly, she met his burning stare directly. "Was it you I heard calling me? Did you bring me home and put me to bed?"

"Yes. Beth helped me get you into bed. She was pretty upset." Dirk sighed tiredly. "And I was scared out of my mind."

Though Tina had to bite her lip, she managed to face his brooding expression. "I . . . I'm sorry, Dirk."

"What the hell were you trying to do?" Dirk demanded raggedly, scraping the floor as he pushed back the chair and jerked to his feet.

Beginning to tremble in reaction, Tina bit down harder on her lip. "Nothing. I . . . I don't know."

"Are you so very unhappy, Tina?" There was an odd sound to Dirk's voice, as if there were something caught in his throat.

"Yes." Unconscious of the pain, at least in her lip, Tina's teeth sank deeper into the tender flesh.

"Is it me?" Dirk asked very softly.

"Yes." Tina was shocked at the sudden taste of her own blood as her teeth pierced her lip. With a distracted flick of her tongue, she removed the ruby drop that welled there, her gaze intent on the spasm of pain that passed over Dirk's features.

"Because I forced you into marriage?" he said huskily.

"No," Tina replied sadly, "Because you don't love me."

"Not love you?" Dirk's amazed expression might have been funny if his features hadn't revealed pure agony. "I adore you. I've always adored you." His body rigid with tension, his face pale, Dirk went on harshly, "Ever since the first day

I walked into this house, into this very room, I've adored you!" Moving jerkily, he started toward her. Tina, I—"

"But that's not the same thing!" Tina cried over his bitter voice. "It's not the same kind of love a man feels for a woman!" All restraint gone, Tina made no attempt to contain the tears that trickled down her face. "I'm not a little girl anymore, or even a teenager. I'm a woman and I need— Dirk!" she cried out as he grasped her by the shoulders and pulled her into his arms.

"I have needs too," Dirk muttered, rubbing his cheek over her hair. "I need you. Oh, Tina," he moaned, seeking the sensitive skin on the curve of her throat. "Tina, hold me. Love me. These last weeks have been sheer hell without you." Lifting his head, Dirk brushed his lips over hers, then paused to draw her lower lip into his mouth, the tip of his tongue testing the texture of the delicate inner flesh.

A heady combination of ripe and sensual excitement bubbling through Tina sent her hands up to cradle his face. Capturing his teasing lips with her own, she let her deep kiss and her softening body convey the barrenness of her own last few weeks.

Even though Tina knew it would solve nothing, she didn't protest when Dirk swung her into his arms, murmuring deep in his throat of a hunger raging out of control. Clinging to him, she buried her face in the curve of his neck as he strode through the house to the stairs.

"Beth." Tina remembered the housekeeper as Dirk attained the landing at the top of the staircase.

Dirk's arms tightened around her tensing body. "Beth left a little while ago to spend today and tomorrow with her sister and brother-in-law in Wildwood Crest," he murmured tersely. "Even though she spends the holiday with them every year, she was undecided this morning whether to go or not. She was very concerned about you, Tina," he chastised softly as he continued on into the bedroom and sat with her on the bed.

"I . . . I'm sorry." Tina lowered her lashes in shame.

"You should be," he chided gently. "You frightened both of us very badly . . . and we both love you, you know."

Tina's lashes swept up, "Do you, Dirk?" she asked tremulously, gazing into his eyes steadily. The tender expression on his face caused a thickening tightness in her throat.

"Yes," Dirk answered simply. "In one form or another, I always have." Raising his hands, he cradled her face in his palms, drawing her to him as he lowered his mouth to hers. "Yes, Tina, I love you," he whispered against her lips. "I suppose I always will. Oh, Tina, please say you love me too."

"I do," Tina sighed, seeking fuller contact with his mouth. "Dirk, you know I do."

Their avowals were repeated, at times in impassioned gasps, at others in replete murmurs through what was left of the morning and into most of the afternoon.

The late afternoon sunlight spilling through the bathroom window struck burnished highlights off Dirk's wet hair, and made Tina's slick body gleam as they lathered each other between bouts of laughter and consuming kisses.

"For a man who had practically no sleep at all last night, I'm feeling pretty damned good," Dirk declared, grinning as he stepped out of the shower and onto the bath mat beside Tina. "You feel pretty good too," he teased, skimming his hands over her water-beaded breasts.

"If hollow from hunger," Tina laughed, slipping away from his enticing fingers.

"Good Lord, that's right!" Dirk's stricken gaze skimmed her too slender form. "You missed dinner yesterday and you haven't eaten a thing at all today." His expression a study in self-reproach, he shook his head. "You know, you were right. I am a selfish bas—"

"Dirk," Tina exclaimed, her feeling of well-being expanding at his obvious concern, "I refuse to listen to you talk that way about the man I love. The problem is easily solved— that is, if there's anything to eat in the house?"

"Anything to eat?" Dirk laughed. "Beth ran amok preparing things for us. The refrigerator is on the point of bursting."

"Well, then, what are we standing around for?" Tossing her sodden towel in the hamper, Tina dashed out of the bathroom, Dirk at her heels. "Let's throw some clothes on and go relieve the poor thing of some of its burden." Inside the bedroom she paused to give him a contemplative look. "On second thought, let's relieve it of a lot of its burden. I feel like I could eat my way through a supermarket!"

An hour and forty odd minutes later, the remains of their feast littering the table, Tina, her robe sweeping the floor, walked to the coffeepot to refill their cups as Dirk sliced thick wedges of fruitcake.

Glancing casually out the window a soft "oh" whispered through Tina's lips at the scene that met her gaze. Approximately two inches of glittering white snow covered the ground and clung to tree branches and fence posts.

Though her exclamation of appreciation was barely audible, Dirk heard it.

"What is it?" he murmured, sliding his arms around her waist as he came to a stop behind her.

"The snow." Sighing, Tina rested her head against the warmth of his hard chest. "Isn't it beautiful?"

"Yes," Dirk agreed readily, then qualified, "Almost as beautiful as my wife."

His wife. For the first time since he'd slipped the narrow platinum band on her finger, Tina truly felt she was Dirk's wife. Loving him until she thought she'd die from the joy of it, Tina leaned against him, reveling in the strength he exuded, growing lightheaded with the musky masculine scent of him.

"Darling?" Dirk's soft voice, close to her ear, enhanced the glow warming Tina from the inside out.

"Hmm?" Snuggling closer, Tina rubbed her cheek against the soft cotton T-shirt he'd pulled on along with washed-out jeans, luxuriating in the play of muscles in his chest and the natural body heat emanating from him.

Absently, reciprocally, Dirk caressed her hip with one palm. "Honey . . . ah . . . have you seen a doctor for a prescription for birth control pills?" he asked in an uncharacteristic hesitant tone.

Sudden tension drew Tina's nerves taut again. "No," she finally responded honestly if breathlessly.

"Good." Dirk expelled the word softly on a long sigh.

Eyes wide with surprise, Tina twisted around in his arms to stare up at him. "You're not angry or upset?" she asked in astonishment.

"No, darling, I'm not angry or upset." Closing his eyes for an instant, he swallowed—noticeably. "I can't describe the relief I'm feeling at this moment," he said hoarsely.

"But, Dirk"—Tina gaped in sheer amazement—"you were so adamant about not wanting a child!"

Dirk's hands gripped her waist reflexively. "No. No, honey." He shook his head in denial. "I never said I didn't *want* a child. I do—rather badly, as a matter-of-fact. And not just one, but several."

Tina frowned. "Yet you didn't have any with your first wife," she murmured. "Why?"

Tina's amazement grew as a faint flush spread from Dirk's neck to his cheeks, and he wet his lips as if suddenly suffering from a dry throat.

"I . . . well, you see . . ." He smiled in self-derision. "Oh, dammit, Tina! I didn't want children from her! I wanted them from *you.*" At her shocked gasp, he smiled softly. "I couldn't give her a child, honey." He shrugged. "Not that she wanted one, she didn't. But even if she had, I . . . I couldn't"

Alarm shot through Tina's mind; was there something wrong with him—something he hadn't told her about? She didn't get the opportunity to ask. Reading her expression, Dirk laughed a little ruefully.

"No, Tina," he assured gently. "I'm perfectly capable of making a child. The problem has been that I have this vision of what my child will look like." Releasing her, he raised a hand to curl his fingers into her hair. "In my vision, the child is a beautiful, scrawny little girl with one braid bouncing on her back."

Though Tina blushed with pleasure, she frowned from confusion. "Dirk . . ."

"Honey, I've spent the majority of the last few weeks cursing myself for telling you I'd prefer not to have children." Raising his hand, he drew his fingertips over her flushed cheek. "I want us to have children, love. I long to watch our child grow inside you." Tilting his head back, he ran a frowning glance over her slim form. "That is," he qualified in a deeply concerned tone, "after you've put some sustaining weight on your body. Have you been overworking and undereating these last weeks?"

"Yes," Tina answered simply. "But most of all, I've been pining for you."

With a strangled groan, Dirk closed his arms around her tightly, as if actually afraid to let her go. "Oh, God, love!" he murmured grittily. "What we've been doing to each other these last five years is criminal." He pressed his lips to her forehead, breathing deeply. Then, raising his head, he smiled gently. "Come, love, it's time to straighten out this mess we've made of our lives."

Clasping her hand, he drew her to the table. "We already know the physical side of our marriage works." He grinned as the color tinged her cheeks again. "Now we've got to work out the practical side."

Her eyes misty with unshed tears, Tina watched him hungrily as he returned to the counter for their coffee cups, filling them again after pouring the now cold brew down the sink, then joining her at the table.

"When I said I loved you, I meant it. I wasn't mouthing the words in the heat of the moment." Dirk's chest heaved a deep sigh. "I've been in love with you since the summer you turned sixteen, Tina."

"Dirk!" Tina carefully placed her cup on the tabletop. "You never—"

"Let me finish, love," Dirk again interrupted gently. "Then you can have your say. Okay?"

Staring at him from glistening eyes, Tina nodded. "Okay."

Dirk swallowed a sip of coffee before continuing, tersely. "I was already a man by the summer you were sixteen. I was more than a little shaken to realize I wanted you as a man wants a woman." His lips twisted derisively. "I fought my share of guilt battles for my thoughts. Then after your father died, and I held you in my arms, I lost the mental battle . . .

and my control. Believe me, the guilt trips I'd suffered before that day were nothing to the one I went through the morning after we made love."

"So you compensated for your guilt by rejecting me," Tina concluded when he paused for breath.

"No!" Dirk's denial held solid conviction. "I never rejected you. I sent you back to school to give you time, Tina." Reaching across the table, he grasped her hand with trembling fingers. "Honey, I wanted you to have all the things young girls are supposed to have. Dates and fun and . . . well, all the things that you deserved."

"But all I wanted was you!" Tina wailed in objection.

"Honey, I thought you were too young to know what you wanted." Dirk squeezed her hand. "You were vulnerable, and you trusted me. I betrayed not only your trust but your father's as well. I . . ." A spasm of pain swept his face and he closed his eyes briefly. "I sent you away because, by looking at you, I had to look at myself—and I hated what I saw.

"When I came to visit you in your junior year, I came to ask you—beg you—to marry me." Again his lips smiled derisively. "I had to come, I couldn't fight myself any longer. You told me to go to hell," he finished thickly.

"I was hurt, Dirk," Tina explained. "I was lashing out. I wanted to hurt you too."

"Oh, you succeeded, love, believe me." Dirk shrugged. "And you continued to hurt me, with your extravagance and, worst of all, with your marriage to that . . . that parasite." His lips tightened almost painfully.

Lowering her eyes, she admitted, "I know . . . now . . . that I chose Chuck deliberately. I used him, Dirk." Raising her eyes, she met his gaze squarely. "I used him to hurt you."

"And all the other men since him?" Dirk muttered raggedly.

Tina stiffened with sudden indignation. "There were no others," she said convincingly. "There was only Chuck. And"—even though she felt her face flush, Tina knew she had to tell him the whole truth—"and even when I was with him, there was only you. Do you understand what I'm saying?"

A smile of commiseration softened his lips. "Only too well," he replied softly. "I used my wife the same way."

"What an utter waste," Tina observed sadly.

"Yes," Dirk concurred. "But I'm through wasting time, or lying to myself, or playing games." Releasing his grip, Dirk began stroking her fingers. "I came back here yesterday prepared to beg you for a real marriage between us."

"But that's—" Tina was about to tell him that that was the same reason she'd come home early, but once more he wouldn't let her finish.

"Honey, I know how much your business means to you, but God, I need you with me!" Leaning forward, he asked, earnestly, "Couldn't you open another salon in Wilmington and make periodic trips to New York?"

"No." A shadow passed over his face at her flat refusal. Aching for him, feeling his pain, Tina rushed to explain. "I have no shop to make periodic trips to New York for, darling. I agreed to sell the business to Paul yesterday. I also gave notice that I'd be vacating my apartment." A smile tugged at her lips when she saw the look of amazement on her husband's face. "As of the end of January, this house is the only home I have."

Kicking over his chair as he jumped to his feet, Dirk circled the table to pull Tina into his arms.

"You could always come live with me, scrawny," he teased in a suspiciously tight voice.

"On one condition," Tina said adamantly.

"Name your terms of surrender." He laughed in relief.

"By next year at this time," Tina said softly, "I want to be decorating a nursery as well as a Christmas tree."

A slow, excitingly sexy smile curved Dirk's lips as he gazed down at her, his blue eyes glowing with love.

"Both here and in Wilmington," Tina added as an afterthought.

"You're a demanding woman, love." Dirk's arms tightened, making Tina thrillingly aware of his need of her. "But as I was planning to keep this house as our getaway anyway, I'll meet your terms . . . on one condition of my own."

"And that is?" Tina asked, molding her soft curves to his angular frame.

"That is"—he paused to kiss her deeply, meaningfully—"we get started on your terms immediately."

MORNING ROSE, EVENING SAVAGE

Chapter One

Tara's fingers flew over the computer keyboard, her eyes steady on the letter she was writing. So intent was her concentration, she didn't hear the office door open and she glanced up with a start when the morning mail was dropped onto the corner of her desk.

"Coffee's just about ready, Tara," Jeannie, the young assistant and head coffee-maker, caroled brightly. "I'll be back with it in a minute, okay?"

Fingers hovering over the keys, Tara nodded and returned the smile of the pretty, eager teen-ager.

"Yes, thank you. I'm just finishing the last of the letters David left me to do. I can take a few minutes and relax with my coffee while I go through the mail."

Jeannie nodded and bounced out of the office and Tara went back to the keyboard. She finished the letter, printed it, then flexed her fingers and arched her back in a stretching motion.

Glancing at the clock, she noted it was nine forty and she'd been writing steadily since eight. On entering her office at her usual time, a few minutes before eight, she'd found a post-it note stuck to her computer screen on which her boss had scribbled:

Tara,
I have an early appointment. Please process these letters I dashed off last night, if you can decipher them. I should be in the office around ten.

David

Tara smiled to herself. *Decipher* had been the correct word. Though David's architectural drawings were a beautiful sight to behold, one might suspect from his handwriting that he was a doctor.

Tara had come to work for the young architect on leaving business college four years ago and the atmosphere had always been informal. From the first day it had been *Tara* and *David,* never *Miss Schmitt* and *Mr. Jennings.* There had been a smaller staff at the time as David had just begun receiving recognition for his work, but as David's reputation grew, so had his staff. Yet the informality remained.

Jeannie delivered the coffee and, after taking a careful sip, Tara gave a small, contented sigh. From the very first day she had considered herself fortunate in finding this job. She enjoyed the work, earned an excellent salary, and, perhaps the best of all, she had made firm friendships with David and his wife, Sallie.

Sallie had acted as David's personal assistant until she was in her seventh month of pregnancy with their first child. She had remained in the office one week after Tara started, to show her the office procedure. In that short time they discovered a rapport that grew into a strong bond between them.

As for David, Tara freely admitted to herself that, if he had not been married, she would have made a play for him. David Jennings was one of the few men Tara really liked. His looks were commonplace. Tall and thin, almost to the point of gauntness, he had thinning, sandy-colored hair and wore dark-framed glasses. His manner was gentle, with a smile that could melt the core of an iceberg. At the same time he was a brilliant architect and an unabashed workaholic.

Tara rose and walked around the desk to ease her cramped legs, then stood with her back to the door as she flipped through the mail. The office door opened then closed quietly and Tara went stiff at the sound of the new familiar, deeply masculine voice of David's newest, and so far most important, client. "I understand you're looking around for a prosperous man to marry. Would I fill the requirements?"

Shock, followed by swift anger at the softly insolent tone,

stiffened her spine even more. Jerking her head up, she turned swiftly to glare into the handsome, mocking face of Aleksei Rykovsky.

"If you are trying to be funny," Tara snapped, "you are failing miserably."

Eyes as deeply blue and glittering as sapphires roamed her face slowly, studying with amusement the high angry color in her creamy cheeks, the flash of sparks in her dark brown eyes, the way she flipped back her long silvery gold hair in agitation.

"Not at all," he finally answered in a silky smooth tone. "I am completely serious. Have I been misinformed about your avowed intention to marry a man who is—uh—well off?"

Tara was not a small girl, standing five feet nine in her three-inch heels, yet she had to tilt back her head to look into his face. *And what a face,* she thought sourly. For any one man to possess such a devastatingly rugged handsomeness was unfair to the rest of the male population in general and to the whole of the female population in particular. The face was the icing on the cake, being at the top of a long, muscularly lean body that exuded pure male vitality and sensuousness. And as if that were not enough, a full head of crisp, blue-black wavy hair was a blatant invitation to feminine fingers. *Too bad,* Tara thought in the same sour vein, *his personality is a complete turnoff.* She did not appreciate the masterful type.

"No," she finally managed to answer, forcing herself to meet that steady blue gaze. "You have not been misinformed."

"Well, then," he drawled, "all we have to do is set the date."

Tara felt the flash of angry color touch her skin. If there was anything she hated more than an arrogant man, it was to be made the object of his humor. She breathed in deeply, trying to keep a rein on her growing temper. For David's sake, she could not afford to antagonize this man.

"You've had your little joke for the day, Mr. Rykovsky," she said through stiff lips, "now if you'll excuse me, I have work to do and—"

"Morning, Tara." David's cheerful voice preceded him into the room. The rest of him followed, a warm smile lightening his otherwise nondescript face. "Have any trouble with my chicken scratches?"

"Not too much." Tara smiled at her boss, sighing in relief at his appearance. "They're all ready for your signature."

David grinned at the other man as she handed him the letters. "Every busy man should have a Tara in his office, Alek." Then, turning, he walked to the door of his own office. Before following, Alek leaned close to Tara and whispered, "I can think of a better place to have you." Then he moved quickly up behind David, who turned and said, "Alek and I are going to be closeted the rest of the day, Tara. I don't want to be disturbed unless it's something you think absolutely must have my attention."

Struck speechless by Alek's whispered words, she nodded dumbly, then stood still, watching the door close. Tara's thoughts exploded. *How dared he, that—that arrogant, over-bearing, conceited*—words failed her. Unclenching her hands, flexing stiff, achy fingers, she made a concentrated effort at control. The emotions raging through her were an equal mixture of anger and humiliation. Anger at his audacity at using her to sharpen his—to her mind—twisted wit. Humiliation at the fact that the basis of his attack was true: she *had* promised herself she'd marry a prosperous man. And although it was ten years since she'd made the vow, she had not changed her mind in the least.

Legs still shaky, Tara walked slowly around her desk and sank into her chair. In a burst of activity she got busy with the work at hand only to pause moments later to stare unseeingly at her computer screen.

She had been fourteen when she'd made that vow, a not unusual thing at that romantic age. Most young girls have been known to declare dreamily that they will marry rich men. But, unlike other girls, Tara had had no dreams of a Prince Charming with gold-lined pockets. Quite the contrary. She had viewed the prospect realistically. A handsome Prince Charming she didn't need; actual wealth she didn't need.

What she had decided she wanted was a reasonably prosperous man and, of equal importance, one who would not be a tyrant. She had already, at the tender age of fourteen, seen enough of the type of man who, to feed his own ego, had to be forever boss. She had seen him in her male teachers, in the fathers of most of her friends, and in her own father.

Tara shuddered as a picture of her mother thrust its unwelcome way into her mind. Trying to dispel the unwanted image, she got to work. She was only partially successful, for throughout the rest of the day, incidents and scenes from her childhood flashed in and out of her mind. And her mother was in every one: her beauty fading over the years; her bright eyes growing dim and shadowed with worry; her flashing smile turning into a mere twist of once full lips that had felt the bite of teeth too often; and, possibly the worst of all, shoulders starting to bow with the weight of hardship and far too little appreciation.

Not for me, Tara had told herself while still in her ninth year of school. *Not for me the scrimping and scraping to make ends meet but rarely even coming close. Not for me the tyrant who would be absolute master in his home, punishing his wife for his own inadequacies.*

She had indulged in no wild dreams or flights of fancy, but had planned carefully and well. She had been blessed with beauty of both face and body and she nurtured it rigidly, getting plenty of rest and exercise and being very careful of what she ate. She had worked at baby-sitting and as a mother's helper from the time she was thirteen, giving most of her earnings to her mother, but always managing to put aside a few dollars for herself. At sixteen she got a regular job working part-time after school in the winter and full-time in the summer. She paid a rather high board at home and hoarded the rest of her money like a miser. She studied hard, receiving high grades in school. After graduation she had applied at and was accepted into a highly reputable business college in Philadelphia. She bolstered her funds by working part-time at a department store. It had not been easy. In fact it had been very difficult. But it had paid off. When she left business college at twenty, she came home to Allentown an excellently trained administrative assistant.

She was hired for the first job she applied for, the one in David's office. That had been four years ago. The first two of those years she lived at home, wanting to ease the burden on her mother. But the situation became increasingly more impossible. She found it harder to accept her father's dictates. She was no longer a green girl, but a well turned-out, highly paid young woman and she could no longer bear being told when to come and when to go, when to speak and when to be silent. A few days after her twenty-second birthday she packed her things and left her father's house for good.

She did not actively hate her father. Herman Schmitt did the best he could within the range of his own knowledge and understanding. What his firstborn daughter resented was that he'd never made an effort to widen his vision past what he'd learned of life from his own straight-laced, Pennsylvania Dutch parents. And more important still, she resented his marrying a lovely, laughing, blond-haired girl and turning her into a nervous, drawn-faced, gray-haired, timid mouse.

No. No. No. Not for Tara this type of man and life. Over the years her resolve had strengthened. It had not taken long for her co-workers and few close friends to ascertain her goals. She rarely dated and then only with carefully selected young men. She was wise enough to realize one had little control over the unpredictable emotion called love. So she operated within the premise that she could not become vulnerable to the wrong man if she had no contact with him. None of the men she'd dated over the years had left an impression on her, and at the present time she wasn't seeing anyone.

She had no idea who had enlightened Aleksei Rykovsky as to her intentions. Who it was did not even matter. What did matter was that that hateful man had used it to amuse himself at her expense.

Tara had felt an immediate antagonism toward him from the day, a few months ago, that David had introduced her to him. He wore his breeding, wealth, and self-confidence like a banner. Arrogance etched every fine, aristocratic feature of his dark-skinned, handsome face. This man, she had thought at once, was probably the most bossy of any boss she had ever met. She hadn't liked him then; she liked him even less now.

The afternoon wore on, her thoughts and memories occasionally jarred by the sound of a low, masculine voice that sometimes filtered through the closed door.

Tara greeted quitting time with a sigh of weariness, and slid one slim hand under the heavy fall of silver-blond hair to rub the back of her neck. She tidied her desk, covered her computer, slipped into her light-weight suede jacket, scooped up her shoulder bag, and left the office with unusual haste. As she walked to the parking lot, she drew deep lungsful of crisp October air in an attempt to clear her mind of the afternoon cobwebs. She unlocked the door of her six-month-old blue Camry and, her sense of well-being returning, she slid behind the wheel, started the engine, and drove off the parking lot and into the crowded line of homebound traffic. In her preoccupied state she didn't hear the low roar of the engine being started up after hers, or notice the sleek silver Lexus that followed her off the lot.

Fifteen minutes later she had left the heavier traffic and five minutes after that she parked the car on the quiet street in front of her apartment house. Thanking the Fates it was Friday, she locked the car, slung the handbag strap over her shoulder, and hurried across the sidewalk and through the street door of the apartment, unaware of the same Lexus parked two cars away from her own.

Dashing up the stairs, she swung into the hall, heading for her second floor apartment, then stopped dead in her tracks. Leaning against the wall next to her front door was the cause of her suddenly intense headache. Looking for all the world like he owned the place stood one totally relaxed Aleksei Rykovsky.

Tara felt anger reignite and the flame propelled her forward. She stopped a foot from him, brown eyes smoldering. "What are you doing here?"

Dark eyebrows went up in exaggerated surprise. "I thought

we had things to discuss." His voice flowed over her like smooth honey, and she felt a tiny shiver slide along her spine.

"We have nothing to discuss," she snapped irritably. "Now, if you'll excuse me, I'm tired." She had turned and unlocked the door while she was speaking, preparing to step inside and close the door in his face, when his voice stopped her. "Of course if you're afraid to talk to me . . ."

Tara turned, her eyes frosty, her face mirroring contempt. "I'm not afraid to talk to any man. What is it you have to say?"

"I usually don't hold conversations in hallways. May I come in?" The taunting amusement in his voice grated on her nerves and, with an exclamation of annoyance, she flung open the door, then spun around and walked into the living room.

On hearing the door close with a soft click, she drew a deep breath for control then turned to watch him come slowly across the room to her.

"What do you want?"

"You."

Tara's breath was drawn in on an audible gasp. "Are you out of your mind?"

"No more than most. If I'm not mistaken, I proposed marriage to you today. I came for an answer."

"No."

"Why?"

Really angry now, Tara was finding it difficult keeping her voice down. "I told you this morning I don't think you're funny. Aren't you carrying this joke a bit too far?"

"And I told you this morning I was not trying to be funny." His own tone wasn't quite as smooth. "I mean it. Will you marry me?"

Tara brushed her hand across her eyes in disbelief. "Why? I mean, why are you asking me to marry you?"

He stepped closer to her, brought up one hand to brush long brown fingers across her soft cheek. "Fair question," he murmured, "but I've already answered it. You're a beautiful, desirable woman. I want you. Would you let me set you up in an apartment in my building?"

"No." It was a soft explosive uttered at the same time she moved back, away from his caressing, oddly disturbing fingers.

"I thought not." He laughed low in his throat, arching one mocking brow at her as she moved away from him. "If the only way I can have you is through marriage," he shrugged, "I'll marry you. I should more than meet your requirements of a prosperous man. I'm a very, very prosperous man."

Tara shivered in revulsion. This man's arrogance was beyond belief.

"Get out of here." Her voice had dropped to a whisper, and she was shaking with anger.

"Tara."

"If you don't get out of here, I'll call the super and have you thrown out." Fighting for control, she spoke through clenched teeth.

Dark blue eyes, bright and glittering with anger, stared into hers; then he moved so quickly, she was left speechless. His hands shot out and caught her face, drawing her up to him. Up. Up, until she was almost dangling on tiptoes inches below his face. She could do no more with her hands than grasp his waist for support, and her voice was a barely strangled gasp.

"What do you think you're—"

Closing the inches that separated them, he caught her open mouth with his, sending a shaft of sensation Tara later told herself was disgust through her body that left the tips of her fingers and toes tingling. His lips were firm, cool, and insistent and, to her horror, she felt her own begin to respond.

Alek's mouth released her slowly. Then with his lips still almost touching hers, she felt his cool breath mingle with hers as he murmured words in a strange language Tara thought must be Russian. His mouth brushed hers roughly before he lifted his head, and his even more darkened blue eyes stared into her soft brown ones, wide with confusion and a hint of fear. "All right, pansy eyes, I'll go," he said softly, then more firmly, "but think about what I said. I could give you a very comfortable life, Tara."

He released her so suddenly, she almost fell, and before

she could form a retort, he was across the room and out the door. Trembling with reaction, lips parted to draw deep, steadying breaths, she glanced around the room as if seeking reassurance from familiar things. *No one in his right mind would say and do the things he had,* she thought wildly. Moving a little unsteadily, she walked to the sofa and sank into it, resting her head back and closing her eyes. *The man had to be mad.* The thought jolted her memory back to something David had said months ago.

Tara had had dinner with David and Sallie and they'd been sitting comfortably in the living room with their coffee when Sallie mentioned Aleksei Rykovsky. Tara had grimaced with distaste and, with a rueful smile, David shook his head. "I don't understand why you don't like him, Tara. Most people do, you know."

Although David and Sallie had long been aware of Tara's preference for well-off men and in fact had introduced her to a few (believing she had an ingrained fear of being poor due to her upbringing), they had no idea of her aversion to the masterful type.

Tara had sighed, reluctant to answer, yet knowing she had to say something. "Oh, I don't know. It's just, well, he seems so damned sure of himself. So completely *in charge. The*"— and here she waved her hand around as if trying to pluck the word out of the air—*"boss,* so to speak. It annoys me."

"I don't know why it should," came David's gentle-voiced reply. "I've never heard him boss you. And anyway, he is the boss. You know what designing his new plants means to me, Tara. This is what I've been waiting for ever since I opened my own office. This is the biggest challenge I've had so far, and Alek has very definite ideas on what he does and does not want. My God, you've seen the proposed budget. In my view, any man who can afford to build a new plant at that cost without batting an eye damned well deserves to be boss."

David's tone had become unusually severe toward the end of his admonition to Tara, and when he finished, the room grew taut with a strained silence.

In an obvious attempt to lighten the mood, Sallie turned

to David with a soft laugh. "Darling, within the last few weeks I've heard several people refer to him as 'the Mad Russian.' Do you have any idea why?"

David's laughter echoed his wife's, and when he answered, all traces of his previous harshness were gone. "Yes, sweets, I do know why. But don't be alarmed; they don't mean crazy-mad. It seems Alek has acquired a reputation for accepting difficult jobs with a close delivery date. Real squeakers, so to speak. The way I hear it, he has, so far, always managed to deliver top quality work—on time. When he first started this practice, those who are in a position to know were heard to say the man was mad to take on such impossible job orders. Ergo—the title *Mad Russian* evolved."

Sallie gave an exaggerated sigh of relief. "Well, that's good to know. I was beginning to think perhaps his attic light was out."

Opening her eyes, Tara shuddered and sat up, Sallie's words of months ago ringing in her ears. After Aleksei Rykovsky's behavior this evening, Tara was inclined to disregard David's explanation and go with Sallie's. In Tara's opinion the Mad Russian's attic light was definitely out.

Reaction was setting in. Tara felt tight and jumpy all over and, glancing down, she stared vacantly at her trembling hands. Closing her eyes, she swallowed around the dryness in her throat and bit hard on her lower lip.

Suddenly she had to move, needed the feeling of some sort of purposeful action. Moving almost jerkily, she went into the kitchen to the cabinet where she kept her cleaning materials. Grasping a dustcloth and a can of spray wax, she returned to the living room.

Slowly, methodically, she applied herself to waxing every piece of wooden furniture in the room. There were not all that many pieces, for it wasn't a very large room. But what there was was well chosen, reflecting Tara's quiet good taste. Not an edge or corner was missed and from there Tara went into the bedroom and proceeded to give the same treatment to the furniture there.

When, finally, she had to admit to herself there was not

one square inch of wood left without a double coat of wax, she returned to the kitchen and replaced the cloth and can.

Straightening from the low cabinet, she stood motionless a moment then said aloud, wonderingly, "What am I doing?" But without allowing any answers to filter through, she was moving again, going to the sink to wash her hands.

Uneasy, because she didn't know why, Tara didn't want to think at all just then. Least of all about *him*.

With single-minded purpose she broiled a small steak, tossed an equally small salad, and brewed half a pot of coffee. Twenty-five minutes after she had seated herself at the small kitchen table, she swallowed the last of her third cup of coffee then stood up and carried her plate to the sink to scrape most of her meal into the garbage disposal.

Tara washed up slowly and carefully, wiping the table, countertops, and stove free of the tiniest imagined spot. When she finally flicked the light switch off, she left the darkened room even more neat and sparkling than usual.

Still moving with the same single-minded purpose, she went to the bathroom, stripped, stepped under the shower, and brought all her concentration to bear on shampooing her long, heavy fall of silver-blond hair.

Later, dressed in nightie and terry robe, she sat in front of her makeup mirror—brush in one hand, blow dryer in the other—and stared with unseeing eyes into the glass. In her mind's eye grew a sharp picture of two glittering dark blue eyes and inside her head, as clearly as a few hours earlier, that deep masculine voice said: "You're a beautiful, desirable woman. I want you."

A shudder went through her body, and she watched, almost blankly, her pale, slim hand grasp the handle of the dryer to still its shaking.

He was beyond her experience. His manner—everything about him—was an unknown. She had gone out with a few carefully selected young men. She had been kissed, thoroughly, by all of them. Most had made a play toward a more intimate relationship. Yet none had shocked or upset her as this man had, with seemingly little effort.

Tara felt vaguely frightened even now, hours later, and she wasn't quite sure why. Was she overreacting? She didn't think so. People who were hitting on all cylinders didn't behave as he had. Did they?

From their first meeting she had felt uncomfortable and strangely on edge whenever he was around, either in the office or on the building site, and now, Tara told herself, she knew why. Not only was he autocratic and arrogant, which were bad enough traits in themselves, but he also had a streak of erraticism. The thing that puzzled her was, if she had sensed this in the man, why hadn't David and the others?

Chapter Two

Tara had a depressing weekend. Not only was she shaken, at odd hours of the day and night, by thoughts of Aleksei Rykovsky's strange behavior, she made the mistake of choosing this weekend to visit her mother.

She walked into her father's house Sunday after dinner to find her mother in tears, her father bellowing at her younger sister, Betsy, and the twenty-one-year-old Betsy screaming back that she was packing her clothes and moving in with her boyfriend.

Tara groaned softly as she hurried across the room to her mother. *This was all I needed to make my weekend complete,* she thought wearily. At that moment she would not have been shocked or surprised if her mother told her her eighteen-year-old brother George had a girl in trouble and that her fourteen-year-old brother Karl had taken their father's car and smashed it.

"Tara." Her mother grasped her arms agitatedly. "Please go talk to your sister. She'll listen to you. I'll die of shame if she moves in with Kenny. And your father will be impossible to live with."

So what else is new, Tara thought resignedly. But she smoothed her mother's once beautiful hair, then gently removed her clutching hands. "All right, Mama, I'll go see what I can do. But will you tell me what this is all about first?" As she was speaking she drew her mother into the kitchen, enabling them to talk without having to shout over the din from the second floor.

In the comparative quiet of the kitchen, Marlene Schmitt drew a deep breath before beginning her explanations. "Well, it started Friday," she began, and Tara thought swiftly. *Didn't everything?* "Your father told Betsy that with inflation and all, he'd have to raise her board. She was very upset because she herself hasn't had a raise in pay for some time. Then yesterday they had an argument just before Kenny came for her to go to a movie. He said her room looked like a pigsty, and it was time she cleaned it." Tara felt a flash of irritation. It was true that Betsy was a little careless with her things, but her room did not look like a pigsty.

"They barely spoke to each other all morning." Her mother's eyes filled with tears, and she twisted her hands nervously. "I guess it's my fault. I was late with dinner, and Betsy asked if she could skip drying the dishes since Kenny was picking her up soon and she had to get ready. Your father exploded. He told her she was not allowed to go with Kenny today and could only see him two nights a week from now on."

"For heaven's sake, Mother, Betsy's twenty-one years old," Tara exclaimed indignantly.

"That's exactly what she said to him. But he told her that she was in his house, and as long as she remained under his roof, she'd do as he said. That's when she said she wouldn't stay here any longer. That she was moving in with Kenny. Oh, Tara, please stop her."

"Okay, okay, calm down. I said I'll do what I can. And you're not to blame yourself just because dinner was late. I'll talk to him, too, if I can, and try to make him see reason."

Several hours later Tara collapsed onto her own sofa with a sigh of exhaustion. After long talks with both her sister and father that would have put a diplomat to shame, she had finally procured a peace settlement of sorts. She smiled ruefully, acknowledging the fact that George had been the one who swayed her father. He had entered the house, and the argument, and declared firmly in favor of Betsy. That her eighteen-year-old brother's opinion was held in higher esteem by her father than her own did not surprise Tara. To a man like her father the judgment of almost any male held more value than that of a female. With bitter amusement Tara thought her father would fall over one Aleksei Rykovsky, seeing in him the absolute top dog of dominant men. Her amusement faded as she considered the probability of encountering that same top dog in the office tomorrow. After Friday night, what could they possibly say to each other? How could they work together if need be?

Thankfully her fears were proved groundless—at least through Wednesday—as the "head honcho," as Tara now thought of him, hadn't appeared.

A mystery did, though, in the form of a single, long-stemmed white rose that was delivered to her at the office Monday morning and each morning after that. When Jeannie brought the first one to her, Tara was delighted. The rose was perfectly shaped and beautiful; its scent heady, almost sensual. As Tara searched through the tissue paper in the florist's box, Jeannie sighed enviously. "You must have a secret admirer, Tara. The delivery man said there was no card and wouldn't even take a tip. Said he'd already been tipped. Do you have any idea who it's from?"

Tara shook her head slowly. "No, but I'll probably find out before too long." Then smiling teasingly at the younger woman, she added, "And you'll be the first to know, I promise."

Jeannie flashed her an impish grin as she left the office, and Tara sat staring broodingly at the rose. Who could have sent it? The first name to jump into her mind was Aleksei Rykovsky, but she dismissed that at once. Much too subtle for the head honcho; he apparently went in for caveman tactics. Who, then? Terry Connors? She mused on the young draftsman in the outer office a few moments, then shook her head decisively. Not Terry. He probably wouldn't think of it, especially after the way she'd spoken to him the last time he'd asked her out. She'd been honest to the point of bluntness. Although he was an attractive young man with talent and a promising future, he was more in love with himself than he could be with any one woman. In so many words she'd told him just that. He'd barely spoken to her since and then only in the office. He lived in an apartment just down the street from hers, and she'd passed him a few times going to and from her apartment and her car. At those times he'd nodded curtly, not speaking. So scratch Terry.

Names kept bouncing in and out of her mind as she hunted up the summer bud vase she'd shoved to the back of her personal desk drawer, and one by one she rejected them. Finally, running out of prospects, she gave up.

She went through the same mental gyrations on Tuesday morning. When the rose was delivered on Wednesday morning, she decided to stop trying to solve the puzzle and just enjoy it.

As she prepared for bed Wednesday night Tara realized the advent of the morning rose had taken the edge off her nervousness about meeting Aleksei Rykovsky in the office. She also told herself the man was probably feeling ridiculous about his behavior and had not come to David's office because he was embarrassed to face her. She should have known better.

She was at the filing cabinet Thursday morning when David, with a pleasant good morning, breezed through her small office on the way to his own. Tara looked up, but before she had a chance to voice a return greeting, two strong hands gripped her shoulders and a caressing voice said, "Morning, darling," as she was turned around and held against a hard, muscular chest. She saw gleaming blue eyes, gave a startled "Oh," then went warm all over as Aleksei Rykovsky's firm mouth covered hers. Again that odd, tingling sensation touched the tips of her fingers and toes but before she could react to push him away, he lifted his head. "I missed that this morning, sleepyhead." While caressing, his tone also held a touch of possession, and Tara was left speechless. He laughed softly as he moved away from her with obvious reluctance to join David, who still stood in the doorway with a patently interested look on his face.

Flushed with embarrassment, wide-eyed in confusion, Tara faced David. "I—I . . ."

David shook his head slowly, smiled gently, and closed the door between the two offices.

Anger flushed her cheeks even more brightly as she stared at the closed door. Who did he think he was, kissing her like that? And what in the world did he mean, he missed that this morning?

At lunchtime, instead of having lunch at her desk as she usually did, Tara left the office and walked. Ever since her teens, whenever she was troubled or had a particularly knotty problem to work out, she walked. She started out at a good pace, her long slender legs eating up the city blocks rapidly. Anger stirred her blood and kept the adrenaline pumping.

This man, this Rykovsky, was beginning to drive her wild. *Banish him,* she told herself severely. *Push him out of your mind completely.* Not an easy thing to do. Mocking blue eyes in a handsome face were beginning to haunt her. Why had he suddenly set out to bedevil her? Had she slipped up, let her dislike and disapproval of him show? If she had, she couldn't think when. For David's sake she had worked hard at always displaying a cool, efficient, respectful attitude toward him.

She could not think of one instance during the last few months when she had let her mask drop even at the times— and there had been several during office meetings and on the new plant site—when his overbearing superiority, his enormous self-confidence and arrogance, had made her hand itch with the desire to slap his haughty, patrician face. She had controlled the urge by removing herself from his presence on one pretext or another.

Sighing softly, Tara shook her head in defeat. She had no idea why he was attacking her. She had avoided his type like the plague and so could not fathom what his motivation could possibly be.

Tara had been striding along at a good clip, oblivious to her surroundings and the gloriously warm fall day. The dry, crackling sound of leaves being crushed underfoot cracked the door of her consciousness; the happy ripple of young children laughing pushed it open.

Glancing around, she shortened her stride; then she stopped

completely. She was passing the park, the still deep-green, well tended grass partially obscured now by the heavy fall of leaves from the various types of trees in the park. Again children laughing caught her attention, and her gaze followed the sounds to the park's small-tot lot. Young mothers stood together talking while keeping a watchful eye on their offspring. Others guided toddlers down sliding boards or stood behind swings, gently pushing each time the seat arced back. Bemused, Tara watched the happy, worry-free youngsters play. She had always loved children, been happy and eager to help her mother when first George and then Karl were born.

A gentle smile tugged at her lips; a tiny ache tugged at her heart. Would she ever meet a man whose children she would not only be willing to raise but wanted to bear with a deep and passionate longing? Had she set her sights too high, made her requirements too rigid? Apparently not, for she had met more than one young man who'd not only met her requirements but had other extra added attractions as well. Yet they had all left her cold, with no desire to continue the relationship, let alone deepen it.

Was she destined to spend the rest of her life alone, searching for some elusive thing that could set a spark to her emotions? Was she never to know the joy evident on the faces of the young mothers she now observed? Did they realize, she wondered, how precious the time was that they held in their hands as their babies grew? Did anyone ever?

Giving herself a mental shake, Tara breathed in deeply, filling her lungs with the sweet, smoky taste of autumn. She had become pensive and moody and, with a determined effort, she drew her eyes away from the children, turned, and began retracing her steps to the office.

A long, low wolf-whistle, issued from the window of a passing car, brought a smile to Tara's lips, a spring to her step. Her long, silvery hair bounced on her shoulders and against her back in rhythm with her stride.

Her walk—*or stalk*, Tara thought wryly—had restored her equilibrium. For all of fifteen minutes, back there at the park, she hadn't given one thought to the head honcho. But now he was back to torment her thoughts. She had walked off the sharpest edge of her anger, but the core was still there, burning low but steadily.

What games was this man playing? And how in the world would she explain her behavior this morning to David? Her worry on that score proved groundless, for she had no sooner returned to her office when David came out of his. Alone.

"I'm going out to lunch with Alek, Tara. He's waiting in the car now. I probably won't be back for the rest of the day. You'll have to handle anything that comes up." David's voice was completely normal, yet Tara felt herself grow warm at the speculative glance he passed over her.

"David, about this morning. I don't know how to explain, except—" She paused, searching for words, and David cut in gently. "Don't worry about it, Tara. You should know by now I'm broad-minded and anyway, Alek explained everything, even though it wasn't necessary. It's really none of my business. Now I've got to go, as we're meeting the contractor. See you tomorrow."

More confused than ever, Tara sat stunned. What in the name of sanity was going on? What explanation could Alek have given for his outrageous actions? And why wasn't it any of David's business? You would think a madman running around loose would be everybody's business.

The more she thought about it, the more convinced she became that Alek Rykovsky was playing some sort of cat-and-mouse game. But to what purpose? More than likely, she thoughts, his pride had been injured and he wanted to make her uncomfortable. Well! He was certainly succeeding there. But why involve David?

By the time the rose arrived Friday morning, she hardly gave the identity of its sender a second thought. After the events of the day before, it didn't seem to matter much. Besides, she had slept badly and was tired, not at all looking forward to round three with the Mad Russian. She was at a total loss as to what he hoped to gain, and so completely missed the clues.

It was a quiet weekend. Too quiet. Tara was not in the habit of running out several nights a week, but she usually went out at least one night during the weekend. Sometimes with a man, but more often with a group of young friends, which included David and Sallie, for dinner or stay-at-home evenings of take-out food, conversation and occasionally a rented video. This was the second weekend in a row she had not received a call or invitation from one of her friends, not even Sallie.

The only unusual thing that happened was on Saturday and Sunday morning when she went to the door to answer the bell only to find the hall empty except for the now familiar florist's box containing a single white rose.

By Sunday night Tara decided the whole thing was very weird. She liked her quiet, but this was too much. Beginning to feel vaguely like the last person on earth, she reached for the phone with the intention of calling Sallie when its sudden jangling ring startled her so badly, she actually jumped.

"I didn't interrupt anything, did I, Tara?" Betsy's voice was as much of a surprise as her words, as Betsy seldom called and then usually only when she wanted something, as it seemed she did now.

"Interrupt anything? For heaven's sake, Betsy, it's after ten thirty. Tomorrow's a working day. I'll soon be going to bed." What kind of a wild existence did her sister think she lived, anyway?

"Well, Sis, you're such a close-mouthed thing, one never knows. Except of course, what one may read in the papers or"—she paused—"hear through the grapevine."

There was a definite insinuation in Betsy's last four words and Tara felt her skin prickle.

"What?"

"Doesn't matter. Look, Tara, the reason I called was, if you decide to give up your apartment, will you let Ken and me know? Maybe even talk to your landlord for us?"

Give up her apartment? What in the world? Her tone was an equal mixture of exasperation and puzzlement. "Betsy, I don't know what you've heard or think, but—"

"Oh! I had no intentions of prying," Betsy interrupted, her

words coming in a rush, tripping over each other. "I've told you how small Ken's place is and I thought I'd get my bid in if you were considering it. You know, I'm a big girl now and I'm hip to the ways of the world and I do understand. I mean, he's such a magnificent . . . fantastic hunk of man."

Skinny Kenny? Magnificent? Fantastic? Tara knew her sister was inclined to exaggerate, but this was too much. Puzzlement won out over exasperation. "Bets, I think some explanation is necessary," Tara began, only to have Betsy interrupt again.

"No, really, just keep us in mind. Okay? Bye." She hung up and Tara stared at the receiver in her hand as if she had never seen one before. Sighing deeply, she wondered if everyone around her was slipping over the edge, or if it was she who was going bananas.

A single white rose continued to arrive daily at the office, and by midweek Tara simply sniffed it appreciatively, stuck it in the vase, and went about her work. She was grateful for one thing: Aleksei Rykovsky hadn't shown up at the office at all and David treated her as if nothing had ever happened.

It was almost noon on Friday when Sallie dashed into the office. "Hi, Tara. Is David terribly busy? I have something I want to check with him and I'm in an awful rush."

"David's never too busy to see you, Sallie." Tara laughed. "Go on in and surprise him."

In less than ten minutes Sallie was back, standing in front of her desk, pulling soft tan gloves over her hands.

"I wanted to check with him about the wine for tomorrow night. I was going to call him from home, but then Mother came to look after Tina, and I didn't think of it again until after I'd left the house." Sallie spoke quickly, glancing at the clock. "I'll miss you tomorrow night, Tara, but David explained everything and I do understand. At least I think I do." Sallie's expression held concern; she seemed almost hurt. "Oh, Lord! I have to run. I'm meeting Dave's mother for lunch and I'm going to be late." She grimaced, threw Tara a half-smile, and dashed out again.

Tara experienced the same prickling sensation in her skin

she'd had the previous Sunday while talking to her sister, and with it a mild sense of alarm. What was this all about? It was beginning to seem that everyone understood everything but her. She was tempted to confront David but she could hardly go in and blurt out, "Why haven't you invited me to your party?"

She worried about Sallie's words and attitude the rest of the day and finally decided the only cause she could think of was Aleksei Rykovsky's extraordinary behavior the week before and her own unwilling involvement in it. But good Lord, she had been unwilling; surely they realized that. Then pride kept her from going in to question David.

As she left the office that afternoon, she hesitated with a sudden aversion to spending the entire evening alone, confined within those few small rooms. Then with a quick, decisive step she walked to the car. Her mother's birthday was the following week and, as she had a sweet tooth that was rarely indulged, Tara decided to take a run to her favorite candy shop and buy her mother a large box of chocolates.

She turned onto Route 222 heading south and was past the consistory building before the beauty of the late October afternoon struck her. When she glanced at the grounds of Cedar Crest College to her right, her breath caught in her throat. The long fingers of the westering sun bathed the fall foliage in a golden glow, setting the russet leaves alight. The glory of the Pennsylvania autumn had always affected her with soul-wrenching intensity and today, caught so suddenly, the beauty of it all cut into her deeply. Hurt, confused by the events of the last few weeks, she was doubly vulnerable to the heart-twistingly beautiful power of nature.

She felt the hot sting of tears behind her eyes and shook her head impatiently. *This is ridiculous,* she thought moodily. The last few weeks she had spent most of her time either in her apartment or at the office. She needed a break, a diversion. She'd visit the gift shop on the floor above the candy shop, make herself a present of some small object. Hadn't she always heard that spending money on something not really needed could always lift a woman's spirits?

In the candy shop she gave her order to the clerk for the special assortment her mother loved, then slipped up the narrow stairway to the floor above. The gift shop was well stocked, the merchandise displayed on tables and shelves along the walls and down the center of the room, leaving a narrow aisle to walk around. Tara moved slowly, her eyes darting around, trying to see everything. Then her eyes stopped and focused on a painting on the wall. Studying the brilliant fall scene intently, she gave a sudden, startled "Oh" when a body jolted into her from behind.

"I'm terribly sorry," a pleasant voice said close to her ear. "I'm afraid I wasn't watching where I was going."

She turned, mouth opened to reply, but the words were never uttered for he exclaimed, "Tara! I don't know if you remember me. Craig Hartman, we met at David's six months ago."

Recognition brought a quick smile to her face. "Of course I remember. You're the guy who was getting ready to go to South America for your company."

"Right. I just got back on Tuesday. As a matter of fact I was going to call you as soon as I'd finished my report to the firm."

"Really?" she laughed. "Why?"

"To ask you to have dinner with me some evening." He grinned boyishly, and Tara remembered she'd liked him when first meeting him. "This is incredible seeing you here, of all places. What are you doing here?"

"Just browsing while I wait for a candy order to be packaged. And you?"

Again the boyish smile spread over his face. "I remembered late this afternoon that my sister's first wedding anniversary is tomorrow and dashed over here, after I left the office, for a gift. I was looking at the paintings and not watching where I was going when I bumped into you."

Tara grinned back. "And I was looking at one and didn't see you coming." She glanced back at the fall scene and his eyes followed hers. "That *is* nice," he murmured. "Are you going to buy it?"

"No," she laughed softly. "I'm afraid my budget wouldn't allow it."

"Then I think I will. Pat has a spot in her living room where it will go perfectly." He motioned to the sales clerk and asked her to wrap it up, then turned back to Tara. "Have dinner with me this evening," he said abruptly. "We can go from here. I know it's early, but we can have a drink or two first, get to know each other a little."

"But I haven't been home," she said, laughing in surprise. "I'm still in my work clothes."

His eyes went over her slowly, appreciatively, before he stated warmly: "You look lovely. Besides which, I've just come from work myself."

Over dinner, she studied him unobtrusively. He wasn't much taller than she and, though slender, was compactly built. Fair, closely clipped curly hair complemented light blue eyes, and she thought that although he didn't posses the devastating handsomeness of one Aleksei Rykovsky, he was certainly a very attractive man. Then she slid her eyes away with a flash of irritation at herself. What in the world had made her think of that miserable man, let alone make a comparison between him and Craig?

"Hey, there."

Tara looked up, startled and wide-eyed, at Craig's laughing voice. "I thought you'd dozed off for a minute. Not very good for my ego at all."

Tara laughed with him, firmly pushing the thought of the Mad Russian from her mind.

It was a pleasant evening. They laughed and talked for hours, discovering they had a few mutual friends besides David and Sallie.

When finally they said good night at the door of her apartment, Craig having followed her car in his own, she felt happier and more relaxed than she had in weeks.

Her lightened mood lasted through the weekend, even though the white rose appeared exactly as before, and the phone remained strangely silent.

She was walking to the filing cabinet early Monday afternoon when the phone rang and she stopped beside her desk to answer it. It was her mother, and she asked Tara, in an oddly strained voice, if they could have lunch together one day that week.

"Of course, Mama," she answered, a small wrinkle forming between her eyes at the strange tone of her mother's voice. "I'll tell you what. I was planning to take you shopping for your birthday present on Saturday. Why don't we wait, and I'll buy you lunch at Hess's?"

Her mother hesitated then agreed dully, and Tara felt a flicker of alarm. Was she not feeling well? Her mother loved the rare treat of having lunch at the large department store, famous for its sumptuous food and large, luscious desserts. Her apparent disinterest now worried Tara.

"All right, Mama, I'll pick you up at nine thirty Saturday morning. Okay?" Her mother agreed in the same strained tone, then said good-bye and hung up.

Her frown deepening, Tara lowered the receiver slowly as the office door opened behind her. A small shiver slithered up her spine, and the instrument clattered onto its cradle from nerveless fingers. She knew, somehow, who had come into the office and felt goose bumps tickle her upper arms moments before she felt his hand lift her hair and his lips touch her neck. She parted her lips but words wouldn't come. Shock, outrage, and something she didn't want to examine seemed to have frozen her mind and body.

His voice was a barely discernible murmur at her ear. "Have a good time Friday night, pansy eyes?"

She made a small, inarticulate sound in her throat, and he laughed softly, deeply before adding in a much stronger tone, "I've tried to stay away from this office, telling myself the nights should be enough, but it seems I've grown greedy and my self doesn't listen."

A shudder tore through her body at the caressing, loverlike tone, and she closed her eyes, willing him to go away. She felt David walk past them and go into his office, closing the door with a soft click, and her moan was a painful thing in her throat: "Oh, God!"

"Don't worry, darling," the fiend with the lover's voice whispered. "You'll understand everything very soon now, I'm afraid." Then he caught her rigid chin with his long fingers, turned her head, and brushed her mouth against his in a soft, tantalizing kiss before quickly releasing her and following David.

She was completely bewildered, feeling shattered and vaguely tearful.

The feeling remained throughout the week, and she hardly noticed the white morning roses. One thing she did notice was the strange, speculative looks aimed at her from her co-workers in the front office. And that made her even more edgy and nervous.

Chapter Three

By Saturday morning Tara had managed to pull herself together yet she still had to force a cheerful smile to her lips when she picked up her mother. The smile faded quickly at her first glimpse of her mother's face. Lines of strain pulled at the corners of her mouth, and she avoided Tara's eyes as she seated herself in the car.

As she drove downtown, Tara made a few vain attempts at conversation but finally gave up as the only responses she received were mumbled monosyllables.

They shopped a few hours, Tara becoming ever more concerned at her mother's lack of interest at everything they looked at. Finally, at eleven thirty, Tara gave up, saying gently, "Let's go have lunch now, Mama. Maybe we'll feel more like it after we've eaten."

She studied her mother during lunch, growing more uneasy by the minute. Her mother barely touched her food, and when they'd finished and were sipping their coffee, Tara asked anxiously, "Mama what's wrong? Aren't you feeling well?"

The eyes that Marlene Schmitt turned to Tara sent a shaft of pain to her heart, so reproachful and hurt was their expression.

"I'm sick at heart, Tara," her mother finally answered sadly. "So much so, I feel physically ill. After the way you talked to Betsy just three weeks ago, I can't believe you're doing this. And Tara, I can't bear it."

Tara's eyes widened at the pain in her mother's voice. What had she done to cause her mother this anguish?

"But Mama, what have I done?" Tara asked anxiously, watching with alarm her mother's eyes fill with tears.

"Oh, Tara, don't. I know I'm a little old-fashioned and naive, but I'm no fool."

"Mama, please—"

"No. I would listen to you, take your side, in most things. But not this." She paused, a sob catching in her throat, then went on, cutting off the defensive words on Tara's lips. "Your father asked—no, told—me to bring you back to the house. I must warn you, he is beside himself with anger."

The last word was no sooner out of her mother's mouth when Tara rushed into urgent speech.

"Mama, if you'll just ex—"

"Tara, please," her mother said softly, glancing around the crowded room. "I can't discuss this here. I won't talk here. I want to go home."

Tara sighed in frustration. "All right. Let's go and get it over with."

They drove in silence, Marlene Schmitt quietly wiping the tears from her cheeks with a sodden tissue.

Tara bit her lip in vexation, frantically casting about in her mind for some transgression she may have committed to cause her mother such unhappiness.

She followed her mother into the house, her steps faltering as she entered the living room. They were all there. Her father, his face flushed a dark, angry red; Betsy; George; and even the fourteen-year-old Karl. Anger stirred, replacing some of her anxiety. *What in the world is this anyway?* she wondered. The words *kangaroo court* flashed into her mind, and she pushed the thought away. Good Lord! This was her family, not a band of enemies. Yet the atmosphere of censure was so thick, it touched her skin chillingly.

Ever defiant, the light of battle gleamed in Tara's eyes. She had no idea what this was all about but she'd be damned if she'd stand before those condemning eyes meekly. Her father's first words took the wind from her sails.

"Well, Tara. I'm surprised you have the nerve to face any of us after your big talk three weeks ago."

"Dad," Tara began patiently, "I haven't the vaguest idea what—"

"Haven't you?" Her father nearly choked on the words. "Haven't you just?" His eyes went around the room, touching every face, then settled again on her. "Anyone else would have the sense to be ashamed, but not Tara. Look at her. Proud as a damned peacock. Not our Tara. Oh, no. Rules were made for everyone else. Tara makes hers up as she goes along. You make me sick, girl."

"Herman—" his wife pleaded.

"Don't 'Herman' me. I've listened to you since she was a teenager. 'Tara's intelligent,' you said. 'She has good sense,' you said. 'She'll make us proud.' *Ha!* What she's doing is intelligent? Makes good sense? It's degrading, disgusting. I should have beat the rebellion out of her years ago."

The defiance in Tara's eyes had slowly changed to bewilderment. Never had she seen her father quite so angry. This was serious. Really serious. And she didn't have a clue as to what he was talking about.

"Dad, please. If you'll just explain—"

It seemed she was not to be allowed to speak, for he interrupted with a shouted, "Me, explain? You think we're dumb Dutchmen, don't you? You think we're so stupid, we don't understand. You think your mother doesn't understand the gossip of her friends? You think your sister and brothers don't understand the behind-the-hand snickers of their friends? You think I don't understand the dirty remarks made by the men I work with?"

Tara wet her suddenly dry lips. Her father's dark, mottled color frightened her, but his words frightened her more. This was more than serious; this was ugly. When she didn't reply at once, her father shouted, "Do you think we haven't heard of this man's reputation with women?"

Tara head snapped up. *What man?* The silent question was answered loudly.

"Do you think we haven't heard how this rich Russian uses them and then kicks them aside? Oh, sure," he added, his voice dripping sarcasm. "He gives them anything they want. Anything, that is, except his name."

"You're wrong," Tara whispered, horrified.

"Of course." His sarcasm grew yet stronger. "That can't happen to you. You're too good for that." His eyes bored into her with hatred. "You've always thought yourself too good. Too good for us or this house. Too good for the nice, hard-working young men who were interested in you. But not too good, apparently, to crawl into bed with that swine Rykovsky."

"Herman, don't." Tara heard her mother scream, but she couldn't help her. She could hardly breathe. Her father's words had hit her like a punch in the ribs, and she stood, white and trembling, staring at his face. Then she spun on her heel and ran, her mother's sobs beating on her ears.

Hours later, as she closed her apartment door behind her, she had no recollection of getting to her car. Or, for that matter, of driving up into the mountains. She had been brought to her senses by the long, blaring sound of the horn of the car she nearly ran headlong into. Shaken, sick to her stomach, face wet with tears she didn't even remember shedding, she slowed down the car then pulled in and stopped at the first observation parking area she came to. She hadn't left the car, as there were many tourists walking around admiring the splendor of the panoramic view of the mountains, which overlapped each other as if trying to push themselves forward in a proud display of their brilliant fall finery.

Tara sat still, hands gripping the steering wheel. Suddenly everything made sense. At least, almost everything. Now she understood her sister's strange phone call two weeks ago. Now she understood David and Sallie's reserved attitude. And now she understood the sly looks of everyone in the office, the odd silence of her friends. They all thought she and Aleksei Rykovsky were—her mind shied from the word momentarily—*lovers*. The word pushed its way forward. They all thought he was her lover. Vivid pictures followed the word into her mind and she gasped aloud. Seemingly of its own volition, her arm lifted her hand to her face and drew the back of it across her mouth, then quickly turned to press cold fingers to slightly parted lips. She could actually feel his mouth against hers. Could feel again that confusing mixture of excitement and fear his lips had aroused. Her fingertips tingled and, lifting her hand, she stared at her fingers as if hypnotized. "Oh, God, no," she whispered.

Now she pushed herself away from the apartment door against which she'd slumped and stumbled across her living room and into the bedroom. Dropping her handbag and jacket onto the floor, she fell across the bed fully clothed, exhausted, her mind numbed into blankness. She had no idea how long she lay staring into space when the shrill ringing of the phone roused her. Reaching over to the nightstand, she picked up the receiver and said, dully, "Hello."

A pause, then Craig Hartman's voice, hesitant and uncertain. "Tara?"

"Yes. . . . Craig?"

"I thought I had the wrong number," he laughed softly. "It didn't sound like you. Did you just get in?"

"Yes," she answered blankly. "But how did you know?"

"I rang your phone a couple of times this afternoon."

"Why?"

"To ask you to have dinner with me, silly. It's not too late. Will you come out with me?"

"Oh, Craig," she answered wearily. "Not tonight. I'm not feeling well."

He was instant concern. "I'm sorry. What's wrong?"

"Nothing serious. I have a blinding headache and I'm going to take some aspirin and go to bed."

"Sounds best. Hope you feel better tomorrow. May I call you one night next week?"

"Yes, any night. Thank you for inviting me."

"You bet! Take care of yourself. I'll call. Good night."

"Good night, Craig."

Tara punched off the receiver then sat staring at the phone, her brow knit in concentration. The numbness that had gripped her mind at the memory of Aleksei Rykovsky's kiss had been swept away, and her brain was asking questions.

What was his reputation with women? Tara had no idea.

She seldom listened to that sort of gossip, simply because she could not care less how other people conducted their private lives. What had her father said? Something about how he used women then tossed them aside. *Very probably true,* Tara thought, her lips curling slightly. The word *womanizer* seemed to fit in perfectly with *tyrant*—arrogant and bossy.

Aleksei Rykovsky's emerging character was an unsavory one. Yet not completely so, Tara admitted to herself grudgingly. His reputation concerning his work was excellent; this Tara knew. Not only from things David had said but also from what she'd observed herself.

According to David, whom Tara wouldn't dream of doubting, Alek was the most ethical businessman he'd ever met. The signing of a contract with Rykovsky, David had told her, was a mere formality. For, once given, his word was as binding as his signature. He managed his plant with a combination of rigid discipline and humane understanding. The finished product, before it left his plant, had to be of the highest quality. And his patience, when dealing either with other businessmen or his employees, was legendary.

This last Tara had found a little hard to believe. She remembered vividly one afternoon in late August at the new plant site. She had gone with David to take notes as he conferred with Alek and the construction boss. It had been hot, the humidity hanging in the seventies. Tara had felt sticky and slightly headachy; the condition was not helped by the fact that Alek had been late, and they'd stood in the hot sun waiting for him. When he had finally arrived with a brief word of apology, Tara had felt her headache grow stronger at the sheer impact of his appearance.

Tara's eyes had run over him swiftly as he approached them. He had left his jacket in the car and Tara wet dry lips, watching the lithe movement of his body as he strode forward. Dark brown chinos hugged his slim hips and muscular thighs and his shirt clung damply to an alarmingly broad expanse of chest and shoulders. His deep tan contrasted strikingly with the creamy color of his shirt and the slim gold watch on his wrist. He still wore his tie but, in concession to the heat, he had pulled the knot loose and opened the two top buttons of his shirt. Frowning, Tara had shifted her eyes away with a flash of irritation at the blatantly sensual look of him. Not once, either then or since, had Tara considered the incongruity of her irritation: She had been on the site some twenty-five minutes and had not been annoyed by, or really even noticed, the fact that most of the workers were either bare-chested or had their shirts opened to the waist.

Other than a nod in her direction on arrival, Alek had seemed unaware of her existence while she stood beside David, pencil flying over her notepad. When the context of the discussion changed to that of not requiring note taking, Tara moved back and away a few feet to give the men privacy.

Flipping the pages as she checked over her notes, Tara had been only surfacely aware of the large, burly workman walking in her direction. As he moved to pass by, not much more than a foot in front of her, he stumbled and Tara glanced up with a startled "Oh!" Arms flailing the air as if to regain his balance, his one hand arced past her face and the next instant she went rigid as his large, grimy fingers clutched her right breast.

The subsequent action had the element of a film viewed from a speeded-up projector; and yet every movement remained clear in Tara's memory. Stepping back and away from those clutching fingers, Tara glanced in dismay at the soil mark on her otherwise pristine white sleeveless scooped-neck top. At the same time, from the moment the man had stumbled, Tara had peripherally seen Alek's head jerk up, then had seen him moving, crossing the few feet of sun-baked yellow-brown earth in two long-legged strides. He reached the man at the same instant Tara stepped back, and her surprise changed to alarm as she saw his arm flash up then down, the edge of his hand striking a blow to the man's shoulder that drove him to his knees. Long hard fingers strategically placed at the back of the man's neck kept him there.

"Are you trying to find out what it would be like to be paralyzed for the rest of your life?"

The tone of Alek's voice had sent a shuddering chill

through Tara's body. Icy, deadly, his words hung like a pall on the suddenly still, hot air. Tara became aware of the work stoppage of the men in their vicinity, the intent look of attraction on the men's faces, including David and the construction boss.

The burly workman at Alek's feet gave a strangled sound in the negative, and Alek's hand moved from the back of his neck.

"If you, or any other member of this work crew, ever make an advance on Mr. Jennings's assistant again, you'll find out pretty damned quickly, so pass the word. Now get the hell away from here and get back to work."

For such a large man, the worker was on his feet and moving away at what Tara was sure was a record pace.

She had very little time to observe the man's retreat, for Alek's eyes, blazing with blue fury, were turned on her. Swiftly they raked the upper part of her body then returned to bore into hers. His voice a harsh whisper, he snapped, "As for you, Miss Schmitt, may I suggest that in the future you dress with a little more decorum when you're on the site. Unless, of course, you enjoy this kind of attention."

With that he turned and walked back to David. Shocked, Tara stood open-mouthed, staring at his back. Shock was at once replaced by humiliation and anger at what she considered his unwarranted attack on both herself and the hapless workman. That his last whispered words had obviously reached no other ears but her own was little consolation.

Turning, cheeks red with embarrassment, Tara spun around and stalked to David's car, slamming the door after sliding onto the front seat. *That arrogant, obnoxious brute,* she raged silently. Where did he get off speaking to her like that? Dress with more decorum indeed! Her clothes were perfectly decent. Moreover, they were in perfectly good taste.

Honest in his business dealings, he may be, Tara thought. *Fanatical in his demand for quality work, perhaps. But patient? Hardly.*

Now, still sitting next to the phone, Tara wondered about his supposed reputation with women. With a manner as abrasive as his, how in the world had he acquired it? No woman playing with all fifty-two of her cards would care to get within shouting distance, let alone close enough to be used then tossed aside. . . .

Her stomach gave a protestingly empty growl, startling her out of her thoughts. She had overslept this morning and had gulped a half glass of orange juice for breakfast. Tara had barely picked at her lunch and now at—she glanced at her watch—eight fifteen her body was sending out a cry for nourishment.

Like an automaton she stood up and walked into the kitchen; she started a pot of coffee, put an egg in the poacher, and dropped two pieces of bread in the toaster. A few minutes later, as she munched her egg and toast thoughtfully, her mind went back to the question: *Who had perpetrated a rumor of this kind? Why would someone want to? And equally baffling, how?* She had seen the man only five times in three weeks. Three times in the office, and then only briefly, once at his plant, and that one time here at her own apartment. Surely not even the most imaginative person could make anything of a twenty-minute visit. And no one had witnessed those incidents in the office except David. David? Tara shook her head firmly. David would have told no one but Sallie, and Sallie, Tara was positive, would not repeat it. But then who? and why? and dammit, how?

Tara got up, walked to the counter, and refilled her coffee cup. As she turned back to the table, she became still with an altogether new thought. *Her* name and reputation were not the only ones involved here. Had word of this reached Aleksei Rykovsky's ears? She somehow felt certain that it had. He was not the man to miss anything. Whatever must he be thinking?

The phone's ringing broke her thoughts, and she went to answer it, carrying her coffee with her.

"Hello."

"Tara, it's me, Betsy." *As if I wouldn't know,* Tara thought wryly. "Look, Sis, I just wanted you to know I don't feel the same as Dad does."

"About what?" Tara asked tiredly.

"Oh, you know," her sister snorted impatiently. "About you and him. I think you would have been dumb not to grab him, he's so handsome and rich."

Tara was quiet so long digesting the greedy sound and intent of her sister's words that Betsy said sharply, "Tara?"

"Good-bye, Betsy." Tara punched the disconnect button. She certainly didn't need any more calls or opinions like that tonight.

Sipping at her still hot coffee, she turned to go back to the kitchen when the door chime rang. *Oh, now what?* she thought balefully. Staring at the door, she considered not answering, but it chimed again.

Sighing deeply, she walked across the pale beige carpet, unlocked the door, pulled it open, and froze. Cool and relaxed, Alek Rykovsky stood in the hall, his hands jammed in the pockets of his black raincoat. *Is it raining?* Tara wondered irrelevantly. *Must be,* she decided, noting the damp spots on his wide shoulders. His coat hung open and he looked trim and muscular in the close-fitting, black denim jeans and a white turtleneck bulky knit sweater. *He's one unnerving sight,* Tara admitted ruefully to herself. If someone had to smear her name in connection with a man, at least whoever it was had chosen a handsome devil.

"May I come in?" he asked pointedly. "Or are you going to just stand there looking daggers at me?"

She jerked her eyes away, feeling her face go hot. Embarrassment put a sharp edge to her tongue.

"Come in if you must," she said cuttingly, pulling the door wider. Perfectly shaped lips twitching, he strolled past her, and in agitation she slammed the door shut. Lifting her cup to her lips, she took a long, calming sip.

"I'd like some of that." He nodded at her cup.

Turning abruptly, she marched into the kitchen with Alek right on her heels. She went to the counter, snatched a mug from its peg on the mug tree, filled it to the brim, then turned and gave an exclaimed "Oh," not having realized he was still close behind her. Some of the hot liquid splashed over the side of the cup and onto her hand, and he snatched the cup away from her with a growled, "What the hell are you trying to do? Scald yourself?"

"I—I—didn't know you were so close," she stammered.

The fires that had momentarily lit his eyes were banked into a bright glitter. "Do I frighten you, Tara?" he chided.

"No, of course not," she snapped. "You startled me, that's all." She turned to refill her own cup, trying in vain to control her shaking hands.

"Hmmm," he murmured judiciously, shrugging out of his raincoat. He draped the coat over the back of a kitchen chair, picked up his cup and drank from it, then, one dark brow arched questioningly, said, "You seem upset about something. Anything wrong?"

Something about his too casual tone annoyed her and, her voice oversweet, she purred, "Have you heard the latest gossip?"

"About us?" he replied, his tone equally sweet.

Anger flared fiercely, and her usually soft brown eyes flashed. "No, the Prince of Wales," she spat. "Of course about us."

He nodded, watching her mounting anger solemnly.

"Who would do something like this?" she burst out angrily.

"Don't you know?"

She jerked her head up to stare at him, suspecting some sort of condemnation. His face was expressionless, his eyes coolly calculating. "No, I don't know! I can't believe for a minute that any of my friends would spread such a vicious story."

"The idea of you and me together is vicious?"

Tara eyed him stormily, hating the theatrically affronted tone of his voice. "You may be amused, Mr. Rykovsky. This kind of thing enhances a man's aura. But my reputation is ruined."

"Is that so very important today?" he asked dryly.

"Of course it is," she cried.

"Well, you may have a point," he murmured. "Come to think of it, you're right."

"What do you mean?"

He drained his cup, walked to the sink, rinsed it, and placed it in the draining rack. Then he turned, took her cup from her hand, and did the same to it before asking, "Wouldn't we be more comfortable in the living room?" Not waiting for an answer, he scooped up his coat and strode out of the kitchen.

Gritting her teeth, Tara followed him, entering the living room in time to see him drop into a chair and stretch his long legs out comfortably.

"If you're sure you're comfortable, Mr. Rykovsky, perhaps you'd explain what you said before."

"What was that?" he asked innocently, then smiled sardonically. "Oh, yes, about your being right. Well, you see, Tara, for all our big talk of equal rights, I'm afraid a great many of us men are still dreadfully chauvinistic. Most will jump happily into bed with any 'liberated' woman who'll have him. But, and it's a very big *but,* these very same men, when they finally decide they are ready to get married, will look around for a relatively untouched woman. I say relatively untouched because even the most naive of us are aware that today there are not really that many virginal women over the age of twenty. So you see, it's the old double standard. While he wants to bed as many as possible, he wants to marry an untouched one. Deplorable perhaps, but nonetheless true. It's the nature of the beast."

As he spoke, Tara felt her anger grow apace with her embarrassment. Now, pink-cheeked, eyes snapping, she jumped up out of her chair.

"Beast is right. How grossly unjust that attitude is."

"That goes without saying. But then, who ever said that life was just?"

He stood up slowly, lazily uncoiling like a large, dark cat. Tara walked across the room to the window facing the street, suddenly, unaccountably, nervous.

"I don't know what to do about this," she almost whispered. "My family's upset. My friends have made themselves scarce. Incredibly, in this day and age, I feel ostracized."

"You have one option that would stop the talk at once." He spoke quietly, his eyes keen on her face as she turned to look questioningly at him.

"Accept my proposal. Marry me." He walked slowly to her and she felt her heart begin to thud frantically, her legs tremble.

Hoping to stop his determined movement toward her, she sneered. "You mean you're unlike other men? You're willing to saddle yourself with a—what is the word—*tainted* woman?"

He laughed low in his throat, the sound slipping down her spine on tiny, icy feet.

"As I'm supposed to be the man who 'tainted' you, I can't see that it makes any difference."

He stopped in front of her, reaching up to touch her silvery hair, which gleamed in the soft glow of the table lamp beside her.

"Such fantastic hair," he murmured. "I want to see it fanned out on a pillow under me, Tara." He pinched a few strands between thumb and forefinger and drew his hand down its long length. "I want to bind myself in it like a silken net." Tara felt the serpent of excitement uncoil in her midriff as he brought the strands to his lips. "I want to draw it across your beautiful mouth and kiss you breathless through it." In unwilling fascination she watched his eyes darken, narrow with desire; felt his hand slide to her nape; felt long fingers curl into the soft thickness and draw her face to his. His mouth a breath away from hers, he whispered hoarsely, "Marry me, Tara." Then he covered her trembling lips with his hard, firm ones in an urgent, demanding kiss.

Tara stiffened, fighting the insidious languor that invaded her body as if fighting for her life. She had been kissed many times but never had she felt like this. Her veins seemed to be flowing with liquid fire that burned and seared and ate up her resistance. His hands moved down her spine, then gripped convulsively, flattening her against the long, hard length of his body. She felt dizzy, light-headed, barely able to hear the small voice of reason that cried, *Step back,* when all she wanted was to get closer, closer. His hand moved up and under her knit top, and she shivered deliciously at the feel of his fingers on her bare skin. The voice of reason broke through when his hand moved over her breast possessively. Using her last remaining dregs of will, she tore her mouth from his and spun out and away from his arms, sobbing, "No. No. No."

He didn't come after her but stood studying her pale, frightened face intently, breathing deeply to regain control.

"You're a fool, Tara," he finally said, his voice calm, devoid of inflection. "I could give you everything you ever wanted. And you are not indifferent to me. I've just proven that."

Tara stood rigid, forcing herself to meet the hard, blue glitter of his eyes. Hands clenched into fists to keep from trembling, she wondered, in a vague panic, why she'd felt chilled to the bone since spinning out of his arms. Then fatigue struck; suddenly her shoulders drooped, and she felt sick to tears, the events of this horribly long day pressing down on her. She turned from him to stare sightlessly through the window and said, wearily, "Go away."

She didn't see the swift flash of concern in his eyes and when she turned back to him, it was gone.

"The offer will stay open, Tara, if you change your mind." His eyes raked her, noting her pallor, the blue smudges of tiredness under her eyes. He took one step toward her, and she cried out, "Will you please go and leave me alone. Mr. Rykovsky, please."

"Since we're supposedly sleeping together, don't you think you could call me Alek," he chided gently.

Her head dropped and her voice was a tired, ragged whisper. "Alek, please, please go."

Her chin was lifted by one long finger and she found herself gazing into surprisingly gentle blue eyes. His mouth brushed hers lightly. "You're exhausted, pansy eyes. Stay in bed tomorrow and think about me. Lock up after me." Again his lips brushed hers, then he whispered, "Good night, lover, for whether you think so now or not, I am going to be your lover."

Then he moved swiftly across the room, snatching up his raincoat without pausing, and went through the door, closing it softly.

Tara stared after him, tears running down her face, feeling unaccountably abandoned. Too tired to probe her emotions or even think, she walked across the room and locked the door as commanded. And it had been a command. Then she turned off the lights and went to her bedroom, where she turned the phone off and fell into a fitful slumber.

Chapter Four

Sunday was a short day, as Tara slept past noon. She woke with a dull headache and equally dull senses and moved about the apartment like a pale, uninterested wraith. What could she do to combat the rumors being spread connecting her name with Alek's? What could she do when she didn't even know the source of those rumors? And could she really do anything if she did know the source? A charge of slander has to be proved, and even if she could prove it, did she want that kind of publicity? The questions tormented her all day and by early evening had turned her dull headache into a piercing throb. At nine thirty, feeling half sick to her stomach, she gave it up and went to bed.

Nine hours of deep, uninterrupted sleep did wonders for her. Rested and refreshed, her headache gone, she faced Monday morning unflinchingly. She dressed extra carefully in a favorite oyster gray pantsuit and low-heeled black boots. Topping the outfit off with a black suede jacket that made her silver-blond hair look almost white, she slung her tote bag over her arm and swung out of the apartment fighting fit.

The long, careful look and silent whistle of appreciation she received from David when he entered the office boosted her morale even more. The smile she bestowed on him was breathtaking and the most natural David had seen in over a week. He stared bemusedly at her then grinned back and headed for his own office, pausing in the doorway to say, "Ask Terry Connors to come to my office, please."

Tara nodded, lifted the phone, punched the interoffice button, and waited for an answer.

A few minutes later Terry sauntered into her office for all the world like he owned the building. "Morning, beautiful, how's tricks?"

The words themselves were innocuous but the suggestive twist to his lips lent them a meaning that sent a cold stab of fear through her midsection. She had no time to question him, however, as he went straight through to David's office.

She sat pondering his words a few seconds, then gave herself a mental shake. She was getting hyper over all this, for heaven's sake; if she wasn't careful, she'd soon be reading double meanings into everything anyone said to her. In annoyance she turned back to her work, soon forgetting the incident.

An hour and a half later Terry left David's office and stopped at her desk. Glancing up questioningly, Tara caught the same twisted smile on his face before he sobered and said softly, "How about having dinner with me some time?"

Tara felt her scalp tingle in premonition, but she managed to keep her voice level. "I told you before that I won't go out with you, Terry."

"Yeah, but that was then and now is now." His smile was an insinuation that made her skin crawl.

"Nothing has happened to change my mind," she said evenly.

"Oh, I don't expect you to two-time him. Not many women have that kind of guts. But when he's through with you—and with his track record it won't be too long—maybe you'll be glad of an invitation out."

While he was speaking, Tara felt her nerves tighten, her fingers grip the edge of her keyboard. With effort she kept her voice cool. "I don't know what you're talking about."

"Come off it, babe," he jeered. "Everyone knows."

He grinned at her crookedly, his head tilted to one side, then he gave a short, nasty laugh. "You're cool as well as beautiful, and I can see what he wants with you, but you can stow the innocent act. Hell, he may as well have taken an ad in the paper." He waved his hand at the bud vase on the corner of her desk. "The roses, the few—how should I say it?—'polite' inquiries he made about you months ago. His car parked in front of your apartment all night—every night—only confirmed everyone's suspicions." Again he gave that nasty laugh. "He even spoke to me one morning as I was on my way to work, after he'd left your apartment."

He stood a moment studying her stricken, wide-eyed face, then snorted, "I told you to can the act. You may think we're a bunch of idiots, but even us peasants can add one and one and come up with two. You must have something special, seeing as how he comes to you rather than move you into his building, the way he usually does with his mistresses."

Tara had been staring in unseeing disbelief, but at his last words her vision cleared and focused on his leering face.

"Get out of my office," she said through clenched teeth, "before I call David and tell him you're annoying me."

"You win, sweetheart," Terry sneered. "But just remember who your friends are after he's through with you." He walked to the door then paused with his hand on the knob and shot over his shoulder, "I mean when the lesser males start calling, more than happy to sample the big man's leavings." On the last word he stepped through the doorway and closed the door with a sharp click.

White-faced, trembling, an odd buzzing sound in her head, Tara stared at the door, devoid, for the moment, of all feeling.

"Aleksei Rykovsky!"

The two words, murmured in a harsh whisper, sounded more like a bitter curse than a man's name. Following the words, which caused actual physical pain, white-hot anger tore through her mind; cleansing anger, motivating anger that unlocked the frozen state she'd been in and set her mind in action. She still had no idea why but now she knew how and, most importantly, who.

With careful, deliberate movement Tara pressed the intercom button and said coolly, "David, I'm sorry but I must leave the office for a short time. I have an appointment."

David, his tone indicating he was deeply immersed in his

work, answered unconcernedly, "Okay, Tara, have Connie pick up on any incoming calls and take as long as you like."

"Thank you."

Tara relayed the instruction to Connie, then, her every movement still careful and deliberate, she slipped her arms into her jacket, removed her tote from her bottom desk drawer, plucked the white rose from the bud vase and dropped it into her wastebasket, and left the office. She was going scalp-hunting.

It was less than a twenty-minute drive from David's office to Alek's large, almost antiquated machine shop. Tara used those minutes to put together the pieces of this bizarre puzzle. His words of Saturday night came as clearly as if he were sitting next to her in the car and had just spoken them.

"Don't you know?"

She had thought, then, that he was in some way accusing her of keeping information from him. Now she realized he had been probing to ascertain if she had any suspicions of him.

She went over and over the whole sordid mess and decided, not for the first time, that this man was not quite on-center; something was twisted inside. If it hadn't been for the anger that had resolved itself into a cold, hard fury, she might have been afraid of what she was about to do.

Alek's offices were located on the second floor of the sprawling old building. As Tara mounted the narrow staircase, she stiffened her spine in preparation to do battle. Steps evenly paced, firm, she walked along the long narrow hallway, glancing at closed doors marked PERSONNEL, SALES, and ACCOUNTING until finally reaching what she knew was her destination, the very last door, marked PRIVATE.

Gripping the knob, she drew a deep breath and walked in. The woman sitting at a desk some five feet inside the door was about thirty with a calm, withdrawn face and cool, intelligent eyes.

"May I help you?"

The impersonal smile and well modulated tones were the

epitome of the super-efficient secretary. Tara matched exactly her tone and manner.

"Yes, I would like to see Mr. Rykovsky, please. If it's convenient."

The cool eyes flickered with a degree of respect. "You have an appointment?"

Tara's lips twitched in wry amusement. This paragon knew damned well she had no appointment.

"No I haven't, but if he is not too busy, I'd appreciate a few minutes. It is rather important."

"I see," judiciously. "If you'll have a seat, I'll inquire, Miss . . . ?"

"Schmitt. Tara Schmitt."

She was left to cool her heels some fifteen minutes before that impersonal voice said, "Mr. Rykovsky will see you now, Miss Schmitt."

Tara's heels may have cooled, but her emotions were still at flash point, although this was not revealed as she rose gracefully to her feet, her outward appearance under rigid control.

"Thank you." Her voice a quiet murmur, she stepped past the secretary, who held open the door, and into the large room, seemingly dwarfed by the overwhelmingly masculine presence of its owner.

"Good morning, Tara." His low, silky voice slid over her, setting her teeth on edge. "You're looking exceptionally beautiful this morning."

And he is looking exceptionally handsome, she thought bitterly. Dressed in an obviously expensive, perfectly tailored charcoal-gray suit, complemented by a pearl-gray shirt and oyster-white tie, the effect of him on the senses was devastating. *How could it be,* Tara wondered, *that someone could appear so shatteringly good on the outside and be so thoroughly rotten on the inside?*

She watched his eyes grow sharp when, without speaking, she stood studying him, even though the voice remained smooth.

"Sit down, Tara."

"I prefer to stand, Mr. Rykovsky."

"Mr. Rykovsky? Saturday night it was Alek." The voice was still smooth but beginning to show awareness of things being not quite right.

"Saturday night I was still an ignorant, innocent fool," she stated coldly.

One dark eyebrow arched fleetingly; the voice matched the eyes in sharpness. "You're upset. What's happened?"

"Upset?" she cried. "Upset? You set out with a deliberate intent to ruin my reputation then dare to stand there calmly and say I'm upset? No, *Mister* Rykovsky, I am not upset. I am red-hot furious."

His face went suddenly expressionless; his narrowed eyes went wary as he watched the pink flares of angry color tinge her cheeks, her soft brown eyes flash.

"All right," he said, evenly. "You know. Now sit down and calm yourself, and we'll discuss it."

Eyes wide in astonishment, she nearly choked. "Calm myself? I don't want to calm myself. And I don't want to discuss it. What I want is an explanation for what you've done and—" The sound of her voice, beginning to rise sharply, made her check her words. Breathing deeply, trying to regain control, she glared at him across the few feet of deep-pile carpeting that separated them.

"Tara"—his gentle voice tried to soothe—"if you'll calm—"

She didn't let him finish. Fighting to regain control, nails gouging into her palms, she ground out: "Were you bored? Was this your perverted idea of a joke? A way to break up a dull time in your life? Well, I don't think you're funny. I think you're sick. You need your head ex—"

"Tara." The silky voice had taken on a decidedly serrated edge, then smoothed out again. "That's enough. Now be quiet and listen a minute. If you let yourself think, you'll know why I did it. I told you twice. It was no joke, and I was not trying to be funny. Also I'm not sick. I simply know what I want and I am not afraid to go after it."

"No matter what method you use," she gasped. "Or who gets hurt?"

"I admit, in this instance, my methods were a bit unorthodox, but really, Tara, you're not all that injured. Good grief, woman, do you really think, today, that anyone gives a damn who is sleeping with whom?"

He had remained so imperturbable, so unaffected through this incredible interview, that Tara was gripped with the urge to scream at him.

"My family gives a damn. *You* don't have to watch my mother cry or face my father's anger."

"That's right, I don't," he stated firmly. "But I will if you give the word. Say you'll marry me, and I'll be at your parents' door within the hour to pacify them."

Tara was beginning to feel as if she'd stepped into some sort of unreal world, a fantasy land. *Things like this just don't happen*, she thought. Shaking her head as if to clear her mind, she said, haltingly, "I don't understand. I'm sure there must be any number of eager females ready and willing to comply with your slightest whim. Why have you singled me out to torment?"

His face hardened and a muscle rippled at the corner of his tautened jawline. "You're right. There are a number of females ready and willing." His eyes, searing like twin blue flames, raked her body boldly, heightening her color still more with embarrassment. "But, for some reason, my body demands the possession of yours. It is as simple as that. I want you. I intend having you."

Eyes wide in disbelief, she stared at him for several seconds. The self-assurance, the powerful drive, the pure, unadulterated arrogance of this man was beyond her comprehension. Throat dry, she whispered, "My father was right. You are a swine."

"No name-calling, Tara." The tone gave a soft warning.

Beyond the point of heeding any warning, soft or firm, she laughed cynically. "Name-calling? I couldn't force past my lips the names I'd like to call you." Tears of anger, frustration, bitterness, blurred her eyes. Grimly she added, "You, in your exalted position of the male, may think that today no one really gives a damn. But then you didn't have to stand and

listen to your father, in so many words, call you a wh-whore."
Her throat had closed, and she barely managed to get the last
word out. Gulping air quickly, she stifled a sob, saying, "You
don't have to listen to the snickering innuendos of the people
in your office or the dirty suggestions of Terry Connors."

"Tara!"

Alek had remained standing behind his desk from the time
she'd entered his office. Now, moving with the lithe swiftness
of a large mountain cat, he was around the desk and in front
of her, his long-fingered hands grasping her shoulders painfully.

"I'll kill him," he snarled.

"And my father?" she cried wildly. "And every other man
who'll think I'm fair game from now on?"

"Stop it," he commanded harshly, giving her a hard shake.

It was the last straw. All the fight went out of her and the
tears that had been threatening for the last five minutes overflowed and ran down her flushed cheeks. Emotionally strung
out, she suddenly felt too tired to care anymore and she stood,
dimly studying the faintly embossed pattern on his tie. The
pattern swirled and swam and she closed her eyes. She heard
him sigh deeply, felt his hands loosen their hold on her shoulders, slide around her back. She felt the muscles and sinews
in his arms tighten as he gathered her close. A strange feeling
of being safe, protected, blanketed her numbed mind. Wearily,
she rested her forehead against the hard wall that was his chest
and, crying freely, released the misery that gripped her throat.

"Tara . . . don't."

The harsh tone of a moment ago had been replaced by a
soft entreaty. He lowered his head over hers in yet another
strangely protective gesture, and she felt his lips move
against her hair. His head lowered again and now, his lips
close to her ear, his words penetrated the mistiness.

"*Dusha moya,* Tara, *ya te lyoob-lyoo.*"

He'd said those same strange words once before, yet it
wouldn't be till much later that she'd wonder about their
meaning. For now the words had a somehow soothing effect,
and she shivered as a momentary peace enveloped her.

Vaguely she became aware of a tiny, nagging voice that told her that she should not be inside the warm, protective circle of his arms. But it felt so right, as if she belonged there more than anywhere else in the world. In the effort to silence that tiny, insistent voice, she turned her head and felt her slightly parted lips make contact with his taut, rough jaw. In bemusement she heard his sharply indrawn breath.

"Don't cry, pansy eyes. Nothing on this earth is worth your tears."

His tone, more than his words, was a gentle seducement. Warm, liquid gold flowed over and through her, seeming to enclose the two of them in a soft, golden world of their own. Without conscious thought her hands slid inside his jacket and she felt vague resentment against the material of his shirt that denied her fingers the feel of his skin.

At her touch he went still, then his one hand moved up and under her hair, fingers spreading, to cradle her head. Slowly he turned her face to his, his lips brushing her cheek lightly, his breath tickling her eyelashes. Time seemed suspended inside that golden circle, and with a soft sigh Tara relaxed, allowing her arms to slide around his waist.

"I shouldn't be here," she murmured, forgetting and not caring, for the moment, why.

"You shouldn't be anywhere else. You belong exactly where you are." *Soft, his tone is so soft,* she thought. It was an inducement that drew her farther into that magic circle.

"Tara."

A hoarsely whispered groan, and then his mouth covered hers, gently, sweetly silencing that tiny nagging voice of reason.

His kiss was a tender exploration of her mouth, making no demands, asking nothing of her. At first she lay passive in his arms, her bruised emotions soothed by the glow of contentment stealing through her. But ever receptive to gentleness, tenderness, she was soon responding, her lips making an exploration of their own.

The kiss seemed to go on forever and ended much too soon. She murmured a soft protest when his mouth left hers, and she buried her face in the curve of his shoulder. Light as snowflakes, his lips touched her closed eyelids then moved to rest against her temple. Strong fingers gently massaged the back of her neck and for a few seconds Tara drifted in a gold-hued void that knew no thought or pain.

His words broke the golden spell, allowing the tiny voice to become a shout. "You're getting yourself upset over this, Tara, when it could be settled so simply by marrying me."

What do you think you're doing? the now shrill voice of her conscience demanded. *What happened to that sense of outrage that filled you on hearing Terry Connors words? What about the fine, bright flame of fury that propelled you to this confrontation?* A feeling of intense self-betrayal shot through her and she shuddered in self-disgust.

Alek misinterpreted her shudder as a sign of surrender, and he murmured, "Well, Tara?"

Tara drew a deep breath, took one step back, and pushed her hands hard against his chest. Unprepared for her action, his hold broke, and she was free of the reason-destroying circle of his arms.

Turning quickly, she ran for the door, her hand groping for the knob. Flinging the door open, shame and guilt strangling her throat, she whispered, "No" to his commanded, "Tara, wait."

Blindly, she ran past his wide-eyed, incredulous secretary, along the hall, down the narrow stairway, and out the entrance door as if a pack of wild dogs were snapping at her ankles.

Trembling almost uncontrollably, she drove straight to her apartment with one thought pounding in her head. *Get home, be safe. Get home, be safe.*

Still running, she dashed up the steps and along the short hall to her apartment. Gasping for breath, she unlocked the door; dashed inside, slammed it shut, double-locked it, and leaned back against it.

On shaky legs she stumbled across the room and dropped onto the sofa. What in the sweet world was the matter with her? Never had she experienced this cloying, panicky feeling. She felt her throat close; then her eyes filled and with a murmured "Oh, Lord," her body fell sideways onto the cushions and she was crying, sobbing like a child, hurt, alone, lost.

For over an hour Tara lay in a crumpled heap, the wracking sobs and tears slowly dwindling to sniffles and an occasional hiccup. Gradually awareness crept back and with a sigh she pushed herself upright. She had to call David.

David's voice was a reassuringly normal sound in a world gone suddenly very abnormal.

"I'm sorry, David," she sniffed, "but I won't be back today, I'm not feeling well."

Instant concern colored David's warm voice. "What's wrong, Tara?" A short pause, then: "Honey, have you been crying?"

"No, no," she reassured hastily. "I think I've had a sudden allergic reaction to something. I've been sneezing like mad and my eyes have been watering and I look a mess." *Well,* she thought, grimacing, *the last part's true.*

"Are you sure?" He sounded skeptical. "What could have brought this on?"

Tara cast about frantically and grabbed at the first thing that came to mind. "I'm not sure, but I think it must be the roses I've had on my desk the last few weeks." *Would he buy it?* she wondered. He did.

"More than likely. Have you seen a doctor?"

"No. I—I don't think that's necessary. I'll take an allergy capsule."

"Well, if it doesn't help you get better by tomorrow morning, get yourself to a doctor. Don't worry about the office but call me and let me know how you feel."

"All right, David, I will. And thank you."

"For what?" he snorted, then warned. "Now take care, Tara, I mean it."

"Yes, sir," came the meek reply. "Oh, and David, would you do something for me?"

"Anything I can."

"Would you call and stop delivery on the roses? The name of the florist is on the box in my wastebasket."

"Sure thing, honey. Be good and get well."

He hung up. Tara smiled gently as she replaced the receiver. David hated saying good-bye and so he never did.

Speaking with David had restored her equilibrium somewhat, and with a firmer tread she went to the kitchen and brewed a pot of coffee. While the coffee perked away happily, she made herself half a sandwich and ate it in grim determination. When the electric pot shut itself off, she placed the pot, a small jug of milk, and a mug on a tray and returned to the living room.

Sitting with the mug of the steaming brew cradled in her hands, she turned her mind to her recent encounter and the events that led to it. She still found it incredible, if not completely unbelievable, that anyone would go to such lengths to amuse himself. In her book, that constituted a pretty weird sense of humor.

"It was no joke, and I was not trying to be funny."

His words slithered through her mind, and she shivered violently.

"Garbage." She said the word aloud and then repeated it silently. *Garbage.* Everything he'd said was exactly that. So much garbage. How she longed to make him pay for what he'd done to her. But how? Reluctantly she admitted to herself that chances of her hurting him in some way were practically nil.

As were her chances of repairing the damage he'd done. How did one combat nebulous hints? Innuendo? Veiled suggestions? She could go to her family and her closest friends and explain exactly what had happened, but would they believe it? Would she if she heard a story like that from someone? Not likely. Oh, yes, he'd been clever. Very clever. So what could she do? Move away? Where? And was it worth it? As he'd suggested, speculation, talk, couldn't cause her any lasting pain. *But he could,* an insidious voice whispered deep in her mind.

In sudden renewed fear, almost panic, she argued with the errant thought. How could he hurt her anymore? She didn't care what he said or did. Wouldn't care if he dropped dead tonight. The sudden twist of pain that clutched at her heart shocked her.

Frantically she moved about, refilling her coffee cup, walking to the TV to switch it on, anything to still those silly thoughts and emotions.

She watched a few minutes of the news then, much calmer, she decided her only course of action was to put on a bright face and brazen it out. In time the talk would die down, become a ninety-day wonder, and in due time she'd be able to forget it—and him.

But will you? that small, perverse voice demanded.

Chapter Five

The following two days went fairly well. She breezed into the office as usual, gave Terry a frosty smile as usual, talked a few minutes with Jeannie at coffee-break time, and breathed a heartfelt sigh of relief that the roses had stopped being delivered. Chalk one up for her.

On Tuesday evening she'd crept outside and scanned the street for his car. There it was, bold as brass, and it left a somewhat brassy taste in her mouth. Where on earth did the miserable man go after he parked it there? Back in her apartment she pondered on what, if anything, she could do about its presence. Should she call the police and report it as abandoned? And if they checked the license number and found out who it belonged to, then what? Alek Rykovsky was a respected businessman. If asked why his car was parked there, he could say he'd been visiting friends or had lent it to a friend in the neighborhood and he'd be believed without further question. And where would that leave her? Looking pretty damned silly. With reluctance she told herself: *Ignore the car*.

Wednesday moved along as Tuesday had, and she was beginning to think she'd get through this mess with some degree of composure. She even had an added bonus discovering Alek's car among the missing. Then the bottom fell out. Craig called. His first words jarred her out of her complacency.

"Look, Tara, I know you're alone because I happened to know Rykovsky's at a testimonial dinner tonight."

"Craig, I—"

"No, don't bother to explain. I understand. The only thing that makes me mad is that you didn't tell me the night we had dinner together. He sure as hell isn't trying to keep it a secret. If you'd told me, I wouldn't have built up any hopes. And I had."

"Craig, please, let me explain."

"Not necessary. You owe me nothing. But look, Tara, if anything happens, I mean, if you split or anything and need a shoulder to cry on, call me, will you?"

Why bother? Why even bother to explain to people who just wouldn't listen, or wouldn't believe it if they did?

"Yes, Craig," she answered softly, a wealth of defeat in her voice.

She went to bed depressed and woke the same way, but plastered a determined smile on her face anyway.

The morning went by without a hitch, and her spirits lifted. In an attempt to keep them up Tara decided to leave the office at lunchtime and treat herself to a fattening lunch of lasagna at her favorite Italian restaurant. She returned to the office a few minutes late but replete in body and restored in well-being.

The low hum of several voices came from David's office, and she checked her appointment book to see if she'd failed to write down a meeting. The space was blank, so she decided, with a shrug, this was probably an impromptu thing that David had called during the lunch hour.

She tackled the filing pile from the morning's work and was busy at it when David's door opened. Before she could close the file drawer, a hand slid around the back of her neck and long fingers pressed against her jawline, turning her face around and up. Eyes wide with surprise, she saw Alek's blue eyes glitter with intent, and then his mouth claimed hers. In the few seconds her mouth was held captive she registered the expressions on the faces of the two men who had followed Alek out of David's office: David's face was a picture of uncertain concern, Terry Connor's of positive envy.

The two men stood watching as if frozen, then moved

quickly toward opposite doors as Alek lifted his head. But not quickly enough to miss hearing Alek's words.

"I'm sorry about last night, darling, but the dinner lasted much later than I thought it would, and I didn't want to disturb you."

The doors facing them closed simultaneously. David's very gently, the other with a sharp snap.

Tara could have wept in pure frustration. Of course that sneaky Terry would have noticed the absence of Alek's car last night. That accounted for the speculative look he'd run over her this morning. And Alek? He was covering his tracks.

Seething with instant anger, she ignored the tingle in her fingers and lashed out, "You son of a—!" She got no further, for Alek cut in a silky warning.

"Careful, sweetheart. I told you before, no name-calling."

"Go to hell," she whispered angrily.

With a swift jerk he turned her fully around and she had to force herself to meet the blue flame of anger in his eyes.

"You're walking on very thin ice, my sweet. Take care you don't break through and find yourself in over your head." His voice was soft but chilling. "Why don't you give it up? Turn over your sword, hilt first, and we'll go on from there."

"I have no intention of going on to anything with you." For some reason Tara couldn't raise her voice above a whisper; she wet her lips, then went on. "So why don't you give it up? Leave me alone. Stop this madness."

"Madness? Hardly that." He laughed softly and planted a tiny kiss at the corner of her mouth. "Just a matter of chemistry. To be blunt, beautiful, you turn me on something fierce. I'd give you proof, but I don't think this is quite the time or the place."

Struck by the blatant audacity of the fiend, all she could find to say was, "Get out of here before I start screaming rape."

He laughed again, an easy, relaxed laugh that caused a vague sort of longing deep inside her; then, thank goodness, he walked to the door.

"Okay, kid, I'll let you get back to work. But I'm not nearly through with you yet."

After he'd gone, Tara turned back to the file cabinet, then paused with her hand on the drawer handle as an odd thought struck her. *Beautiful, sweetheart, kid.* The same words Terry had used on Monday morning. Alek had even thrown in *darling* and *my sweet.* Coming from Terry's mouth, the endearments had been offensive, an insult. Why then did they sound so exciting, somehow natural, from the lips of that hateful devil? The thought made Tara uncomfortable, and she pushed it away.

The remainder of the afternoon was a shambles. Try as she would, Tara could not seem to pull herself together, to still her trembling fingers. She made numerous entry errors, kept dropping things, and in the space of a few hours, almost wiped out her beautifully kept filing cabinets.

By the time she left the office, she was on the verge of tears. She ached, literally hurt all over, as if she'd been pulled through a hedge backward. While her teeth were punishing her lower lip as she walked to her car, her mind cried fiercely, *Why does he keep on with this?* Surely he knew by now how much she disliked, disapproved of him.

Sliding into the car, she slammed the door, jabbed the key into the ignition. She had thought, after that fiasco in his office on Monday . . . her hand paused on the key; hot pink color swept her cheeks. She could not, would not, let herself think about that.

Her fingers flipped the key, the engine fired into life, and with unthinking recklessness Tara drove off the lot and into the flow of traffic, ignoring the angry horn blasts from several irate drivers.

Where to go? What to do? she asked herself. She just couldn't face that apartment alone tonight. She was becoming positively claustrophobic in those small rooms. *Sallie?* Tara shook her head. *Explanations would have to be made. Who in the world would believe something like this?* Tara was having trouble believing it herself. Besides, Tara felt she had no right to endanger the working relationship between David and Alek.

Tara drove aimlessly for some time. Up one street, down another. Glancing around uninterestedly as she sat at a corner waiting for the light to change, Tara's eyes passed then came back to rest on a small tavern on the opposite corner. She had been in that tavern several times with friends. The food served was plain but good, the prices fair.

The light changed to green, and with sudden decision Tara hunted up a parking space, parked, and locked the car.

The tavern was family owned and run. The wife did the cooking and serving, the husband tended the bar, and their son worked in both places, wherever he was most needed.

Though she rarely had a drink, Tara had suddenly decided she needed one. Hell! At this minute she felt she needed a dozen. Leaving the car, she skirted around the front entrance that led into the bar and entered the side door that opened into the dining room.

The room was half full of what Tara judged were neighborhood regulars. Moving toward the front of the building, Tara stopped at a small table, just inside the large open archway, that gave full view of the barroom. Young Jake Klinger, Jr., was working the end of the bar near the entrance to the dining room, and as Tara sat down he glanced up, grinned, and waved.

"Hi, Tara, howzit?"

Somehow she managed to return the grin convincingly.

"Fine, Jake, how are things with you?"

"Fair to middlin'," he replied laconically, then turned to serve his customer with the glass of beer he'd just tapped. That done, he sauntered around the end of the bar and to her table.

"What can I get you, gorgeous?"

Tara smiled, her eyes on the menu written in chalk on a blackboard hanging on the wall. After the lunch she'd eaten and the afternoon she'd put in, she didn't feel at all hungry. But she knew that if she drank and didn't eat, she'd be out for the count, or sick, in no time.

"I think I'll have a Caesar salad and a glass of Pinot Grigio, please."

"You got it, baby."

Tara smiled again as Jake walked through the swing door into the kitchen to give his mother the order. He was well named, truly a junior, for he looked remarkably like his father. Both Jakes were not very tall, but broad, built strong as bulls; they both had open, pleasant faces and gentle, compassionate brown eyes.

He paused on his way back, long enough to slide her plate in front of her, then went on into the bar to pour her drink. When Jake set the glass on the table, he said quietly, "This one's on me, sweet lips." Then he winked broadly, pursed his lips in a silent kiss, and went back behind the bar.

Tara laughed softly as she started on her salad. Eating without really tasting it, she pondered the different reactions male and female had to each other.

Jake's teasing familiarity amused her, whereas Terry's use of endearments on Monday had made her feel cheap. As to the way she reacted to the same brand of teasing from Alek, well . . . she did not even care to think about that. Was it, as Alek had suggested, simple body chemistry?

By the time she pushed her empty plate to the center of the table, Tara was working on her second drink and telling herself to go home. Hearing a vaguely familiar voice say, "It's all right, I know the lady," Tara glanced into the barroom as a young man detached himself from the bar, a drink in each hand, and headed toward her.

As Tara watched him approach, her mind nibbled at recognition. Her memory clicked, and she put half a name to his face. Barry something-or-other, an architectural engineer she'd met last summer at a clambake she'd attended with friends. At the time, he'd appeared easygoing and well-mannered and Tara had agreed to go out with him the following week. It was a mistake for, although the evening had been a pleasant one, he had no sooner parked his car in front of her apartment when he was all over her like a bad rash. She had had literally to fight her way out of his car. And there was the reason she could not remember his last name. After she'd safely reached her apartment, she had dubbed him Barry Octopus. And now Mr. Octopus had come to stop at her table.

"Hiya, Tara, all alone?"

His grin was engaging (very probably practiced), revealing stunning white teeth (very probably capped). In tight, faded blue jeans and snuggly fitting polo shirt, he was very attractive and knew it.

"Yes, Barry, I'm alone."

Placing one of the drinks in front of her, he said quietly, "May I join you for a few minutes?"

Tara didn't want the drink. She didn't want his company either, but shrugging lightly, she murmured, "For a few minutes only. I'm leaving soon."

"Why? The night's young."

And you're so beautiful, Tara added, finishing his line wryly, somehow managing to keep a straight face.

"I've got a date later, that's why," she lied.

"Ah, yes, I've heard about your latest . . . date. Really moving up in the world, aren't you?"

Tara's voice was as cold as the glass her fingers clenched.

"If you're going to be offensive, Barry, you can go back to the bar, and take your drink with you."

He eyed her steadily a moment then he laughed easily.

"Truth hurt? Never mind. Hell, I wasn't trying to be offensive or then again maybe I was. After the cold shoulder I'd received, the pure-as-the-driven-snow act you'd put on, well, I'll admit when I first heard about it, I was shocked. He has a rather overwhelming reputation with woman. But then he has a rather overwhelming bankroll also."

"Good-bye, Barry."

Tara was hanging on to her temper as tightly as she was hanging on to her glass.

Reaching across the table, his hand caught hers.

"Aw, come on, Tara," he coaxed. "With all the ladies he's got on the string, surely he wouldn't object to you and I having a little fun together."

Eyes flashing with contempt, Tara snatched her hand away.

"Maybe *he* wouldn't, but I would," she said through clenched teeth. "Now go away and leave me alone."

Grasping for her hand again, he began urgently, "Don't get mad—"

"You having trouble, Miss Schmitt?"

With an audible sigh of relief, Tara looked up to see Jake senior leaning across the end of the bar, looking broad as a tank and just as menacing, eyeing Barry dispassionately.

"He was just leaving and so am I, Jake. Could I have my check please?"

"Sure thing," he nodded, then added, "Why don't you come back to the bar, Barry? I'll buy you a drink."

Barry hesitated then gave in gracefully.

"Okay, Jake, you're on. Sorry if I was out of line, Tara."

Ignoring Barry, Tara paid her check and left, feeling even worse than when she entered. The sight of Alek's car parked directly in front of her apartment plunged her spirits even lower.

Filled with rage, frustration, and humiliation, she paced the apartment for hours. First Terry, now Barry. How many others believed he was paying her rent, keeping her? Tears of weariness and defeat blinding her, she finally fell into bed. Teeth clenched, she whispered aloud, "Damn you, Aleksei Rykovsky."

Friday was a drag. Tara had never been so glad to see quitting time before in her life. As she left the office, she massaged her temple distractedly; she had a headache. Her eyes felt puffy and irritated from the hours she'd spent crying the night before. Lord, it seemed she'd had a headache and done nothing but cry for the last month. Was there no end to it?

Feeling too uninterested and dispirited to prepare a meal, she ate dinner at a small diner close to her apartment then went home. Home? The lonely hours spent in solitude in those few small rooms were beginning to make what was once a haven into a cage. She felt trapped. Trapped by the unbridled passion of a man too used to getting what he wanted.

The tears were flowing again before she reached the door of her apartment, and the pain in her head had intensified into sharp, stabbing blows. Tara dropped her jacket and handbag on the nearest chair and went to the bathroom, groping blindly inside the medicine cabinet for the aspirin bottle. She swallowed the two white pills then stood regarding her reflection in the cabinet-door mirror. Watery, haunted eyes stared back at her, black-smudged mascara adding a clownish touch. What a pale, pitiful sight she was, she thought abstractedly. At nine thirty, head still pounding, she swallowed two more aspirin and went to bed, positive she wouldn't sleep.

She was wrong. She slept deeply and well and woke Saturday morning with at least some of her usual vigor restored. As she consumed a light breakfast of juice, toast, and coffee, her eyes roamed around the small kitchen. *What you need, friend,* she told herself bracingly, *is some physical activity. Today you clean the kitchen.*

Within minutes she'd thrown herself into the job at hand, saving the most hated chore, the kitchen stove, till last.

Tara had the rangetop in a half dozen assorted pieces, scrubbing the drip pan under the burners, when the door chimes pealed.

"Oh, hell," she muttered, tugging the rubber gloves off her hands and dropping them in the sink. Walking to the door, she wondered if she should slide the chain into place, then shrugged and opened the door.

"May I come in, Tara? Or are you still mad at me?" Betsy eyed her uncertainly on the other side of the threshold.

"I'm not mad at you, Bets," Tara denied. "A little disappointed, maybe, but not mad. Come in."

Betsy stepped inside, slipped out of her long coat, and tossed it over a chair, all the while glancing around unobtrusively.

Tara watched her cynically, sighing softly with the knowledge her sister was looking for occupancy of a man.

"I'm cleaning the kitchen and was about ready to take a break," Tara said quietly. "Would you like a cup of coffee?"

"Yes, thanks," Betsy answered. "It's cold out there this morning. A hot drink will taste good."

Tara didn't miss the strained edge to her sister's voice, but she made no comment as she poured the coffee then placed the mugs, sugar bowl, and a small jug of milk on the table.

They sipped their coffee in an uncomfortable silence for a few minutes, then Betsy blurted, "Tara, I think you should call Mama."

"Why? She hasn't bothered to call me." Tara was surprised at the bitterness of her own voice.

"I know," her sister said placatingly. "But I still think you should. I'm worried about her, Tara. You're the only one she ever opened up to at all. She won't talk to me. I've tried."

"Is she sick?" Tara asked in alarm.

"Not sick exactly," Betsy replied. "But she's not eating or sleeping well and she's been crying a lot."

Welcome to the club, Mama, Tara thought wearily, convinced her mother's trouble stemmed directly from the controversy surrounding her oldest child. "All right, Bets," she promised. "I'll call her later today and see if I can find out anything. Will you stay for lunch?"

"No. Thanks anyway. I've been skipping lunch." Then she added at Tara's raised eyebrows, "I've gained a few pounds and with the holidays coming up, I thought I'd better be careful or come January first, I'm liable to find I can't get into my clothes."

Tara smiled and relaxed at the more normal tone Betsy's voice had acquired. Not much later Betsy left, saying she had some shopping to do, and Tara went back to the stove.

After a hurried sandwich-and-coffee lunch, Tara went to the phone, drew a deep breath, and quickly dialed her mother's number. Her heart sank on hearing her father's gruff hello.

"Hello, Dad. Is Mother there?"

There was a noticeable pause before her father replied. "Yes, she's here. But she doesn't want to talk to you, Tara, and neither do I." And with that he slammed down the receiver.

Tara stood still, a look of hurt disbelief on her face, before slowly replacing her own receiver with trembling fingers. Feeling her eyes beginning to mist over, she shook her head in swift anger. No, she would not cry anymore; she was going to fight. *I don't know how I'll fight him,* she thought fiercely, *but I'll find a way. I have to. I can't take much more of this.*

To keep depression at bay she sprang into frenzied activity, giving the rest of the apartment its weekly cleaning, running to the basement laundry-room with a basket of wash, shampooing her hair, and manicuring her nails.

Sunday she walked for hours, coming back to the apartment cold and tired and nowhere near a way to get at Alek. A little after ten she sat moodily trying to concentrate, without much success, on a movie on TV. Though Tara was unsure exactly what the movie was about other than a philandering husband, one scene, near the end, caught then held her attention. The wronged wife was speaking to a friend in a harshly bitter tone. "He's offered me a large settlement if I'll give him a divorce." She laughed hollowly before continuing. "He should live so long, the bastard. Oh! I'll get that money. That and a lot more. He'll pay through the nose. I'll make his life a living hell. By the time I'm through with him, he'll wish he'd never looked at a woman."

Tara sat nibbling her lip, a germ of an idea beginning to wriggle to life. Her breath caught painfully in her throat. Could she do it? Did she want to?

She set off to work Monday morning, her step firm and determined. No definite plan presented itself. She'd have to play it by ear, wing it, as it were. The morning passed slowly and although Tara became exceedingly more nervous, her resolve strengthened and set. All it needed now was the opportunity.

That arrived shortly after lunch when David came into the office, followed by a deceptively lazy-looking Alek. Before either man could speak, Tara said haltingly, "I—I'd like to speak to you, David. It's important."

David's voice mirrored the surprise on his face.

"All right, Tara." Then, turning to Alek, he murmured, "If you'll excuse us a few minutes."

Alek began, "Of course—" when Tara interrupted, "No! Please David, as this involves Alek, too, I'd like him present."

Alek's eyes turned sharp, watchful, while David's expression changed from surprise to confusion.

"Whatever you say. Come into my office, both of you."

David waved his hand at the leather chair in front of his desk as he seated himself in his swivel chair opposite. Alek indicated he was quite comfortable where he was, perched indolently on the side of the large desk, which suited Tara, as she had an excellent view of both men's faces.

She let the silence hang a few seconds before stating quietly, "David, I want to give notice. I'm leaving."

"Give notice!" David exclaimed. "Leaving? But why?"

Tara's eyes sliced to Alek, then quickly away. In that brief glance she could swear he was holding his breath. She gulped in air, then said boldly, "I'm getting married and, even though we haven't discussed it, I don't think he wants me to work afterward." She swung her gaze directly to Alek's hooded blue one and added, "Do you—darling?" then held her breath.

He was a cool one, she had go give him that. For, other than a slight tightening along the jaw, he betrayed no reaction. One dark eyebrow arching slowly, he drawled, "While I would enjoy you giving your undivided attention to me, if you want to continue working, that is entirely up to you—my love." As he finished, the corner of his mouth twitched with amusement.

Tara gritted her teeth. *The fiend. I call his bluff and he has the gall to be amused.* She was beginning to wonder just who had called whose bluff.

David looked and sounded stunned. "Getting married? When?"

Tara hesitated only a moment. "The second Saturday in December."

"The second Saturday," he echoed, his eyes flying to his desk calendar. "But that's less than a month away. Why didn't you tell me sooner?" He turned to Alek, his voice sharp. "Or you? My God, man, we see each other nearly every day, and I've made no secret of how Sallie and I feel about Tara. Couldn't you have said something?"

Alek's smile was totally disarming. "I've been waiting, impatiently I might add, for the lady to set a date. This is as much of a surprise to me as it is to you." Glittering blue eyes were turned on Tara. "I didn't realize you had such a flair for the dramatic, my sweet."

"I think you'll find, my liege"—Tara's smile was pure saccharine—"I'm full of little surprises."

"I'll just bet." He laughed softly.

Throughout this exchange David's head swiveled from one to the other, a frown of consternation on his face. Catching the expression, Alek's laugh deepened. "Don't worry, David, you're not going to lose her, either as a friend or, apparently, as an assistant. That is, of course, if you're agreeable to her taking two weeks for a honeymoon, and the rest of the day."

Neither of the men seemed to notice Tara's gasp, as David was too busy shaking Alek's hand while acquiescing to his demands, and Alek was too busy grinning fatuously while accepting his congratulations.

Before Tara had time to gather her wits, Alek was grasping her arm and propelling her from both David's and her own office, pausing only long enough to snatch up her handbag and jacket. Flinging the latter around her shoulders, he led her out of the building and into his car.

"My car!" she squeaked.

"We'll get it later," came the brusque reply.

He drove without speaking for some time, leaving the city behind as he turned onto a country road nearly devoid of traffic. At the first roadside rest area, he pulled off the road and stopped. After turning off the ignition, he sat staring out the windshield, his silence somewhat ominous. When, after countless minutes, he finally spoke, she jumped, startled.

"You're committed now, you know. There will be no backing out." The hard edge to his tone softened somewhat as he asked, "Has something happened to effect this sudden change in your attitude?"

"It was brought home to me that I had very little choice," she replied softly, suddenly having to fight to keep tears from spilling over. "You have made a farce of all my hopes and plans. I'm afraid you're in for a shock if you're expecting an experienced woman. I'm one of the unmodern ones. I . . . I had thought to save my virginity for my husband, give it to him as a g-gift." Her last word was spoken on a strangled sob, and she turned her head away.

Tara heard his indrawn breath, felt him move a moment before his fingers, gently grasping her chin, turned her face back to him. His face was close, his voice very low. "And so you shall."

His mouth covered hers in a kiss both reticent and possessive; possession won. He drew her as closely to him as the console between the bucket seats would allow. Suddenly he released her and was moving away, cursing softly. Before she knew what he was about, he was out and around the car, yanking open the door next to her. In one unbroken movement he leaned inside, grasped her shoulders, pulled her out and into his arms. Shifting his weight to balance hers, he stood with his feet planted firmly a foot apart, crushing her body against the long, hard length of his.

He groaned softly and muttered, "God, Tara, I want you." Then his mouth began plundering hers hungrily, drawing from her a response she had had no idea she was capable of. His hands moved urgently over her body, arching her to him, giving her shocking proof of his words.

First the ground rocked, then the world spun, and she was drowning in a sea of intense, electrifying pleasure. Fire whipped through her veins, igniting pulse points and nerve ends in its wake. Arms tightening convulsively around his neck, teetering on the very edge of total surrender, she moaned a soft protest when his mouth left hers. Opening her eyes, she saw him glance around before murmuring huskily, "Where the hell can we go?"

His words brought a measure of unwanted sanity and with

a choking sob she wrenched away from him to stumble sharply into the side of the car. She cried out in pain, but the pain brought further sanity, enabling her to plead, "No, Alek, stop," when he reached for her.

"No?" he rasped. "Stop? What are you trying to do, drive me mad?"

She was sobbing openly now, frightened badly, as much by her own body's astonishingly urgent need as his. Shaking her head, she sobbed wildly, "I'm frightened. You as much as promised me, not fifteen minutes ago, that you'd wait. I can't go on. Not here, not like this. Alek, please."

His face went hard, a muscle kicking in his taut jaw. His hands clenched into hard, white-knuckled fists, and he drew deep, long breaths. "All right, Tara." He groaned through clenched teeth. "We'll do it your way. But you can be grateful you set the day as closely as you did, for I'm damned if I'll wait one day longer."

His words chilled Tara, promising difficulties for her nebulous plans. It was not until later, on the way back to town, that she admitted ruefully to herself that he had gained control much more quickly than she. For while he was cool and withdrawn, handling the car with smooth expertise, she was still a humming bundle filled with awareness of him. And she knew that if he touched her now, she'd melt as quickly as a snowflake in August.

As they entered the city, Alek glanced at the expensive, slim gold watch on his wrist and said, "We have something to do before dinner. I want you to pick out your engagement ring."

His words jerked Tara away from her confusing emotions. "I don't want an engagement ring," she said flatly.

"Don't want . . . ?" he began, giving her a startled glance. Then his eyes hardened, grew icy. "Don't try playing games with me, Tara. You'll wear my ring." He finished grimly: "You said you'll marry me, and marry me you will."

"I'm not playing games," she replied coolly. "I have no intention of backing out of the marriage. But if you buy an engagement ring, I won't wear it. The only ring of yours I'll wear is my wedding ring."

His beautifully chiseled mouth flattened into a thin line. "Why?"

"I simply do not want one."

Tara could feel his anger crackling outward, touching her, and she shivered.

Grimly, he punched a series of numbers into his cell phone. Speaking to his mother, he made the announcement that he was engaged and would like his parents to meet their future daughter-in-law. After another minute of conversation, he hung up and turned to Tara, giving her a smile that didn't quite make it to those glinting blue eyes.

"We've been invited to dinner so you can meet my parents. I'm sure you'll want to bathe and change, as I do." His smile changed, becoming cruelly sardonic. "But first we'll stop at your parents' home. I'm sure your family, especially your father, will be delighted with our news."

Tara felt her blood turn to ice water and she shivered again. This was a ruthless man she was dealing with. Did she really have the courage to carry out her idea?

Chapter Six

The closer they drew to her parents' home, the more tense and withdrawn Tara became. How would her parents react to Alek? Especially her father? He might fly into a rage. Hadn't he referred to Alek as "that Russian?" *"That swine Rykovsky"?* On the other hand he might be so relieved to know Alek was going to make an honest woman of her, he might accept his future son-in-law gracefully. *Too many mights,* she told herself nervously; *I might just be sick.*

Alek said nothing, but Tara caught the several eagle-eyed glances he threw at her. As they turned into the street her parents lived on, Tara noted the long fingers of golden afternoon sun. *Oh, great!* she thought. Not only would her father be home from work but by now Betsy would be too. One was never sure of her brothers, but this close to suppertime, they probably would be too. Her mother, of course, was nearly always home. Tara grimaced inside. A regular family conclave.

Alek parked at the curb in front of her parents' small frame home and said quietly, "Stay put," as her hand jerked to the door handle. Almost lazily, he left the car and moved around to open her door, helping her out as a lover would. Leaning close to her, he teased, "Someone may be watching from the window."

At any other time Tara would have walked, unannounced, into her father's house but not now, after his crushing words to her on Saturday, she hesitated. Ignoring Alek's questioningly raised eyebrows, she placed a none-too-steady finger on the doorbell.

The door was opened a few inches by Karl, who gave her a disgusted look and complained, "What did ya ring the bell for, for cripes' sake?" He turned back into the hall at once, yelling, "Mom, Tara's here," not having seen Alek at all.

As she moved a few steps into the small hallway, Alek close behind her, she heard her father curse, then the rustle of a newspaper being flung to the floor.

Her father reached the doorway to the living room, George at his heels, just as her mother came hurrying along the short hall from the kitchen and Betsy came clattering down the stairs to stop abruptly in back of Karl, who had started up but had stopped and turned at their father's curse. All five began speaking at once.

"Tara, I told you on Saturday—"

"Oh, Tara, I'm so glad to see—"

"Tara, I thought you were going to call—"

"Gee, Tara, did you come in that car out—"

"Tara, what's going on any—"

"Be quiet, all of you."

The barrage ceased. Alek had not raised his voice, but the tone sliced through the babble like a rapier through butter. The tone of a man used to giving orders and having them obeyed without question: there were none.

The same tone broke the stunned silence as, eyes hard as the stone they matched, Alek addressed her father. "Mr. Schmitt, I'd like to speak to you in private a few minutes."

Eyes softening, he turned to her mother. "Perhaps you could give Tara a cup of coffee in the kitchen?"

"Yes, of course," her mother fluttered. "Come along, Tara. I just made a fresh pot for supper."

Tara hesitated, watching her father's angry red face, until he mumbled, grudgingly, to Alek. "All right, come into the living room." Then: "Make yourselves scarce, boys."

George threw a curious glance at Alek, then went up the stairs after Karl, and Tara followed her mother into the kitchen, Betsy right behind her.

Marlene poured coffee into two cups, placed them in front of Tara and Betsy, then asked, tremulously, "Who is that man, Tara? Why does he want to talk to your father alone?"

Before Tara could draw her attention from her mother's tired, unhappy face, Betsy answered excitedly, "That's none other than Mr. Aleksei Rykovsky, Mama." Turning wide eyes to Tara, she went on. "Why does he want to talk to Dad?"

Tara had been asking herself that same question. Surely it would have been easier to tell them all while they'd been gathered in the hall.

She contemplated what to answer as she sipped her coffee. "Well, I'm not quite sure—"

"Marlene," her father's voice cut her off. "Come in here and bring Tara with you."

Biting her lip, her mother turned apprehensive eyes to Tara. Forcing a light laugh, Tara quipped, "I guess we'd better go and face the music." Swinging out of the kitchen, she answered, "May as well," to Betsy's "Can I come too?"

The two men stood facing each other across the room, Alek in front of the worn sofa, her father in front of his favorite chair. Tara took one step inside the room and stopped, her mother on one side, Betsy on the other. Apprehensively she glanced at Alek, then her father, then back to Alek again, unable to read anything in the face of either man.

"Come here, Tara."

Alek's voice was low, his tone gentle, and without question Tara went to him, her eyes trying to read his impassive face, the small smile playing at his mouth.

Her mother and Betsy followed her into the room and out of the corner of her eye she saw her brothers slip inside the doorway. Deliberately, it seemed to Tara, Alek had kept his eyes on her face until they were all in the room, then he turned that brilliant blue gaze on her mother and said quietly, "Mrs. Schmitt, your husband has just given me his permission to marry your daughter. I sincerely hope you will give yours also."

He had asked for permission! Alek Rykovsky! Incredible, Tara thought. Tara felt her breath catch, heard Betsy's small "oh," saw her mother go pink, glance at her husband then back at Alek before stuttering, "I-I—if Herman says—"

"He does," Herman interrupted. Then, as if suddenly becoming aware that they were all standing, he said, "Won't you sit down, sir?"

Too much! Tara thought. She stared at her father. The only other men she'd ever heard her father speak to in that deferential manner were their priest and doctor. And not always their doctor.

Alek murmured "Thank you," lowered himself to the sofa, then held his hand out, palm up, and said softly, "Tara."

Bemused, Tara sat down next to him, placed her hand in his large, well shaped one, and felt it squeezed as he said to her mother, "Tara and I would like to be married on the second Saturday in December. I hope there will be enough time to make the necessary arrangements."

Her mother's eyes flew to her, and Tara answered hurriedly, "Yes, of course there'll be enough time. A small wedding really doesn't take much arrange—"

"You'll naturally want to be married in your own church," he cut in smoothly. "But I hope you'll have no objections to my own priest presiding."

Tara turned astonished eyes to him. "You're Catholic, Alek?"

"Yes, my love, I am." Again that small smile played around his mouth. She watched it in fascination, then his actual words struck her.

"In church?" she choked. "But that's not necessary. I thought a quiet wedding, no fuss."

She heard her father snort, her mother exclaim, "But Tara!" But Alek again commanded the floor.

"We will have a full Catholic wedding, darling. Including mass. We're only going to do this once; we may as well do it right. You may have as few or as many attendants as you wish." The devil danced in his eyes as he added, "Just don't exhaust yourself with the preparations."

Tara felt her cheeks flush at his meaning: He didn't want an overtired bride on his wedding night. She felt his arm slide around her waist, draw her closer to him. *What's he playing at now,* she wondered fretfully. Then was surprised at the explanation that leaped into her mind. The endearments, the touching, the tone of voice were all calculated to assure her father, all of them, that she was loved, cared for, protected. *But why would he bother to do that?* she argued with herself. *He had what he wanted. At least he* thought *he did.* Nevertheless the feeling persisted that he was deliberately acting the role of a man very much in love simply to reassure her parents.

The action of Alek glancing at his watch forced Tara's attention back to the conversation. He was speaking to her father, and his words jolted her alert.

"And, as I just said, the number of the wedding party, the type of wedding, is entirely up to Tara, but if you have no objections, I will arrange the reception." He held up one hand as both her father and mother started to protest. "Let me finish, please. I'm afraid it will be, by necessity, both rather large and expensive. I have quite a few friends and business associates. I would not want to have any one of them feel slighted because they were not invited. Many of them will be coming from a distance. Not only from out of town, but out of state as well. Arrangements must be made for their accommodations." Until this point his voice had been smooth, almost soft. Now it took on a thin, hard edge. "I insist on paying for it, as the majority of the names on the guest list will come from me." He glanced at her mother, and again the tone grew gentle. "I would appreciate it if you could have your guest list completed within a few days. We have less than a month, and I'd like the invitations in the mail by the end of the week."

"The end of the week!"

"But Alek, that's impossible."

Tara and her mother spoke in unison. Tara was too surprised to say anymore, but her mother continued. "That's not nearly enough time. Not only do we have to make up the guest list but we have to see the printers, pick out the invitations—"

"That won't be necessary," he interrupted. "Just make up your list as quickly as possible. My staff will take care of the rest. The invitations will be handwritten. Believe me, you will be satisfied with the result."

"Well, if you say so," her mother murmured.

Tara was beginning to feel very uneasy. When had she lost control of this farce? She was actually not being consulted at all, for all his talk of the size of the wedding being up to her. Feeling that she had to make some sort of stand she said, firmly, "Alek, I really do not want a large wedding. I had thought a small, quiet affair with just the families and maybe a few close friends."

The wicked gleam in his eyes alerted her, yet his words shocked her, causing a momentary hush in the room. "My sweet love, would you deprive the rest of our friends, everyone, the pleasure of witnessing the culmination of the union about which there has been so much speculation?"

Tara felt tears sting her eyes. "Alek." It was a low cry of protest, almost instantly covered by the hurried speech of nearly everyone in the room.

"It is settled." Alek's tone indicated he would listen to no arguments.

"Well then, Tara," Marlene said briskly. "You and I had better get working on a list."

"Not this evening," Alek stated. "Tara and I have a dinner engagement with my parents." He paused a moment then went on. "Darling, as it appears you are going to have to be spending a lot of time here anyway, why don't you pack what you'll need and move in here until the wedding. We can empty your apartment at our leisure later."

Tara stared at him in stunned amazement, unable, for a minute, to speak. Too fast, she told herself. *Everything is happening much too fast.* Why had she told David the second Saturday in December? She was beginning to feel rushed, stifled. And who did he think he was? *We? Our?* And she definitely did not want to move back here. She opened her mouth to say no, but not fast enough.

"Tara, that's a wonderful idea." Her mother's eyes were bright with excitement and enthusiasm. "It would save you all that running back and forth. Oh, honey, please, it will be such fun."

The word *no* trembling on her soft mouth, Tara sighed in defeat, unable to utter the word that would extinguish the light in her mother's eyes, cast a shadow on the happy face. But Alek would hear more about this later.

"All right, Mama," Tara answered tiredly. "I'll bring my things one night this week."

"I'll bring her and her things," Alek inserted. "Tomorrow night. If that's convenient." He didn't look at Tara's angrily flushed face, but kept his polite gaze on her mother, acknowledging her nod with a smile.

"I have my own car," Tara said through gritted teeth.

"Yes, darling, I know that." His words came slowly, evenly measured, as if he were speaking to a child who was not too bright. "Nevertheless, I will bring you tomorrow night. Now I think we really must go, as Mother is expecting us in an hour and a half."

His hand firmly grasping hers, he stood up and strode across the room, hand outstretched to her father. "A pleasure to meet you, sir. I assume we'll be seeing quite a bit of each other during the next few weeks?"

"Yes, yes, of course," Herman hastened to assure him, "and a pleasure to finally meet you, Mr. Rykovsky."

"Alek. I insist." His tone was so silky-smooth, Tara felt her teeth clench. He wished her mother a gentle good night, then started to move out of the room. He paused to raise an eyebrow at Betsy and murmur, "I'm depending on you to help Tara with all the arrangements. Will you do that?"

"Are you kidding?" Betsy laughed. "I'd like to see someone stop me."

He grinned, then moved on only to stop again at George.

"You're in your last year of high school?" he asked abruptly.

George nodded, eyes guarded.

"You're going to college?"

"If I can get a scholarship. Why?"

Alek studied him a second, then, as if reaching a swift

decision, gave a brief nod and said, "If you want a job after school, come to see me. And if the scholarship doesn't materialize, we'll have a talk. Good night." He turned his head to include Karl, then made for the hall and their coats, tugging Tara behind him.

He held her coat for her, then shrugged into his own, bid them all a collective good night and, his hand at her back, propelled her out of the house. By the time he had seated her in the car, the dazed, steamrollered feeling had passed and Tara was doing a slow burn.

"How dare you," she seethed the instant he slid behind the wheel.

"How dare I what?"

Her hands clenched at his innocent tone. "Damn you, you know what," she snapped. "I do not want a large wedding and I certainly do not want to move back home and I damn well will not have you arranging my life."

"Don't swear at me again, Tara." His voice, while soft, had a warning edge of steel in it.

"All right," she sighed, "I'm sorry. But I mean it, Alek. Don't think for one minute that just because I agreed to marry you, I have any intention of playing the meek little hausfrau, blindly obeying your every dictate. I won't."

"Whatever you say, sweetheart. Now please stop nagging at me as if we were already married and look at that lovely moon. Not quite full but beautiful anyway."

The sound of his soft laughter seemed to wrap itself around her heart, and Tara had to remind herself sharply who he was and what he'd done.

"I don't want to look at the moon," she said irritably. "And I don't really want to have dinner with your parents, although I suppose we owe them a courtesy visit. And don't call me 'sweetheart.' Save your breath, and the endearments, for your next audience."

She heard his sharply indrawn breath, saw his hands tighten on the steering wheel before he growled, "I will call you anything I wish, when I wish. I'm sorry if the prospect of meeting my parents is repellent to you, but you may be in for a surprise. I'd be willing to bet you'll like them. They are very nice people."

In this he was proved correct. They *were* very nice people, and she did like them. He had dropped her at the apartment with a terse, "I'll be back in a half hour. Can you be ready by then?" At her nod he said, "Good," sharply. The moment she was out of the car, he shot away from the curb, still obviously very angry.

The drive to his parents' home was completed in tense silence, which Tara herself broke unconsciously when he drove along the driveway and parked in front of the sprawling redwood-and-glass ranch house.

"Oh, it's beautiful!" she breathed softly. Tara had expected something large and formal and this lovely rambling house was a delightful surprise.

"Yes, it is," Alek replied softly. "And so are the people who live in it."

Tara had known she'd angered him with her waspish words about not wanting to meet his parents, but now something about the tone of his voice told her he had also been hurt. *Impossible,* she said to herself, pushing the thought away. Nothing she could say to this unfeeling man could hurt him.

On entering, Tara was delighted to find the inside as lovely as the outside. It was decorated beautifully in soft, muted tones, the overall effect one of warmth, welcome. The warmth and welcome were reflected on the face of the woman who came to meet them, hands outstretched.

"Darling, you're right on time." The low, musical voice of Alek's mother's was not a surprise, coming from such an exquisitely beautiful woman. Small, splendidly proportioned, she had the most perfect bone structure Tara had ever seen. *So this is where he came by his devastating good looks,* she thought.

Before Alek could murmur more than, "Good evening, Mother," she was speaking again, taking Tara's hands in her own. "And this is Tara. Such a lovely name, and what a lovely thing you are too. No wonder Alek is in such a rush to get you to the altar. But come in, please, we have just enough time for a drink before dinner. And here's Peter, right on time to mix them."

Tara was forced to change her opinion of a few moments ago. For coming toward her was the original mold from which Alek had been made. One glance and Tara knew exactly what Alek would look like in twenty-five years. After the introductions were made, Peter Rykovsky tilted one dark brow at his son and said quite seriously, "Well, son, I didn't think it possible, but you have found yourself a woman whose beauty matches your mother's. My deep and sincere congratulations."

"Thank you, sir."

Pink-cheeked, Tara glanced at Alek in astonishment for the tone of respect he'd conveyed in those three short words.

As they sipped their drinks, Alek filled his parents in on the wedding plans they had made earlier. Peter and Alene's reaction to Tara's idea of a small, intimate wedding was the same as her own family's had been.

"Oh, no, my dear," Alene reproved gently. "I'm sure that would be a mistake. Every woman should be able to remember her wedding day as being as perfect as possible. By all means keep the wedding party small, if that's what you prefer. A wedding doesn't have to be large to be beautiful. But I do think Alek is right in his insistence on a church ceremony." Her soft laughter gave proof of the happiness bubbling inside as she added, "I must admit to a degree of selfishness in my considerations. I have waited so long for this day. When Alek celebrated his thirty-fourth birthday last spring, I decided, perhaps I had better resign myself to the idea of his remaining a bachelor and never giving me the grandchild I so long to hold."

Tara started, paling visibly, although her reaction went unnoticed. Alek and his father wore identical expressions of deep love and tenderness as they gazed on the misty-eyed, wistful, but adoring face of Alene. Tara felt terrible. Motivated by anger and frustration, she had acted without thought, now the ramifications of that act were piling up around her like so many stones, imprisoning her inside a cell of her own making. Panic gripped her throat, and she gulped the remains of her drink in an effort to dislodge it.

A grandchild! Not once had she considered that possibility. Why hadn't she? It was the natural order of things. First the wedding, then . . . A shiver rippled through her body. Her own parents had not said anything but they, too, would be looking forward to their first grandchild—after a decent interval. *Oh, Lord!* Tara's mind clung to her last thought. *A decent interval!* Everyone thought she and Alek were already lovers. Now suddenly they were being married within a few weeks. How many of her friends would be counting the months? Watching for signs? *But I've done nothing, nothing,* her mind cried silently, envisioning the different type of speculative glances she would probably now be receiving. A feeling of intense dislike—almost hatred—for Alek burned through her and she closed her eyes.

Locked in a pain-filled world of her own, Tara was startled by Peter's voice, heavily laced with concern, alerting her to where she was.

"Tara, are you ill? You've gone positively white."

She saw Alek's gaze swivel from his mother's face to her own an instant before he was moving to her side. His eyes, his face, puzzled her, for he looked almost frightened. Alek frightened? His softly murmured words chased all contemplation of his expression from her mind.

"What's wrong, darling. Are you ill?"

The endearment set her teeth on edge and she had to fight to keep from screaming at him, *You fraud, you are what is wrong. You and the scheming and plotting you've done.* Using every ounce of willpower she possessed, she brought her emotions under control. "I'm afraid the drink has hit rock bottom," she lied shakily. "I've eaten very little all day, and my empty stomach doesn't seem to want to tolerate the alcohol."

Long, unbelievably gentle fingers brushed her cheek, felt the moisture that had gathered at her temple.

"Would you like to go home?"

Jerkily she leaned back, away from his caressing voice,

his disturbingly light touch. *Yes,* she pleaded silently, *I want to go home. I want to hide myself away until everything that has happened the last week is long forgotten.*

"Would you like to lie down, my dear?" Peter asked anxiously.

Before Tara's confused mind could formulate an answer to either man, Alene was helping her to her feet, stating practically, "What this child needs is some food. Come along, Tara," she coaxed. "Something solid inside your stomach will banish this queasy feeling in no time." Leading Tara into the dining room, she shook her head in mock dismay, chiding, "Men are so helpless in situations like this. For some reason the strongest of them, and these two must be close to the top of the list, fall apart when someone they love is unwell."

A bubble of hysterical laughter became trapped in Tara's chest. If Alek was close to the top of the list of the strongest, he had to be even higher on the list of best actors if he could convince his mother with his performance.

Alene's diagnosis proved correct, for by the time they were halfway through the meal, Tara, her color restored, was laughing at Peter's obvious attempts to amuse her.

Tara was totally captivated by Alek's parents and under any other circumstances would have loved having them as in-laws. Strange, she mused, Peter and Alek were so much alike, yet she failed to detect any sign of the tyrant in Peter. His treatment of his wife was the type great love stories were written about; after nearly forty years of marriage his eyes touched her with an expression that Tara could only describe as adoration. Tara quickly learned where Alek had acquired the art of using endearments with such ease of manner. Peter seldom spoke to Alene without some form of endearment. That his feelings were returned in full was evident: Alene made no attempt to hide the fact that her world revolved around her husband and son.

As Tara basked in the warmth Alene and Peter generated, the evening slipped away from her. The only thing that marred her enjoyment was the caressing, possessive tone Alek used whenever he spoke to her.

When he drove her home, he pulled up in front of her building and said, "It's late, I won't come up with you." Tara breathed a sigh of relief then tensed as his hands cupped her face and drew her close. He kissed her slowly, lingeringly, and Tara felt the tenseness seep out of her, tiny little sparks igniting all over her.

When he lifted his head, he again whispered those same Russian words then said, "As your car is still on the office parking lot, I'll drive you to work tomorrow. Is seven thirty all right?"

"Y-Yes, that will be fine," Tara stammered. "I—I must go in. Good night."

There was no conversation exchanged between them the next morning other than a polite "Good morning, Tara," and an equally polite "Good morning, Alek," until he drew up at the office. Placing a hand on her arm as she moved to get out of the car, he said, "I'll come by at seven thirty to help you with your things."

Impotent anger surged through Tara and, pulling her arm away from his hand, she snapped, "All right,"then thrust open the door and slammed it shut, his laughter following her as she hurried into the building.

"Tara, you really know how to keep a secret. Why didn't you tell us?" Jeannie's words hit her as she came through the door, but she was saved from confusion by the newspaper Jeannie shoved in front of her. In a lower corner of the front page was a picture of Alek with the caption LOCAL INDUS-TRIALIST TO WED. Tara skimmed the small column that ran the length of the picture than pasted a smile on her face as she looked up at Jeannie. "If I'd told you, it wouldn't have been a secret. Besides, we wanted to discuss it with our parents first."

When did he do this? she thought furiously. Somehow she managed to maintain the smile as she glanced around the room murmuring thank-yous to the good wishes being called out. Her eyes brushed Terry then came back. The only words to describe the expression on his face were utter disbelief. His eyes seemed to ask, How did you do it when all the others failed?

With a forced note of happiness she asked Jeannie if she could borrow the paper then, still smiling, she went into her own office, dropped into her chair, and read the article more thoroughly.

Mr. Aleksei Rykovsky, son of Mr. and Mrs. Peter Rykovsky, owner-manager of the Fine Edge Machine Company, has announced his forthcoming marriage to Miss Tara Schmitt, daughter of Mr. and Mrs. Herman Schmitt. A December wedding is being planned. Miss Schmitt is the personal assistant of Mr. David Jennings, one of the city's up-and-coming architects and the designer of the new plant Mr. Rykovsky is having built.

David came in the office, paper under his arm, as Tara was finishing the article. "I brought you the paper, but I see you already have one."

"Yes," she replied sweetly, lifting the sheet. "Plugs for everyone. Isn't that nice?"

David gave her an odd look then shrugged and headed for his office. "Oh, yes. I almost forgot. Sallie asked me to give you her very best wishes."

Sallie! Oh, Lord, Tara groaned inwardly, *I should have called her. But when?* She reached for the phone and dialed David's home number. Sallie answered on the third ring.

"Hi, Sallie. It's Tara."

"Tara! Oh, I'm so glad you called. Did David give you my message?"

"Yes, thank you." Somehow she managed to instill the lilt of happiness into her voice. "Sallie, I know it's short notice, and we'll be rushed like mad, but please say you'll be my matron of honor."

Sallie's light laughter betrayed her delight. "Of course I will, I'd have been crushed if you hadn't asked me. When can we get together?"

"Could you get away for a few hours tomorrow night? Come over to my mother's?"

"Yes, certainly. Your mother's?"

Tara knew she'd have to make an explanation that was convincing. Sallie knew all too well how she felt about living at home.

"Yes, I'm going to move back home until the wedding. With so much to do in so little time, I'm hoping to save wear and tear on my nervous system."

"Probably the best idea," Sallie replied, musingly. Tara exhaled very slowly with relief as Sallie added, "I'll come over right after dinner, okay?"

"Fine, I'll see you then. Now I'd better get to work before the boss catches me goofing off. Bye, Sal."

Tara hung up, Sallie's happy laughter ringing in her ears. She felt a growing sense of panic, as if she were caught in a net and someone was drawing it tighter and tighter. What had she started?

Chapter Seven

That evening Tara stood in her bedroom, suitcases open on the bed, clothes scattered around them, when the doorbell rang at exactly seven thirty.

"Damn," she muttered under her breath, then stormed out of the bedroom to the door. Turning the lock, she flipped the door open, spun on her heel, and stalked back into the bedroom without even glancing into the hall.

Staring in disgust at the cases and clothes a few minutes later, Alek's voice, low, menacing, touched her like a cold breeze. "Don't ever do that again, Tara."

Surprised turned to shock when she swung her head to stare at him. He was standing just inside the bedroom doorway, and his stance, everything about the hard look of him, was more chilling, menacing than his voice had been.

"Do what?" Tara wet her dry lips, suddenly frightened. "What did I do?"

His tone was harsh, the words clipped. "Don't ever unlock your door and turn away without looking to see who it is again. Are you looking to get robbed, or mugged, or worse?"

"But I knew it was you." Tara made her voice hard in an effort to hide the fear curling in her chest.

"You thought it was me," he rapped. "Not quite the same thing."

Unable to face that brittle blue stare, she turned her head to gaze unseeingly at the bed. Shock was added to shock at his lightning change of mood. His tone now light and teasing, he sauntered across the room to her, eyes flicking over the cluttered bed.

"I thought you'd be almost finished packing by this time."

Anger replaced the fear inside and, without pausing to think, Tara flashed, "I don't know what to take and what to leave. I don't want to go to my mother's. I want to stay here in my own place. I'm used to my freedom. Do you realize that not only will I lose my privacy, I'll have to share a bedroom with Betsy?"

"Get you used to the idea of sharing a room," he teased laughingly.

In exasperation she turned glaring eyes to him. "Damn you, Alek, it's not funny."

Before the last word was out, she knew she'd gone too far. His face went hard, and his hands shot up to grip her upper arms, his long fingers digging in painfully. "I told you not to swear at me again," he growled dangerously.

She opened her mouth to apologize but not quickly enough. He pulled her against his hard chest, and his mouth crushed hers punishingly, brutally. Her hands, flat against his chest, pushed futilely at him, and she tried vainly to pull away from him. His one hand released her and, with a low, swinging arc, his arm swept the cases from the bed. His hand regripped her arm and he turned her, pushing her back and down. Her back hit the bed, his full weight on top of her, and she felt her breath explode inside her chest. The fear she had experienced earlier was nothing compared to the blind panic that now clutched at her throat.

Like a wild thing she struggled against him, hands pushing, legs kicking. Twisting her head frantically, she finally succeeded in tearing her mouth away from his cruel, bruising lips. Gasping for air, she choked, "You're nothing but a savage. You're hurting me."

He was still a moment, then his hand moved from her arm, sliding slowly to the beginning swell of her breast. Lips close to her ear, he groaned, "Tara, in a few weeks I'll be your husband. Surely a few weeks can't make all that much difference." His hand slid caressingly over her breast and, his voice a harsh whisper, he urged, "Tara, let me. Let me."

Tara had to fight a different kind of fear now. The fear of betraying, yielding softness invading her body.

"No," cried. "Alek, you promised me."

His cool breath caressed her cheek as he sighed, then lifted his hand and pushed himself up and away from her. He stood tense, staring at her broodingly for a long minute before snapping, "All right, let's gather this stuff together and get the hell out of here before I change my mind." The thought flashed into Tara's mind that this was the reason for his insistence she stay with her parents. Was he afraid that the inevitable would happen if they were alone here? She shook her head in negation. *No, not Alek. Too out of character.* His reason was obvious. While she was surrounded by her family, there was less chance she'd change her mind, call the whole thing off.

By nine o'clock Tara was settled into her sister's room. Betsy had emptied some drawers and made room in the closet for her things, then stayed to help her unpack.

After the scene in her apartment bedroom, they had made fast work of the packing. Alek had carried the heavier things down the stairs and stowed them in his trunk. Then he had followed her car in his own to her father's house, where her brothers had taken over, lugging the cases up to Betsy's room.

Tara and Betsy were stowing the cases under the twin beds when their mother called, "I've made coffee, girls. Come have a cup while it's hot."

The sisters grinned at each other at the term *girls* then, side by side, went down the stairs and into the living room to join Alek and their parents.

"Well, Tara, come sit down. You look so tired, you're pale." Her father's changed attitude toward her was a secret source of amusement to Tara, and she had to work at controlling the twitch on her lips—a job made almost impossible when she encountered the wickedly laughing gleam in Alek's eyes.

"Yes, darling, come sit next to me and have some coffee. It will help you relax."

Although she did as he asked, Tara was convinced that if she was to relax, the last place in the world for her to sit was next to Alek.

As they drank their coffee, they discussed their plans for the next few days. Tara told her mother about having Sallie for her matron of honor, and that Sallie would be coming over tomorrow night. Then, glancing at her hopeful-faced sister, she grinned and said teasingly, "I hope you'll agree to be my maid of honor, as I'm planning on it."

"Oh, Tara." Betsy laughed shakily. "I was beginning to be afraid you weren't going to ask me."

"Not ask you? You nit, do you think I'd get married without you?"

Tara's voice was a little shaky, and she was glad when her mother turned the conversation to Alek.

"Have you decided on a best man yet, Alek?"

"Yes, I have. As a matter of fact I spoke to him today. My cousin Theo assured me he'd be delighted to prop me up, so to speak."

"Your cousin lives here in Allentown?" her father asked.

"No, Theo lives in Athens." At her parents' startled expression he explained briefly: "My mother's sister married a Greek. The Zenopopoulos family is a very old, respected one. Their firstborn son, Theo, runs the family shipping line now that my uncle Dimitri has retired."

"You have something of an international family, it appears," Tara said quietly.

His eyes came back to hers; his smile was pure charm.

"Yes, my sweet, I suppose I have. But only on my mother's side. She was born in Great Britain and her mother, now widowed, still lives in London, as does her brother, my uncle Edward. Her eldest brother, William, married a girl from Scotland. They live in Edinburgh. My father is second-generation American. He and I are the only ones left, as his parents are both dead, and he was an only child. As I am."

"I see," Tara replied, not quite sure she understood the underlying inflection he'd placed on his last words.

"Do you, my love? I wonder."

Confused, feeling as if she'd missed an important point, Tara changed the subject. "I think we'd better work on the guest list tonight," she said to her mother. "Have you had a chance to work on it at all today?"

"I've finished it." Marlene slanted a quick glance at her husband before adding, "Your father and I worked on it last night after you left."

Will wonders never cease? Tara asked herself wryly, somehow managing to keep the surprise she felt from showing. Her father's complete change of face since Alek had spoken to him the night before was both a source of amusement and irritation. It was as if he felt that now he had to handle her with kid gloves so as not to damage the merchandise Alek had claimed as his own. Tara couldn't decide if she wanted to laugh out loud or scream at him. What she had suspected weeks ago had been proved correct. Her father, recognizing in Alek the top dog of arrogant tyrants, had capitulated completely. Mentally tossing her head at the funny little games men played, Tara offered, "I'll go over the list later and add my own to it. It will be ready tomorrow, Alek."

He left soon after that, drawing her with him when he stepped out the door. Her hand firmly on the doorknob to prevent the door from closing entirely, she shook her head when he asked, "I won't be seeing you at all tomorrow night?" His eyebrows went up in question when she replied, "Or Thursday." At his expression she added hurriedly, "I want to go shopping. The dresses must be selected as soon as possible."

He frowned but murmured, "All right, but don't make any plans for Friday. We're having dinner together. I'll come for you at seven."

She had no time to answer, for, bending his head, his lips caught hers in a light kiss that proceeded swiftly to one that was hard and demanding. She stood passive, her lips cool under his, for a few seconds. Then, frightened by the warmth spreading through her body, she pushed her arm against the door and stepped back into the comparative safety of the brightly lit hallway. His eyes flashed with irritation, and she whispered breathlessly, "I must go in, Alek, I'm cold."

"I could have warmed you," he murmured harshly as he turned abruptly and walked to his car.

I no longer doubt it, Tara admitted to herself somewhat fearfully.

Sallie stopped by, as planned, the following evening and after a few hours of haggling with everyone in the house, Tara had her own way. They all protested, but Tara was determined to keep the wedding party small. Betsy and Sallie would be her only attendants.

Right after dinner Thursday evening, Tara, her mother, Betsy, and Sallie set out for the most exclusive bridal shop in town. Tara had no preconceived idea of what she wanted but she chose the second dress she looked at, paling slightly when the salesclerk told her the price. The other three women took much longer in selecting their outfits, enjoying themselves immensely, trying on dress after dress, while Tara sat, shifting restlessly in her chair.

She and Alek did not go out for dinner on Friday evening after all. As Sallie was preparing to go home after they'd returned from shopping, having gone from the bridal shop to a shoe store, she said gayly, "Tara, David and I have planned an engagement party for tomorrow night. Just a small gathering, casual dress, so I'll see you then."

Tara felt suddenly panicky at the prospect of facing the rest of her friends for the first time since the wedding announcement and she stammered, "But, Sallie, I—I don't know, I mean, I don't think Alek—"

"Don't be silly," Sally interrupted. "David spoke to Alek about it this afternoon and he said Alek was delighted. Now I've got to run. See you tomorrow night. Bye."

The party was an ordeal for Tara. She dressed casually but carefully in a sapphire colored raw silk shirt and matching pants. After a light application of makeup, she stepped back from the mirror to observe the overall effect and smiled with satisfaction. Alek's expression, as he ran his eyes slowly over her, was an added boost to her confidence. But it was short-lived, slipping away to be replaced by growing nervousness and tension, as she fought to maintain the picture of the happy bride in front of her friends.

The evening seemed to drag on forever, Alek's possessive attitude and endearments making her alternatively angry and more nervous. When it was finally over and they were back in Alek's car on their way home, she let her head fall back against the seat and sighed with exhaustion. There would be more parties of this type, and she knew it and prayed for the strength to get through them with at least some degree of aplomb.

Her mind was drifting aimlessly when he brought the car to a stop in front of her parents' house, and her body jerked in alarm when his hands cupped her face, and he touched her mouth with his own. Turning her face, sliding her mouth from his, she whispered, "Alek, please, I'm so tired. All I want to do is go to bed."

Her action had placed her ear close to his lips and he replied, urgently, "Not nearly as badly as I do."

The words, his tone, sent a shaft of such intense longing through Tara, she was shocked, suddenly frightened. She didn't understand these feelings he could so easily arouse, and in sheer self-defense, she whipped up her anger. Her hand gripped the door handle and pushed the door open as she moved away from him. "I'm going in," she snapped. Then she turned to look directly at him and observe, "It seems to me that the only things men think about are sex and money."

"And that's bad?" He laughed softly.

"Don't laugh at me, Alek," she warned.

"All right, I won't," came the indulgent reply.

"And don't patronize me either," she cried, turning to jump from the car.

His hand grasped her arm, forced her around to face him. "Whoa, take it easy." His eyes glittered, his voice held a touch of concern. "You *are* tired. Sleep in tomorrow. I told you, I didn't want you wearing yourself out."

His last statement brought color to her pale cheeks, a flash to her tired eyes. Who the hell was he to tell her anything?

"Let me go, Alek." She spoke through gritted teeth to keep from screaming at him. "I'm going inside."

Slamming the door as she got out of the car, Tara ran up the walk and had the key in the door lock when Alek caught up with her. His arms slid around her waist, pulling her back against him.

"Tara, I know this evening wasn't easy for you, but don't you think you're overreacting a little?" His breath was a soft caress against her hair, and in a weak moment Tara let her head rest on his hard chest. "If you allow yourself to get this uptight every time we're in the company of our friends, you'll be a total wreck in no time. Relax. Enjoy the attention you're receiving as the bride-to-be. The decision to marry was yours, you know."

Renewed anger banished weariness temporarily and, twisting away from his arm violently, she said bitterly, "Oh, yes, I know, the final decision was mine. But I was left with little choice and I didn't want, nor can I enjoy, the attention of my friends." Sarcasm overlaid the bitterness as she added, "Now, if I have your permission, I'd like to go in."

"Tara!"

"Good night, Alek."

With that she turned the key, pushed the door open, stepped inside, and shut the door firmly in his face.

The following two weeks rushed by hectically, Tara constantly fighting down the growing feeling of panic. What had she started? Would she go through with it? Was there any way she could stop it now? She knew the answer to that. Her mother's happy face, as she sat carefully numbering the increasing flow of wedding gifts and arranging them on a long folding table her father had set up in the living room, gave it to her. There was a sparkle in her eyes as she smoothed work-reddened hands over the white tablecloth and touched, again and again, the obviously expensive gifts. She looked years younger and laughed often, and Tara felt trapped, afraid to go ahead, unable to step back. Betsy and Sallie were enjoying the preparations almost as much as her mother and through it all Tara plastered a smile on her face.

She could find no escape, even in the office, and the smile grew brittle. Suddenly all the friends who'd been silent for weeks became very vocal and Tara had to fight down a mushrooming cynicism. God! She had never been so popular in her life. Totally unimpressed, she moved through the days, giving all the proper answers, laughing at all the proper times, and withdrew into her own hiding place inside herself. Denied even the solace of a room of her own, she cried inside, bitter, resentful tears that never touched her cheeks but lent a sparkle to her eyes that was mistaken for happiness, excitement. She drove herself in the office, rearranging files that were already in perfect order, cleaning desk drawers that had always been neat. She knew David attributed her industry to a desire to have her office in order for her replacement while she was on her honeymoon.

The very word *honeymoon,* which she was beginning to hear more and more frequently in teasing tones, was enough to send a tiny flutter—of what? Fear—up her spine. And she was tired. Lord, was she tired.

Tara looked forward to Thanksgiving as to an oasis in the desert. Although she would be spending most of the day with Alek, she hoped that, surrounded by family, she would be able to rest, relax, be herself. *It seems,* she told herself at the end of the day, *that fools never learn.*

The arrangements were for her and Alek to have the traditional Thanksgiving dinner at one o'clock with her family then, in the evening, go on to his parents' for a cold buffet. Alene and Peter had invited a few close friends to join them, Sallie and David included.

Tara was blissfully alone in the kitchen Thanksgiving morning, humming to herself as she prepared vegetables for a salad, when Alek's soft voice stalked across the room to her from the kitchen doorway.

"Good morning, my love. Happy Thanksgiving."

As Tara jerked around from the sink with a startled "Oh," the paring knife she'd been using slipped from her fingers and bounced around on the floor tiles, dangerously close to her ankles.

"Careful!"

Alek was across the room in three long strides, his hand outstretched to grasp her arm and pull her away.

"Are you hurt? Did it hurt you? Why the hell did you let go of it?"

The sharp, staccato questions struck her like blows and, feeling attacked, she answered defensively, "I—I . . . you startled me."

He bent, retrieved the knife with his free hand, dropped it into the sink, then turned her into his arms, holding her loosely.

"That is the second time you nearly injured yourself because, as you say, I startled you. Tara," he said probing gently, "what is it about me that unnerves you so? Are you afraid of me?"

How could she answer him? She didn't know the answers anymore. She felt confused, uncertain. Oh, why had she started this? She was afraid of him. But why? And did he really think she'd ever admit it?"

Shaking her head in negation, she said, lying, "Don't be silly. I was deep in thought and—"

"You won't let me near you, will you?" he sighed. "You're hiding behind that invisible fortress you've built around yourself. Tara, don't you realize that while you're locking me out, you're also locking yourself in?"

She didn't want to listen to any more. Making a move to turn out of his arms, she snapped, "I don't know what you're talking about. Now go away so I can finish the salad."

His arms tightened, refusing to let her go. Bending his head, he whispered, "You didn't return my greeting."

"I—"

"But that's all right, I prefer a silent one anyway."

His mouth caught hers, locking on firmly. Tara steeled herself to remain passive then felt a jolt in the pit of her stomach as his lips forced hers apart, demanding a response. Panic crawled through her when she felt the tip of his tongue, and her hands pushed against his chest. He reacted by dropping his hands to her hips, pulling her roughly against him. The hard muscles of his thighs pressed against her urgently.

Her resistance weakened, and as her mouth grew softer, his became harder, bolder. She felt floaty, light-headed, and, her breath quickening in unison with his, her arms snaked up around his neck and clung.

Tightening his arms, he drew her even closer, his hands moving gently along her spine, pressing her softness against the long, hard length of his body. Thought disappeared and was replaced by sensations. The golden curtain dropped around them, and she felt a strange contentment seep through her. For the first time in weeks she felt safe, secure. Sighing softly, she allowed her lips to be parted yet farther, wanting to drown in the firm sweetness of his mouth.

The slamming of the front door reverberated through her like shock waves, setting off an alarm in her mind. Her father's voice, chastising Karl for letting it slam, brought both shame and reason. What did she think she was doing? Was her mind slipping? Was a soldier ever so weary, he sought rest in the camp of his enemy?

With a small cry of self-disgust, she backed away from him, eyes closed in pain, her hand covering her quivering lips.

"Tara?"

Shaking her head wildly, she turned away. "Don't say anything."

"Tara, this is ridiculous. If you'd—"

"No! You make me sick. I make myself sick." She spun around to face him, eyes wide, frightened, refusing to see the almost desperate expression in his eyes, to hear the almost pleading note in his voice. "You can go to—you can go to the living room. Keep my father company while I make the salad."

She had been speaking softly, tremulously. Now her tone went hard: "Go away, Alek."

He started toward her then stopped as the kitchen door was pushed open. Marlene's voice preceded her into the room.

"You should have come to church with us, Tara—" On seeing Alek she paused, hands behind her back as she tied an apron around her still slim waist. "Oh! Good morning, Alek. Happy Thanksgiving. I swear, if it wasn't for the mouth-watering smell of that turkey in the oven, I wouldn't believe it was Thanksgiving, it is so mild outside. Why—" She stopped, eyes swinging from Tara to Alek then back to Tara, suddenly feeling the tension that danced between the two. "Is"—she paused, wet her lips—"is anything wrong?"

At the look of anxiety that had replaced the happy glow on her mother's face, Tara caught herself up sharply. Marshaling her rioting emotions, she managed a shaky laugh.

"Of course not, Mama. I was just trying to chase Alek into the living room to Dad, so I can get on with the salad."

Tara saw, but refused to let register, the small sigh Alek expelled before he turned a composed, warm face to her mother.

"Hello, Marlene. Happy Thanksgiving." He had been using her parents' Christian names, at their request, for several days now, yet each time he addressed one of them, Tara felt an uncomfortable twinge. He did it so easily, so effortlessly, as if he'd known and liked them for years.

"I suppose," he went on teasingly, "that if I want to taste said bird in the oven, I had better retreat to the living room, and Herman, as graciously as possible. And you were right. The aroma is mouth-watering. If you've taught Tara all your little kitchen secrets, I'm afraid I'll have to watch my waistline very carefully after we're married."

Tara's fingers curled into her palms, the nails digging into her flesh as she watched her mother's expression change from worry to flushed pleasure. He had completely captivated her mother. Had in fact captivated every member of her family. Betsy became all flustered and pink-cheeked whenever he favored her with one of his teasing, devastatingly gentle smiles. Her brothers trailed around behind him as if in the wake of some vaulted, invincible hero, their expressions bordering on awe. And her father! That was the kicker. Her father walked around with his chest expanded, eyes bright with pride, whenever Alek slipped and called him *sir* instead of *Herman*.

Their attitude, the whole situation, filled Tara with disgust. *They act as if he were one of the lords of the earth,* she had thought scathingly several times, rather than the devious, arrogant, tyrannical boss he in fact was. Not once did she question her own deeply ingrained opinion of him. He was the enemy. Period.

Tara spent the rest of the day in cold resentment; he had ruined the holiday for her. By the time they reached his parents' home, her resentment had changed to simmering anger. His possessive attitude, his endearments, had her fighting the urge to hit him.

Alene had planned a casual evening and, after the cold buffet supper had been cleared away, they gathered in the living room. As there were more people than chairs, Tara sat on the floor between Alek's and Peter's chairs. The conversation ran the gamut from fashion to politics.

Tara was just beginning to relax and enjoy herself when Alek's hand dropped onto her shoulder and his cool voice drawled, "I wonder if most women really know what they want?" His eyes rested briefly on his mother's face, then he added, "The most contented women I know are the ones who realize their happiness stems from being well cared for and cherished by the men they belong to."

The obnoxious bastard! Red flares exploded inside Tara's head. Trembling in anger, she turned her head to stare pointedly at his hand before lifting her head to give him the full blast of fury in her eyes. To keep from shouting Tara had to push her words through her teeth.

"If a slave is your secret desire, Alek, count me out. I will be a slave for no man."

Alek's face paled and, in soothing tones, he murmured, "Tara, I didn't mean—"

"I have reason to know," Tara interrupted bitingly, "you

mean exactly what you say. *Belonging to* means ownership and ownership of a human being means slavery. I am, and intend to remain, my own person. With or without your approval. And will you please remove your hand."

Tara's last words were spoken so cuttingly, Alek snatched his hand away as if he'd been burned. A tide of red crawled across his cheeks, and his eyes held an unfamiliar look of humiliation.

A deathly silence covered the room for some minutes, then Peter's quiet voice eased the tension.

"You deserved that, son," he said easily. "Strangely enough, your mother put me in my place much the same way forty years ago."

"And hard as it may be to believe, Tara," Alene chimed in laughingly, "Peter was even more cocky then Alek."

Her teasing gibe relieved the strain in the room, and everyone began talking at once. Even so, Alek did not touch her for the remainder of the evening.

By the Saturday before the wedding Tara was bewildered and near tears. She couldn't or wouldn't understand her own emotions any longer, and she felt depressed and somehow scared. That afternoon she sat doing her nails, nibbling at her lower lip. There was to be yet another party—the last of many—that night at the home of a lawyer friend of Alek's. From what she had gleaned from Sallie, it was to be a large one, some forty or so guests. This was to be the first really formal party for them, and Tara had shopped for hours till she found the right dress. The fact that her beautiful future mother-in-law would be there was an added spur to her choice. Alene had exquisite taste and always looked as if she had just stepped out of the pages of a haute couture magazine. Also Alek had told her she'd be meeting his cousin Theo at this party, as he was arriving Saturday morning.

The dress she'd chosen was a beautifully cut, form-fitting lilac cocktail dress that fell to her delicate ankles. Elegant strappy evening shoes in a matching shade completed the outfit.

As she walked into the living room that evening, she was glad she'd taken more care than usual with her appearance. Alek, in black evening wear, was a devastating threat to any female's senses, and Tara felt her heartbeat quicken. The glittering, sapphire gaze he slowly ran over her didn't help her breathing any, and she drew a deep, calming breath when he murmured, "We had better be going," and turned his eyes away from her to say good night to her parents.

In the car Tara was quiet, her mouth and throat felt dry as bone, and she admitted to herself that she was scared. Tonight, for the first time, she would be meeting Alek's more important friends, and she was naturally anxious.

As he turned the car into the private drive leading to his friends' home, Alek slanted her a sharp glance, then, as if he had been monitoring her thoughts, said gently, "They're only people, you know. Very little different from other people. Some may have more money, some more intelligence, and most, more ambition and drive. But people, just the same. I doubt there'll be a woman there more lovely or poised than you. I wonder sometimes if you fully realize how beautiful and desirable you are." He parked the car in the midst of dozens of others, then turned to face her fully. "Chin up, my sweet. Let's have one of those heart-stopping smiles of yours," he teased.

Feeling a soothing warmth flow through her, Tara did smile, if a little tremulously. Bending his head, he brushed his mouth across hers and whispered, "Now go in there and knock their socks off."

The house was very large, very imposing, and more than a little daunting. As they entered the large, impressive hall, Tara unconsciously straightened her shoulders and lifted her head, completely unaware, as she walked into the room full of people, that she had the graceful bearing of a young queen.

Her first impressions were of lights and sounds and colors. The room was brightly lit, the light reflecting even more light as it struck fiery, rainbow-colored sparks off the jewelry that adorned the throats, wrists, fingers, and earlobes of the fashionably dressed women. The sound was a blend of laughing voices and muted background music coming from several speakers positioned at different spots in the room.

She was vaguely aware of Alek introducing her to her host and hostess, John and Adele Freeland, and they in turn were introducing her to the people standing closest to them. In amazement Tara heard herself responding in a tone of cool self-assurance. Then the press of people separated her from Alek, and what little confidence Tara had, left her completely. She was beginning to feel panic rise when, on a sigh of sheer relief, she saw Alek's father making his way to her through the crowd.

"Good evening, my dear." Peter Rykovsky's voice was a warm caress to badly fraying nerves. Without so much as a by-your-leave he took her cold fingers in his warm hand and said imperviously, "I've been ordered by my lady to bring this delectable young thing to her, and, as you know, Alene's wish is my command."

Warm laughter followed them as he led her adroitly through the milling people, not stopping until Tara stood directly in front of Alene. "Ah, there you are, darling," Alene's lovely voice greeted her. "Come meet my nephew Theo."

Tara turned and felt the breath catch in her throat. Standing next to Alene was a young man who could easily have posed for at least a half dozen Greek statues. His face and form were classically beautiful; his dark, curly hair appeared sculpted to his head; and his eyes were clear and blue as a summer sky. Even, white teeth flashed as he smiled at her and in a voice that held only a hint of an accent he said, "All my life I've secretly thought that Alek was not only the shrewdest but also the luckiest devil alive. Now my beliefs are confirmed. I think I've fallen in love on sight. I don't suppose, beautiful creature, you'd care to run away with me this minute and leave old Alek at the altar, would you?"

In speechless confusion Tara heard Alene's laughing comment and Peter's dry retort. *This guy is almost as outrageous as Alek,* Tara thought. What surprises would the rest of the family have for her?

She was saved from answering him as Sallie joined their small circle, and once again she was being led away. They had taken only a few steps when she had to stop short, her path being barred by an exotically lovely woman whose black eyes glittered maliciously at her. In a tone of barely controlled fury, she purred icily, "I haven't yet met the bride-to-be, Sallie."

A flicker of alarm touched Tara's spine at the hostility underlying the woman's tone, and she looked at her sharply. She was of average height, voluptuously built, with full breasts, a small waist, and full hips that tapered to long, slender legs. Her skin was olive-toned, and right now a dusky pink tinged her cheeks. Hair as shiny black as sealskin lay smooth and sleek against her head in a short cap-cut. Beautifully arched black brows set off snapping black eyes, which were surrounded by long black lashes. The almond shape of her eyes added to the exotic look of her. The feeling of alarm grew stronger at Sallie's obvious reluctance to introduce them. After what seemed like a long pause Sallie said hurriedly, "Tara Schmitt—Kitty Davenport."

Kitty! *More like the jungle cat,* Tara thought as she acknowledged the introduction. Her thought was proved correct with the woman's next words: "I hope you're enjoying yourself now," she purred. "It won't be long before the novelty of innocence wears off for Alek, and then your nights will be very cold and long."

"Kitty!" Sallie's voice held shocked reproof, even though she'd managed to keep it at a normal tone. Grasping Tara's arm, she drew her away from the nasty laugh that broke from Kitty's dark-red lips. When they were a few feet away from her, Tara whispered, "What was that all about?"

Sallie began to shake her head, then paused and finally said, "I may as well tell you. You'll find out sooner or later anyway." Still grasping her arm, she drew her into a relatively quiet corner, glanced around, then said softly, "Until a few months ago Kitty was Alek's—uh—girl friend. She has been vocally bitter about their breakup. I can't imagine why she was invited to this party."

The searing stab of pain that tore through Tara at Sallie's words stunned her, and she turned her head to hide her pain-filled eyes. She was jealous! Fiercely, hotly jealous, and the knowledge of it frightened and confused her. As if looking for a lifeline, she glanced around the room frantically, and her glance was caught, held by a glittering blue one. Even across the width of the large room Tara saw Alek's eyes grow sharp, questioning. As her eyes stared into that sapphire blaze, a small voice cried out inside, *Dear God, no. No, no, no. I can't, I won't be in love with him.* . . . *But you are* came a silent taunt.

Remember how he's hurt you, what he is, she told that silent voice, then she deliberately turned back to Sallie and said coldly, "Girl friend? You mean *mistress,* don't you? Did he pay for an apartment for her in his building or did she just share his?" It was a futile effort to reject her emotions. The pain and humiliation grew to the dimensions of torture, and she was only vaguely aware of the concern in Sallie's voice. "Oh, Tara, does it really matter? It was over months ago."

Yes, Tara thought. *But for how long?* How long would it be before Alek, once having acquired the one thing he'd been denied, became bored and began looking around for a diversion. And Kitty would be there in his sight; of that Tara felt quite sure.

Chapter Eight

Tara opened her eyes the morning of her wedding and closed them again quickly, tightly. The weather matched her emotional condition. The sky was weeping hard, and although Tara's eyes were now dry, inside her heart the tears fell as swiftly as the raindrops. The days she lived through since the party—a week ago tonight—had been pure hell.

Vainly and painfully she had fought against the realization of her love for Alek. She had spent as little time with him as possible, telling him she had too much to do. His skeptical eyes questioned her, although he didn't voice his doubts. She went to her apartment several evenings, ostensibly to pack her things for removal to Alek's apartment, only to pace from room to room crying bitter tears. She didn't want to love him. She didn't even want to like him.

What was she to do? The desire to make him pay for what he'd done to her had been cauterized by that searing knife of jealousy on Saturday night. She hurt badly yet she knew, somehow, that the pain she now knew was nothing to what would come later. Twice she had left the apartment to go back to her parents, firmly determined to tell them she could not go through with the wedding. Both times the words died on her lips at the sight of her mother's face.

The rehearsal last night had been an ordeal that was not helped by Theo's light banter. When it had finally been over, Alek had led Tara outside to his car, brushing aside her protested "Alek, my car," with a curt "I'll bring you back for it."

He had not driven far, parking the car again on a dimly lighted street. Resting an arm on the steering wheel, he slanted a long look at her before asking tightly, "Last-minute jitters, Tara? You've been withdrawn and jumpy all week. Is something wrong? Aren't you feeling well?"

"I feel fine," she murmured, twisting her hands in her lap. "I'm a little tired, that's all."

He turned to face her fully, his one long hand covering hers, stilling their agitated movement. Head bent, Tara studied his slim-fingered hand, felt its warmth seep into her cold skin. A small shiver rippled along her spine as his hand moved, slid up her arm to grasp her shoulder. "Look at me, Tara."

When she didn't comply at once, he released her shoulder and caught her chin in his fingers, lifting her head and turning her face to his descending mouth. She forced herself to remain passive, silently fighting down the tingling in her fingers, the warmth spreading through her body. Feeling somehow that if she didn't break contact with his persuading mouth, she'd be lost forever, she pulled her lips away from his with a small sob.

"Alek, please take me home. I'm very tired, and isn't Theo having a bachelor party for you tonight?"

"Yes he is, but there's no hurry." His fingers caressed her cheek, brushed lightly at the few strands of silky hair that had fallen across her face. His mouth followed the progress of his hand and, as his fingers slid into the deep waves of her hair, his lips, close to her ear, whispered, "Only one more day, pansy eyes, and this mad rushing around will be over. You can rest then, and I'll help you. The medicine I've got for you works better than any tranquilizer ever made." Then his mouth found hers again, hard, demanding a response from her. Trembling, breathless, she could feel her resistance slipping away, and in desperation she brought her hands up to his head and pushed him away. "Alek, don't."

He flung himself back behind the steering wheel, breathing hard, smoldering, darkened eyes roaming her face.

"You're right," he rasped. "I'd better take you home before

I decide the hell with the party and take you to my place." He paused then added roughly, "I want you badly, Tara. Tomorrow can't come soon enough."

Now, lying in her bed, Tara groaned aloud at the memory and turned her face into the pillow. Why hadn't she backed out of this days ago, as soon as she'd felt that soul-destroying stab of jealousy? She wanted to run away and hide, and it was too late. Within a few hours she would be his wife. His words, like a scratched record, kept repeating in her head. *"I want you badly." I want you. Want. Want. Want.*

The rain still poured from leaden skies when Tara, pale, ethereal, and unknowingly beautiful, was dressed and ready to leave for the church. A bubble of hysterical laughter caught then lodged in her throat at the incongruity of tugging clear plastic boots over her white satin slippers and carefully catching her long, full skirt around her knees, under the protective rain cape her father placed around her shoulders. From house to car, from car to church, George held a large golf umbrella over her.

The feeling of unreality that had gripped Tara from the minute she'd begun dressing mushroomed and grew until now, poised, ready to follow Betsy down the aisle, she felt cold, numb. The signaling organ chord was struck, her father's shoulder nudged hers, and she moved in measured step beside him, unaware of the several small gasps or open stares of admiration that greeted her appearance.

The gown Tara had chosen was of white satin, starkly beautiful in its simplicity. It fit snugly from the high collar that encircled her throat to the nipped-in waist, and from her shoulders to where the sleeves ended in a V point on the back of her hands at the middle fingers. From the waist the skirt belled out full and voluminous, ending in a short train in back. It was completely without adornment of either fabric or jewelry.

In a strangely withdrawn state Tara walked slowly down the long aisle, drawing ever nearer to the two cousins, both handsome in different ways. They watched her progress with different expressions: Theo's smile was soft, his eyes warmly appreciating her beauty. Alek's unsmiling countenance was held in, taut, expressionless. His eyes blazed with a fierce possessiveness, and something Tara couldn't define.

The withdrawn, cold state lasted throughout most of the ceremony, and not until the blessing was being given did Tara feel the first pangs of guilt. She had agreed to marry this man for a very unholy reason. Revenge. In any way that presented itself, she had decided to make him pay for what he'd done to her. The fact that his reason—lust—was equally sinful didn't matter. The face that she now loved him didn't excuse her either. She was in the house of God and she was committing a reprehensible act; she felt, if possible, more miserable than before.

Finally it was all over. Not just the ceremony, but the picture-taking as well. And now the hand that tugged the plastic boots over her slippers felt weighted from the heavy, wide gold band Alek had slid onto her finger. And the car that whisked them to the Hotel Traylor for the reception was shared by her husband.

She was thankful for the numbed coldness that had enveloped her again during the long period of picture-taking, and it carried her through the reception. A smile cramping her neck and jaw muscles, she went through the motions of the lead-off dance, the cake-cutting, and the tossing of the bouquet, all the while blinking at the incessant flash of light from the hired photographer. On the point of thinking it would go on forever, Tara felt the firm clasp of Alek's hand and walked beside him as she made a determined move to the door.

The plan had been for them to change clothes at Alek's— now their—apartment, then go on to New York for a week. It had grown colder, and the rain still slashed against the windshield. After Alek had maneuvered the car into the steady stream of late-afternoon traffic, he said abruptly, "I wouldn't be a bit surprised if this rain turns to snow in a little while. We're not driving to New York in this tonight, we'll wait and leave in the morning."

At the sound of finality in his tone, Tara gulped back the

protest forming on her lips, her panic at the prospect of being alone with him that much sooner closing her throat to speech.

His apartment, in a fairly new modern complex, was large and luxurious. Tara had been in it once before, on Thursday night, when they had transported her clothes from her father's house. She had been given the grand tour of: Alek's large bedroom and a smaller one, both with their own baths; a roomy, well-equipped kitchen and cozy dining area; and a huge living room, part of which had been sectioned off as a bar area. The furnishings were Scandinavian modern, the lines straight and clean, yet overall the impression was one of the kind of comfort that comes only with money.

Alek turned the key in the lock, pushed the door open, reached inside to flick on the light switch, then ushered Tara in, saying dryly, "I think I'll save the over-the-threshold tradition until we move into a home of our own, if you don't mind."

Tara shook her head and walked into the room, only to stop and glance around irresolutely. The sound of the door being closed softly, the click of the lock springing into place, set her in motion, and she hurried toward the bedroom, her voice breathless. "I—I think I'll change. The bottom of my gown got wet and it's heavy and uncomfortable."

She dashed into the bedroom, closed the door behind her, and leaned weakly against it, gasping for air. Dear Lord, what was she going to do? She didn't think she could face him again, yet she was trapped inside this apartment with him. Moving away from the door, she walked around the room nervously, her eyes not registering the light-wood tone of the double dresser, the chest of drawers, the desk, the big overstuffed leather armchair, the deep rich green of carpeting and draperies or pristine white of walls, ceiling, and woodwork. But mostly her eyes avoided the wide double bed with its plump down comforter and crisp linen shams.

Without thinking, her trembling fingers slid open the zipper on the inside of her sleeves, moved to tug at the long one that ran from the back of her neck to her waist. She managed to get it halfway down, then no amount of stretching or reaching would move it an inch farther. In agitated frustration, Tara tugged on her sleeves, hoping to slip the gown off her shoulders, enabling her to twist the zip around to the front. She was on the verge of tears when the bedroom door opened and Alek asked softly, "Need any help?"

"I can't get the damned zipper down," she cried irritably and heard his low laugh as he came across the room to her. She felt his fingers at her back, then the zip was sliding easily to its base. A pause, then his hands parted the material, slid inside and around her waist, scorching her skin through the thin fabric of her slip. As if his fingers actually burned, she jerked away from him.

"Alek, I'd like to take a shower." Trembling, she turned to face him, a plea in her eyes. "Please."

His eyes glowed darkly as they roved over her body then came back to study her face. "That is a strikingly beautiful dress." His voice was a blatant caress, rippling over her skin like warm satin. "It almost does you justice. All right, my sweet, have your shower. I'll use the other bathroom and take one too." Then his voice sounded a mild warning note. "You have exactly one half hour." With that he calmly walked to the closet, yanked out a long terrycloth robe, and sauntered out of the room.

Tara released her tensely held breath on a long sigh then quickly removed her dress and lingerie, tossing the lot onto the overstuffed chair. Plunging her hand into the closet, she grabbed the long white satin robe she'd hung there Thursday night and ran into the immaculate bathroom.

Standing under the hot, stinging shower spray, she longed for a few extra minutes to stand and let the fingerlike jets work the tenseness out of her body. But she didn't have a few extra minutes, for she had made up her mind to dress and leave the apartment before Alek finished his shower.

In fumbling haste she dried her hair and body, slipped into her robe, and scrubbed her teeth. Her hair a silver-blond mass of damp waves rioting over her shoulders and down her back, she pulled open the bathroom door, stepped through it, and stopped cold at the sound of Alek's sharply indrawn breath.

He was standing just inside the bedroom door as if he'd just that minute entered. The robe hung to the top of his bare feet, the belt looped tightly around his lean waist.

Tara stood motionless, as if mesmerized. His softly spoken words, as he moved toward her, startled her into awareness. "God, Tara, you're beautiful."

Cautiously she moved away from him, toward the far-window wall, her voice sounding hoarse and strained to her ears. "This is a mistake. I can't stay here, Alek. I'd like you to leave the room so I can dress. I'm going home."

He paused, then continued to her, stopping a foot in front of her. In growing alarm she watched his face harden, his eyes change from confusion to wariness to anger.

"Like hell I'll leave this room." She flinched at the whip-flick cutting sting of his voice. "If there's been a mistake, you made it and you'll live with it, and me. You're not going anywhere. You *are* home."

Shrinking inside at the coldness of his tone, Tara drew a deep breath and, moving quickly, she circled around him and made for the door. Her hair was her undoing, for as she swung away from him, it fanned out and around her head. With lightning swiftness his arm shot out, and he caught a handful, making her cry out with the pain that stung her scalp. He gave a tug to turn her around to him and she lost her balance and crashed to the floor on her knees in front of him. Giving another sharp tug he jerked her head back, turned her face up to the cold, hard planes of his. Through tightly clenched teeth he growled, "You're my wife, Tara, and you'll stay my wife. I've waited long enough; I'll wait no longer."

Defiance blazed out of her eyes and in an attempt to inflict pain on him, as he was on her, she flashed, "You're a savage. Underneath that thin veneer of civilization you're as wild and unruly as a mountain man."

His glittering blue eyes never leaving hers, he dropped onto his knees in front of her. "I hear you," he rasped. "And this evening, my love, you are going to find out what it feels like to be made love to by a savage."

With all her concentration centered on remaining passive, unaffected by the disturbing pressure of his mouth crushing hers, Tara was only vaguely aware of his fingers relaxing, sliding away from her hair. His other arm was around her tightly, pinning both of hers to her sides. Slowly he began to move, sideways and down, drawing her with him. His free hand braced on the floor, he lowered them both to the soft pile carpeting, his lips still locked on hers.

He turned her at the last moment, and her back hit the floor with a dull thud at the same time his hard chest struck hers, knocking the wind out of her. Feeling suffocated, Tara managed to turn her head away from him, gasping for air. Not once breaking contact, his lips slid across her soft cheek to her ear, and she uttered a tiny gasp when his teeth nibbled at her lobe.

"Tara, I don't want to force you." Tara shivered at the impassioned whisper. "But this marriage will be consummated tonight. I *will* make you mine. Never have I wanted to own a woman the way I want to own you. Don't fight me, love, or, in different ways, you'll hurt us both."

Fleetingly she wondered at the meaning of his words, then all thought fled, for his lips were sending small tongues of flame into every vein in her body. With tiny, devastating kisses his lips moved from her ear to the corner of her mouth where, along with the tip of his tongue, he teased and tantalized until every one of her senses cried out with the need to feel those lips, that tongue, against her own.

"Alek."

His name broke from her throat with a small sob as she moved her head the fraction of an inch needed to slide her mouth under his. She heard the breath catch in his throat, as if in disbelief, then his mouth crushed hers more savagely than before, in an excitingly desperate kind of way, plundering, seeking every ounce of sweetness there.

It seemed the whole world was on fire, and she was the very center of the blaze. Filled with a sudden, urgent need to touch him, her hands broke free of his imprisoning hold and, parting the lapels of his robe, she slid her hands across his chest, exhilaration singing through her when she felt him shudder at her touch.

With a groan his mouth left hers and he buried his face in the curve of her neck, his hand brushing her robe aside roughly. She felt his warm breath tickle her skin, heard again the same incomprehensible Russian words he'd spoken before. Moving quickly, he lifted her and removed her robe, then shed his own, his eyes scorching her body as they roved slowly over her.

Having him away from her, even that short distance, brought a measure of sanity. What was she doing? She had to stop this. But she loved him so. Needed him so. Two tears escaped over the edge of her lower lids and rolled slowly across her cheeks into her hair. Instantly he was beside her, his hands cupping her face.

"Tara, darling, don't be frightened."

Frightened? Yes, she was frightened of her own response, of the overwhelming longing to be close to him, belong to him.

Dropping tiny, fiery kisses, his lips surveyed her face while his hands caressed and aroused her body. His softly murmured words added fuel to the rapidly spreading flames inside her.

Moaning softly, she curled her arms tightly around his neck, gave up her mouth in total surrender. Somewhere in the deep recess of her mind she knew she'd have to pay for it for the rest of her life. Yesterday was over. Tomorrow was far away. The only thing that held any meaning for her was here, and now, and him. The apartment, the city, the world dissolved, and it was as if they were alone on a tiny island, soaring through time and space.

His hard body moved over hers, and his lips close to her ear whispered, "I must hurt you, love, but I will promise you the pain will not last long, and it will set you free. Free to give me as much or as little as you wish. Free to accept everything I have to offer."

On his last words pain ripped through the lower part of her body and, stiffening with outrage and shock, she arched away from him, the cry of rejection that tore from her lips drowning inside his mouth. With infinite patience and surprising restraint he kissed, caressed, soothed her tension-contracted body until the pain receded and was replaced by a fierce urgency inside her to know a oneness with him.

The gentle appeaser was gone with her first renewed stirrings, replaced by a hard, demanding lover, intent on fulfillment. When he exploded off the edge of their tiny island in space, he took her with him. Shuddering, gasping for breath, for one small moment she seemed to face the pure white light of the sun, then she went spiraling through the darkness of space, held softly, securely, within the steel-like coils of his arms. If someone had told Tara one week, one day ago, that surrendering herself completely to Alek would fill her with such ecstasy, she would never have believed it, as much as she loved him. This beauty and contentment that engulfed every part of her being were part of the make-believe used in romantic literature and films. The idea that all the passion that ever poured out of the pen of poets or lyricists had to be based in some fact had never occurred to her.

Slowly the awareness of time and place crept back to her. She felt the soft carpet against her skin, the night-colored air in the room lightly cooling her flesh. She felt Alek's thumping heart return to a normal beat, heard his ragged breathing grow more even. Still held tightly against his hard body, she felt his breath stir her hair as he whispered in an almost awed tone, "Never in all my wildest fantasizing have I dreamed that anything could be so perfect." His arms tightened possessively and his mouth covered hers in a deep consuming kiss. When he lifted his head, his voice was firm, though still soft. "The marriage has been fully consummated, Tara, with the joining of our bodies, and the coupling of our souls. If what we've just experienced is savagery, then I give up all claims to civilization."

Tara slept, then was jarred awake again when Alek lifted her from the floor and carried her to the bed. It seemed very late and she was shivering; goose bumps covered her arms and shoulders. He left her a moment and the room was plunged into darkness. Then he was back, sliding onto the bed next to her, drawing the covers up and around them before pulling her into his arms hard against him.

"I'm so cold." The words trembled from her lips shakily.

"I know. I'm sorry. I fell asleep. I haven't sleep that deeply since I was a child."

His murmured words were revealing something of importance to her, but the deeper meaning of them was lost to her sleep-hazy mind.

Slowly, as warmth returned to her body, heat returned to his, and within minutes he was whispering her name between fierce, demanding kisses, his hands possessive, his body pressing hers into the mattress urgently.

If she'd have thought, she would have believed it impossible to experience that same oneness as before. Yet if anything, their wild, explosive flight through space this time ended in a more perfect unity. More slowly, languorously, she drifted back to an awareness of Alek's mouth lazily branding small kisses over her face, her throat, her shoulders, and lingeringly, her breasts. Sighing in deep contentment, she was beyond wondering at the strangely fervent tone of his voice, or the meaning of the oft repeated Russian words. Almost purring, she curled against him like a well-petted kitten, her fingers idly stroking his muscle-ridged back. One minute she felt more vibrantly alive than ever before in her life, and in the next, sensuously drowsy, she slipped into a deep, relaxed sleep.

The early-morning rays of sun touching Tara's face wakened her. Closing her eyes again quickly, she moved to roll onto her side and grew still, suddenly aware of a weight on her chest. Turning her head slowly, she opened her eyes and stared at Alek sprawled beside her, one arm flung across her breasts.

Memory returned in a flash, and she felt the hot sting of tears behind her lids. Afraid to move, barely breathing, her eyes roved over him lovingly. The comforter was twisted about his slim waist, leaving his broad shoulders and chest exposed to the chill air in the room. Slowly she curled her fingers into her palm, fighting down the urge to touch, to slide her fingers over his smooth skin, to feel the curly spring of dark hair tickle her palm.

Eyes moving slowly, missing nothing, trailed up to the strong column of his throat and rested a moment on the steady pulsebeat there. Her throat closing with emotion, she lifted her eyes to his head. Silky black waves were tousled, one swath lying endearingly across his forehead, and Tara felt a pang remembering it was her fingers that had caused the disorder. Long, thick, inky lashes threw shadows onto his high cheekbones, the lines of which, along with his firm jaw, were somewhat softened in sleep. Her eyes rested on his beautifully chiseled mouth; her lips ached with the need to kiss him.

Her lashes glistened with tears; consumed with the desire to wake him, to beg him to hold her close, she tore her eyes away and stared at the ceiling. Her mind working furiously, Tara tried to find an alternative to what she knew she must do. Finally her lids closed in defeat. It was no good. It would never be any good. And she knew it. Her heart cried at the realization, but she knew she couldn't stay with him. Gone were the vaguely formed plans to make him pay for what he'd done to her. Before, she'd been angry, hurt. Now she was terrified.

Why did the night have to end? she thought bitterly. Why had she slept and wasted so much of it? He had been so gentle, then so demanding, his hands and mouth awaking a sleeping tiger of passion she had never dreamed she possessed. She shivered with remembrances, then her eyes flew open. What must he think of her now? She didn't even want to think about that, so she pushed the thought aside, then felt a shaft of blinding pain as a new consideration slithered its way into her mind. His love-making had been so completely mind-shattering. It had affected her two ways, physically and mentally, striking to the very core of her being. She had known she was in love with him for some days; now she belonged to him. What would it be like to be actually loved by him?

The thought drove the pain deeper, and she stirred restlessly. There was the cause of her misery, the reason she could not stay with him. For he did not love her. What had his words been? She had no need to ask herself the questions, for she could hear his voice as if it had been yesterday: *"If the only way I can have you is through marriage, I'll marry you."*

Just in time Tara caught back the sob that rose in her throat. If she stayed with him now, slept with him, he'd crush her spirit and independence. Loving him so deeply, she'd be like clay in his hands. His nearness made her ache; his touch set her on fire. Her dependence on him would grow, and within a short amount of time he could make a near-slave of her. And being the epitome of dominance, he would relish the enslavement. She would end hating herself and probably him also.

No, no, no, she told herself. She would not, she could not, let that happen. She must end it, now, this morning.

As if it were a sign, he moved in his sleep, lifting his arm from her and flinging it back over his head. She was free and with a shiver she slid her naked body off the bed. Their robes lay in a heap where he had tossed them last night and, scooping hers up, she slipped into it and wrapped it around her slim form, tying the belt securely.

Like a sleepwalker she moved to stand at the windows, staring down at the Sunday morning street empty of traffic, her arms wrapped around her trembling body.

"Good morning, pansy eyes. Come back to bed." Alek's sleepy soft voice reached out across the room to envelop her like a caress. "There's something I want to tell you. Something I forgot in the—uh—heat of the moment last night."

Tara shook her head, her fingers biting deeply into her upper arms in an effort to still her increased trembling.

"Tara," he crooned, "this bed is getting colder by the second. It's early yet. Come back here and we'll warm it together."

"No." It sounded like a frog's croak and Tara cleared her throat nervously.

"No, Alek, I'm not coming back to bed with you. Not now. Not ever again."

The silence that blanketed the room had the cold stillness of death. Tara's nails dug unmercifully into her flesh. Why didn't he speak? Swear at her? Anything but this silence that seemed to stretch forever and tear her nerves apart. When he finally did speak, the sound of his voice was as chilling as the silence had been.

"When you speak to me, Tara, please have the courtesy to look at me."

The insolent tone of his words had the same effect on Tara as if he'd smacked her with a cold, wet towel. She spun around, head up, eyes blazing with defiance. The sight of him stole the stinging retort from her lips. He had pushed himself back and up against the pillows, more in a reclining than a sitting position. His long torso, exposed to at least two inches below the naval, had a golden, toast-brown hue in the morning sun. He didn't move or say anything, and yet the invitation was as clear as if he'd held out his arms and whispered, "Come to me."

And she wanted to. With every fiber and particle of her being, she wanted to. She had lain in this man's arms all night. He had opened doors, shown her beauty she had never dreamed existed. For one sharp instant she felt not only willing to be his slave, but longed for it. She actually took one step toward him when her eyes touched his face, and she was stopped cold, pinned to the spot by two rapier-sharp points of glinting blue.

"That's better," he said coolly. "Now what the hell is this all about?"

Tara drew a deep calm breath. Somehow she had to match his coolness. "Exactly what I said, Alek. I won't sleep with you again." Lord, was that detached voice hers?

"You can say that to me after last night?" Anger ruffled the coolness now. Anger and a touch of disbelief. "Do you have any idea how rare an experience like that is?"

Without realizing it, she was shaking her head. She didn't know, not really, but she was beginning to. So many things that she'd never quite understood began to make sense. "The world well lost for love"—that had always baffled her. The idea that anyone could turn his back on the world, or his own small corner of it, had been beyond her comprehension. Yet now, if he loved her, just a little, she would happily do just that. But he didn't, and the knowledge was tearing her to shreds.

Catching back the urge to put her pain into words, to cry out, "Alek, please love me," she replied hoarsely, "It doesn't matter."

"It doesn't matter?" His words were barely whispered, and yet the astonishment in them had the impact of a shout. His eyes closed briefly, and Tara told herself she misread the emotion she'd glimpsed in them. She knew she did not have the power to hurt him. The truth of this hit her forcefully when he lifted his lids, for his eyes were hard and cold and filled with contempt for her. He moved abruptly to get up and, startled, Tara stepped back, catching a glimpse of his long, muscular thigh before her lids veiled her eyes.

"You can open your eyes now," Alek murmured sardonically a few moments later, then his voice went flat. "Would you care to tell me what you intend to do?"

He had put on his robe, and as Tara opened her eyes, he paced in front of her with the masculine, dangerous grace of a jaguar. Tara exhaled slowly before answering equally flatly, "Go back to my apartment. Go back to work. Get a divorce."

"Of course. This is the way you get your revenge. Right?"

His voice was ominously soft and his eyes watched sharply, through narrowed lids, for her response.

She didn't disappoint him. Swallowing with difficulty she gasped, "You—you knew?"

He sighed almost wearily. "Credit me with at least a little intelligence, Tara. You ran up the white flag too abruptly. Did an about-face too quickly to be believable. I knew at once you were up to something. It took me all of about ninety seconds to come up with the word *revenge*. You had decided to make me pay. My mistake was in thinking you were planning to make me pay through the wallet. I have to admit, you threw me when you refused an engagement ring. But then I decided you were waiting until everything was legal to put the bite on me."

Tara flinched and whispered, "You don't have a very high opinion of me, do you?"

"I pushed you pretty hard," he said quietly. "You were hurt and angry and wanted to retaliate." Shrugging carelessly, he added, "I wanted you and I was willing to pay the price."

His words stung, brought a flush of color to her cheeks, and she said angrily, "Pay the price? Like I was a common—"

"Don't say it, Tara," he cut in warningly. "That's not true, so don't ever say it." He was quiet a moment, then he asked softly, "Last night wasn't part of the plan, was it?"

Tara wet her lips nervously and slid her eyes away from his, unable to maintain that hard blue contact. "There—there was no actual plan. I just felt I had to make you pay, somehow."

"And now you're going to walk out of this room and out of my life?" She should have been warned by the silky sound of his voice but, in trying to hang on to her own composure, she missed it and answered calmly, "Yes."

"Think again." Startled eyes flew back to his at the finality of his tone. Before she could protest, he went on blandly. "Have you thought what you are going to tell people? Sallie and David? The rest of your friends? The people you work with?" He paused, then underlined: "Your parents. Yesterday you were the picture of a gloriously happy bride. What can you give as a reason for leaving me? That you suddenly fell out of love? Hardly. That I beat you? Where are the marks? That I'm a terrible lover? Well, as everyone was convinced we anticipated our vows anyway, I don't think that will do. So what can you tell them? Can you imagine what your father is going to say?" He paused again before adding ruthlessly, "Or your mother's face?"

Her mother! A low strangled moan escaped Tara's lips. *Dear Lord.* She hadn't thought. Had been too full of thoughts of him to spare any for anything or anyone else. A picture of her mother's face the day before, serenely happy, looking almost young again, formed in front of Tara's eyes. In pain she closed her lids against the image.

Insensitive to her distress, words hard, measured, as if underlined darkly, Alek drove on ruthlessly. "Which do you think will be harder for her to take? The *idea* of her daughter sleeping with a man without benefit of clergy or the *fact* of her daughter leaving her husband the day after a full Catholic wedding?"

As he spoke, he walked slowly to her, coming to a stop so close, she could feel his breath on her hair. She kept her eyes tightly closed, vainly trying to control the shudder that ripped through her body at his nearness.

"Look at me, Tara."

It was a command. One, his hard tone warned her, she dared not disobey. Slowly, she lifted her head and her eyelids, then swallowed with difficulty. His eyes were as cold and hard as the stone they matched.

"As I said, you'd better think again. For if you go through with this, I won't make it easy for you. In fact I'll make it very hard. I'll fight you publicly. Make an unholy field day for the newspapers." His voice dropped to a menacing growl. "In short, Tara, I'll tear you apart."

"But why?" Eyes wide with confusion and more than a little fear, Tara's cry was one of despair.

"The Rykovskys do not divorce." Flat, final, the words struck her like blows. "You seem to forget, I also have parents. Who, by the way, love you already. I will not have them hurt."

His hands came up to cradle her face; long brown fingers, unbelievably gentle after his harsh words, brushed at the tears that had escaped her lids and rolled down her morning-shiny cheeks. His voice was now low, husky, yet still firmly determined. "No, Tara, You've made your bed and now we'll lie in it. Together."

"No!" In desperation she jerked away from him. Away from his warm, caressing fingers. Those hard, compelling eyes. That hypnotic, druglike voice that was sapping the resistance from her body. She put the width of the room between them before she turned to face him again, eyes blazing. "I'll stay with you. Play the role of the adoring wife. But I want nothing from you, either material or physical. I will not share your bed." She paused to draw a deep, calming breath, then added quietly, "And if you try and force me, I'll go, and to hell with the consequences."

"Don't do this, Tara." His quiet voice seemed to float on the angry silence left by her bitter words. "We could have a good life together if you'd—"

Weakening, and frightened of it, Tara cut in scathingly, "If only I'd agree to every one of your dictates. Thank you, but no thank you. I've given you my terms, Alek. It's the only way I'll stay."

His face a mask, he studied her a moment, then turned away with a shrug so unconcerned, so indifferent, it sent a shaft of hot pain into Tara's heart.

"Now, if you don't mind, I think we'd better dress." His detached tone deepened Tara's pain. "I'm hungry, and I'd planned to stop for breakfast on the way to New York."

"You still want to go?" she gasped.

He turned back swiftly, eyes hard and cold. "My dear wife, do we have a choice? The reservations are made. Everyone thinks we're there now. Our only other option is to pen ourselves in this apartment for a week. Would you prefer that?"

"No!" Tara answered quickly, then more slowly, "No, of course not. I—I'll be ready in half an hour." As she turned to escape his unyielding stare, his taunting voice stopped her on the threshold. "One more thing, Tara. I'm a normal male, with all the natural drives. I was fully prepared to live up to the vows I made yesterday, as regards fidelity. Your attitude changes that. Do you understand?"

Tara froze, unable to force herself to look back at him, a

picture of the smirking Kitty locked in her mind. Fingers like ice, she pulled the door wide and stepped into the hall.

"Do you?" Alek insisted.

"Yes."

It was a hoarse whisper hanging in the air. Tara had fled.

Chapter Nine

The following Sunday afternoon Tara sat in a state of be-musement listening to her husband's smooth, quiet voice as it blended with the low hum of the Lexus's engine as they neared home.

It had been a surprisingly relaxing week. Alek had re-vealed a facet of his character unseen by Tara up till now. He had been courteous and considerate, easygoing and al-most light-hearted, as he squired her around New York.

They had walked the city until she thought her legs would drop off, and she doubted there were any elaborate Christmas decorations anywhere that they had not ad-mired. Secretly her favorites were the angels and the enor-mous tree in Rockefeller Center. They had started early every morning and had gone full tilt until after midnight every night. They had dined at a variety of restaurants, from The Four Seasons and Tavern-on-the-Green to The Russian Tea Room and Lûtece.

One night he took her dancing, surprising her even more on the dance floor with his perfectly executed, somewhat sensuous step. And Tara had to admit to more than a twinge of pride and jealously at the blatantly admiring female glances cast over his long, slim form clothed in black shirt and pants that were as simple as they were devastatingly sexy.

As they were having breakfast Wednesday morning Tara said suddenly, "Alek, if you don't mind, I'd like to do some shopping today. I haven't finished my Christmas shopping and I think it'd be fun, especially for Mama and Betsy, to receive gifts from New York."

"Why should I mind?" he asked blandly, then added sardonically, "It's your honeymoon too, you know. I'm sure I can amuse myself for a few hours. Where would you like to go? Bloomingdale's? Saks?"

"I don't know. The few times I've been in New York have been on day tours. Just time enough to see a show, squeeze in some sight-seeing. I've never done any shopping here."

"Bloomingdale's," he stated firmly. "If you've never been there, it'll blow your mind."

It did. Tara was fascinated with the store. When she had the time and money, she loved to shop. This morning she had both. When Alek had deposited her at the entrance, he had handed her a no-limit platinum card with her name embossed on it, told her he'd be outside the same entrance at three o'clock, and added dryly, "Have fun."

Three o'clock? she had thought. What in the world was she to do for five hours? Time slipped away easily. At first Tara was content to stroll around aimlessly, delighted with the unusual and varied selection of merchandise. When she finally did get down to serious shopping, she spent long minutes on her choice of gifts for her mother, Betsy, and Sallie, feeling a pang of guilt as the total of her purchases climbed alarmingly.

With her father and brothers in mind, Tara wandered into the men's department, growing suddenly taut with an intense longing. It seemed every third article her eyes touched screamed Alek's name at her. Alek was always well groomed, and though Tara knew he had a huge closet full of beautifully tailored clothes, she wanted to buy him everything.

For a few moments, a small smile on her lips, she allowed her thoughts to run riot, picturing low-slung expensive sports cars, sparkling white yachts, sleek-lined Thoroughbreds. Pulling her thoughts up short with a mental shake, she lovingly touched fine-knit cashmere sweaters, beautifully made raw-silk shirts.

On the point of walking away, she stopped. Well, why not? It was Christmastime, wasn't it? The time for buying gifts. Also the excuse she needed. With a determined step she turned back, a happy gleam in her eyes, and promptly lost all sense of time. She bought discriminately but lavishly, this time using a credit card from her own wallet, not caring about the rate of speed with which the bill totals rose.

Tara could have gone on for hours, but a glimpse of her watch brought her shopping spree to an abrupt halt with a disbelieving gasp. It was a few minutes after three. She was keeping Alek waiting.

Alek's eyebrows rose in amusement when she finally staggered out of the store under the weight of her packages.

"When the lady says she's going to shop, she's going to shop," he teased. "Did you enjoy yourself?"

"Oh, Alek," she replied happily, unaware that for the first time since they'd met, she had responded to him warmly, spontaneously. "I've had a wonderful time and I'm starving."

She missed the quick narrowing of his eyes, his brief hesitation, for they were gone in a flash, and he was chiding her gently. "Didn't you take time to have lunch?"

"Lunch?" she laughed happily. "I never even thought of food."

Relieving her of the bulk of her burden, he helped her into the cab he had managed to hail and smiled dryly. "In that case I think we can find you a crust of bread and a glass of water somewhere."

After dropping her purchases in their room, Alek led Tara to a small table in the hotel's bar. When he gave the waiter an order of a sandwich and coffee for her and only a drink for himself, she turned questioning eyes to him.

Smiling easily, he murmured, "I didn't forget to eat lunch."

Happy with her day and for the first time in weeks at

peace in her own mind, Tara returned his smile with a brilliant one of her own. The waiter appeared at their table at the same moment, and Tara missed the low sound of breath catching in Alek's throat, the fleeting expression of longing, of hunger in his eyes.

At no time during the week had Alek made a move of a physical nature toward her. Other than taking her elbow while crossing streets and occasionally sliding his arm around her waist in extra crowded places, he did not touch her. Every night had been the same. He'd see her to their hotel room then go to the bar for thirty or so minutes to give her time to get into her nightgown and into one of the two double beds in the room.

Now, not more than forty-five minutes from home, the atmosphere in the car was the exact opposite of that of a week ago. Tara sat back comfortably, her bemusement stemming from Alek's homebound conversation. Some stray remark had touched at a memory, and he had been relating anecdotes from his boyhood. It was the first time he'd opened up to her and, at her hesitant query about his ancestors, he'd gone quiet and she was afraid he'd withdrawn again when he resumed his smooth, quiet tone.

"The Rykovskys go back a long way and were, at one time, entertained by the czars. My great-grandparents were uneasy under the rule of Alexander the Third and possibly read the handwriting on the wall. At any rate, they transferred as much of their property as possible into cash and left Russia around 1883, when my grandfather was still quite small. They landed and stayed in Philadelphia for a while, and then a merchant my great-grandfather had met and made friends with invited them to come and visit him in his neck of the woods. That, of course, was the Allentown area. They came, liked what they saw, and settled. My great-grandfather was an intelligent, well-educated man who liked to tinker with machines and tools. After he was settled, he built a small shop and put his hobby to work. Although my grandfather and then my father added to it, the original shop is still there."

"And now you're building a new one," Tara said softly.

"Yes, we've outgrown the old."

Again he was quiet a few moments, then he slanted a glance at her and smiled. "You said once that I have an international family, and in a sense you're right. While doing the grand tour, my grandfather met and eventually married the shy, youngest daughter of a wealthy French wine-producing family. I still have some relatives somewhere in the Loire district. My father met and married my mother when he was stationed in Great Britain during World War Two. So, to that extent, there is a European flavor to the family, but it stops with me. I'm a straight-down-the-line American. My cousins delight in referring to me as 'the Yankee capitalist,' and they're right—I am. I've been all over Europe at one time or another and although I've always enjoyed it, the best part was coming home. I'm afraid what you see here is a true-blue patriot. I love my country."

The devil danced in the eyes that slanted her another quick look, before he added teasingly, "I'm also hung up on American women. I've known, since the time I was old enough to notice girls, that I'd marry an American woman. I've met and, quite frankly, made love to some stunning women all over the world, and yet I wouldn't exchange what I have sitting next to me for any one of them."

At once pleased and flustered, Tara sought vainly for something to say. When she didn't reply, he went on, "I've inadvertently broken a few Rykovsky family traditions, but there was one I was very happily looking forward to breaking—deliberately."

"What was that?" she murmured, an uneasy premonition snaking up her spine.

"For six generations the Rykovsky brides have been blessed with only one child. A male." Alek paused, and with growing unease Tara watched his jawline tighten, his knuckles whiten as he gripped the steering wheel. "I wanted a son, of course," he went on tersely. "Maybe two. But I also wanted a daughter, possibly more."

Tara found it impossible for a moment to speak around the lump in her throat. When she did finally get the words out they came jerkily. "I—If you'd agree to a divorce, you could get on with finding a proper mother for your children." She could barely push the last word past the pain in her throat at the sudden vision of a dark-haired little boy with devilish blue eyes. Suddenly her arms ached with painful longing to hold that child close to her breast.

"A proper mother." His low, bitter tone was like a slap across her face, and Tara averted her head to hide the tears that stung her eyes.

He cursed savagely under his breath, then ground out, "I told you the Rykovskys do not divorce. I have no intention of blazing a new trail in that direction." The grim determination in his voice sent a shudder through her. He meant it. He had no intention of giving her her freedom. She felt caught in the trap she'd set herself. They were close to home, and the remaining miles were covered in the hostile silence; the companionable atmosphere of before had been shattered.

Tara lived through the week until Christmas with a growing feeling of unreality. In the short periods of time she and Alek were alone together, they maintained a sort of armed truce. When they were in the company of their respective families or friends, they played the blissfully happy newlyweds.

Tara filled her days by emptying her apartment, disposing of the furniture she didn't want, arranging in Alek's apartment the things she did. And moving her clothes and personal things into the spare bedroom. Alek went back to his office, snapping, "If I remember correctly, your stated wish was that you want nothing from me. I assume that includes my help, so go to it."

Alek rarely came home for dinner and in fact was seldom home by the time she went to bed. It didn't take much speculation on her part to come up with an answer to where he was spending his nights. She spent her own nights alternately hating him, and curled up in bed, arms clutching her midsection, trying to fight down the aching need to feel his arms closing around her, his mouth seeking hers. *God!* she thought. She loved him. And if she had thought she had cried a lot before, she knew now, those tears had been just for openers.

Saturday morning Tara was brushing her hair when she heard the door to the apartment open, a strange rustling sound, then the door close again. Intrigued, she left the bedroom, walked along the short hall to the living room and stopped, staring in wonder at the live tree Alek had dragged into the room.

Standing the tree straight, he asked blandly, "Do you like it?"

"Yes, of course. I love live Christmas trees, but why?"

"Because it's Christmas," he snapped. "And because, although we won't be doing much entertaining, I'm sure the families will stop over sometime during the holidays. And I don't feel up to lengthy explanations as to why there is none. So," he gestured disinterestedly, "the tree." He then proceeded to surprise her even more by removing a large carton of tree decorations from the storage closet.

Tara tried to show little enthusiasm as she helped him trim the tree. It wasn't easy. She really did love live Christmas trees and had always enjoyed fussing with the decorations, thinking it one of the best rituals of the holiday. She was also glad she now had a place to set her gifts. Even if she was a little apprehensive about Alek's reaction to his. As soon as the tree was finished, Alek showered, dressed, and left the apartment, telling her he didn't know what time he'd be back.

On the morning of Christmas Eve Tara stood in the kitchen dully watching the coffee perk. It was late, almost eleven, and although she had just awakened, she did not feel rested. She had lain awake, tense and stiff, until after three in the morning.

The apartment was so still and quiet that Tara was sure she was alone and so turned with a start when Alek walked into the kitchen. He looked terrible, pale and weary with lines of strain around his eyes and mouth. Tara was torn between deep compassion and vindictive satisfaction at his obvious exhaustion.

Without a word he walked across the room to her, then tossed a small, gaily wrapped gift onto the counter in front of her.

"Your Christmas present," he said shortly. "I'm giving it to you now because I'd like you to wear it to my parents' party tonight."

Tara eyed the small package with trepidation, then removed the wrapping with shaking fingers. With growing alarm she lifted the lid of the tiny, black-velvet-covered box then gasped aloud at the ring nestled in its bed of white satin. The single sapphire was large and square-cut and reflected exactly the color of Alek's eyes.

"Alek, I told you—" she began in a tremulous voice when he interrupted with a low snarl, "I know what you told me. But you will wear this, at least in the presence of my parents. They expect it. The Rykovsky men have always adorned their brides with jewels. So you'll do me the favor of wearing it. Not for me, for them. Other than that, I don't care what you do with it. Toss it to the back of the drawer, where it won't offend your eyes."

Tara winced at his harshly bitter tone and, fighting back tears, whispered, "All right, I'll wear it tonight. It—it is beautiful and—"

"Don't strain yourself, Tara, and don't look so frightened, I'm not going to demand payment in return."

Tara had no doubt as to what *payment* he meant, and she turned sharply back to the counter to hide her pain-filled eyes. "Alek, that's not fair." Try as she would, she could not keep the hurt from her voice.

"Not fair?" he snapped. "Lord, I don't believe you said that." Then his tone changed to one of utter weariness. "Oh, the hell with it. I don't want to argue, I have a headache that won't quit and I'm dying of thirst. Isn't that coffee finished yet?"

By the time they left for his parents' party, his bad

humor seemed to have vanished along with his headache, and he was his usual controlled, urbane self. Tara wore his ring and tried not to see the cynicism in his eyes as she replied properly to the exclamations of admiration from the other guests.

Christmas morning, still wearing his ring, Tara slipped out of the kitchen as Alek read the paper while drinking his coffee. Gnawing nervously on her lip, she placed his gifts in a neat pile, returned to the kitchen, and set them on the table in front of him. The paper was lowered slowly. Face hard, free of expression, he stared for long moments at the presents.

"You tell me you'll accept no gifts from me. Then you turn around and buy some *for* me. Why?" Alek's tone confused her, made her feel as if he were asking far more than the actual words stated. For a moment she was tempted to blurt out the truth. That because she loved so deeply she had not been able to resist the urge; she had in fact wanted to buy him the earth.

His eyes, so guarded, so unreadable, stopped her. Swallowing around the dryness in her throat, she managed a careless shrug and answered, "As you said yesterday, it is expected."

The packages were opened silently, his eyes piercing hers each time another lid was lifted. When finally the last one was opened, he stood and came to her, kissed her mouth gently and murmured, "Thank you, Tara. I'm sure our families will be as pleased with your taste and choices as I am."

For a moment he seemed far away, as if caught up in a memory, then he added quietly, "I don't understand you at all, Tara. There are times when I'm sure I have you all figured out, then you say or do something that completely baffles me, and I wonder if I'll ever understand you."

Slowly, over the next few days, as they attended numerous holiday parties and gatherings, she noticed a subtle change in him. It started on Christmas Day, when they made a quick stop at David and Sallie's to deliver their gifts. After unwrapping the exquisite doll they had bought her, the three-year-old Tina had run to Alek, her cubby arms outstretched, laughing, and he had scooped her up into his arms. Tina's small head hid Alek's face from all but Tara, and she felt a hard contraction around her heart at the expression that passed across his face fleetingly as he hugged the child to him. Deep, painful longing had been revealed in that instant, and Tara felt overwhelmed with guilt at her unwillingness to give him the child she now knew he wanted desperately.

From that moment on he seemed to withdraw from her. No longer did she receive his tender glances or softly spoken endearments when in the company of others, and he left her side often and for longer periods of time. By New Year's Eve it became apparent that their friends were aware of his attitude also.

They were attending a rather large party at a private club some distance outside of town and, from the covert glances she was getting, Tara knew her friends were asking themselves if the honeymoon was over. Alek disappeared several times for very long periods, and the fact that Kitty was also conspicuously absent at the same time filled Tara with both jealous fear and embarrassed fury.

Fury conquered fear when midnight came, and then passed, and Tara stood alone in a room full of celebrants kissing and toasting in the new year. Head held high, her step determined, Tara made her way out of the room, ignoring the speculative looks turned her way. She was almost to the cloakroom when she heard a familiar voice call to her to wait and with a sigh she turned and watched Craig Hartman walk up to her. Both his expression and voice held concern.

"Are you leaving?"

She nodded, and when he asked how she was going to get home, she answered briefly, "Taxi.

"No you're not," he stated firmly. "I'll take you."

"But—"

He didn't wait to hear her protests but walked into the

cloakroom, emerging seconds later shrugging into his coat and carrying hers.

He helped her into her coat then said softly, "Come along," and Tara moved with him out the door, unaware of the alarmed expression that had replaced the usually placid one in David's eyes as he watched them leave.

They drove in silence for about five minutes, then Craig stopped the car on the gravel-covered shoulder of the dark country road. Tara turned in her seat in surprise. "Craig, what—"

"It's not working, is it, Tara?" he interrupted gently.

"Craig, really. I don't want to talk—"

"No, I can understand that," he interrupted again. Then his tone changed, became angry. "But how he could prefer that overblown, destructive bitch over you, I'll never—"

This time it was Tara who interrupted. "Craig, you don't know—"

"No, you're right," he cut in. "But I know her, and she's not worth one minute of your unhappiness."

Before she could think of a reply, Craig added earnestly, "Tara, I told you once that if you ever needed a shoulder to cry on, mine was available. It may not be as broad as his but—"

That was as far as he got, for the door next to Tara was yanked open, her arm was grasped in a grip of steel and she was jerked unceremoniously from her seat. Her outcry was drowned by the low, menacing growl of Alek's voice. "Get the hell out of there and go wait for me in my car."

"No look here, Rykovsky—" Craig began, only to be cut off by Alek's snarled, "No, *you* look, Hartman." That was all Tara heard before she fled to the Lexus and slid onto the front seat.

Chapter Ten

The drive home was completed in ominous quiet, and as soon as she stepped into the apartment, Tara dashed for her bedroom, locking the door behind her. She dropped her coat onto her small rocker then spun around, breath catching in her throat, when she heard Alek call her name and saw the doorknob twist sharply. The next instant her eyes flew wide with disbelief as she heard Alek's foot smash against the door, saw the wood splinter around the lock, and on the second blow from his foot the door slammed back against the wall. Alek's advance on her was reminiscent of the stalk of a predator, and he had the same wild, savage look.

Badly frightened, Tara raised her hands in a defensive movement. With one careless swing of his arm Alek knocked them down then, grasping her upper arms, dragged her roughly against him.

"What is this man to you?" he spat.

"A—a friend," she stuttered.

"He looked *very* friendly," he snarled. "Has he made love to you? The truth, Tara." His fingers tightened and his eyes blazed furiously into hers.

"No! Alek, please," Tara choked

As if he hadn't heard her, past all reason in his anger, his fingers tightened still more, and Tara groaned softly in pain and fear.

"I'll be damned," he rasped, "if I'll let another man have what's legally mine yet denied me."

"Alek, don't," Tara could barely whisper. "I give you my word, I—"

"Damn your doe-soft eyes," he groaned, then his mouth was crushing hers punishingly, bruisingly, as his hands released her arms and slid urgently down her back, molding her body against his.

"Did you really think a locked door would keep me out?" he sneered, when finally his mouth left hers. "Have you been locking your door all this time?"

Shattered, unable to speak, Tara shook her head dumbly.

"Then why tonight?" he asked silkily. "Is there some reason you tried to hide away tonight?"

Tara strove for control, for a measure of calmness in her voice.

"You were so angry. You frightened me, Alek."

"You have every reason to be frightened, my sweet." His soft laugh was not a pretty sound, and his use of the present tense had not escaped her.

"Alek," she breathed desperately, "can you really believe that I—"

"Can't I?" he cut her off harshly. "Why not? You forget, I held you in my arms all night, felt your response, your need. Whether you admit it to yourself or not, you wanted me as badly as I wanted you. Those needs cannot be turned off like a faucet. I know because right now my body is screaming for possession of yours, and I no longer intend to deny myself that satisfaction."

Tara struggled against him frantically, but it was a losing battle, for in truth she was fighting two opponents, Alek and her own rising desire for him.

Later, lying beside him, replete and spent, she closed her eyes in pain at her own deflections. His possession of her had been as wild and savage as his appearance had been and she had gloried in it, soaking in his lovemaking as thirstily as a drunk slaking his thirst after a long abstinence.

Seconds later a small shiver rippled through her as Alek's lips moved slowly across her cheek then stopped at her own, teasing, tormenting around the outer edge of her mouth, until with a soft moan, she reached up and grasped his head and brought his mouth to her own. When finally he lifted his head, he whispered harshly, "Damn you, Tara, there's no end to my wanting you."

The words, his tone, cut into her like a knife and in self-defense she said fiercely, "I hate you, Aleksei Rykovsky."

He went still for a breathless moment, then his fingers dug painfully into her hair and, his lips close to hers, he groaned, "Well, I guess that's better than indifference. Hate me some more, Tara Rykovsky."

It was late in the morning when Tara woke, wondering why she ached all over. Memory returned in a rush and, turning her head, she gave a long sigh of relief on seeing she was alone. She felt unrested, not very well, and worst of all, used—badly, unjustly used. The thought made her wince, and with a dry sob she covered her face with her hands. Silent tears of conviction running down her face, Tara knew she had to pack and leave, today, before she found herself blabbering her love to Alek like some demented, love-starved idiot, and cringing under his amused triumph.

Giving herself a mental shake, Tara left the bed tiredly, her eyes avoiding the rumpled sheet and comforter. Feeling drained, she went to the kitchen and made a pot of coffee, watching it perk dully while she sipped her orange juice. Where was Alek? The answer that presented itself brought pain, and she rejected it with a sharp shake of her head. She didn't know why, but somehow she knew positively that Alek would not leave her bed and go to another woman.

Impatient with the coffeepot, she left the kitchen, stopped at the closet in the short hall, removed her suitcase, and went back to the bedroom. With swift, jerky movements she straightened the bed covers then opened the case on the bed.

For some reason the mild exertion had brought a light film

of perspiration to her face and hands and she turned from the case to go to the bathroom. As she stood under the hot, stinging spray in the shower a shudder tore through Tara's body. What was she going to do? For the time in many years she was uncertain about the direction of her life. Her mind gnawed away at that thought as she dried herself, dressed quickly in jeans and a white rib-knit sweater, and slid her feet into sneakers.

Since her early teens she had set goals for herself and one by one had achieved them. And now all of them seemed unimportant. The thought shook her, and she stopped in the act of placing underwear in her case, her arm motionless in midair. Suddenly she felt very, very old, while at the same time very, very young and she was consumed with the need to talk to someone. Someone older, with more experience of life.

The filmy underthings dropped into the case from numb fingers at the face that flashed into Tara's mind. Her mother? She hadn't sought her mother's counsel since her thirteenth year and yet she had an overriding urge to go to her now.

Before she could change her mind, she dialed her mother's number. While her mother's phone rang, she walked to the kitchen and poured herself a cup of coffee, only to set it onto the counter with shaking hands when her mother's voice said hello.

"Mama. It's Tara," she said breathlessly, then went on in a rush: "Are you busy? I—I need someone to talk to and I wondered . . . oh, Mama, can I come talk to you? Please?"

There was a short pause, then her mother's voice, strangely calm, responded quietly. "Yes, of course, Tara. Come right away. I'll be waiting for you."

Hands still shaking badly, Tara hung up. She dashed into the bedroom, shrugged into a Navy pea jacket, scooped up her handbag, and left the apartment. The untouched coffee sat cooling on the counter; the half filled suitcase lay open on her bed; the dresser drawers remained ajar.

On entering her father's house, Tara stood inside the door, glancing around in question at the unusual quiet.

"I'm in the kitchen, Tara," her mother called. "Come have a cup of coffee."

Marlene Schmitt stood at the sink, pouring coffee into two heavy earthenware mugs and, as Tara seated herself at the table, she turned and said, "We can talk here. Betsy is spending the day with Kenny and his parents, and your father took the boys out to give us some privacy."

"Mother!" Tara exclaimed. "You didn't say anything to Dad, did you?"

Marlene's eyebrows went up as she sat down opposite Tara. Then, her tone slightly chiding, she murmured, "There wasn't much I could tell him, other than that you seemed upset and were coming over to talk. He didn't ask questions, simply gathered up the boys and left."

Tara eyed her mother wonderingly as she sipped her coffee. Never before could she remember hearing quite that calm, unruffled tone and for the moment she was left speechless. Her next words left her stunned.

"Your father is not the unfeeling brute you think he is, Tara." And when Tara tried to speak out in protest, her mother held up her hand and added, "Nor am I quite the blind fool. No, don't interrupt. Please, let me finish. Failure to do all you'd like to for your family can do strange things to some men, and that is what has happened to your father. I've watched it happening for a long time. But he is a good man, Tara. I love him. I always have."

Tara stared at her mother as if at a stranger. Had she been wrong all these years? Misread the situation? She had thought her mother stayed with her father because of her and her sister and brothers, and out of a sense of duty. But now?

Marlene's soft voice brought her attention back to the present and her own situation.

"There's a problem with Alek, isn't there?"

Looking at her mother through different eyes, Tara felt her throat close and she whispered, "Yes."

"I thought so. I have for some time now. For all your bright smiles and happy chatter, I knew you were unhappy. And so is Alek."

"Mama, you don't understand," Tara cried. And her mother came back, "Possibly not, but I understand this. Alek is a bright, ambitious, very attractive man. And he is a man, Tara. The kind of man who needs a mature woman beside him. One who is willing to give, as well as take."

Tara felt tears sting her eyelids. Was that the type of woman that, in her single-mindedness, she had projected? One who was not willing to give? Before she could form an argument, her mother said, "Less than a month ago you made a commitment to that man. Have you lived up to it?"

Vision blurred by tears, unable to speak, Tara shook her head.

"Honey, do you love him?"

Tears now unashamedly running down her cheeks, Tara sobbed, "Yes. Oh, Mama, yes. But he doesn't love me." She paused, then added bitterly, "He says he wants me, and that's not the same, is it?"

"No, it isn't," Marlene answered very softly, her fingers brushing gently at the tears. "But that's something, and as long as there's something, some emotion, there's reason to work at it. It probably won't be easy, Tara. But then nothing worth having ever does come easy."

As Tara drove back to the apartment, her mind went over what her mother said. There had been more, much more, but in essence, what it had amounted to was this: Tara had worked hard for everything she had wanted; surely the one thing she wanted most in the world was worth twice the work.

Tara was still unsure of what she'd do or say to Alek, if anything, when she got home. But she was grateful for one thing: This new and deeper understanding between her mother and herself. She had been on her own for some time; now, for the first time, she felt really grown-up.

Suddenly Tara knew she was not yet ready to go home. She had to think this through, make a decision one way or the other. Eyes steady on the road, she drove into the mountains. All the splendor of fall was gone now, but even denuded of their summer finery, the Poconos were a balm to her mind.

Time slipped by unnoticed as did the large and small billboards advertising the lodges, motels, and many points of interest and activities offered.

Her mind drove on in rhythm with the car's engine, paging back over the last few months, going over everything, step by step. And over and over, threading through her thoughts, her mother's voice asked softly, *"Honey, do you love him?"*

What should she do? The events leading up to this day, many of which were caused by Alek, no longer held any importance. The question driving her on now was: *Did* he still want her? Her body still hurt from last night. Every muscle felt sore. She felt sure he had not set out to make love to her, but to punish her. He had been rough with her, as if deliberately acting out the role of savage she'd cast him in. His stated intention had been to own her. Now that he did, had he lost interest?

He had become so cool, so withdrawn over the last week. A shudder rippled through her as she remembered the previous Thursday. She had left the office to find a mist-shrouded fairyland of ice, glittering and treacherous. She had driven home at a mere crawl, holding her breath each time she felt the tires lose their grip and begin to slide. By the time she had shut off the engine inside the apartment building's covered parking area, her palms and forehead were damp with sweat, and she had felt totally exhausted.

As she'd thrust her key into the apartment door, she'd

had one thought in mind: to soak in a hot tub and forget that world of ice outside. She took one step through the doorway when Alek's voice rapped, "Where the hell have you been?"

He was standing at the bar, phone at his ear, his one palm covering the mouthpiece. Before she could answer, his hand slid away and he said shortly, "Yes, it's her."

Just as she was about to close the door, Tara had stopped, frozen by his next words.

"Yes, Kitty, I know, but I don't know what else to tell you. Perhaps in a week, maybe less."

What had possessed her? Even now Tara didn't know. At the time she had not stopped to think, to ask for an explanation. She had run out of the apartment to her car and back to that ice-covered world that had nothing on her heart.

How long she'd slithered around aimlessly, she had no idea, but when finally she had turned back to the apartment, it was raining hard, the ice fast disappearing. There was no sign of Alek when she got back, and as she soaked in the tub, Tara wondered dully if he was with Kitty. The searing pain of jealousy she'd felt on the night she'd first realized she was in love with him was nothing compared to the agony she'd gone through while sliding around on the glassy streets. And now, tired to the bone, she was almost beyond feeling.

She was lying on the bed, staring at the ceiling, her bedside lamp still on, when she heard the front door slam moments before Alek was standing in her doorway, face cold, eyes blazing.

"How long have you been here?"

"A—a half hour or so."

"While I've been running around nearly killing myself looking for you." His voice had been ugly, not much more than a snarl. "Would that have made your revenge complete, I wonder?"

"Alek, please, I'm sorry—"

But it had been too late; he was gone, slamming out of the apartment as violently as he'd entered.

Tara's hands gripped the wheel as she shivered again. Vaguely she registered the road sign indicating the number of miles to Camelback. Then last night, she wondered, had his neglect, indifference, been his way of showing her he no longer cared if she left him? got a divorce? But then why had he been so angry about Craig? His pride? Of course. She could hear him now. *"Has he made love to you?"* That fierce Rykovsky pride would not be able to bear the thought of someone else having what he still called his own. The thoughts swirled and whirled, leading nowhere.

Camelback! Good grief, she had to turn this car around, go home. And there was her answer, clear as a perfect spring day. She had to go home, and Alek was all the home she ever wanted. Silently she answered her mother's question. *Yes, Mama, I love him. More than I ever thought it possible to love any one person. I'm afraid, Mama, so afraid. For if he no longer wants me, I'll be devastated.*

Alek's car was parked in the apartment lot and with trembling fingers, Tara let herself into the apartment. She stood listening to the silence in the empty living room a moment then, slipping off her jacket, she went to her bedroom to stand staring at the open case on her bed. Alek's voice, from the doorway, went through her like an electric shock.

"Where have you been?"

"Alek, I—"

"No. Never mind. As long as you're all right. The way you left the apartment, I thought something had happened." His voice was so cool, so withdrawn, Tara shivered. His eyes left her face, rested long moments on the suitcase, then came back to hers. "Before you leave, I have something to say to you. If you'll come into the living room, please?"

He turned and walked away, and Tara was left staring at the empty doorway, fingers of real fear digging at her stomach. She didn't know what he had to say, but she was almost positive she didn't want to hear it and she actually had to force herself to follow him.

He was standing gazing out of the window when she entered the room, and the sight of him clutched at her heart. Why, of all the men she had known, did it have to be this one who could rob the strength from her knees, make her ache in anticipation? He was everything she had avowed she had not wanted in a man, yet he was the only man she wanted.

He was standing very straight, almost stiff, and as he turned from the window, Tara felt the breath catch in her throat. His face had an austere, lifeless cast and the usually glittering blue eyes looked flat, empty. His eyes went over her slowly as if studying every detail, and when he finally spoke, it was in that same cool, withdrawn tone.

"I'm a proud man, Tara, as you know. This is possibly the hardest thing I'll ever have to say, and I'll only say it one time. Don't leave me." He paused and his tone became softer. "I beg you, stay with me. I give you my word I'll do everything in my power to make it a good life for both of us."

Eyes wide with astonishment, Tara stared at him, unable to move for a full fifteen seconds. Then, with a small incoherent cry, she was across the room, flinging herself against his chest.

"Oh, Alek," she whispered. "And here I was, about to beg you to let me stay."

"Let you stay?" he repeated incredulously, his arms hard and tight around her. "I never wanted you to go. You know that. I've been berating myself all day for what happened last night. For giving you what I thought was the perfect excuse for leaving me."

Her hand slid underneath his sweater, then up and over his warm skin, with an urgency in her to touch him. She felt a shudder ripple through his body as he buried his face in her hair and groaned, "Oh, God, Tara, I love you. These few weeks have been pure hell, wanting to hold you like this all the time I tried to work during the day, lying alone in that damn bed at night."

"Which reminds me," Tara stepped back and looked up into eyes now alive and glowing with love and tenderness. "Where have you been every night? You didn't spend very many hours alone in that bed."

"Are you jealous, Tara?" he laughed down at her.

"Yes, damn you. And what were you and Kitty up to last night?"

He laughed again, kissed her fast and hard, then said softly, "Simmer down, hellion, and don't swear at me. Kitty wants to open her own boutique and needed some backing. I've looked over her plans and decided to invest. And that's all."

"On New Year's Eve?" she cried in disbelief.

"Well, I may have been trying to punish you a little. Damn it, Tara, you've been driving me crazy for months. I thought, after that unbelievable wedding night, that you'd realize what you meant to me. What you have meant to me since not long after I met you. In the last week I've felt at the end of my wits and patience. It was either stay away from you or drag you off to the nearest bed. It seems I did both."

He stopped long enough to give her another hard kiss, then a little shake. "As for Kitty. There is nothing between us but business. Anything else was over some time ago. And she never lived in this apartment or slept in our bed." His arms loosened and his hands came up to cup her face, long fingers sliding into her hair. Lips close to hers, he rasped, "Tara, if you don't soon tell me you love me, I won't be responsible for my actions."

Soft brown eyes gazed into anxious blue ones then, quietly, but very clearly, Tara said, "I love you, Alek."

"Dear God," he moaned. "I was beginning to think I'd never hear you say it." Then his mouth was crushing hers, his hands moving down her back, molding the softness of her body to the hard strength of his. Tara's mind whirled, then the room spun as he scooped her into his arms and strode into the bedroom. Their bedroom.

As he lowered her gently onto the bed, Tara whispered, "Since right after you met me, Alek?"

"Yes, pansy eyes."

"But, I don't understand."

"Oh, Tara. You were so cold. You seemed to take such an aversion to me. I guess, at first, my vanity was stung. I made up my mind to find out more about you."

Kicking off his shoes, he slid onto the bed beside her, then proceeded to drive her slightly mad with tiny, fervent kisses, until she caught at his head and pulled it back with a pleaded, "Alek?"

"All right," he sighed. One long finger tracing the contours of her face, as he went on. "It didn't take long to find out you went out only with men who had—ah—shall we say, good prospects? But somehow that didn't seem to quite fit you. So I dug a little deeper, observed a little harder, and came up with the answer. You were scared to death of strong-willed men. By then I was so damn in love, I knew I had to have you, by whatever methods. But how to get close to you, get under the fence you'd built around yourself? You avoided me whenever possible, cut me dead whenever I spoke to you. That's when I put my plan into motion. I didn't want to hurt you, for when you hurt, I hurt. But I did want you."

"And in all this time, until today, that's all you've said. 'I want you.' "

"Not true, pansy eyes. I've been telling you I loved you since the first night I came to your apartment. I knew you were not yet ready to hear it, so I said it in Russian. If you remember the morning after our wedding I said I had something to tell you when I asked you to come back to bed. I was fully prepared to lay my heart and my life at your feet. In English."

"Those Russian words!" Tara exclaimed. "But how could I know?"

Then, her arms snaking around his neck, she whispered, "Translate at once—please."

Alek's breath was a cool caress against her mouth as he murmured the Russian words, then whispered, "Roughly translated, it's 'My darling, Tara, I love you.' "

ABOUT THE AUTHOR

Joan Hohl lives with her family in Pennsylvania and is currently working on her next Zebra contemporary romance, which will be published in 2002. Joan loves to hear from readers and you may write to her c/o Zebra Books. Please include a self-addressed stamped envelope if you wish a response.